WESTERING WOMEN

Center Point
Large Print

Also by Sandra Dallas and available from
Center Point Large Print:

The Patchwork Bride

**This Large Print Book carries the
Seal of Approval of N.A.V.H.**

WESTERING WOMEN

A Novel

SANDRA DALLAS

CENTER POINT LARGE PRINT
THORNDIKE, MAINE

For my brother, Michael
One of the good guys

ATTENTION
Young Women *of* Marriageable Age

If you are an adventuresome young woman of high moral character and fine health, are you willing to travel to California in search of a good husband? Do you want to instill God and Civilization and Righteousness in the western-most part of our country? The below-signed Ministers of the Gospel propose escorting a group of Eligible Women to the gold mines of Goosetown in the California Diggings, where hundreds of God-fearing men are seeking wives. You must be strong enough to withstand the rigors of a 2,000-mile trip. Only good Christian Women with the highest principles need apply. For particulars, you may attend a meeting at three in the afternoon on February 22, 1852, at Lord's Grace Church, City.

REVEREND WILLIAM PARNELL
REVEREND JOSEPH SWAIN AND WIFE

One

February 22, 1852
Chicago, Illinois

Hidden beneath her black umbrella, Maggie stood in the shelter of the church and stared at the woman reading the broadsheet. She was big, perhaps the largest woman Maggie had ever seen, not fat but solid, and she towered over two men who stood in front of her, their eyes on the announcement.

"I expect they will have the biggest collection of ugly spinsters ever assembled in Chicago," one of the men said.

"The most desperate, too. Imagine going two thousand miles to find a husband," his companion replied.

They laughed as they turned, almost running into the woman, and even through the sleet, Maggie could see their embarrassment. It served them right. No woman should be mocked for her looks. "Ma'am," one said, as they started down the street. He poked his elbow into the other man's side, and the two of them smirked.

The woman should have been embarrassed, too, but she only stared after the men a moment before she turned back to the broadside, her lips moving as she read the words.

Maggie moved silently to her side. The woman was a head taller and even broader than Maggie had thought. Maggie herself was tall, with dark hair and blue eyes, but she felt dwarfed beside this woman. "Are you going in?" she asked in a low voice, pushing her umbrella aside so that she could see the woman's face. She shivered as the wind hit her, but the tall woman seemed oblivious to the cold.

"I am thinking of it. There is no mention of age," she said. "I am thirty-five, but I am strong as a horse."

"I can see that," Maggie said, then bit her tongue, hoping she had not offended.

"I read the message three times this week. It is posted all over Chicago. I am of a mind to consider it. I do not see as it would hurt to find out."

"No," Maggie said. "I imagine you are just the sort of woman they want."

"I can plow and harvest, milk, tend to animals, anything to do with a farm. That is my horse over there." She pointed to a red horse that was as oversized as the woman. "My brother owns it, of course. He owns everything—he says the law gives him the right—but I borned that horse, raised him myself. Nobody else but me ever rode him."

Maggie stared at the animal and saw it was fitted with a man's saddle, not a sidesaddle. Did the woman ride astride? She had never seen a woman ride a horse that way, but it was likely this woman could do anything she wanted.

"You coming in, too?" the woman asked. She adjusted the shawl that covered her head. It was damp from the sleet, but she paid no attention. Maggie saw that her eyes were a little crossed.

Here it was, then, the time to make a decision. Maggie, too, had seen the broadsheets, had read them so many times that she could recite the words from memory. The message had brought her to the church, but would she really go inside? Could she leave Chicago? Did she have the stamina to go all the way to California? Did Clara? Was there even a choice? "I do not know if they would take a woman with a child," she said, moving aside to reveal the small girl hidden behind her skirts.

The big woman's face softened, and she smiled at the child, then held out her hand. "There is some that might like a ready-made family. I believe I myself would not mind if I were to be given such a sweet little thing. Has she a name?"

"Of course. It is Clara. She is four."

At that, the child curtsied and smiled at the woman, then slowly put her tiny hand into the big one and murmured, "Hello."

Maggie was surprised. "She is shy and does

11

not often take to strangers. You have a way with children."

The woman nodded, accepting the truth of it.

"You will not know if they will allow children unless you ask. Go in with me, then. It is a strange undertaking. If we are both to make the journey, we can start now by being friends." She picked up Clara, who did not protest. Then, as if she were a man, the woman held out her hand. "My name is Mary Madrid." She smiled with her brown eyes as well as her mouth.

"I am Maggie—" Maggie started to give her last name but stopped. That would not do. Instead, she said, "And as you know, my daughter is Clara." She shook Mary's damp hand, feeling the strength in it.

Mary stared at Maggie for a moment, and Maggie was afraid she would demand her full name. But the woman held her tongue, and the two joined the crowd swarming into the church.

Maggie selected a pew in the back of the sanctuary where she would not be noticed, and she stared at the other women as they walked past. They were a varied lot, most of them young, although some looked as old as Mary, a few even older. Many were dressed in their Sunday best, some wore the black dresses and white aprons of domestic servants, and others, such as Mary, had on the rough clothing of farm girls.

Maggie was startled to recognize a woman in

a fur coat and diamond earrings, a Negro servant girl beside her. They were sitting in the front of the church. It was Mrs. George Whitney, a Chicago society leader, and Maggie had made the silk dress she wore. Why would a woman like that attend such a gathering? Surely she was not going to California to find a husband. A rich widow such as Mrs. Whitney could have her choice of husbands. Perhaps the Negro girl hoped to go, and her mistress was there to speak up for her. Mrs. Whitney was a kind woman, Maggie remembered. Still, Maggie did not want to be seen, not that a woman like Mrs. Whitney would pay attention to a dressmaker who had made her only two or three gowns.

Maggie spotted a red-haired girl with bright green eyes marching down the aisle, her head back. That one was more likely to recognize her, because the girl worked as a maid in one of the fine Chicago houses—the Fletcher mansion. Her name was Winny, Winny Rupe, and she had told Maggie that she'd come from Ireland a few years before with her brother. She had been kind, too, and she would surely recall Maggie from the time Winny had picked up a dress for her mistress. Servants were likely to recognize tradespeople, and the two had been more than casual acquaintances. Winny might even be her friend if both of them went to California. Maggie couldn't risk being recognized, however. Not now, anyway.

Maybe later, when they were far away and it was too late to turn back, Maggie would introduce herself. When Winny glanced her way, Maggie ducked her head and straightened the bow in Clara's curls.

Maggie heard the laughter and nervous chatter around her, although she also glimpsed one or two dour women. She nudged Mary as a woman who apparently had changed her mind about attending the meeting stood up and marched back down the aisle, muttering, "You are a bunch of fools."

"That we are," a girl called to her, then laughed with her companion. Maggie looked away, thinking perhaps the woman was right. *What could be more foolish than going all the way to California to find a husband?* she wondered. But then, she didn't care about finding a husband. She slunk down in her seat, hoping she would not be noticed.

The sanctuary filled quickly, with many women standing in the aisles or at the back of the church. The talking stopped when a tall man who had been seated in the chancel stood and walked to the pulpit. Maggie stilled Clara, who had begun to squirm, and studied him, wondering if someone so impressive could be a preacher. She hadn't known many ministers, but the few she did know had been old men who were wizened and unctuous. This man, while gaunt, was tall and well built. His hair was gray, although he looked to be not yet forty. He strode to the pulpit as if he owned the world. Maggie straightened up. "I'd go to California for him," a woman behind her said in a loud voice.

The man acted as if he hadn't heard. "Good afternoon, ladies. I am Reverend William Parnell," he said in a rich voice. "And the man behind me is my brother-in-law, Reverend Joseph Swain."

Maggie thought he had the voice of God.

"I welcome you here. It is a fateful journey we plan, and I am sure you wish to hear the particulars."

Joseph, dark and far more handsome than William, stood and came forward at that, saying in a voice with the slightest tone of censure, "First, brother, we must start with prayer."

"Of course. You are right as usual," William said with a slight sigh. Joseph stepped to the pulpit, as if he would offer the prayer, but before Joseph could speak, his brother-in-law bowed his head and asked the Lord for His blessing on the venture they were about to undertake. The supplication was brief, and Maggie wondered if Reverend Swain's prayer would have been longer. She glanced at the woman sitting behind the men, who nodded at her brother, then patted her husband's hand after he returned to his seat, as if in support, and whispered something to him.

She, too, was familiar, although Maggie could not place her.

"Now, ladies," William began again, looking out over the crowd. He stopped at Mrs. Whitney, the woman dressed in furs, and gave her an almost imperceptible nod. "You have come here because you have seen the sheets posted around the city and are curious. Some of you may think this is a joke, but I assure you we are deadly serious." He paused to let that sink in. "As the posting says, myself, my brother-in-law, and his wife—my sister"—he gestured at the woman seated next to Joseph—"propose to organize a wagon train of young women of high moral character who are willing to make the arduous journey to the California gold fields in search of husbands."

He paused as Maggie gasped. She had read the broadsheets, but until that moment, she had not fully grasped that the two men were in earnest.

"For shame," a man called, and Maggie turned to stare at him. She had not seen any men come into the church.

"No, sir," William said. "The Bible instructs us to marry, and it says nothing forbidding women from going by wagon train to do so."

Mary chuckled, and the man disappeared into the shadows at the back of the church. Maggie tried to get a good look at his face, although it was unlikely he was there because of her. She'd never said a word to anyone about attending the meeting. Nonetheless, she felt a wave of fear and drew Clara closer to her. As if sensing Maggie's turmoil, Mary took her hand and smiled at her. Despite the crossed eyes, Mary had a pretty face, although it was roughened by sun and wind. *Mary would never be afraid of anyone,* Maggie thought.

"You may not know me, because I have only recently come to Chicago, but many of you are familiar with Reverend Swain," William continued. "You know him for a godly man, a man of the highest character. I am proud to claim kinship with him." He gestured toward Joseph, who bowed his head in acknowledgment. "Reverend Swain would not commit himself to the venture we propose with any but the most respectful motives.

"And I believe there are few among you who do not know my sister, Caroline Swain. She has agreed to join us in our adventure. As noble as our purpose is, it is still a brave undertaking, and she is up to the mark."

Maggie turned to stare at Caroline and realized then who she was. She had seen her at a place called the Kitchen, where Caroline served food to the destitute. Maggie had gone there sometimes with Clara and had been grateful the woman didn't preach or look down on her for being poor. In fact, Maggie had seen Caroline welcome fancy women, treating them with kindness.

"Mrs. Swain will look after the welfare of those of you who elect to join us. She will provide succor and comfort as only a woman can."

"Can she drive a mule team?" Mary called.

The audience turned to stare at Mary, and a few laughed.

"She will learn. You will all learn. And it is oxen that will take us there, not mules," William said. "I can tell you that she can ride a horse bareback better than any boy I ever saw."

Caroline bowed her head in embarrassment.

Joseph cleared his throat, and William said, "Of course, this venture is no laughing matter. The trip will be arduous, but we do not intend for it to be all drudgery. We will have prayer and laughter to go with the hardship."

He was still for a moment as he looked out at the women, who were leaning forward to hear more. He had a commanding presence, and he inspired confidence. "The broadsheets have told you the purpose of our venture. We propose to take women to Goosetown in the California diggings, where you will choose husbands from among the many men there. I expect there are a hundred men for every woman, maybe a thousand."

He stopped as several women chuckled. Maggie did not care about a thousand men. She glanced at Mary, who was listening intently. *Why does she feel the need to go all that way to California just to marry?* Maggie wondered.

"Of course, not every man is worthy of a wife. Some are too far gone in wickedness to be acceptable. Still, I believe the majority lack only a good woman by their side to overcome the temptations of greed and gambling and . . ." He paused and cleared his throat and tried to hide a smile. "And other temptations." He looked out at the congregation a moment, and then he gave them the details of the trip. "This will not be an easy journey," he concluded. "Only those of you in good health should consider making it. We will have wagons to carry provisions and your belongings, but you will walk most of the way."

"Two thousand miles?" a woman shouted.

William nodded. "Walking will be the least of your challenges. You will sleep on the ground and cook over a campfire. You will encounter dust so bad you must tie a bandana over your face, and even then, it will get into your nose and mouth until you cannot breathe. You will feel a prairie heat as hot as the final resting place of the sinful. Then, in the mountains, you will be chilled by rain and hail and maybe even snow before we reach our destination. There may be Indians, although they will not be as dangerous as cholera and other sicknesses. Or accidents. Some of you may die." He stopped to underline the seriousness of his words. "I advise you not to sign up if you are unwilling to face the hardships. We want only the ablest and purest of women."

19

I am neither, Maggie thought.

"And the most moral," Joseph added in a loud voice. He stood and looked out over the congregation. "We will accept no degenerates nor harlots nor those fleeing the law."

"Yes, of course," William agreed. He raised an eyebrow at Caroline.

"We expect the trip to take five months, perhaps more," he continued. "That means some days we will go ten or fifteen miles or more a day. Some days will be slower. Others faster."

"Why will we not go by stagecoach?" a woman asked.

"There are no stage lines to California, and if there were, the fare would be too costly. Besides, I have been to California and back, and I doubt that a coach could survive such a trip. Nor could horses. They are a poor choice for such a long journey. Mules are better, but we will use oxen. They are cheaper and more docile. Have any of you worked with oxen before?"

Mary raised her hand, and so did several others. Maggie wished she knew about animals. Dressmaking was a poor skill for an overland journey. *A needle won't be much good fighting off an Indian,* she thought.

"That is good. The rest of you will have to learn to drive them."

"Us?" Maggie muttered.

"You. We will employ men"—he glanced at

Joseph—"righteous men for the most strenuous work, but you women, too, will be expected to participate."

"What if I do not find a husband I like?" someone asked, and the audience laughed.

"With a thousand men to choose from, you would have to be mighty particular," he told her.

"What are those men like? I would not want a degenerate."

The minister laughed then. "Yes, there are degenerates among them, but most are good men. They are your brothers and friends and neighbors who have preceded you to California. No man will be forced upon you. The choice is yours."

Clara was bored and began to fidget. Mary took the child from Maggie. She drew a handkerchief from her pocket and with a few quick turns made it into a rabbit. Clara was fascinated with the animal as it leapt from Mary's hand to Clara's shoe. Mary put the rabbit on her arm, where it jumped up and down. Clara laughed and said, "Again."

"Tell them what they must take with them," Caroline said, and Maggie leaned forward to hear the answer. Perhaps they would be required to purchase their supplies.

"As little as possible," William answered. "We will provide the wagon and tents, the food and other provisions. You will need to bring sensible clothes, boots and two pairs of sturdy shoes, medicines, and personal items."

"I shall personally supply each woman with a Bible," Joseph interjected.

"Thank you, brother."

"What about my furniture, my dishes. I could not go without my spinning wheel," a woman called.

"There is no need for furniture, and likely you would have to discard it along the way if you brought it. As for dishes, we will have tin ones. China would be broken before we get to Fort Kearny. I would allow you to take your spinning wheel only if you would agree to carry it in your arms for two thousand miles."

My dressmaking things, Maggie thought. *They will not take up much room.* She glanced down at the large bag she had brought with her and set on the floor. It contained her thimble and threads and measuring tape, her scissors and needles and pins. There was fabric, too, including scraps for mending and quilting. If she had to, she could tie some of the contents to her belt.

Reverend Parnell spoke again. "Ladies, I cannot emphasize too much that this will be a rigorous trip. A dangerous trip. None but the hardiest should undertake it. I do not want any of you to agree to it without knowing what will be expected of you."

Mary raised her hand, and Reverend Parnell

nodded at her. "How much you going to charge us?"

There was a chorus of "Yes, how much?" and "I wondered about that."

Maggie had not thought about the cost. Of course there would be a charge. It didn't matter how much. She had no way of paying it. She had been imprudent in coming here.

The minister paused and smiled at the women. "Not one copper. We have raised the cost of the trip from generous members of the community."

Mary and Maggie exchanged glances, and others murmured words of surprise. Caroline took her husband's hand.

"Many have supported our venture with their purses, but we are indebted to one member of the congregation in particular who has generously agreed to underwrite most of the journey. That person wishes to remain anonymous."

"So we don't need to pay anything?" Mary asked.

"You will need to supply your clothes and anything else you wish to take with you. And you should bring along an amount of cash to pay for necessities along the way."

"How much?" someone shouted.

"A hundred dollars should suffice." When a woman groaned, he added, "Many can make do with half that, perhaps even less."

Maggie touched her pocket. She had little more

than twenty dollars, but she would make that do.

The woman beside Maggie stood up and walked out with several others. Most stayed until the questions were done and William held up his hand. "We would like to see how many of you are interested in joining us. You have a week to commit yourselves, but if you would line up now, Reverend and Mrs. Swain and I will interview you. Do not be offended if we say you are not suitable for the trip. As I have told you, only the hardiest women should make it."

Two

"Will you go, Maggie?" Mary asked. She removed her shawl, revealing thick yellow braids wrapped around her head.

Maggie shrugged. "I do not know. I have to think on it. What about you?"

A woman stepped aside to allow Mary into the aisle. "My brother and his wife will call me puddin' headed. They will surely try to talk me out of it. Perhaps they are right, but I believe they are not," Mary replied, setting Clara on her feet.

The little girl smiled up at Mary, who for the first time, it appeared, saw the bruise on the side of the child's face. "Fell, did you?"

The girl buried her face in her mother's skirt.

Maggie didn't reply as Mary pushed up the veil on Maggie's hat and studied the bruises on her face, too. After a moment, Mary said, "I help raise my brother's young 'uns. They are all the time falling." She reached over and touched Maggie's nose. "It looks broken. I guess you fell yourself."

"There are stairs," Maggie said, although that didn't explain it.

"Stairs," Mary said and nodded. She stepped

aside to let two women retreat up the aisle to the door. One muttered she would not walk two thousand miles for any man, even Millard Fillmore. Her companion replied she would not walk even a mile for the president, such a bungler was he.

Mary watched them for a moment, then said, "I have made up my mind to go. They—my brother, Micah, and his wife, Louise—they cannot stop me, but they will make me feel as if I have lost my mind." She paused. "If you would come, I would help you care for the girl."

"She likes you," Maggie said.

"Children and cats, but maybe not men."

"You have not found one to your liking here?" Men were fickle, Maggie thought. They cared more for a woman's pretty face and slim waist than for her intelligence and hard work. She would have pitied Mary but suspected the woman would reject such sentiment.

"He has not found me."

"Surely you do not need to go all the way to California to acquire a husband."

"Oh no. There is old Howard Hale. He has the farm next to ours, that is, my brother's farm. In truth, it is half mine, was left to me in partnership by our parents, but Micah says that by law, a woman cannot hold ownership if she has a man to act as guardian, and so it is my brother who claims it. Micah thought it would be a good thing for me to marry our neighbor and bring the land into the family. Howard is as old as the saints, and he had no children by his first wife. As the second, I would inherit his holdings."

"Would it not be a good thing, then, to have your own land?"

"If I inherited it, Micah, as my guardian, would take control of it, too."

"Perhaps you would have a son by then."

Mary snorted. "Not by that old man. I would as soon sleep in the woodshed, begging your pardon, Maggie. I live on a farm and know the doings of the animals and sometimes do not watch my tongue."

"You do not offend me. Little does anymore. So you will not marry him?"

Mary laughed, and Maggie thought she had a merry laugh, like a girl. "Would you marry a man who bathes only twice a year, on the days he changes his underwear, a man that is likely always drunk whenever he is awake? He is a lazy sort, who has let his land go to ruin and would expect me to farm it and care for the animals, as well as cook his meals and warm his bed. When he proposed, he inquired as to whether I could repair a roof." She laughed again. "There was good reason. When the rain came through a hole in the roof onto his bed, he moved the bed."

While Mary talked, other women pushed past them, and now the two were near the end of the line. "Do you want to sit a minute while you think it over?" Mary asked.

Maggie nodded.

"Is it the hardship you worry about?" Mary asked.

"No, I am used to it."

"I would be pleased to carry Clara when you tire."

"Thank you."

"You would have time to make ready, more than two months."

"That is a problem. I had thought we would be staying here until we left, that we would prepare ourselves or learn to drive the wagons, whilst we lived in the church. Clara and I are wearing all of our clothes, and I have brought our personal things in a bag."

"And you cannot go home?"

Maggie jerked up her head. She had said too much. "Oh, yes, of course."

Mary did not say more, as the two seated themselves in the shadow of a pillar in the front row. Maggie drew Clara into her lap. They could hear the ministers, but the men did not appear to notice them. She watched several women sign the applications. Others carried them off, perhaps to be read at their leisure—or maybe only to be laughed at. Reverend Parnell turned away a woman who was tubercular and another old enough to be his mother. Maggie and Mary smiled at each other when a woman who gave her name as Lavinia Mercer said she already had a wedding dress and wanted to find a husband to go with it. Her fiancé had proved wanting, and she did not want the dress to go to waste, she told them. "I shall not forgive him," she said, raising her chin in the air. She was plump and had a haughty face.

Joseph accepted two women who were widows but was not sure about one who had completed four years of college. "She would not make a good wife. She would want to be in charge of her husband," he said.

Winny, the maid Maggie had recognized, went up to the men and declared she had made up her mind to go.

"Are you able to walk that distance?" Joseph asked, sizing up the girl, who was barely five feet tall.

"I walk a hundred miles a day going up the stairs with water and down them with the slops," she replied.

Maggie smiled as she listened to the conversation. It was likely the girl had done more manual labor than either of the ministers.

"I ask because you are small," Joseph said.

"My mistress does not think I am small when she has me scrubbing stairs and hauling buckets of coal. I work twelve hours a day and often more."

"What do you think, Willie?" Joseph asked.

"Women know their strength more than we do. Sometimes I think they are better suited to the rigors of the trail than the men. I say she will do." William handed Winny an application.

"Begging your pardon, sir, but as you have been to California, I ask if you have heard mention of my brother. David Rupe, he is. He left for California in '50 and expected to find a fortune. I believe he must be very rich now."

"California is a large place, and many men are there. They all expect to get rich," William replied. "Nobody ever goes west to get poor."

"He was one of the Rough and Ready boys."

"From Maine?"

"Illinois."

"I know of half a dozen Rough and Ready companies. I cannot say I have heard of a David Rupe, however, but some men change their names."

"Oh, Davy would not. You would remember him. He is very strong and handsome, with hair redder than mine. It is bright enough to glow in the dark."

"Many who leave are strong and handsome, but they do not always arrive in such condition in California."

"You think he did not make it?"

"Oh, I cannot say that at all. There are dozens of diggings. Do you know the name of the place he intended to go?"

Winny shook her head. "His last letter came to me while he was still on his way to the gold fields. But I am not worried. When he discovers I have come looking for him, he will find me." She slowly printed her name on the form and signed it. Then she sang out, "I'm off to California with my banjo on my knee."

Maggie watched the girl as she left the chancel and went out a side door, glad the ministers had accepted her, because Winny was a good person. Later, if she joined the company, Maggie would take Winny aside and tell her they had met before and thank her for her past kindness. She wondered if Clara remembered her, too, but the girl was playing with Mary's handkerchief rabbit and hadn't paid attention.

The ministers interviewed scores of women, and the line was getting shorter when one stepped forward and picked up the pen and dipped it into the inkwell, only to have Joseph snatch it away. "Just a moment, madam, a few questions first," he said, looking hard at her. The woman wore a gaudy dress, and her cheeks were rouged. Her hair was an unnatural color of red. Despite her tasteless embellishments, she was a beautiful woman, with white skin and deep-set eyes that were almost turquoise. "Who are you?"

"Sadie Cooper," the woman replied, defiant.

"And what is your occupation?"

Sadie frowned. "I am a widow."

Caroline smiled and turned away at that, and then Maggie herself recognized the woman. She was a fancy woman, a Magdalene who sometimes went to the Kitchen. Caroline had always greeted her with affection, and that thoughtfulness had impressed Maggie.

"And your husband, what was his occupation?" Joseph asked.

"None of your business," Sadie said.

William looked up at that, then glanced at his sister and suppressed a grin.

"Such impertinence does not serve you well. Do you believe this woman is qualified to join us?" Joseph turned to his wife.

"Oh, but dearest, she will be perfect. I know her from the Kitchen. She keeps the women in line, makes sure they do not fight or steal each other's food. And she loves the children so. I believe she would be an asset on our venture." She glanced at her brother and added, "We do not want to take only timid women."

"Her appearance, her dress, her face . . . ," Joseph protested.

"I know you would not be so un-Christian as to judge by appearance." Caroline added in a whisper just loud enough for Maggie to hear, "Her dress is not her fault. Perhaps it was given to her and is all she has."

Caroline's brother had listened to the conversation and caught his sister's eye again. "Her

32

face will soon be covered with dust. Of course, if you judge her to be unacceptable . . ." Maggie thought that, like his sister, he had used the word "judge" on purpose.

Joseph stared at his wife a long time. "If you will vouch for her, then I will accept her," he said, handing Sadie the pen.

"Noted," William told him.

Sadie scribbled her name, then looked at Caroline with what might have been an air of triumph. After the woman left, Maggie saw Caroline exchange a smile with her brother.

The church was almost empty now. A few women lingered at the back, perhaps out of curiosity, but when the line was finished, they left. In a few minutes, only Maggie and Mary and Mrs. Whitney, the woman in furs, and her servant were seated in the pews. Maggie started to rise, but Mary touched her arm as Mrs. Whitney stood up. She was as stylishly dressed as any woman in Chicago. She was not pretty, not even handsome, but still, she was striking because of her stately demeanor. It was clear she wanted to talk to the ministers privately. None of them seemed to realize two other women waited behind a pillar.

Mrs. Whitney went up the steps to the chancel, the Negro servant behind her, and Joseph bowed to her. "Why, dear Mrs. Whitney. I hope you approve of our beginning," he said.

"It was good of you to come and give us your blessing." He turned to William. "As I have confided to you, Mrs. Whitney is the woman who is financing nearly all of our trip. She gave the rose window"—he pointed to the window behind them—"in memory of her dear husband, George."

"I thought the financing of this venture a more suitable way to memorialize him. He was a fine man."

"Your generosity overwhelms us," William said. "As you can see, we have much interest in our venture. Twenty or thirty applications have been signed, and we may have more by the end of the week."

"The women will be most grateful to you," Caroline said.

"The women are not to know," Mrs. Whitney told her. "That was our agreement, was it not, Reverend Swain?"

"It was indeed. My wife and my brother-in-law will keep your confidence." He fetched a chair and set it in front of the table for Mrs. Whitney. She sat down, spreading her skirt over the edge of the chair, and Maggie saw a tiny tear in the fabric. She had made the dress only a few months before, and her fingers itched to repair the rip before it got bigger.

Mrs. Whitney reached for two applications. Then, to the surprise of the ministers, she filled them out and handed them to Joseph. "For my servant and me."

Joseph looked aghast. "You are going?"

"I am."

"You are going to California to find a husband?"

"That remains to be seen. I have been lonely since Mr. Whitney died. I have not found a suitable replacement among the mealy-mouthed men who court me. They primp and fawn and lie to me, telling me I am a great beauty." She turned to Reverend Parnell. "Tell me, sir, am I a beauty?"

Maggie and Mary exchanged looks, and Mary grinned.

"Of course—" Joseph began, but Mrs. Whitney cut him off. "I know what you would say. I ask Caroline's brother."

William studied her. The woman was younger than her manner would suggest, probably not yet forty, but her face was lined, and gray hair escaped from her bonnet. Her eyes were an ordinary brown. "You have strength of character in your face, and you have a stately demeanor, but no. I cannot say you are so very pretty."

Joseph started to protest, but Mrs. Whitney held up her hand. "There, I want such an honest man, and one who does not mind soiling his hands to earn his living. I have found no such person in Chicago, and so I believe I will try California. Evaline"—she indicated the servant behind her—

"has agreed to go along to take care of me. She is thirteen. I shall fit up a wagon for myself and hire my own driver."

"That would not be possible," William spoke up.

Mrs. Whitney frowned at him. "Do you object because Evaline is a Negro? Are you saying there are no Negro men in California?"

William looked down at his hands for a moment. "No, her color is of no consequence. There are plenty of men who would find her to be desirable. It is your demand that you take your own wagon. I believe it would cause dissent among the women if you accompanied them as you suggest. All are equal on the trail. If you were to play the great lady, you would find the others turning against you. The women must work together or they will not make it to California. Suppose you or your servant were to contract an illness—cholera, perhaps. You would need one of the women to nurse you. What if your driver were to be injured? Would you drive the wagon? No, madam, as grateful as we are for your support, we would not allow you to join the company unless you were on an equal footing with the others."

"Surely we can make an exception. This is Mrs. Whitney," Joseph said, wringing his hands.

"What do you say, Caroline?" Mrs. Whitney asked.

"I?" Caroline glanced at her husband. She was

standing next to him then, and Maggie wondered how so handsome a man had come to marry such a plain woman. She was short and squat with a large nose and small, close eyes. Perhaps he saw the goodness beyond the unimpressive looks.

Mrs. Whitney nodded.

"I believe my brother knows best."

Clara hit her foot against the pew, and Maggie held her tight. What would the ministers think if they knew she and Mary were listening?

"Would I be allowed to take my Chippendale chairs? They have been in my husband's family for many years."

"You could take them, but they will be thrown out before we reach Fort Kearny," William told her. "Or perhaps used as firewood."

"What about my dresses and hats? I would not care to arrive in California looking like a scullery maid. They were made by the finest dressmakers, here and in Paris."

Maggie felt a surge of pride, since she had made several of Mrs. Whitney's garments. She worried then that the woman would indeed recognize her and was glad it was dark where she sat.

"You should take only those clothes that will not wear out on the trail. Calico is best. As for hats, yes, but only if you have a sunbonnet."

"My little dog?"

"If you do not mind him going into some Indian's cooking pot."

Mrs. Whitney looked startled, and Joseph said, "Willie, how could you!"

"Your servant is going, then?" William asked, glancing at the black girl.

"I would not leave without her. She is very dear to me." Mrs. Whitney put a protecting arm around the girl. "What do you say, Evaline? Shall we go or stay?"

"I will abide by your decision, but I would not mind the challenge," the girl said. Maggie's eyes widened at the girl's proper speech. She had never heard a Negro speak like that, but then, she knew few Negroes.

"No, you would be up to it. The question is, am I?" Mrs. Whitney asked.

"You won't . . ." William began, then paused as if not sure he should ask the question.

"Take back my money. No. But I shall think seriously about taking my dog, Whitey, with me, and woe to the Indian who tries to turn him into supper."

After Mrs. Whitney and the servant girl left, the ministers gathered up the applications. Mary took Maggie's hand and said, "It is time. I am going to speak to them. Will you come?"

Maggie nodded. She was nervous. What if they asked her reason for going to California? "Come, Clara," she whispered.

"Where are we going?"

"Perhaps as far as the moon."

"Sirs," Mary said.

Joseph looked up, startled, and glanced at the door Mrs. Whitney had used.

"We would speak with you, too," Mary said. "The child was resting, and we did not wish to disturb her. She had our full attention." She stood, and the men stared at her.

"You heard?" Joseph asked.

Mary did not lie. "I have heard many things. I keep to myself that which is not my business."

William nodded. "Would you go to California, too?"

Mary, big as a barn, stepped forward and stood in front of the men, turning her head to the side, perhaps to hide the cast in her eye. "I would. I am fit and healthy."

"And you know how to drive oxen," William said. "I saw you raise your hand."

"I can shoe them, too, if need be. You will not find me wanting."

"No, I can see that. I question whether you might find our men wanting." He paused, then asked, "Are you wishing to escape debts or leave a husband behind?"

"No, sir."

"Are you a moral Christian woman in good health?"

"Yes, sir."

Maggie smiled to herself as she wondered how

39

many women had actually admitted to being immoral.

"Your age?"

"That is my business, sir. There was no mention of age in your advertisement."

"You will do." William smiled at her; then, without looking to his brother-in-law or sister, he handed her the pen.

Mary signed her name in plain block letters, then turned to Maggie. "My friend will go, too."

Maggie came out of the shadows, gripping Clara's hand. She shook with fear. What if the ministers asked questions? She should have thought of a story to tell them.

"A child?" Joseph asked. "We said nothing about children."

"You let the woman who is sponsoring the venture take her servant, and she is only a girl," Mary interjected.

"Plenty of children have made the journey," Reverend Parnell said. "They are as well suited to it as the adults."

"She is all I have. She must go with me," Maggie said.

"Where is your husband?" Joseph asked.

Maggie started to answer but found the words would not come. What could she tell them?

"Have you a husband?" he demanded. "We take no runaway wives. If you are among them, I

40

counsel you to return to him and beg his forgiveness. It is your duty."

"I . . . ," Maggie began but was too shaken to finish.

"Go along with you, then," Joseph said. He glanced at his wife, who looked down. She would not contradict him.

"She has no husband," Mary said suddenly, and Maggie looked up at her in surprise.

"Are you saying she is a sister of misfortune and the child is a bastard?" Joseph asked.

Mary glared at him so hard that he leaned away from her. "No such thing. She is a widow, so newly fresh a widow that she cannot speak of it, can barely say his name without breaking down. Her husband"—Mary cleared her throat—"perhaps you read about him in the newspapers. Henry his name was, such a good, hearty fellow. He was run down by a coach and four. He dashed into the street to rescue a boy who was in the path of the horses. Oh, it was a brave and terrible thing to do."

As Mary put her hand to her eyes as if to wipe away tears, Maggie stared at her in astonishment. She had known the woman for little more than an hour, and yet she had come to her defense with this story.

"Ah, the tragedy of it, to leave behind a widow and child, to leave them to the harshness of a Chicago winter."

41

"I have not read of it," Joseph said.

Caroline studied Maggie, then looked at Clara. "I am sure I did, my dear. Perhaps you forgot it. Was it not before Christmas?"

Maggie realized Caroline had addressed the question to her, and she nodded, too astonished to speak.

"I believe we must accept her," Caroline said. "After all, it is not only the men in California who need succor. The Lord calls on us to aid all of our brothers and sisters." She reached around her husband and handed Maggie a pen.

Maggie took it and signed "Maggie."

"A last name, please," Joseph said.

Maggie froze. Then Mary spoke up. "I believe you will be pleased with Maggie Hale."

Maggie leaned forward, wondering whether the name was spelled "Hail" or "Hale," but chose the latter. She was glad the men had forgotten to ask her the questions Mary had been asked to answer. As she stepped away from the table, she recovered her voice and said, "The boy lived."

Maggie went to retrieve her umbrella and her bag, which she had left in the pew, and when she looked up, she did not see Mary. She was sorry, because she should have liked to thank her.

The sleet had turned to snow, and a harsh wind swept it down the street. Clara shivered and said, "It is too cold, Mama." Maggie took off her shawl and wrapped it around her daughter. She did not know where to go. Maggie had told Mary she could go home, but she would not. It was too dangerous. Perhaps she could return to the church and find a corner in which to hide, leave her bag in some out-of-the-way spot. But what if the ministers found her? She would look for a doorway that would shelter them. She had a little money, but she dared not spend it unless she had to. The ministers had said she would need at least fifty dollars for the trip, and she had only half that amount. Still, it would not do for Clara to sleep on the street on such a cold night.

As she tried to make up her mind, Maggie saw Mary loom out of the blizzard, leading a horse. "I am sorry about the name Hale. It was all I could think of."

"It is a good name," Maggie said.

"Have you a home to go to?"

Maggie knew the woman understood the truth of it. "I shall find something."

"And in the meantime, you will freeze. Come home with me. We can all three ride the horse. He is strong enough to carry two of me."

"Oh, I cannot put you out."

"It is no bother."

"You said you live with your brother and his family. Surely they will not want me."

"They do not want me much either and would put me out if I did not do the farm work. The

43

house is half mine. If they do not welcome you, I will. We can always sleep in the barn."

When Maggie gasped, Mary said, "I am only joking. There is room in the house. Come." Before Maggie could reply, Mary lifted Clara and placed her on the horse. The little girl clapped her hands with delight. Then Mary picked up Maggie and set her behind Clara, handing her the heavy bundle she had brought with her. Finally, Mary herself mounted the horse and, holding tight to Maggie, kicked the chestnut into a trot. As they headed out into the swirling snow, Maggie wondered what she had committed herself to. It could not be worse than what she had left behind.

Three

Louise Madrid thrust an armload of clothing into Maggie's hands and said, "If you are eating my cooking and sleeping in my bed, you might as well earn your keep. These need mending." She sat down in the rocking chair and picked up a book.

In fact, Maggie did the cooking now, and she and Clara slept on the floor, but Maggie didn't mind the sewing. She longed to busy her hands with needlework, and she was grateful to the Madrids for allowing Clara and her to stay. Maggie had heard Louise complain what a nuisance the two visitors were, but Mary had stood firm. "If you want me to finish preparing the fields for spring planting, you will welcome them. Truth is, I have more claim to the house than you do, Louise, it being left to both me and Micah. I have a mind to find a solicitor who will tell me my rights. Might be I could sell my portion of the farm," Mary had told her sister-in-law. No one had ever stood up for Maggie, and she was grateful. She tried to pay for her keep by doing work that Louise considered beneath her.

Now Maggie took out her needle and thread

and concentrated on her stitching, listening to the clamor outside. Louise's two children were as smitten with Mary as Clara was. The three followed her everywhere. Maggie recalled her friend's comment that cats and children loved her, although not men. Women didn't seem to care for her either. The news was about that Mary was going to California to find a husband, but not a single woman had called to wish her well.

As if knowing what Maggie was thinking, Louise said, "She is a queer one, Mary is. All the girls she grew up with are married now, with children, some even with grandchildren. They think her odd, and she is, no husband and working the farm like a man. They do not understand it, and neither do I. She could have married our neighbor, Howard Hale—" Louise stopped and looked up from a book she held in her hands. "Is he kin to you?"

"No," Maggie replied.

"Odd, you having the same name."

"Mary will find a husband in California," Maggie said.

Louise snorted. "The shame of it, her going away like that. What about me? Did she consider Micah and me? Did she give a moment's thought to all the work I will have to do when she is gone? I am already worked to the bone."

Maggie smiled to herself. Louise sat in the house most of the day, reading or doing useless needlework. She had recently painted grapes on a piece of velvet that Maggie had made into a pillow for her, and now she was making drawn-work doilies. The fancywork sat in a basket beside her chair. Did the woman really have any idea how much work Mary did and how she would be taxed when Mary left? "Mary wants adventure," Maggie said.

Louise rolled her eyes. "That is unnatural. Women do not want adventure. They want a husband and children. If Mary leaves us for California, Mr. Madrid will not allow her to return. He has made that clear to her. He does not want her back after all the embarrassment."

"I thought Mary owned half of the farm," Maggie said. It was none of her business, but she wanted to prick Louise for her harsh words about Mary.

"Who says that?"

Maggie shrugged. She should have kept her mouth shut.

"Mr. Madrid owns the farm for the both of them," Louise said sharply. "It is unseemly that a woman should work a farm for herself. Although Mary is . . . well, look at her. She might as well be a man."

As far as Maggie could see, Micah left the farming to Mary, who enlisted the children to help her plow and plant. Mary acted as both hired man and hired girl. She had told Maggie that when she was a girl, she had had her own bedroom upstairs, but as the children were born, Louise claimed the room for them, and now Mary slept on a pallet near the fireplace in the kitchen. When Maggie showed surprise, Mary said she didn't mind. After all, it was the warmest place in the house in winter, and she did not wake others when she rose before dawn to prepare breakfast.

"I shall miss her, I suppose. She is company of a sort," Louise said suddenly. "I am lonely here. Mary is not interested in the finer things, in fancywork or poetry. I have never seen her read anything but a newspaper. She talks mostly of seeds and planting and reaping. I have tried to improve her mind, but she does not care for novels, and she will not gossip. When she talks of something besides the farm, it is politics. Perhaps that will please a man in California, but not here. Politics is for men, not women. I myself would not be able to name the president of the United States if Mary had not talked so much about him."

"Then her political knowledge has accomplished some purpose," Maggie said, choosing to misinterpret Louise's words.

The remark confused Louise, and she cast an accusing eye on Maggie, as if Maggie were criticizing her. Then she asked, "Why will *you* go to California? Surely someone as pretty as you could find a husband in Chicago."

As if prettiness is all that is necessary for a good marriage, Maggie thought. She knew better. "I wanted to leave Chicago," she said. "I could not bear to stay there. I determined to get as far away as possible, and California seems like it is the end of the earth."

"Yes, I suppose I understand it, your husband getting killed like that." Mary had told her sister-in-law the same story she'd told the ministers, that Maggie's husband had been run down by horses while saving a child.

"It was in the newspaper," Mary had said, and Maggie had swallowed a smile when she overheard that, because she knew Louise did not read newspapers. "You must have read it."

"Oh yes, I suppose I did," Louise had replied.

Now Louise closed her book and picked up her needlework. "I must say I enjoy your company more than Mary's. It is nice to take a few minutes away from all my chores to sit and talk." When Maggie only nodded, Louise continued. "You may think me harsh in my view of Mary, but she resists my attempts to instruct her in women's ways. Perhaps it goes back to an incident when she was young."

Maggie knew Louise wanted her to ask what had happened, but she did not care to know Mary's secrets, did not want to gossip about her.

When Maggie didn't reply, Louise continued.

"I do not like to carry tales, but I believe you should know of it. The thing happened when Mary was fourteen or thereabout. She was always a big girl, and by then she was unnaturally large. The boys did not care for her, not only because she was an oddity but because she was always besting them at games and would not defer to them." She stopped as if waiting for Maggie to nod in disapproval.

Maggie kept on stitching, however, and after a moment, Louise went on. "There was one fellow. I believe his name was Andrew—Andy for short. He brought her sweets in his lunch bucket and sat beside her in the schoolroom. The boys did not tease him for it, and Mary should have known from that that something was wrong. But she was foolish about him and paid no attention to the others. In fact"—Mary leaned forward—"I believe Mary was quite smitten with him and thought he was with her. Imagine that!" She sat back and dipped her chin to emphasize the absurdity of what she had just said.

"Sometimes Andy walked her home, and on one particular day, he suggested they go a round-about way through a copse of trees. Mary was imprudent enough to agree. After they were hidden by the foliage, he pushed her against a tree and kissed her. When Mary did not protest—I do not know this for sure, but it was what the boy claimed—he ripped the bodice of her dress and grabbed her breasts." Louise stopped to gauge Maggie's reaction, but Maggie, her face flushed, kept her head bowed. She did not want to hear about Mary's humiliation.

"I suppose Mary pushed him away, but by then it was too late, of course. He ran off shouting to his friends, 'Touched them! Touched them! You owe me a nickel!' You see, the boys had followed them and had seen the entire incident. It had been a dare. A boy asked what they felt like, and Andy replied, 'Like shoats.' For weeks, the boys made oinking sounds whenever Mary passed. She never let on she knew what they meant, but everyone in the school had been told what had happened and laughed. I myself was so embarrassed that I could hardly stand next to her. You see, Micah was already courting me."

"Her brother did not defend her?" Maggie asked.

"He could hardly fight the whole school. Besides, we were both so ashamed of her." Louise laughed and looked at Maggie for her response, but Maggie kept her eyes on her sewing. Not for anything in the world would she laugh at her friend's terrible experience. Louise should have offered sympathy, not censure, and Micah, who like Mary was tall and broad, should have beaten the boys within an inch of their lives.

When Maggie said nothing, Louise cleared her throat. "I tell you this out of the goodness of my

51

heart, so that you understand why Mary does not care for men."

"I must start supper, Mrs. Madrid," Maggie said, rising. "I shall finish the mending later."

Louise was irked and said, "You may put it aside. I should like you to make a dress for me. I have the fabric already. Mary says you were a dressmaker in Chicago, Mrs. Hale."

Maggie was startled. She still was not used to her new name.

Her last name was actually Kaiser, Maggie told Mary after she had been at the farm for a week and knew Mary would keep her secret. She hadn't said anything at first for fear the truth would make Mary reconsider taking her in. She would have changed her first name, too, if she had been quick enough to think of it.

"You should know who you have brought under your roof," Maggie said one night after the others had gone to bed. Maggie had mixed up the bread dough and set it near the fireplace to rise overnight.

Mary was putting away the supper dishes the two had washed and dried and was about to pour the water remaining in the teakettle into the tin cans holding the geraniums, which she had taken from the windowsill to keep them from freezing. She held the kettle in her hands for a moment, then said, "Louise is in bed upstairs. What do you say to a cup of the good tea?"

Maggie grinned. Louise allowed them to drink only the cheap tea that Mary brought home from the store, keeping the expensive tea for herself, for her nerves, she insisted. "I say you deserve it," Maggie told Mary.

Filling the kettle, Mary set it on a grate in the fireplace and added kindling to the fire, then took out a small china teapot with pink flowers painted on it. Louise had claimed the teapot was a wedding gift to her from Mary's mother, but Mary confided that the pot had been in the Madrid family for years, and her mother had promised it to her. Louise did not allow Mary to touch it, for fear the big woman would break it, although Maggie had noticed that Mary was not clumsy. "We will have a tea party. Shall we go into the parlor?" Mary asked and reached for china cups and saucers instead of the tin cups.

The parlor was cold and fussy, however, and Maggie said she would rather sit at the scrub-top kitchen table near the fireplace. Besides, Clara lay sleeping on a pallet in the kitchen. Maggie sat down at the table, enjoying the homey scene. She once had thought marriage would be like this—a fire, a sleeping child, tea with someone she loved.

Mary settled herself in a chair, then said, "I do not require you to tell me anything. You are my friend, and I know you for a good woman."

Maggie reached across the table and squeezed Mary's hand. Then she said, "I am a married woman, and it is possible, even probable, that my husband is still alive, although I wish to God he was not. I tried to kill him. His name is Jesse Kaiser."

Mary only nodded, and Maggie continued. She had never told anyone what had gone on in her marriage and had believed it would be difficult, but the words poured out as she unburdened herself.

"It was true love when I met him. He was so thoughtful. He brought me violets, and when my hands were cramped from sewing, he rubbed them with oil. My parents did not approve of him, and they told me if I married him, they would be through with me. But I was in love." She shook her head. "How foolish we are when we are young. I never thought to inquire what work he did and discovered too late that it was gambling, and he was not good at it. We were not married a month when he hit me the first time. I had been brought up in refinement and never considered that I would have to earn my living. He said I must help support us. My only skill was stitching, and so I set myself up as a dressmaker and was quite fortunate to attract some wealthy clients. Among them was that Mrs. Whitney, although I do not know her well and have made only two or three dresses for her. Jesse said my earnings as a seamstress belonged to him as my husband. When I protested, he struck me. He beat me again after a coachman came to pick up a dress, saying I had been unnatural with the man, and another time he accused me of holding back money from him. After a while, he did not need a reason to hurt me. I thought the beatings would stop when I conceived, but they only grew worse."

"And after Clara was born?"

"I had a son first." Maggie's throat contracted, and she blinked back tears. "Richard. We called him Dick." Maggie paused to gain control of her voice. It hurt so much to talk about the boy. "Jesse was thrilled. For a time, he was once again the loving man who had courted me. Then I conceived again, and the beatings became worse than ever. He asked how I expected him to support two children, although it was I who brought in the money. I hid enough to buy food for Dick and me and gave Jesse the rest, which he gambled away. After Clara was born, Jesse said he had no use for a daughter, and he left us.

"I was glad. I did not make a great deal of money, but it was enough for a room and what we needed, although sometimes when the women were late in paying me, I took the children to the Kitchen. Reverend Swain's wife operated it, and at the church I was afraid she would recognize me, because Jesse once caused a scene

55

there, saying I had embarrassed him by seeking charity."

Mary had poured the hot water into the teapot and added the tea leaves to steep. Now she went to the stove and poured the tea into the cups. "I can chip a little sugar off the cone if you want it," she said, but Maggie shook her head, saying she was not used to sugar in her tea. Mary set down the cups and seated herself. "If it is too painful, you need not go on. It is not necessary that I know."

"I will be all right. It is like a weight off my chest to tell of it." Maggie took a sip of the tea and smiled. She had rarely had such good tea and understood why Louise wanted to keep it for herself. "Jesse came back to see me from time to time. If he had won at gambling, he brought us sweets and once a diamond ring, or so he claimed. I tried to sell it and discovered it was glass. Then he would lose again and demand money and beat me. When he was in the room, I sent Clara to stay with a neighbor for fear he would hurt her, too. He never touched our son." *No,* Maggie thought, *he did not touch Dick, but he treated the boy so abominably that Dick shook whenever his father entered the room, and I had to hold him to stop the trembling.*

"It appears he did strike Clara," Mary said. "I saw the bruises."

"That was later." Maggie stared at the tea

in her cup, remembering that once a wealthy woman had given her a tip for finishing a dress ahead of time, and she'd taken Dick and Clara to a tea shop for cakes. She smiled to remember that Clara had stuffed her cake into her mouth, while Dick had eaten his in small bites to make it last. She realized now that the generous woman was Mrs. Whitney. "This is very good," she said, putting down her cup.

"Louise requires the best—for herself," Mary said with a laugh. "Isn't that nice for us tonight?"

Maggie swirled the leaves in the cup. "We lived like that for a long while. I would have moved, but my ladies knew where I was located, and I was afraid they would not follow me to a new address. Jesse visited on occasion but did not stay long with us. I think he had another woman, and the truth was, I hoped so. I wanted him to keep away."

"Did you consider divorce?" Mary asked.

"Oh, no. Jesse would have taken the little ones from me for spite, and who knows what he would have done with them. My business would have suffered, too, and I had to feed the children. My customers would not care that my husband hit me, but they would be shocked if I were a divorced woman." She paused. "Besides, Jesse told me he would kill me if I ever left him, and I believed him."

Maggie was quiet for a moment. It was painful

to go on, but still she continued. "My son got sick. I think he had pneumonia, or maybe typhoid. You remember how there was rain and hail and such cold in the fall that people stayed in their homes and did not go out. I had made several dresses, but the women did not send for them since, due to the weather, many parties had been called off. So I was not paid, and money was scarce. I had to choose between food and fuel. I knew we would starve if we did not eat, so I purchased bread."

For a time, Maggie did not go on. She stared out the window into the darkness, remembering. She remembered that the rain had mixed with the soot on the outside of the windows, making black streaks down the panes. She had sat with her sewing in dim light that came through the glass, her hands stiff with the chill. Clara was wrapped in quilts in the rocking chair, numbed by the cold. The boy lay on the bed, his head hot with fever. Maggie wanted to tend him, to rub his head with cool water. But one of her clients had demanded she finish a dress in time for a party. The garment had been completed the week before, but the woman, a Mrs. Fletcher, decided she did not like the sleeves and wanted them removed so that she could display her diamond bracelets. There would be no extra pay for the additional work.

Maggie had had to leave the children behind when she went to the Fletcher mansion for the final fitting. A neighbor had promised to look after them, but when Maggie returned the woman was drunk, and Dick was screaming from the fever. Maybe if Maggie had been there, Dick would not have gotten worse, but how could she have stayed? There would have been no money if the dress had not been completed. Mrs. Fletcher, at least, paid her bill on time.

"Mrs. Fletcher told me her maid would pick up the dress," Maggie said. "The maid was that girl Winny, the Irish one with the red hair we saw at the church."

Mary smiled. The two had discussed the other women who had signed up for the trip, and they had both thought Winny was among the nicest.

"Winny saw how tired I was and said she would watch Dick and Clara while I napped. She did not have to get back for a time, because Mrs. Fletcher was not going to the party after all. I was so grateful that I did not argue and lay down and went to sleep. When I awoke, I saw that Dick was better, and Winny was rocking him in the chair. It was a brave thing for the girl to do, since she could have caught Dick's fever. He was laughing, and I thought Winny must be an angel. She offered to stay longer, but I knew she would be missed by Mrs. Fletcher, and I said my husband would be there soon, although I did not expect him at all. As she left, Winny told me Mrs. Fletcher put ice on her children's foreheads when they had fevers. I thought that was a good idea and went outside for it. The ice in the street was dirty, and I had to hunt for some that was clean. It took longer than I wished. When I returned to the room, Clara was sitting beside her brother, holding his hand. Dick was dead." Maggie took a deep breath and stopped. She closed her eyes to hold back the tears.

She glanced over at her daughter, who was curled up on her pallet. Maggie remembered it all so vividly. She had wrapped Clara in quilts and set her on the bed to sleep, then held Dick in her arms, rubbing the ice over his head as if it could ease the fever of the dead boy. Tears ran down her face as she rocked him back and forth until the little body was cold. She could have taken him outside, left the body in the street, but she would never abandon him. She took Mrs. Fletcher's money and paid for a proper burial. Then, with Clara in her arms, she made her way through the snow to her parents' house and begged them to take her in. They refused.

"And so you came to the church," Mary said, finishing her tea.

"Not then. It was sometime later. There is more," Maggie told her, bowing her head.

"There is more tea, as well," Mary said, when Maggie did not continue. "In fact, I believe there is enough that we can have a cup every night when Louise is in bed. She will not know until we are on our way to California that it is used up."

As she stood, she gripped Maggie's shoulder, and Maggie clutched her friend's hand.

"Perhaps the rest should wait for another time. I do not wish to add to your sorrow," Mary said, after she had added more tea leaves to the pot and poured in the water from the kettle.

"No, it needs to be said now." Clara stirred and muttered something, and Maggie went to her, covering her with the quilt the girl had thrown aside. "I wonder if she dreams of it," Maggie said but did not explain what she meant. She sat back down at the table and waited for Mary.

"Jesse came back. I had thought he was gone for good, but he was not. It was the week before the meeting at the church. When he discovered that Dick was dead, he was furious and knocked me down, accusing me of killing our son. Clara tried to tell him that it was not my fault and blurted out that she had held Dick when he breathed his last because I was not there. I said I had only gone for ice to help with the fever, but Jesse would not listen. He was like a madman. He hit me again and again until I could no longer feel the pain. I think I passed out. When I came to, I saw him on the bed with Clara. He had beaten her, too. You saw the bruises. He had pushed up her dress and was using her as he would a wife." Maggie turned her head to the side and covered her eyes with her hand. "I cannot say more."

"You do not have to," Mary said, reaching

across the table and putting her hand on Maggie's arm. "I know what animals do."

"He is indeed an animal. His own daughter," Maggie whispered. "I could not imagine such a thing. Clara was crying, and he slapped her and told her to be still." Maggie stopped to wipe tears from her eyes. "I told him to stop, and he said I was jealous. Jealous! How could he? I went as mad as he was at that, and I grabbed a poker and slammed it down on his head. I did it again, maybe twice more, until he was still."

"And you left then?"

Maggie shook her head. "I was horrified at what I had done. I went outside and hailed a hack and took him to the hospital."

Wordlessly, Mary poured more tea and set Maggie's cup in front of her. The two were silent until Mary asked, "You say you do not know if he is dead?"

Maggie shook her head. "Three days later, two policemen came to see me. They asked what had happened. I should have told them the truth, but I could not. I said Jesse had beaten me, and I had defended myself. One of the coppers, the older one, asked what I had done to deserve the beating. Had I said something to him? He even asked if I had burned supper. I replied that Jesse was angry because our son had died, that he blamed me for it. The man said that explained it. He told me I'd had no cause to hit Jesse, that it was a man's right to beat his wife. He said I ought to make it up to him." She paused. "I could not tell him what Jesse had done to Clara. I could not shame her."

Mary struck the table with her hand. "The beast! It is all right for him to beat you, but not all right for you to defend yourself and your daughter?"

"I suppose that is the law."

"And what did the other copper say?"

"Nothing. Not then, anyway. He returned a day later. He was by himself. He said that Jesse was in a bad way and that if he died, I would be charged with murder. He told me to take Clara and hide somewhere." Maggie gave a little smile. "I thought he would want something of me for his help, but he did not. In fact, he said, 'My sister's husband, he sometimes . . .' He did not continue, but I knew he meant the husband beat his wife, too. When he left, he handed me a dollar and said he wished he had more to give me.

"I did not know what to do. The next morning, I packed as much as I could and took Clara, and we roamed the streets. That was when I noticed the broadsheets about the California venture. I had seen the sheets before, had read them, but until that moment I did not think that I would be one of the women to sign up. Perhaps God was speaking to me then, was showing me a way. I had thought I might rent a room in another part of the city or perhaps leave Chicago, but I did not have the money. Besides, I feared Jesse would come after me."

"And will he?"

"Oh yes, if he lives. He may be looking for me even now."

"And so you go to California to look for another husband, even though you still are married."

Maggie looked up, shocked. "I had not thought of it that way."

"Perhaps he *is* dead," Mary said.

Maggie turned her head to look at Clara. "God willing," she said.

Four

May 9, 1852
St. Joseph, Missouri

Never in her life had Maggie seen so many wagons, not even at midday on Lake Street in Chicago. She watched the throng of emigrants and their canvas-topped vehicles swarming along the banks of the Missouri River at St. Joseph. Wagons and prairie schooners drawn by horses, mules, and oxen were lined up, waiting for the ferry to take them to the far side of the river. People were in a hurry. It was late in the season to depart for the gold fields. The ministers had hoped to leave earlier, but they had been caught up in the myriad of details that planning the trip required.

Maggie pointed to the painted wheels on the wagons and asked Clara which color she liked best.

"Blue," she replied. "No, yellow. Yellow is my favorite color. Like the sun."

Maggie smiled, remembering that Dick had preferred red.

Drivers, impatient at the delays, cracked whips over their teams as they inched along. Women and children walked beside the wagons, dodging the animals and riff-raff. A driver cursed, incensed that someone had shoved in line ahead of him. He and the other driver swore at each other over the sounds of cattle and horses and the howls of two dogs that were fighting to the death. Maggie, gripping her daughter to keep her out of the traffic, hoped Clara did not notice the swear words but thought it unlikely the child would get to California without picking up some of the profanity.

Peddlers called to her, naming their wares. One sold tinned oysters and sardines. "Last chance till California," he said. Maggie ignored him but was tempted by the woman who offered loaves of fresh bread, although she would not waste her money buying one.

She had had just twenty dollars when she signed up for the California trip, but now she had a great deal more, thanks to Mary. Not long before the two women left, Micah had told his sister he would not sell her half of the farm so that she could go larking off to California.

"I did not tell you to. Three hundred dollars, enough for Maggie, Clara, and me, will do," Mary said.

Maggie held her breath at the amount. Three hundred was a fortune.

Micah thought so, too. " 'Tis a great amount."

"There is that and more in our account."

"Is it true?" He seemed surprised, and Maggie realized that Mary kept the books.

"I will not see you again in this life," Micah said suddenly, and tears came to his eyes. Maggie supposed the two had been close as children. Later, when his wife was not listening, he told Mary to take the red horse. It might have been a gesture of kindness, although he had never ridden the horse and perhaps knew that Mary would have taken the animal anyway.

Louise did not soften. Maggie had to beg her for an old dress that Louise had put aside to be torn into rags, as well as a pair of overalls that Louise's son had outgrown. In exchange, Louise insisted on a length of silk that Maggie had brought with her. Louise thought herself generous when she threw in an old hat that had been set aside for a scarecrow. Maggie was so disgusted with the way Louise treated Mary that for spite, she hid the china teapot with the roses on it in the trunk Mary had given her. It was not stealing, Maggie told herself. She was only taking what belonged to Mary, and she would give it to her friend once they were on their way.

Now Maggie steered Clara away from a wagon where men were sharing a bottle of whiskey. A crude sign advertised liquor by the bottle or the drink. Maggie hated liquor.

Mary pointed to an Indian lying near the whiskey vendor. Maggie thought at first that he was injured or perhaps even dead. Then she saw a woman nearby, an empty bottle beside her, and realized the woman was drunk, her husband most likely passed out. She had seen Jesse lying senseless like that, and the sight repelled her. A small boy sitting beside his mother picked up the bottle and rolled it back and forth. Then the child began banging it on the ground. Maggie stepped forward to take the bottle from the boy before he broke it and hurt himself.

"Let him be," Joseph told her. She had not seen him come up beside her.

"He is only a child with an empty bottle," Maggie protested. She knew that the minister and Caroline had no children, and perhaps he did not realize the child could cut himself on the glass shards.

"They are heathen, an inferior race. There is nothing you can do."

"He could injure himself," Maggie said.

"It is said about them that nits breed lice."

Maggie opened her mouth to tell him that was a horrid thing to say about any child, but she stopped herself. It would not do to anger the minister. She had tried her best to blend in with the other women. She had changed her hairstyle from a fashionable center part with long curls to a knot on the back of her head and bangs, so she would be less recognizable in case Jesse followed her or sent someone after her. She did not know if he had survived, but if he had, he would have searched Chicago for her and realized she was no longer there. She did not want to give the reverend a reason to remember her in case a man inquired about her and described her appearance.

She and Mary had been cautious when they met with the other women in Chicago to board the boat that would take them on the first part of their journey. Mary had insisted Maggie wear an old coat of hers, one that was outsized and sloppy and would hide her trim figure. She also wore Louise's large hat with a veil that shaded her face. At the boat, the two women had separated, Mary taking Clara with her. The little girl was dressed in the outgrown clothes of Mary's nephew, and she wore a cap over her hair, which had been cut short like a boy's. "I'm just like Dick," Clara had said when she donned the clothing. If Jesse was there, he would assume the child was Mary's son and ignore her.

The minister left, and Caroline joined Maggie, taking a handkerchief from her pocket and holding it to her nose as she looked around the camp. The smell of rancid grease, filthy clothing, and human and animal waste was overpowering.

"I had not expected the Overland Trail to be like this," she said. "I thought it would be like the paintings—green valleys with white-topped wagons moving west into fiery sunsets."

Maggie nodded. In finishing school, she had

been taken to a museum to see such pictures. She felt more comfortable around the minister's wife now that they were far from Chicago. She still didn't know if Caroline recognized her. "It is quite a sight," Maggie said.

"My brother tells me that tomorrow we will cross the river and be away from it. He says we will like it better on the other side." She smiled. "We could scarcely like it less."

"Have more women left us?" Maggie asked. She knew that two women already had deserted. Forty-four had signed up for the journey and boarded the boat for the first leg of the trek, the trip from Chicago to St. Joseph. One had quit halfway, debarking and finding passage back to Chicago. Then, just that day, Maggie had seen the second one point to the crush of people and wagons at St. Joseph and announce that she, too, did not care to go farther. "I would rather be an old maid," she told the ministers.

"It is just as well," William had said. "These are the easy parts of the trip. If a woman cannot tolerate a few days on a boat or camped beside a river, she will never make it to California. Frankly, I am surprised so many are going ahead with us."

"We will tolerate no slackers," Joseph had said.

Maggie had expected Mrs. Whitney to be one of the go-backs. The other women showed up at the boat with only what was necessary—clothing,

70

bedding, medicine, and a few personal items such as photographs and books. Some, like Mary, had brought farm implements and even guns, not ladies' pistols but rifles and shotguns. They knew how to use them, too, they said. Joseph had presented each of them with a Bible when they left Chicago, but Maggie had seen several Bibles abandoned on the boat. Perhaps they'd been given to women who couldn't read, she thought charitably. She realized that Mary had forgotten hers and picked it up, but Mary had refused it. "I shall share yours on the unlikely chance I shall need it," she said.

Mrs. Whitney was different from the others. She arrived with a four-burner sheet-iron stove, twelve apple trees, and three trunks that she said contained only necessities. "I have put not a single thing in them that is not of the greatest importance," she insisted.

"Of course, dear lady," Joseph told her.

Mary whispered that perhaps he didn't object because he himself had insisted on taking along a black-walnut pulpit.

William surveyed Mrs. Whitney's heavy items and said, "Take what you want. I would wager half will be discarded before Fort Laramie."

Mrs. Whitney seemed surprised when she found that she and her servant were sharing a cabin on the boat with Maggie and Clara. Mrs. Whitney had been a gracious roommate, however, and had not murmured a word about returning to Chicago. The night before, she had slept in a tent near the river with the rest of the women instead of finding lodging in a hotel. Nonetheless, she invited Maggie and Clara along with Caroline to go into town in search of a tea shop, where she treated them to tea and pastries as a farewell to civilization.

"Ghastly fare, but I suppose it is no worse than what we will eat the next five months. Pray God, it will not be *that much* worse," she said as they returned to camp.

"You are not used to this," Caroline said.

"Are you?"

"No."

"I should think you would find it no worse than the smell of hypocrisy at the parsonage, Caroline."

"My husband—" Caroline began, defending Joseph.

Mrs. Whitney interrupted. "I am not speaking of Reverend Swain. I mean those self-righteous women who gather to cluck their tongues over the sins of the poor. An unforgiving lot they are."

"But you are one of them," Caroline said, then added quickly, "I did not mean . . ."

"Do you not think that is one of the reasons I chose to escape Chicago?"

"You are a contradiction, Mrs. Whitney."

"Bessie. You are to call me Bessie, and so are

72

the other women. I will not stand out as different. We are equals."

Caroline chuckled. "Since we are equal, then, I shall enjoy seeing how you drive the ox team."

Bessie thought a moment and said, "I had not intended to be that equal."

Bessie went on ahead, taking her servant's hand and pointing to the wagons lined up to cross the river, chatting happily with the girl.

"She is a good mistress. Do you know she is a supporter of the abolitionist movement?" Caroline asked.

"I am not surprised. She is very kind to the Negro girl."

They stopped because Clara had found something in the mud. Maggie told her to leave it be, but Clara held up a dirty coin. "Look, Mama," she cried and gave it to Maggie. "Are we rich?"

"Of course you are. You have each other," Caroline answered for Maggie.

Maggie smiled and started to respond, but Caroline cleared her throat. "Something odd happened not long before we left," she said.

The smile left Maggie's face as she caught the seriousness in Caroline's voice. "What was it?"

"Oh, it has nothing to do with you. It was just a strange thing. I do not know why I even remark on it." She smiled. "A police officer came to the church a day or two before we embarked. There were a few of the broadsheets still posted in Chicago, and I suppose he saw one."

Maggie didn't want Caroline to see her fear, so, using her skirt, she wiped off the coin Clara had found and put it into her pocket. Clara was busy searching the mud in hopes of finding more money. "What did he want?" she asked.

"He said a woman murdered or tried to murder her husband; I cannot be sure which, because at first I was not listening. At any rate, the police believe the wife ran away with their child. He wanted to know if they might have joined our company."

Maggie looked off into the distance. "What did you tell him?"

"I said we had no one like that. He showed me a photograph of the couple. The woman was quite indistinct, but I remember the man. He had come to the Kitchen, a place where I volunteered my time. Perhaps you have heard of it. He was a boorish fellow who berated his wife for being there. I hope his wife found a safe place to hide from him. The man seemed unbalanced."

"Did the officer believe you?"

"I do not know. I looked for the husband when we boarded the boat but did not see him. That does not mean he does not believe the woman is with us."

"Why do you tell me?" Maggie's hands were damp. Caroline knew, she thought. Otherwise she would not have told her about the policeman. What if she had told the ministers, too, and they would refuse to let her go on? Would she have to return to Chicago? Perhaps she could stay in St. Joseph. Would there be employment for a dressmaker? She held her breath, waiting for Caroline's answer.

"No reason. Only that you are a woman with a daughter. Perhaps if you see another widow with a child, you will warn her to stay close to her wagon. I think this man must have been evil. I do not blame his wife for running away. I would not want her to be arrested."

"That is a good idea," Maggie said, as Caroline slipped an arm through hers. Jesse had been evil. But if she had known evil at his hands, she had just experienced goodness, thanks to the understanding of the minister's wife. "Thank you," she murmured, knowing Caroline might have saved her life.

They spotted the two ministers up ahead, and Caroline, still holding Maggie's arm, hurried to them. Clara followed, her head down, still searching for coins.

Joseph was frowning as he and William surveyed the wagons and oxen and the mountain of supplies that William had purchased. He had ordered fifteen wagons made from hickory, the beds and wheels painted blue, and six teams of oxen for each wagon at sixty dollars per team. "A steal, as the animals are young, only five years old," he was explaining when the women reached him. He had supplied the train with tools, guns, powder and ball, and cooking equipment. And he'd purchased enough sugar, flour, bacon, beans, and other foodstuffs to last for five months.

"So much, Willie? Do you not think a hundred and fifty pounds of flour and twenty-five of sugar for each woman excessive? If we run out, surely we could supply ourselves along the way," Reverend Swain said.

"Yes, we could if we were lucky. And if we had the money. The prices at Fort Kearny and Fort Laramie are usurious."

"We could resupply in Salt Lake City, then."

"Of course, if we go that way. I have not yet decided. Still, the Mormons are shrewd people. They charge what the market will bear. And the market bears a great deal."

"They would rob us? Do they not profess to be Christians?" Joseph protested.

"As are the merchants in St. Joe, but as you have seen, they drive a sharp bargain."

"Well, I do not believe we need so much coffee," he said.

His brother-in-law laughed at that. "Coffee is perhaps the most important item we will have with us. We can face Indians, rain, snow, dust, even starvation, but we will not make it without

76

coffee. By the time we reach California, you will willingly sell your soul for a swallow of it."

"I heartily doubt it. Do not blaspheme," Joseph told him.

"Just wait, and you shall see."

Caroline drew Maggie aside and said, "Joseph does not approve of stimulants. I am grateful William bested him in that argument. I do not know if I could travel two thousand miles without my coffee. Do you drink it?"

Maggie nodded. She had considered coffee and tea a luxury when money was scarce and had not bought them in a long time. Until she went to Mary's farm it had been months since she had had a cup of either one. "I believe I could travel a long way on coffee," she said.

"They are like brothers, those two. They were roommates in divinity school, and it was William who introduced me to Joseph. William and I are close, and William thought so highly of Joseph that he considered him a suitable match for me. I had always been too plain and headstrong to attract a husband on my own. William sought to save me from spinsterhood. As you can see, I am fortunate. Joseph is steadfast and has strong religious convictions. I could not imagine that a man so blessed with a fine face and body as well as a strong intellect would find me suitable. The Lord blesses me."

And you repay the Lord by seeing Joseph in the

77

best light, overlooking both his humorlessness and his intolerance, Maggie thought.

Clara had stopped searching for coins and was now caught up in watching the men load the wagons, so Maggie lingered with her, holding her daughter so that she did not get in the way.

"I hope the men you have chosen to go with us are of a religious bent," Joseph said to his brother-in-law, as he, too, watched the wagons being loaded. He called to the men to be careful with the pulpit. It had been a gift from his congregation.

"I am sure they are, although I did not think to inquire. I selected them because they are young and strong, and many have knowledge of the trail. In fact, I turned down several who were too anxious to accompany a wagon train of women. I have told those we hired that the women are intended as brides for the miners in California."

"And we do not pay the men?" Joseph asked.

"No, most want to go to the gold fields and think it is a stroke of luck that we will provide them with food and companionship in exchange for their work. Some will go only as far as the Great Salt Lake."

"Mormons, are they?"

"I did not ask, but I hope so. Mormons are known as hard workers, and they are honest."

"They also have more than one wife."

Maggie gasped. She had heard of the strange

78

sect. She wondered if the women were allowed to have more than one husband. The thought made her smile. If that were true, she might then find someone to marry even if Jesse were still alive.

"Perhaps they would want the women for their harems," Joseph said. "Women are not as smart as we are. Who knows what will turn their heads. They can be foolish."

"Not Caroline," William protested.

"No, but I must tell you that she does not always show good judgment. She would rather dish up dinner for poor women than meet with the ladies of our prayer group."

"Imagine that," William said and turned to Caroline. His sister was gone, however. Only Maggie, Clara beside her, stood there, and he gave her a sly smile.

He turned to the wagons, checking the packing of each one. He told a driver to put the water where the women could get to it on the trail. Another man, who had filled a bucket with water and hung it on the back of the wagon, was told, "Pour out the water. We will add cream to the bucket before we leave camp each morning, and the movement of the wagon will churn it into butter."

"You will make the women lazy," Joseph said.

"No one will be considered lazy who makes the trip to California," William told him.

79

• • •

Although William fretted at the delay, saying they should have been under way weeks earlier, the company lingered in St. Joseph for a few days. Maggie had thought they would leave the day after they arrived. She was anxious to be gone, now that she knew that an officer of the law had been looking for her. It was unlikely he had gone all the way to St. Joseph searching for her, but still, she did not want to chance encountering him. If the man found her later on, she hoped she would be so much a part of the wagon train that the ministers would deny she was the woman who had killed her husband.

Mary and William used the time to teach the women how to drive the oxen, while Caroline developed their morning routine of preparing breakfast over a campfire and storing dishes and cooking utensils in the wagons. Cooking over campfires and sleeping on the ground were a surprise to some of the women, although Maggie had known the accommodations would be primitive. To her delight, she discovered that Clara loved the freedom of living that way.

"I shall marry the first man in California who tells me he has a feather bed," Sadie told Maggie as the two sat together, Maggie hemming the other woman's skirts. They had been told their long skirts would be ragged in no time from dragging on the ground and must be shortened.

Maggie had already hemmed her dresses as well as Mary's, but Sadie confessed she did not know how to sew. At first, a few of the women refused the shortened hems, saying it was improper, but after walking in the muck by the river, they agreed that long skirts would hamper them. Maggie thought Sadie had asked for her skirt to be too high—well above her boot tops—but said nothing. After all, Sadie had shown up at the boat in a plain calico dress instead of the fancy satin frock she had worn to the church and seemed to be making every effort to blend in.

"Are them the marrying women, like the kind that advertises for a man in a magazine?" an immigrant lady asked her husband as the two stopped to stare at Maggie and Sadie. The word was out that two ministers were taking a wagon train of unmarried women to California, and many of those who were camped along the river had come to inspect them. Some made unkind remarks, but others were merely curious. One woman glanced over her shoulder at her husband, who was spitting a chaw of tobacco onto the ground, and said she wished she'd married after she reached California instead of before.

"Bunch of old maids," the husband of the nosy woman replied now. "They's touched in the head going all the way to California for a pig in a poke."

"Better than marrying a hog with his breakfast

on his beard," Sadie told him. The couple hurried off, the man brushing crumbs and bits of sausage from his face.

A few minutes later, after Maggie had finished Sadie's hem and was biting off the thread, a young woman who had been sitting on a rock watching them approached the two. "Is it true? Be you truly a wagon train of women?" she asked.

"We did not advertise for husbands, but we are going to California in hopes of finding them," Maggie replied.

"You the one that's in charge?" The woman was thin and poorly dressed, and she could not look Maggie in the eye.

"There are two ministers who organized the company."

"Are you filled up?"

"Are you of a mind to join us?" Maggie asked.

"Would you take me?"

Maggie studied the girl a moment. "Why do you want to go with us?"

The girl pushed aside her sunbonnet to show that half of her face was bruised and there was a cut near her eye. She might have been pretty at one time, but her face was now thin and haunted, like a mask of sorrow. She was of medium height with gray eyes and hair so pale it was almost white. It was snarled and uneven and as lank as a horse's mane. Maggie saw that her arms were bruised and scraped. She was sure that worse injuries were hidden by the girl's dress.

Without realizing it, Maggie reached out and took the young woman's hand, knowing she had been beaten by some man, probably her husband. Her heart went out to the poor creature. Maggie was well aware of the pain, the constant worry of being hit again, the fear that the next time would be fatal. She wondered if all men were like that, if all wives were afraid of their husbands. She could not imagine that Reverend Swain hurt his wife, who worshipped him. But what did she know about what was hidden behind closed doors?

The girl's eyes flicked back and forth, as if she were afraid of being spotted. "Yesterday he beat me awful with his whip. I can't walk hardly. Last time it was his belt, although mostly he uses his fists. Next time he'll kill me." She removed her hand, and Maggie saw that two of the fingers were bent, as if they had been broken and hadn't healed properly.

The words brought back Maggie's own pain. "How awful! Your husband?"

"Asa says he is, but we never had the words said over us. He was real nice at first, said I was the prettiest thing he ever saw and brought me flowers he picked hisself."

Maggie remembered how Jesse had brought her violets.

"He got me to go off with him. 'Course he

didn't have to say much, because it was bad at home. Pa died, and Ma married a man . . ." She shook her head. "Getting beat ain't new, but beat like this is. Sometimes I wish I could die. I stood it for a time, because he's always sorry later, always says he wouldn't do it no more if I didn't rile him. I try. I don't talk back, and his supper's always ready, but it don't do no good." She paused and said in a rush, "I got to get away. You think I could join up with you?"

"Yes," Maggie said. She had never told anyone but Mary what Jesse had done to her. This woman seemed to have been beaten even worse than she had. She wanted to put her arms around the girl and hold her safe. How could she refuse to let her join them?

"Won't your husband—that is, your man— come after you?" Sadie asked.

"I thought it all out. He don't plan to leave for a week or two, maybe longer. We are waitin' here for his least brother. There's three of them Harvey boys—Asa, Reed, and Elias. I can tell him I'm going in town. When I don't come back, he'll be thinking I found a place there to hide." She shivered. "I fear the other two as bad as I do Asa." The girl shook her head. "Them brothers together, they do things to me . . ."

Maggie frowned, not understanding, but Sadie spoke up. "They take you at the same time?" she asked.

The girl turned away, as Maggie blurted out, "All of them?" Maggie had never imagined such a thing, and her face reddened.

"It shames me."

"We could hide her in one of the wagons until we leave," Maggie told Sadie.

"We would have to ask the ministers first."

Maggie's face fell at that. Of course. The ministers would have to approve. She had a thought. "Perhaps we should ask Caroline instead."

"And she would ask Reverend Parnell." Sadie grinned. She spotted Caroline and waved her over. "This is . . . What is your name?"

"Pennsylvania House," the girl said.

"That's your name?" Sadie asked.

"I ain't picked it. Ma named me after where she come from. She called me Penn for short. My step-pa called me Girl, and Asa, he knows my name, but he just calls me Woman—or God-damn Woman."

Caroline looked at the girl curiously, and Maggie said, "She wants to join us. Look at her face." Quickly she told Penn's story.

"I will have to ask my husband," Caroline said.

"Ask your brother," Sadie told her.

Caroline gave a faint smile. Then she called to William and explained about the girl. "She is not married, so it would not be bigamy if she found a husband in California," she said. "You know one of our women quit yesterday, so we already have provisions for her."

William thought that over. "I would worry the man would come after her and put the others in danger," he said. "Still, if we hid her in one of the wagons, that might work. He would not know she had gone on west, and if he did, he would not know which train she had joined. We will have to have Joseph's permission, however."

Caroline sighed, and Maggie's heart dropped. If they turned away the woman, she would die. That was as true as anything. Maggie herself might be dead if the ministers had not allowed her to join the train. She reached out and took the girl's hand again and nodded, as if to say they shared the same pain. Maggie understood what it was like to hear footsteps and pray that her man was not angry, that he would not strike her because a carriage had splashed mud on him. Or take her by force because he was upset that he had been refused credit at a saloon. She wanted to tell the girl they were sisters that way, but the others thought Maggie's husband was a loving man who had died.

"It would be best if you did not mention she has been living with a man," Caroline told her brother.

William smiled. "Joseph is a good man. He will take her in. We shall ask him now."

The two turned to see Joseph striding up to them.

"We were talking of you just now. We have a dilemma," William said. "A young woman has just approached and asked to join our train. She would replace the woman who quit yesterday. I believe it is a fine idea."

"What do you know of her? Is she a Christian?"

"Of course. She spoke to me of God," Caroline said. It wasn't a lie. Penn had said the man called her a God-damn woman.

"Perhaps she is a troublemaker."

"No, she is just a poor woman. She was with another train and has had an unhappy experience. She has been abused. She is unmarried and would feel safe with us. I believe we should take her into our fold. It is our duty as Christians."

Joseph thought that over, then nodded his approval. "If you put it that way," he said, adding, not unkindly, "You always do."

Caroline touched her husband's arm and smiled. "I do not believe we will be sorry."

"I suppose she is running away from something," her husband mused.

William glanced at Maggie and Sadie. "We all of us are running from something," he said.

Five

A t last the wagons were packed and the oxen harnessed, and Maggie and the other members of the women's train slowly made their way alongside them to the river crossing. Mary had offered to drive an ox team, she told Maggie. But Joseph had thought that unseemly.

"But all the women will drive before we reach Fort Kearny," William protested.

"That may be so, but I expect to start our journey in a way that befits us as a group of proper Christian souls."

"Even if some of those men he engaged don't know the front end of an ox from the back end of a mule," Mary whispered to Maggie.

They had hoped to be among the first at the ferry, but when they arrived, they discovered that a long line of teams had already formed. Clara laughed at the sight of a wagon driven by a man in a top hat and military jacket who slapped the reins over six matching white horses. "I want to ride with him," she said.

"You would not get far," William told her. "Those animals will not last half the way to Fort Laramie. Our oxen may be slow, child, but they will feed on prairie grass instead of grain. In time, you will like them better than horses."

Clara stared at the minister and gripped her mother's hand. Maggie wasn't surprised that after the way her father had treated her, Clara was frightened of men. At the thought of Jesse she looked around, but no one in that nearby throng of dirty, bearded men looked familiar.

Clutching Clara's hand lest she be trampled, Maggie pointed at wagon covers—or sheets, as they were called—decorated with pictures of elephants and buffalo and maps of California. "We are going to see the elephant," Maggie said, but Clara did not know what an elephant was, did not understand the popular gold-rush expression. It meant they would see what there was to be seen.

The covers were emblazoned with the names of companies—Wild Kentuckians, Gold Diggers, Never Say Die, and Rough and Ready. Maggie showed that last one to Winny, who rushed to inquire if anyone knew the whereabouts of her brother Davy. But those Rough and Readies were from Georgia, not Illinois.

"Should we have thought up a name to be painted on our wagons?" Maggie asked Caroline.

"Joseph suggested 'God's People,'" Caroline replied. "Fortunately, William said that by the time we reached California, the wagon sheets would be a disgrace to God."

"A wise decision," Maggie said. She studied the bearded men in fringed buckskin and rawhide boots or flannel shirts, corduroy trousers, and broad-brimmed hats as they walked along, and could not help staring at half-naked Indians, their hair powdered red, who begged for "ko-fee" and crusts of bread.

"When it is your turn to drive a team, I will watch Clara," Mary offered. "I think the men will drive until the oxen are broken in. They are green yet. I am glad we are not driving mules. They are hard to break and mean. I do not believe the women could drive them. Oxen are not so difficult, as you know."

Maggie did indeed know. On the farm, Mary had taught her how to handle the brutes. She knew to tap the lead ox on the rump and yell, "Move out! Giddup!" to start the team, and to stop it by calling "Whoa!" with a tap on the head. "Haw!" with a tap on the right ear made the team turn left. "Gee" and a slap on the left ear, and they turned right. "Back!" and a knock on the chest or the knees sent the team backward. "At least that is what they are supposed to do," Mary had told her after one of her lessons. "Oxen are dumb. And stubborn, as stubborn as Reverend Swain sometimes."

"Maybe we should smack *him* on the side of the head with the whip handle when he is put out with us," Maggie said. Joseph was now complaining that the wagon line was untidy. Did he think the oxen cared?

I wish we would hurry, Maggie thought as she watched Mary stride off with Clara to examine a goat. Just that morning Mary had told her she had heard of a man inquiring about a woman and child. Maggie shivered as she thought that someone might be in St. Joseph searching for her. Although the man could have been looking for anyone, the two women thought it a good idea for Clara to stay with Mary and to continue to dress like a boy. Maggie would feel safer once they crossed the river. The companies would spread out, and there was a smaller chance she would be recognized. She glanced at the crowd near the ferry but did not see anyone familiar. So many of the emigrant men looked alike in their mud-spattered clothing and formless hats. She scuffed her toe in the dirt and spotted a blue flower in the grasses that somehow had escaped getting crushed. Intending to give it to Clara, she picked it, but as she rose she spied a woman she had noticed on the boat. The woman, a girl really, who was young with the blond hair and pale face of a bisque doll, seemed sad, and Maggie thought perhaps she was sorry she had come. "I'm Maggie," she said, handing the girl the stem.

The girl looked at the flower as if wondering how such a pretty thing had survived the wagon wheels and boots of thousands of travelers. She took it and held it in her hand, not knowing what to do with it. "Dora Mifflin," the girl said at last.

"You are peaked. Are you thinking you made a mistake? It is not too late to turn back. Others have." Maggie wondered if she should have spoken so. The girl was none of her business, and Maggie should not have intruded on her thoughts. Still, Dora was alone, and it seemed as if she needed a friend.

"No. I had no choice."

"Perhaps you are ill, then. They say the river bottoms breed disease."

"Only a little. Breakfast did not sit well."

"Are you saying you do not enjoy a coarse meal of pancakes covered with dust instead of sorghum?" Maggie laughed a little at her joke.

Dora gave her a slight smile, showing small, even teeth, then glanced at the flower in her hand. "I wonder if we shall see such flowers on the trail." She fastened the stem in her long flaxen braid. "I hope so. It is very brown here."

"I think we shall get used to it," Maggie said.

Dora nodded. "I suppose we must get used to many things—sleeping on the ground, for instance. But I cannot complain, for I want to go on in the worst way."

"I hope you are not a criminal, then." Maggie tried to lighten the conversation. When the girl did not reply, Maggie apologized. "I overspoke. Forgive me."

"No, it is all right." The girl put her hands in the small of her back and stretched, bending backward a little, and Maggie saw the swelling in her belly.

"Oh!" Maggie said before she could stop herself.

Dora straightened up and put her hands over her belly. "You will not tell, will you?" The girl sounded desperate. "The truth is I do not want to go to California at all, but nothing else presented itself. The father—he is married. I did not know, and when I told him of my condition, he would not have a thing to do with me. He denies the baby is his. But it is! I have never been with anyone else."

"Were you in service?" Maggie asked. Maggie knew that pretty servant girls were often violated by the sons of their employers—or the employers themselves. She thought of Evaline. Perhaps Bessie had joined the company to prevent the Negro girl from encountering such foul behavior. She glanced around until she spotted Bessie, Evaline beside her. Bessie always kept her servant close.

Dora shook her head. "A teacher. I was a schoolgirl. I was going to be a teacher, too. I loved to learn. He read such beautiful poetry that I could not help but give him my heart."

"And there is no one to take you in?"

"Mam and Pap would turn their backs on me

if they knew. I never told them. I just ran away. Likely the ministers would do the same as my folks if they found out. So you must not tell them," Dora pleaded. "What would I do if they turned me out? I am hopeful I can go far enough toward California before I show so that they cannot leave me behind." She grasped Maggie's hand. "You will keep my secret, will you not?"

Maggie nodded solemnly, thinking how alike their stories were. Both had been betrayed by men, and both had families who would not help them. Of course she would keep Dora's secret. She would do what she could to help the poor girl. She remembered the minister saying they were all running from something. That was true for her, for Penn House, perhaps for Sadie, and now Dora. "Your secret is not mine to tell. Besides, there are other secrets here that the women do not want known." She leaned forward and whispered, "I know of a fancy woman among us."

"Who?" Dora asked, shocked.

"I shall not tell that either. You see, I can keep a secret. But yours, it will be known long before we reach California." She laughed. "The ministers believed some of the women would drop out. They did not know we would add to the company. When is the baby due?"

Dora shrugged. "I cannot be sure, but I think maybe four months, perhaps five." Then she mused, "I wonder what I shall do when I reach California. Do you think I shall be an outcast?"

"They say there are many outcasts there already. Surely you will find a husband, if you want one. I am told that many a man would be pleased to acquire not just a wife but a family. You see, I have a four-year-old child with me." She put her arm through Dora's and said, "We will walk on the shady side of the wagon. Lean on me if you feel faint."

"I will not do it! If I cannot go to California on my own strength, I shall throw myself under an ox team."

Maggie laughed and said, "You are too proud. Before we reach California, we will all of us lean on each other."

All morning, Maggie looked for Pennsylvania House, the girl who had approached her the day before about joining the company. Maggie had expected Penn to show up first thing to make sure she didn't miss the train, because there was no way she could join the caravan of women after they crossed the Missouri. As the day drew on, Maggie wondered if Penn's man had discovered her plans and beaten her, maybe tied her up—even killed her. Jessie had threatened to kill her if she ever left him, and Maggie knew he'd meant it. She peered behind her so often that Dora asked who she was looking for. "A woman who hoped to join us," she said, no more willing to tell Dora about Penn than she was to share Dora's situation with the others.

She saw Sadie and asked if she had spotted Penn. "Maybe she changed her mind," Maggie said, although she doubted it. If Penn House had been desperate enough to share her situation, she had already made up her mind to run away.

Sadie shook her head and said, "She was frightened. I seen women like that before. A man promises to be good, and they believe him, the fools. He's nice for a day or two. Then back it is to what they had before, only worse. If he finds out she's going to leave him, he will beat her bad." She paused. "I ain't trying to shock you. I know you for a widow, and I expect your husband was a good man."

Maggie didn't trust herself to respond. Instead she said, "We may be Penn's only chance to get away from such an evil man."

"No, there is another. She could go in a pine box."

Caroline, who had joined them, said, "We must pray for her."

"I never did much praying," Sadie told her.

"I have found it helps. At least it does no harm."

Maggie looked over the crowd and at last spotted a girl hurrying toward them. "There she is," she said, relieved.

Penn rushed up to them, glancing back over

her shoulder to see if she was being pursued. The gesture made Maggie herself look around again, searching for anyone watching her. "I could not get away. Asa asked where I gone yesterday, and I says I was seeing the sights," Penn told them. "Then he says I was looking for another man, and he whipped me something terrible. I think he broke my nose." She touched her nose, which was red and swollen. Her eyes were black, too.

"How *did* you get away?" Maggie asked.

Penn scanned the crowd again. "He went for the borrow of a sledge. Soon as he disappeared, I run off. All I brought is what I got on. I got a dollar in my shoe that I stole last night, but I ain't got no more clothes."

"I will share mine," Maggie said, thinking she could cut down one of the dresses Louise had let her take so that it fit Penn, who seemed as thin as the flower stem she had given Dora.

"We must get you hid before he discovers you are gone," Sadie said.

The three women helped Penn climb into one of the wagons, then covered her with a quilt.

"Do not show yourself until we have crossed the river," Maggie ordered. "We shall keep a sharp watch for Asa." Then she turned to Sadie. "Do you know his appearance?"

Sadie shook her head. "No, but I know the look of him. We got to watch for a man with a sledge in his hand and hate in his eye."

Caroline shivered. "Do you believe we are in danger, then?"

"If he finds out she is with us, I say we better watch out."

It was midafternoon before the company reached the head of the line and the fleet of boats and rafts that ferried the travelers and their wagons and animals across the Missouri.

"The prices are usurious," Joseph complained in a loud voice as William negotiated a rate with a ferryman. "Tell him we are men of the gospel, taking a train of women to civilize the gold fields."

William only laughed. "In that case, he would likely charge more."

Maggie was apprehensive as she watched the loaded boats set off. "The Missouri looks like a giant mud puddle. You cannot see an inch below the surface," she said to no one in particular. Water frightened her.

"I never saw a river so dirty," the woman beside her said.

Maggie turned to see who had spoken and recognized her. She was Lavinia Mercer, the woman who had wanted to join the company because she already had a wedding gown.

"I do not understand why the ministers do not engage a steamship to take us across. If men in California want us as their wives, they should be willing to pay for our comfort," she complained. "It is bad enough that we should be expected to sleep on the ground. Why are there not wagons with beds for us?"

The idea was so preposterous that Winny, standing nearby, laughed. "I have made up a thousand beds in my life and am glad not to make up another for five months." She and Maggie exchanged a look.

"The mosquitoes are terrible," Lavinia continued, slapping at her arm. "And I do not care for the food. The trip is not what I had expected. Why was I not told more of the hardships?"

"You could quit. There is still time," Maggie said, thinking Lavinia's fiancé was lucky he had not married such a complainer.

"And do what? Where would I go? This is the best I can do, and a bad choice it is." She turned toward the river, a look of distaste on her face. "I do not believe it is safe to cross in such a way. Perhaps I should speak to the ministers."

Suddenly there was a cry of "Look!" The three turned to see a man topple off a boat into the Missouri. He flailed his arms. His head bobbled up and down, and then he disappeared under the water.

Maggie looked for Clara, but the girl was safe with Mary. She rushed with the others to the edge of the river to watch.

"Maybe he cannot swim. Someone must jump into the river after him," Lavinia said.

"Then two would drown," Winny told her. "You could not see the body under all that dirty water. If he cannot save himself, then he is done for."

"But the boatman—" Lavinia protested.

Maggie interrupted. "What could he do? If he jumped in, what would become of the raft? It would overturn, and all those aboard would be drowned."

The women stared in horror at the water, hoping to spot the man's head. They heard a piercing wail from the river and saw a woman standing at the edge of the raft, her arms raised in supplication. Beside her were small figures—children.

"What will she do?" Winny asked. "Will she go on?"

"She might," William replied. He, too, had seen the man fall into the river and had joined the women on the bank. "There are single men who would marry a widow for her wagon and provisions."

"It is a horrible thought," Lavinia retorted. "A woman who would marry while her husband is barely dead."

"That may be," William replied. "But what else can she do? It is likely they sold everything to outfit themselves for the trip west. What is there to return to? Sometimes the unknown ahead is preferable to the known we have left behind."

Maggie turned to stare at him. Was he speaking of himself? He was certainly speaking of her.

The raft reached the far side of the river, and the wagon was unloaded. William watched as it disappeared into the crowd of vehicles and people. "We will never know," he said.

"We shall pray for his soul and the well-being of his family," Caroline said, as she wrapped her hands in the apron she wore to protect her dress.

Dora was somber, staring at the spot where the man had disappeared. "I did not think it would be like this," she said.

"It will get worse. Some of us will die, too, I think," Mary told her.

"You are right," Maggie said. "But most of us will live, and we will make it to California."

"God willing," Caroline added.

"Hurry it up!" the ferryman called. Drownings were nothing new, and a long line of wagons waited to board the rafts. "Who be the first among you?" he yelled.

Maggie expected Mary to step forward, but even the big woman seemed to have second thoughts. For the first time on the journey they had witnessed death, and that sobered them. Maggie had thought only of getting away with Clara. Now she was faced with what lay ahead. Had she been too hasty in agreeing to the trip? Still, what else could she have done? Perhaps the other women realized the enormity of their undertaking, too. None of them volunteered to be first.

"Others be waiting. You want to go or not? Makes no difference to me. Who's next?" the ferryman repeated.

William, who had bowed his head in prayer, looked up then and said, "Joe, you and I will set an example—"

Mary cut him off. "I shall be first."

Maggie looked around to see who would speak next. When no one did, she took Clara's hand and stood beside Mary. "And we shall go with you."

Six

May 15, 1852
Gold Rush Alley, or the St. Joe Road

After a week on the road to Fort Kearny, Maggie was used to the routine. Still, it was not easy. The dust and smells of the animals, along with the smoky campfires, made her irritable. Clara often refused to wear her cap, and the sun burned the child's face. Maggie herself limped because of blisters. She wrapped her feet in strips of cloth, but the grit of the trail worked its way into her shoes and under the bandages. She tried going barefoot, but the rocks and thorns tore at her feet. She had mended her dress—Mary's, too—because it caught on the underbrush, and she wondered if her clothing would be rags before she reached California. She might have ridden on one of the horses that Reverend Parnell had purchased, but he had brought only men's saddles, and Maggie was not willing to try one—not yet. Only Mary, often with Clara sitting in front of her, rode astride on her big red horse.

The days were dictated by the sun. Maggie rose at four and breakfasted with Clara and Mary,

Winny, Dora, Penn, Sadie, and Lavinia. Then they packed their belongings. The men William had engaged to accompany them harnessed the oxen. Mary helped, and Maggie tried, but even with Mary's training, she felt useless. *Will I always be found wanting?* she wondered.

By six, the company was ready to move out. Maggie was glad they could travel in the cool of the morning, because by ten her face was covered with fine dust, and she felt sweat trickle down her sides. She had thought she would ride in a wagon, but the board seat was hard, and after an hour she was bored by the slow pace of the oxen and the monotonous landscape. Besides, Clara did not want to sit still, and Maggie worried she would jump down and be trampled by the oxen.

The prairie was covered by long brown grass that waved in the wind. The grassland seemed to stretch on forever, so far that Maggie thought she could see the earth curve. Sometimes there was not a single thing to mark the plains except the sight of another wagon train. "I wonder why God did not see fit to plant a tree here," Mary complained to Maggie.

"It would block the view," Maggie replied with a laugh. Clara was beside her, on the hunt for treasures, while Maggie searched for berries and wild onions. Neither was very successful.

At noon, William called a halt so the company could eat a cold meal and the animals could rest.

After an hour, he set the wagons on the trail again until four or later, choosing a campsite when he found a suitable spot. He instructed the women to form a circle with the wagons, with the oxen and the horses and the dairy cows that Caroline had insisted they take along corralled in the center. By dark, Maggie was asleep, wrapped up in quilts and lying on a gutta-percha tarp spread on the ground.

She shared cooking duties with the others. Even Penn crept out of the wagon to take her turn at the campfire. Except for meals, however, Penn stayed hidden, until after a week Maggie convinced her to walk by her side. Still, if Penn saw men on horseback approaching from the east, she disappeared into the wagon. The entire train knew that Penn had run away from a man who had beaten her and that she feared he was following. Most were sympathetic, but Lavinia complained that Penn put them all in danger. "Who knows what she done to cause that man to hurt her. I do not trust her. Who said she could join us? Besides, she is mighty common," Lavinia said.

"She is all right," Maggie told her. *A better companion than you,* she thought. Penn never complained. In fact, after she felt safe leaving the wagon, she was quick to offer to help others. She knew almost as much about oxen as Mary and was happy to walk beside the brutes when others were tired. Maggie came to love her, because Penn had extracted a thorn from Clara's foot, then rubbed it with a salve made of herbs to keep it from swelling. And when a rattlesnake curled up beside a wagon wheel near the little girl, Penn took a pistol from her pocket and shot the snake.

Maggie and Mary protected Penn. Whenever a group of men passed them, the two insisted they take over Penn's chores and let her ride in the wagon. "I should be about," Penn said once when there had been no sign of Asa.

Maggie told her, "We are all safer if you are hiding when he passes by."

When the wagons were corralled at night, Mary told Penn to sleep in the center. "Asa will not sneak up on you," she explained.

Maggie hemmed Penn's skirt, and Sadie gave her a blouse and drawers and a petticoat, because Penn had joined them with only the dress she wore. Bessie gave her gloves, and Evaline presented her with hair ribbons.

Penn ran Evaline's gift through her fingers with wonder and said, "I never had a ribbon in my life, nor underwear, nor a present neither."

"There is not one of us here who is not concerned with your well-being," Maggie told her.

Maggie liked it when her wagon was in the lead and she did not have to deal with the dust from wagons in front of her. Of course, the next day, the lead wagon returned to the rear, and the others moved up a place. Maggie often tied a handkerchief over Clara's nose and mouth to keep her from breathing in the dust and brushed the child's hair each night to remove the dirt and sticks that blew into it. One night, Clara's hair was like mud because they had marched through a rainstorm. Maggie had suggested they stop and seek shelter under the wagons, but Reverend Parnell said they had to keep moving. "We are already late in the year to be on our way, and we are not keeping up with other trains. Every day, every hour counts if we are to reach California before the snows. Besides, there will be worse days ahead. You will be glad later on that we did not stop now."

"But it would be for only an hour," Maggie protested.

"In a snowstorm, an hour is as important as a day," he said.

Maggie looked forward to Sunday—they all did—because it was their only day of rest. That first Sunday, William and Joseph disagreed on whether to stop or to keep going. "Honoring the Sabbath in that way will add two weeks to our journey," William protested. "I believe we can praise the Lord as we go along."

"I will not break the commandment to rest on the holy day," Joseph said. "The women and animals need it. They will be refreshed for the following week. Go if you choose, but I shall stay and catch up with you later."

"There are other commandments we shall willingly break on this trip," William told him.

"Not I."

Maggie, who had fretted at Reverend Swain's sense of righteousness, was glad then that he held steadfast on that issue. She needed the rest, although the Sabbath was not a day of leisure. It was a day for catching up, for doing laundry, mending clothing, washing themselves, and cooking what they could for the coming week. Maggie discovered that preparing meals over a campfire was not a pleasant task. The fire sent out sparks that burned her skin and made holes in her clothing, and the wind blew smoke into her face and hair. The food was tasteless, and after just a week, she found it monotonous—side pork, beans, cornbread or biscuits, a few greens only if they were discovered along the road, and prairie chicken if Mary was lucky enough to shoot one.

"I'll be bloated big as a sow by the time we reach California," Lavinia complained. When she thought no one was looking, she reached into her trunk for a box of sugar candies, slipping one into her mouth but offering none to the others, even Clara. Maggie saw the little girl stare at the sweets, and she was disgusted with Lavinia's greediness. Lavinia had refused to take her turn at cooking, and that evening, after the others complained about her, Lavinia told Mary, "I was never expected to cook at home, so why should I do it now?"

"Do not hold yourself above the others. If you do not cook, you will not eat," Mary chided. "Do your part, or you will be sent home."

"And how'll you do that?" Lavinia asked defiantly. "You think the ministers are going to turn me out to walk back to St. Joseph?"

"If need be. After all, we cannot spare a horse." Lavinia stamped her foot. "I was never treated this way!"

"You should have been," Mary said, turning her back.

"You never cooked over a hearth?" Maggie asked. She took out beans from the night before and put them into a kettle over the fire. She was angry at Lavinia, too, but they had to eat. Despite Lavinia's selfishness, Maggie felt sorry for her.

"We always had us a cook," Lavinia said.

"But you knew it was expected of us. The preachers made it clear. Did you not hear them?"

"I never expected to come this far. I never expected to come at all." Lavinia watched as Maggie cut slices off a slab of bacon and laid them in a cast-iron pan, then set the pan on the coals.

"What do you mean?"

"I thought Arthur—he was my intended—was coming for me. We had us a quarrel. He said he wouldn't marry me then, but he never meant it. He loved me too much. He should have come for me when he found out I was going to California. He should have begged me back. He was at the boat. I know because I saw him plain as anything."

"You did not talk to him?" Maggie asked, thinking perhaps Arthur was not there to ask Lavinia to stay in Chicago but to make sure she was leaving.

"No. It was his place to come for me and apologize. I turned my back. Why should I make it easy for him? He should have boarded the boat and taken me away. I cannot think why he did not." She pouted. "If he loved me as much as he said, why didn't he go to St. Joseph to win me back? There was other boats for him to take."

"But he did not." *The irony of it,* Maggie thought. She and Penn were both running away from bad men when Lavinia had purposely left behind a decent one.

Lavinia shook her head. "Maybe he got there too late. I can't think of any other reason. Maybe he'll be waiting in Fort Kearny. Maybe he's taking a different route."

"How would he get there ahead of us?"

"Oh bosh! We are going so slow, a horse could carry him there and back in the time it takes us to go one way."

"Do you want him to be waiting for you?"

Lavinia turned away. "Well, I don't care to walk all the way to California now that I know what a beastly trip it is. Why do you have to ask so many questions?"

"It would be best for all of us if he was there," Winny interjected. She and the others had been listening to the conversation as they set out the tin plates and forks and filled the cups with coffee that Winny had brewed.

Lavinia whirled around. "Why do you say that?"

Maggie stooped and stirred the bacon with a long fork. She held her hand over the beans to see if they were warm yet. She glanced at the other groups of women. They had finished eating and were sitting around the campfires, singing and mending dresses and stockings. A few knitted. Caroline had taken out quilt pieces and was stitching them together. Maggie had brought along her own scraps and thought that perhaps one evening she would join Caroline, and the two would sit side by side piecing their quilts. She longed to relax and stitch with other women. Someone nearby laughed. Penn it was. Maggie had not heard her laugh before.

When Winny did not answer Lavinia, Mary spoke up. "We are tired of your complaining, of your shirking your duty. You make us pick up your share of work. Do you think we want to drive oxen and cook over a campfire? No, but it is required of us. You force us to do more than our share. Even Maggie, with a child to care for, does not complain. She is doing your portion now. We would not miss you if you left."

"That is unkind, Mary," Maggie said

"There are others here who are highborn, but they do not complain. Just look at Bessie. It is not our fault Lavinia has enjoyed a soft life," Mary continued. "I say if you want to eat, Lavinia, you must learn to cook."

"No one has ever spoken to me in such a mean way," Lavinia said. She began to cry.

"Save your tears for a man. They do no good with women, at least not tears of self-pity."

Maggie knew Mary was right, but nonetheless, she tried to make up for her friend's sternness. She touched Lavinia's arm. "The cooking is not pleasant, but it is not hard either. I will teach you." She handed Lavinia the fork and told her to stir the beans. "Tonight, I shall show you how to soak the beans in water so they will soften. You put them over the fire when we stop at the end of the day. We shall look along the trail for greens to give them flavor. We make soda biscuits with flour and water and a pinch of saleratus, or cornbread with cornmeal and salt. It is not hard. On Sundays, when we lay over, there will be time to bake yeast bread. And maybe pie if we can find berries along the way."

"I can't ever make a pie here."

"Of course you can." Maggie herself had made a molasses pie, using a tent post instead of a rolling pin to roll out the dough on a wagon seat. She had thought herself quite clever. "I can show you how to do that. By the time we reach California, you will be a fine cook. Come now. Stir the beans so they do not burn. Stir the bacon, too, and here are the ingredients for biscuits."

Lavinia did as she was told, then dished up the supper onto tin plates and handed them around to the women. They did not remark on the fact that both the bacon and the beans were burned and the biscuits were as hard as brickbats.

Despite the hardship of travel, Maggie loved the freedom of the prairie, the late-day sun glinting off the brown grasses, the sounds of birds, the long vistas. She had never seen so far in her life. She smiled as she watched Clara romp through the prairie grass searching for flowers and pretty rocks. She did not have to worry about the girl because everyone looked after her. Still, Maggie could not bear to let Clara out of her sight, as if her vigilance alone kept the girl safe. Perhaps if she had stayed with Dick, he would have lived. At that very moment he would be running across the prairie with his sister, his hair, as fair as Clara's, shining in the sunlight. For a few seconds, the thought of Dick playing with his sister, helping with the oxen, gathering wood for the campfire, made her smile.

After the bleak streets of Chicago and her early impression of the prairie, Maggie enjoyed the vast rolling land that stretched into eternity, the occasional copses of willow and oak and cottonwood, the flowers that studded the grasses like bright bits of glass. She found morning glories and wild roses and giant yellow flowers that had no name. Each step took her farther from Chicago and made her feel safer. Most of all, she loved the women, talking to them as they walked along, listening to their fears of the trail and hopes for California. As a dressmaker, she had discovered that her clients often confided in her. She was a good listener, and they trusted her with their secrets. The women on the Overland Trail confided in her, too, and Maggie came to care about them. As Reverend Parnell had said, many were running away, but others were running to something. Winny was one of them.

As the two walked together, Winny claimed that the trail was preferable to the hard work she had done as a servant in Chicago. She was older than Maggie had thought—twenty-four, she said— and had a joyous nature, although she had had a hard life. "Me and Davy's all that's left," she said. "The rest, they died—of starvation mostly. The least ones went first. I found the baby cold as river ice, his little hands curled up and hard as walnuts," she said, looking away.

"Then the two-year-old, and after him, the one who was five. Six of them and then Ma and Pa. Ma surely died of the starvation, because she would not eat a crumb and gave her portion to the rest of us. When only me and Davy was left, Davy says we have to leave Ireland and go to America. 'I cannot lose you, Win,' he says. 'If we stay, we will die, too.' So we found us passage on a boat and made our way to Chicago. Davy got a job building houses, and I went into service. We saved our money so we could buy a farm one day, saved two hundred dollars."

"You have two hundred dollars?" Maggie asked.

"Davy took it. We used to meet on Sunday, my day off. One day he told me he was of a mind to go to California. 'Where?' I asks because I never heard of it.

" 'It is a far-off place by the sea,' he says.

" 'By Ireland?'

" 'No, Win, the other way.'

"I ask why we would go there, and he tells me, 'Not we, Win. Me. It is not a place for a woman.'

" 'You would leave me, Davy?' I asks. He says it is only for a little while, until he gets rich. He says when he comes back, we will buy a farm, and I will never have to be in service again. He even promised me my own hired girl. Then he says, 'I would have to take our money. There is a company forming, and I need the two hundred to join. It is our stake, girl. I promise to come back with a hundred times more, a thousand times.' "

"But he did not come back," Maggie said. It was a statement, not a question.

Winny shook her head. She and Maggie had been walking beside the wagon, and Winny cried out and looked at her foot. She was barefoot because she'd brought only one pair of shoes and wanted to save them. A burr was stuck to the bottom of her toe. She pulled it out, then stared at a drop of blood. Winny wet her finger and placed it over where the burr had pricked her.

"He did not come back?" This time Maggie asked a question.

Winny shook her head. "He wrote me two times. He said he would write every month, but I only got two letters. I guess maybe he had no paper."

"Perhaps the letters got lost," Maggie said, although she was thinking that perhaps Davy had forgotten his sister—or died. What a blow it would be to that sweet girl to arrive in California and discover her brother had not given her a second thought.

Winny frowned for a moment, then looked up. "Or maybe they got throwed away. Mrs. Fletcher, the lady I worked for, was always saying she hoped I would not ever leave. Maybe the letters came, and she was afraid I would take out after Davy. What do you think?"

Maggie shrugged. "How would I know?"

"Because you—" Winny stopped suddenly. "I'm just asking."

Maggie knew then that Winny had recognized her—perhaps on the boat or in St. Joseph, or maybe even as early as the church. She would have realized that Maggie had changed her name and that she might have something to hide. The girl must have thought it over and decided not to reveal she knew who Maggie was. But she'd slipped just then. "Because I sewed for her, is that it?" Maggie asked.

"Oh, did you?" Winny asked, pretending she had not known.

"You know who I am." Suddenly Maggie grasped Winny's hand. "You were kind to me. I never thanked you for it."

"Your little boy?"

"He died. I tried to find ice for him, as you suggested . . ." Maggie did not continue. She could not tell Winny that Dick had passed on while she was searching for the ice. It still brought too much pain to know she was not there when he died.

"I am sorry. I know how it hurts. I lost too many brothers and sisters." Winny studied Maggie for a long time. Then she said, "I expect your husband died, too."

"Of course," Maggie replied. "I cannot talk about it."

117

"I shall not talk about it neither," Winny told her. Then she grinned. "I am glad you came along. You are always so cheerful and ready to help everybody. You and Mary, I am thinking we might not make it without you."

Maggie was startled. She did not consider herself indispensable. She knew Mary was necessary to the company, however. In just a few days, Mary had become the acknowledged leader of the women. They asked her advice, and Mary took their concerns to the ministers. In turn, the two men consulted Mary about the women. It was strange, Maggie thought. At home, she had seen how Mary was an oddity, but on the trail, Mary was admired and even loved by the women. Maggie wondered if her friend was aware of that. She thought again of what Winny had said about Maggie herself. Maybe the others, too, thought she was a worthy addition to the group.

One evening, just as they stopped for camp, Penn complained of a headache. A few minutes later she began vomiting. A wagon train had overtaken them earlier that day, and Penn had thought she'd seen Asa among the men. The fear of Asa finding her and dragging her away never left her. She had hidden herself in a wagon, and when she peered out, she realized she had been wrong. But the incident had been stressful, and when she tried to eat, she retched.

"Most likely it is her fear that causes her to be ill," Caroline told Maggie, who understood. There were times that Jesse's threats had caused her to be sick to her stomach, too. The two women helped Penn lie down on a quilt on the grass.

Lavinia was standing near the water bucket, and Caroline asked, "Would you bring her a dipper of water? She may have a fever."

Lavinia stared at Caroline, then said, "I will not do it! I will not go near her. Send her away. She has the cholera!"

Maggie, shocked, looked around for Clara. If Penn did indeed have cholera, Maggie must keep her daughter as far away as possible. She spotted Clara playing a game with Evaline and thought her safe for a time.

Cholera, she knew, was the scourge of the trail, more deadly than Indians or accidents, weather or starvation. Reverend Parnell had told her so after they passed a corpse that had turned black.

"Stay away," he had said. "It could be the cholera."

"Cholera?" Maggie had asked.

"It starts with diarrhea and vomiting, and in minutes, a thirst you cannot quench and terrible pain. The victim turns gray-blue, and death is not far away. I have seen men left to die alone because their companions will not go near them for fear of catching the disease. It is a wretched, lonely death."

Maggie was horrified to think that Penn might have contracted the disease. "Is it cholera?" she asked.

"We know no such thing," Caroline said.

"*You* may know no such thing, but it is as clear as daylight to *me* that she has it," Lavinia said. "She must have brought it with her from St. Joseph, from that man she lived with, and now she'll infect the rest of us. Leave her behind, I say." She repeated in an even louder voice, "Get her away from us before she kills us."

The anger in Lavinia's voice shocked Maggie. What was more, she realized then, even if Lavinia did not, that they were a group of women banded together. If they did not help each other, no matter the cost, they would not make it to California. "I shall get the water," she said.

She started for the water bucket, but Mary stepped in front of her and took the dipper. "You have Clara to think about," she said. She took a dipperful of water to Penn, who drank a little. Mary put the dipper aside so that no one else would touch it. Then she picked up Penn. "She will be more comfortable under the wagon, out of the sun. When the tents are set up, I shall put her in one."

"You touched her," Lavinia cried. "Now you'll get it, too. Stay away from our campfire."

Maggie gripped Lavinia's arm. "You do not speak for the rest of us. Keep your distance if you will, but do not tell Mary what to do."

Lavinia gave her a furious look, then grabbed her quilts and found a place for herself away from the others. "If that woman isn't dead by morning, we'll leave her behind," she said.

Maggie and the others were solemn as they ate their supper. Maggie was afraid for the fate of the young woman. It would not be right that she had put her old life behind only to die after barely starting on the new one. Maggie knew some of the women might not make it to California. The ministers had told them that at the meeting at the church. Now she was faced with the possibility that one of the women she loved best would die so soon after leaving St. Joseph.

Because the evening was pleasant, with no wind and no sign of rain, the women did not set up tents but spread their quilts inside the wagon circle. From time to time, Mary checked on Penn, asking if she needed water or a cool cloth on her forehead.

Penn was asleep and seemed to be resting well when the others turned in. In the night, Maggie heard someone vomiting, and then there were cries of pain. She started to get up, but Mary murmured, "Stay. I will see to her." She returned in a moment and said, "There is no fever. Penn is sleeping soundly."

"Help me," a voice cried.

"This time, I shall see what is wrong," Maggie said, rising from her quilt.

"Help me," the voice repeated. The plea was cut off by the sound of retching.

"Who is it?" Caroline called. The cries had awakened her, too.

"I believe it is Lavinia," Maggie said. "Do not trouble yourself." She crept to Lavinia, who had arranged her bed apart from the others. "Are you ill?" she asked.

"Can't you see I'm soaked, and my bowels . . ." Lavinia began to shake. "Such pain. I cannot stand it. Do something!" she said.

Maggie went to the campfire and lit a fagot in the coals, then held it over Lavinia's face, which was twisted in pain and had turned a dark color. The woman smelled of bile and excrement. Maggie dropped the flame.

"What is it?" Caroline had gotten up and put a handkerchief over her nose because of the stench. Now she put her hand on Lavinia's head.

"I believe it is the cholera. Stay back. I shall tend her since I am already contaminated," Maggie said. "I think there is nothing we can do for her except to make her as comfortable as possible."

Penn, who had awakened, rose and crept near the women. "I will get water for her."

"No, you keep away. It would not do for someone else to contract the illness and spread it to the rest of the camp."

"But you can come down with it, too. You have a little girl."

Maggie thought about that for a moment. She had been injudicious in going to Lavinia's aid, but she had risen half-asleep when she heard her, as if Clara had been the one who had cried out. Now she dared not go to Clara for fear of carrying the disease to her. "I have already been close to Lavinia. I shall tend her. You can pray," Maggie said.

"I never done so."

"We shall all pray," Caroline said. She told Penn, "It is easily done. You just ask the Lord for what you want, then thank Him for it."

"You mean He gives it to you."

"Not always, but He answers in the way He believes best."

The talking awakened Joseph, who came to Caroline's side. "And you, dear husband," Caroline said. "You must keep a distance. The women need you more than they do me."

"It is not the Lord's way to turn our backs on those in distress," he said.

Maggie looked at him strangely. Until now, he had not seemed a brave man or even a sympathetic one. "It is the cholera," she said, thinking Reverend Swain might not have understood.

"As I said, I shall attend her, too. She should not be moved. It would do no good and would only bring her pain," he told them.

"No, Maggie and I are already exposed. You have responsibilities elsewhere. We will stop the train until she is well," Caroline told him.

Joseph shook his head. "We cannot delay our journey. The rest of you will go on, and I shall stay with her. If she recovers, I will bring her along. If not, I will bury her. It is my duty as a minister."

"No!" Caroline said sharply. "God has ordained you to care for these women. He has chosen Maggie and me to administer to Lavinia. I shall not allow you to stay with us."

"You would defy me?"

"If I have to." He started to protest, but she put up her hand. "Do not ask it of me. Maybe it is God's will."

Joseph thought that over. "I have learned that God speaks to you, perhaps even more than He does to me. I shall pray for you. For Mrs. Hale and Miss Mercer, too." He glanced over to where Clara slept. "And for the little girl. She should not be deprived of her mother."

"Mary . . . ," Maggie pleaded.

The big woman nodded. "I shall care for Clara as if she were my own." Then she added firmly, "Until you return to us."

Joseph stretched out his hand to his wife, but she did not take it. "I shall tell William that Miss Mercer has cholera. We will keep the train moving. I shall leave one of the horses so that you can catch up with us . . . when the disease has run its course."

"Will they be safe, two women alone?" Sadie asked. She had awakened and approached Reverend Swain.

"Except for the cholera. What traveler—or Indian, for that matter—will come near two women exposed to such a deadly disease?"

"If anyone approaches, we shall cry out, 'Unclean!' as if we were lepers," Caroline said, adding a little levity to the situation.

Lavinia screamed then, and her cries woke the rest of the camp. "Tell the others what has happened. Tell them to stay away from us," Maggie told Mary.

Dora prepared breakfast and left two tin plates of it for Maggie and Caroline. "We will wait an hour, perhaps two, in case . . ." She did not finish, and Maggie knew she meant in case Lavinia died.

But Lavinia did not die then, and after a time, William shouted, "Move out!" The women waved or held their hands in prayer. "God will protect you," they shouted, and "Trust in the Lord."

Maggie watched as Mary and Clara disappeared in the distance, Clara turning once to wave. Then Maggie returned to Lavinia, who was crying in pain, cursing, demanding that someone help her. Caroline forced her to swallow water, but she only threw it back up. The woman was delirious, and she called out the name of the man to whom she had been betrothed. She cursed him, too. Maggie dipped a rag in water and placed it on Lavinia's head, but the woman flung it off.

In the afternoon, Lavinia's cries stopped. She moaned in pain and had the strength to speak only a little. The two women could do nothing but sit beside her, shading her from the sun and running water-soaked rags over her blackened body. Maggie saw that Reverend Parnell had left a shovel beside Lavinia. She would wait until Lavinia was dead before digging her grave.

As evening came on, Lavinia breathed her last. "She is gone," Caroline told Maggie.

"It is over," Maggie responded. She had not liked Lavinia much. The woman had caused trouble. Still, Maggie mourned her death. No woman should have died in such agony. She wondered why it had been Lavinia. Why did she catch the cholera and not Penn or Caroline or herself? Or Clara? There was no order to it. Fate seemed to select its victims at random, just as it had once chosen Dick. One moment Lavinia had been as healthy as the rest of them, and then, within hours, she was dead.

She and Caroline washed Lavinia's body, then dressed her. Because, as Caroline said, there was no sacred ground in a hundred miles, they buried her on the prairie. They took turns digging a grave in the hard soil, then wrapped Lavinia in a quilt as a shroud and placed her body in the earth. The grave was shallow, and they covered it with rocks to keep out the scavengers. No Bible had been left for them, so Caroline recited verses from memory. Maggie said a prayer. "It is done. She is with God," Caroline said.

The two women washed themselves and changed into dresses that had been left behind for them. They burned Lavinia's belongings and their own soiled clothing.

They waited a day to make sure neither one of them had caught the cholera from Lavinia. Then they mounted the horse Joseph had left for them and hurried to catch up with the wagon train.

"She died in the evening," Maggie said after she and Caroline reached the others and Caroline's husband helped them off the horse.

"God have mercy on her," Dora said.

"And on us," Caroline added.

Maggie bowed her head at that. Lavinia was the first of them to die. How many more would not complete the journey to California?

A few days after Lavinia's death, as the women nooned, a troop of dragoons stopped at the camp. They were on their way to Fort Kearny.

"So you are the wagonload of spinsters we heard about in St. Joe," the lieutenant who commanded the company said. "We have been on the watch for you."

"Indeed. Are we such a curiosity?" Mary asked.

"To some, perhaps. We have never heard of women crossing the country by themselves."

"We have a dozen men with us, but we are sharing their work," Maggie replied. "I do not believe we should be considered oddities."

The soldier blushed. "No, ma'am. We are not here out of curiosity but because a man with us is searching for one of your number."

Maggie felt a chill go through her. Had she been followed? She looked for Jesse among the soldiers, but he was not there. She glanced around the camp for Penn but could not see her and thought that the girl had hidden herself. Maggie hoped the soldiers did not insist on searching the wagons. "A soldier?" she asked.

"A civilian. He joined a wagon train behind you but begged to ride with us because we travel faster." Maggie searched the men until she spotted one who was not wearing a uniform. She felt a sense of relief. He was small and looked something like a dandy, not at all like Penn's Asa. Surely such a man would not be searching for her.

"I believe this is the group you have been seeking, sir."

The man rode forward and spoke to Maggie. "My fiancé is among you. I have come all this

128

way to beg her to return to Chicago with me."

Maggie shuddered as she looked off into the distance, realizing who the man was. The sun shone on the prairie, turning it as gold as a wedding ring. It should have been a happy day, but she was gripped by sadness as she turned back to the man. "Her name, sir?"

"Lavinia Mercer. I know she left with you. I saw her board the boat in Chicago, although I do not see her now. It may be she is in a wagon, hiding from me. I mean to convince her to return east as my wife. Perhaps one of the ministers with you will officiate. We would have been wed long since. The wedding was planned, we had engaged the church, and Lavinia had already made her wedding dress. But we quarreled. I broke the engagement. I hoped to teach her a lesson by turning my back. I thought if she knew I was willing to let her go, she would become more docile. As you can see, it did not work. Now I will admit to her my error and apologize. I love her dearly, and I believe she loves me, and I will do all in my power to make her happy."

Just then, Caroline came up to them, and Maggie said with a catch in her throat, "This is Lavinia's fiancé, come to fetch her back home."

The man dismounted and removed his hat. "If she will have me," he said. "Will you explain to her that I am here?"

"She . . . ," Maggie began but could not go on. She tried to blink back the tears, then turned away, and because she had no handkerchief, she wiped her face with her sleeve.

Caroline stared at the man, wringing her hands in her apron. "Oh, that you had come just a week ago."

The man frowned. "What do you mean? Do you say she has gone off with another?"

"Only God," Caroline told him. "Arthur? That is your name, is it not?"

"She has mentioned me, then?" He looked hopeful.

Maggie nodded. "She would indeed have married you. She told me so."

He shook his head in confusion.

"She is with the Lord now," Caroline said. When the man still did not understand, she added, "Lavinia is dead."

"Dead?" Arthur stared at Caroline, then turned to Maggie. "How can she be dead? Did she tell you to say that because she does not want to see me?" He gave a hopeful smile. "She does love to play silly games."

"She died of the cholera," Caroline told him.

He gasped and put his hand to his cheek. "Did she suffer? Tell me she did not suffer."

Caroline turned away, and Maggie, knowing lying would distress Caroline, answered for her. "Only a little." She stepped forward and took

130

Arthur's hands. "She hoped you would be at Fort Kearny. It is what she told me."

"She would have come home with me, then?"

"Oh yes."

For a moment the man wept, rubbing his eyes with his fists. Maggie wept, too.

"I was with her at the end," Maggie said. "She thought of you till the last. That final day, in her suffering, she called out your name." Maggie did not add that the name was followed by curses. "Your name was on her lips when she died. 'Artie' was the last word she spoke in this life."

"And I was not there to comfort her," he cried.

Maggie took his hand. "I believe the *thought* of you brought her comfort. Mrs. Swain and I granted her last wish."

Arthur waited. "Her last wish?"

"We buried her in her wedding dress."

Seven

Lavinia's fiancé left that day with a group of men returning east. The dragoons, too, prepared to go on, but before they left, they warned William to be on the alert for Indians. In fact, the soldiers had been charged with watching for the hostiles on their way to Fort Kearny.

"We have not seen any since we left St. Joseph," William said.

"You can presume they have seen you every day," the lieutenant told him.

"Are they dangerous?" Maggie asked. She remembered the drunken Indians she had seen in St. Joseph and thought that if the rest of their tribesmen were like them, they posed little problem. Still, there had been stories among the emigrants they encountered of Indian attacks and depredations, of men hacked to death, of women ravished and children stolen away. She glanced at Clara, making sure the girl was near the wagons.

"They can be," the lieutenant replied. "With the cholera, most Indians are staying away from the trains just now. Cholera is as deadly for them as for you. Still, it is best to be prepared. If they are painted and are riding without their women and little ones, they may be warriors. They are a noble race who are defending their way of life. Still, they are vicious fighters and give no quarter to women and children. If you see them, you must corral your wagons at once and be prepared to fight. If they are accompanied by their families, they are most likely beggars. You would be wise to keep them as far away as possible, for they are thieves, the women the worst. You cannot blame them, of course. We have taken much away from them. Give them a few biscuits and a trinket or two, then send them on their way. Guard your belongings and your children, if you have them among you. If they attack, you must shoot to kill."

Maggie knew she was not the only one who was alarmed. "I could not kill a person, even an Indian," one woman said.

"You had best do so," the lieutenant told her. "What an Indian will do to a woman . . . well, to tell of it is not fitting. If you had the choice of putting a bullet through your head or being ravished by a red man, do not think twice."

"I mean I do not know how to shoot a gun," the woman said.

"We taught the women to handle the animals and build fires and load and unload the wagons. We did not feel it necessary, what with the men accompanying us and a few women already familiar with firearms, that the others learn to handle guns," William said.

"Besides, it is unwomanly," Joseph added.

"And you think dying at the hands of a savage is womanly? You must teach them now, before you go farther," the lieutenant said. He turned to the women gathered around him. "Which of you knows how to handle a gun?"

Mary and several other women raised their hands. The rest shook their heads.

The soldier looked at the dragoons. "I believe we can wait for morning to leave." He turned to Joseph. "I advise you to let us teach these women to protect themselves."

"The commandments say thou shalt not kill," Joseph told him.

"Do the commandments tell you to watch while your women are raped and mutilated, while your children's heads are bashed in?" the soldier asked. "Do the commandments say stand idle while the Indians hack off your manhood? If so, then by all means, do not let your women learn how to shoot a gun."

Joseph blanched, but William spoke up. "We should be grateful for your instruction."

Maggie did not know how to shoot. She lined up with the others in front of the wagons so that the dragoons as well as the men who were members of the company could show them how to load and fire the pistols, rifles, and shotguns they had brought with them.

After what the lieutenant had said about rape,

the women were anxious to learn how to handle guns and were apt students, although not all of them. "You ain't never going to learn to shoot, miss," a soldier informed Dora after he instructed her how to aim at a bush. She'd shot through a wagon sheet instead. "If a Indian comes riding by, you just throw the gun at him."

Several of the dragoons were amused at the women and treated them like children. "I already know how to shoot a gun," Penn told a soldier who had taken her arm. She removed the pistol from her pocket.

"A pepperbox like that ain't going to cause much damage, 'less you hold it right up next to a Indian's head," the soldier replied. "Guns and womens don't mix is my way of thinking. It's a good thing you're going to California to find you a husband to protect you." He handed her a rifle and told her to aim for a tree.

"Which branch?" Penn asked.

The soldier laughed at her. "The one with the crow on it." He turned and winked at another soldier.

"I reckon I'll get the crow in the eye." Penn held the rifle steady and sighted on the bird, then slowly squeezed the trigger. The crow toppled off the branch in a shower of feathers. "I guess maybe I ain't needing a husband to protect me in California," she said.

Another dragoon came along the line looking

the women over and stopped beside Maggie. "You know anything about guns?"

"No."

He grinned at her. "Come over here behind the wagon so's you won't hurt nobody. You stand out here with a gun, you're liable to shoot one of them preachers."

Maggie didn't like the looks of the man and thought to tell him no, but she wanted to learn to shoot. He led her past several wagons until they were beyond view of the others and showed her how to load a shotgun and aim it. He stood behind her and held his hand over hers to explain how to pull the trigger. Suddenly he placed his hand on her breast.

Maggie drew back in horror, too shocked to say anything more than "Sir! Keep your hands off me."

"Oh, don't be high and mighty with me, miss. I know you."

Did he know about Jesse? Had Jesse followed her? Maggie began to shake and wanted to cry out, but she could not because she was afraid that he indeed did know about her. "I have never met you," she insisted.

"Maybe not, but I knowed all about you. I knowed you womens got a reason for joining the wagon train. You're running away. You behave, or I'll tell them ministers about you."

Did he really know something, or was he

bluffing? Maggie wasn't sure, and she didn't dare risk the chance he might be telling the truth. "You don't know me," she insisted.

"Oh, you reckon not? I seen you in St. Joe. I been expecting to meet up with you. You're a whore."

Maggie stared at the man. Had he mixed her up with Sadie?

"Ain't no better than a whore. Myself, I can tell. You got something to hide. You ain't no old maid going to California for a husband. I seen you right off when we got here, and I says to myself, 'Wilson, she is going to give you a good time.'"

Maggie was sickened by the man's words. "Let me go or I'll scream," she said. Her voice was high and tight and too shaky to sound convincing. Besides, she had waited too long to protest. The soldier surely knew she was hiding something.

"You do that, and I'll tell them preachers who you are. They'll turn you out at Kearny." He threw back her skirt and tore at her petticoat. Then he added, "You whore!"

What would Clara think if she heard her mother called such a horrible name? Maggie wondered. But if she allowed the soldier to touch her, she was no better than what he had called her. "Take your hands off me," she screamed. She drew back her hand and slapped the soldier hard across the face.

"You bitch! Look what you done now!" he cried.

The others heard the commotion, and the preachers, Caroline with them, hurried to Maggie. "What is this?" William demanded.

"I was trying to learn her to shoot, and she turned crazy on me," he said.

"You were teaching her to shoot by ripping her dress?"

The soldier grinned. "She done that herself, said if I didn't kiss her, she'd holler."

The other women had reached them and looked at the man in disgust. No one would want to kiss the filthy, bearded dragoon.

"Mrs. Hale?" William asked Maggie.

"He tore my dress. He put his hands on me and demanded—"

"Soldier!" The lieutenant came up to the man. "Explain this."

The grin left the dragoon's face, and he looked frightened. "It ain't my fault, sir. She's a cat. She come up to me and asked for money, said she'd fix me if I didn't give it to her."

By now the entire company of women as well as the soldiers had surrounded Maggie and the dragoon. Maggie clutched at her torn dress. Ever since she had signed up for the trek west, she had been afraid the women would discover she had tried to kill her husband. Now she wondered if they believed the man when he claimed she was a prostitute. They stared silently at her as Caroline stepped forward and took her hands.

The soldier glanced at them and grew bold. He turned to William. "You got took, sir. She ain't no old maid."

"He lies."

The women turned to see who had defended Maggie. For a moment, Maggie thought it was Mary, but Mary had taken Clara to see the horses. Instead, Sadie stood defiantly with her hands on her hips. "Maggie's the sister of my school friend. We went to the church together," Sadie said in a voice that allowed for no dissent. "She ain't no more a fancy woman than me."

Penn and Dora came up beside Maggie and put their arms around her waist.

"She's just a plain old cat. Most likely, she's going to California to set up a whorehouse, make these other women work at it."

"She is no such thing. I believe I know her family," Caroline put in. "She is a woman of good character, and you slander her."

The dragoon was furious. "They's lying, sir."

"Have a care, soldier. You have accused this woman of a shameful act. I will not stand for it," a voice said.

Maggie turned, thinking Reverend Parnell was speaking, but it was the other one, the self-righteous one, Joseph Swain.

"I demand you take action against this man for his foul attack," he continued.

"No," Maggie said. "Let it be over. I do not want to think of it again, or speak of it." She was embarrassed and shamed at what had happened. She did not want the others to wonder why she had waited to cry out. Nor did she want anyone to look too deeply into her past.

"You see, sir," Joseph said to the lieutenant. "Only a woman of pure heart would forgive a man for such an abomination."

The lieutenant nodded and turned to Maggie. "I am sorry for this and thank you for your compassion, ma'am. Filing charges against a soldier would take time away from protecting wagon trains. I will keep a watch on him, and so will the others." Then he said to William, "It is better we be on our way now instead of waiting for morning." He ordered the dragoons to be ready to move out.

The women crowded around Maggie then, offering words of sympathy, and she realized they had not doubted her at all. Penn proffered a salve she had made from herbs that she'd picked along the trail, for where the soldier had dug his nails into Maggie's breast. Evaline told her that Bessie had gone to build up a fire and prepare a cup of tea for her. Dora said she would fetch Maggie's other dress and a needle so she could mend the torn one. As if they did not want to embarrass Maggie, the others slowly turned away, until only Sadie was left standing with her arm around her friend.

"What you said . . . ," Maggie began. "If you had not spoken up . . ."

Sadie smiled. "I knew you weren't a whore." She gave Maggie a sly look. "I hope I was not in error about our knowing each other. I did not recognize you until a few minutes ago. I ask you to give my regards to your sister next time you write."

"I do not have a sister."

"You do now, more than forty of them."

Maggie climbed into a wagon to change into her other dress, then sat down by the puckered opening at the back of the wagon to mend the torn one. After a time she heard footsteps, but she paid no attention until she heard Joseph ask, "Did you in truth know Mrs. Hale's family?"

"No," Caroline replied.

"Then I think it has cost you much to tell a falsehood."

"It was necessary. I believe God will forgive me."

"It was generous of Mrs. Cooper to speak up. She took a chance." He paused a moment. "I believe you are aware that it was Mrs. Cooper who was a woman of the streets. Did you know of her profession when you allowed her to join us?"

Caroline paused as she considered the question. "I suspected."

"And William, did he know?"

"He may have guessed."

"And yet you approved of her."

"Yes."

"Will you tell me why?"

Caroline did not reply at first. Then she said, "I knew her at the Kitchen for a good woman. I believed she had had a hard life and wanted to change. We could give her that opportunity. It was not for me to judge her, no more than Our Lord judged the Magdalene."

"I believed the same," Joseph said.

"You knew?" Caroline sounded incredulous. "Was it because of her appearance?"

"Not that. I knew because she once approached me on the street."

"And yet you did not refuse to let her join us."

"My dear, I saw that you were her champion, that you were bringing a sinner back into the flock. How could I have gone against such a powerful advocate as my beloved wife?"

A little later, the dragoons, their gear packed, were ready to mount their horses when the lieutenant approached Joseph and Caroline. Maggie was sitting on a log near them, a quilt around her shoulders. "The woman?" the lieutenant asked.

"She will be fine," Caroline replied. "It is good of you to inquire."

He nodded, then cleared his throat. "I had another reason for stopping with you that I have not mentioned." He glanced at Maggie, but she was not listening. Instead, she stared out across the prairie, which was dotted with flowers. There was the sound of birds, and she took comfort in their little songs.

"What is it?" Joseph asked the lieutenant.

"You will excuse me," Caroline said, but the lieutenant told her to stay.

"You should be as aware of this situation as your husband," he said. He looked again at Maggie, who sat with her eyes closed.

"I have information about a criminal who may be among you," the lieutenant said.

"What?" Joseph asked. "One of our men? My brother has conducted interviews with each and is confident they are all of good character."

"I am not talking about your men."

"A woman?" Caroline asked.

Although she did not open her eyes, Maggie was aware of the conversation now. She heard the shock in Caroline's voice.

"It appears she is charged with a very serious crime—the worst."

Maggie held her breath. Jesse was dead. The news tore at her heart. He couldn't hurt her anymore, or Clara either, but she could not help remembering the man who had brought her violets. Perhaps there had been a part of him that was decent. Now she would never know. She was safe, but at what cost?

"She is among us?" Joseph asked.

"It is thought she may be."

"Who is she?"

"Her name is Margaret Kaiser. She is traveling with her daughter, who is four or thereabout."

Caroline reached behind her and gripped Maggie's shoulder. "We have no one of that name in our company," she said.

"She may have changed her name."

Maggie tightened the quilt around her shoulders in an attempt to stop shaking. Would the soldier take her all the way back to St. Joseph? Or perhaps she would be tried at Fort Kearny. What if she was found guilty? Would she be hanged in front of her friends? And what would happen to Clara?

"What has she done?" Joseph asked.

"It appears she may have murdered her husband." He held out a piece of paper. "This is a notice I received. It says right here, 'Murder.' "

"Perhaps she had a good reason," Caroline put in. "Perhaps he beat her or threatened her child. I have seen women like that in Chicago, women so cruelly treated that they are reduced to the state of animals. They fight back only when their children are threatened."

The three were silent for a moment. Then Caroline said, "Well, whatever her name is, she is not in our company. And as you can see, we have only a boy with us and a Negro girl. Do you know that this woman is going west?"

"It is presumed so."

Maggie heard the dragoon's boot kick at the dirt, and she remembered how Jesse had struck her with his own boot after she had fallen to the floor. Tears slipped from under her eyelids. The world was unfair. Why was it all right for him to beat her so savagely but wrong for her to fight back?

The lieutenant continued, "I didn't join the cavalry to track down runaway wives. To my way of thinking, it is not my business." Maggie heard the rattle of paper. "I just thought I would mention it. There's a reward—two hundred dollars."

Two hundred dollars? Maggie wondered why the government cared so much about the killing of a gambler.

"This is the information. I believe the description could fit several women in your train," the lieutenant said. "I do not need it. As I say, it is distasteful to me to have to track down a woman. Maybe one of your people will recognize her."

Although Clara was dressed like a boy, the women in the train knew she was a girl. If they heard of the reward, one of them was likely to recognize Maggie as the runaway wife. Two hundred dollars was a great deal of money.

Perhaps if she confessed to Reverend Swain, he would take pity and help her. She thought of that as the dragoon walked away.

Joseph's voice shook her out of her reverie. "Mrs. Hale, what do you have to say to this?"

Maggie looked up to see the minister staring at her. Slowly, she stood, letting the quilt fall to the ground. She could deny she was that woman, but he already knew better. "It is true," she said.

"Will you tell us why?"

"He beat me. He beat Clara. He did terrible things to her . . ." She stopped. "I cannot shame her."

"There were children at the Kitchen who had been used as prostitutes, some by their fathers," Caroline said. "Maggie's husband was a cruel man. I believe she had no choice but to take the action she did."

Joseph turned to his wife. "You knew?"

"I suspicioned it. A man came to the church asking for her. I remembered him. Maggie was familiar to me when I first saw her."

"And you did not tell me?"

Caroline did not answer his question. Instead, she said, "I did not like the look of him. I have seen his kind before. I thought Maggie was wise to leave him."

"The Bible says a woman must cleave to her husband."

"The Bible does not say she must submit to

abominable behavior. It does not say she must allow him to beat her to death and accost her child. You saw the bruises on their faces when Maggie applied to come with us."

"Yes." He was silent a moment. "She is a married woman, however. Did you not consider that? After all, our purpose is to find Christian brides for the miners."

"We have many purposes. I believe the Lord called on me to rescue a downtrodden woman."

Caroline put her arm around Maggie and drew her close as Joseph considered the situation. Then he ripped the paper in half and in half again. "I shall add this to the campfire."

Eight

A wagon was stuck in the deep prairie sand, and Maggie and several other women helped the men unharness the oxen from the wagon behind and harness them to the first one so the animals could help pull out the mired vehicle. It was the second time that day that they had had to double-team the oxen because of a wagon that had bogged down.

"We must lighten the load," William told Joseph. "The oxen will never make it to California if they have to haul all this."

Maggie had already seen the piles of discarded items along the way—trunks and bureaus, chairs, farm implements, feather beds, curling irons, buttonhooks, even food. At first the women had viewed the discards as treasure to be plundered. Maggie had opened a trunk of clothing and watched Sadie sort through silk dresses and corsets, lace shawls and bonnets, adding a few to her own trunk. Winny had taken a skillet, a coffeepot, and a slab of bacon that was only a little spoiled. Penn had found drawers and a petticoat. And Maggie had searched for a dress to replace the one the dragoon had ripped. She had mended that dress but could not bear to wear it. She also hunted for boys' clothing for Clara. She had expected the girl to wear overalls only until they left St. Joseph, but after she found out the law was searching for a woman and her daughter, she decided Clara should continue to dress like a boy. Besides, sometimes when she saw Clara running across the prairie, Maggie was reminded of Dick, and for an instant she had two children. The little girl did not protest, because she found pants less confining than a skirt.

After a time, the items discarded along the trail no longer interested Maggie. Anything picked up only added to the weight in her own wagon and would have to be thrown away farther down the road. Now she and the others took only what was better than what they had. Dora found a good skirt to replace one of hers that was ragged. It was also larger in the waist, Maggie noted. Caroline exchanged a sturdy kettle for her own, which had a hole in it.

Some of the discarded items had been burned by the emigrants who abandoned them. If they couldn't have them, nobody would. But other travelers were more generous. Caroline picked up a fine sampler dated 1840. Embroidered at the bottom was "This was done by Fanny Kirk, who hated every stitch of it." Maggie came across a pile of quilts, pieced in intricate patterns and put together with tiny stitches. Someone had laid a board on top of them with a note: "Please take and love my good quilts. C. Morrow."

"She must have cried when she left them," Maggie said, peering at the even stitches. Maggie had brought only the plain quilts she had pieced when she stayed on Mary's farm, and now she exchanged them for the ones left on the trail. "I believe this one is far finer than any I made," she said.

"And yours is finer than anything I have," Sadie told her, picking up one of Maggie's discarded quilts and leaving behind her own shabby bed covering.

Maggie didn't protest Reverend Parnell's order to lighten the load. By then, she had pushed too many wagons out of the sand and mud holes to object. Although she had brought little with her, she nonetheless searched through her belongings to see what could be discarded. She set a pair of kid slippers beside the trail. Jesse had bought them for her after he won at gambling and was in a good mood. They were soft and fine, but they would be ruined in a minute if she wore them through the sand.

"My books can go," Caroline said.

"My frame. I will keep the picture," Mary told Maggie, who was surprised that Mary had brought along the daguerreotype of her brother and sister-in-law.

"My flute." A woman opened a case lined in

velvet and touched the instrument longingly. Then, as she wiped a tear from her eye, she placed it back into its case and set it on the ground.

"The Bible Reverend Swain gave me," Sadie put in.

"Mine, too," another woman said.

"My stove," Bessie told them. Her wagon had been stuck more than any of the others, and Reverend Parnell had suggested a few days before that she discard the sheet-iron stove. Bessie had refused. "I do not intend to cook over a campfire once I arrive in California," she had replied. "Besides, my stove may be my greatest attraction as a bride." Now, however, she and Evaline removed the stove lids and tossed them out of the wagon. The men lifted the heavy stove and set it on the ground. "Perhaps someone will come along who can use it," she said, setting a lid lifter and a can of stove blacking on one of the lids. That was unlikely, Maggie thought. The stove would surely rust into the ground.

"What about the pulpit?" William asked Joseph.

"Absolutely not!" Joseph was incensed. "It was a gift from our Chicago congregation, and it will grace a house of worship in California. I would rather throw out my gold watch than abandon the pulpit."

"It is walnut and very heavy. It weighs more than all the clothes and books and personal items the women are throwing away. Surely it will

151

mean more to the men in California that they have a preacher than that you brought the furnishings of a church," Caroline told him.

"I could never explain it in Chicago. No, I will take it to California if I have to carry it on my back."

"As well you might," William muttered.

Bessie was more sympathetic. "It is hard to discard possessions that are dear to us," she told the ministers. "I find that most distressing."

Maggie could see that. She glanced at the rocking chair in the back of the wagon. Bessie had not offered to abandon it. But that was not Maggie's business.

William looked at the chair, too, and smiled.

"You think me too materialistic?" Bessie asked.

"I cannot say that of someone whose generosity made this trip possible."

"But you would say that of someone else, would you not?"

"You are not someone else."

"Much as I try," she said. She turned and studied the rocking chair. "Will it go before we reach California?"

"No doubt."

Bessie sighed. "Then it might as well be discarded now." She turned to Maggie. "Will you help me lift it out of the wagon?"

William went over to the wagon to take the chair, but the women had already picked it up.

152

Once it was on the ground, Maggie said, "It is very pretty."

"My husband made it—my first husband."

Maggie had not known that Bessie had been married twice. "He painted the homey scene on its back," Bessie said. "The rocker is a little crude and of no value to anyone else, but I prize it more than the Chippendale chairs that belonged to my second husband. It is the only possession of his that I retained."

William, too, examined the rocker. Then he lifted it back into the wagon. "You have already discarded your stove, and you did not bring the little dog of which you were so fond. I believe the rocker can survive a few miles more. Who knows, perhaps it can make it all the way to California after all."

"On my back?" Bessie asked.

"Would you prefer mine?"

Maggie saw the two exchange a glance before Reverend Parnell walked away. "You have lost two husbands, then," she said to Bessie.

"Two good ones. I do not believe I shall find a third."

"Then why do you go to California?" Maggie remembered Bessie's conversation with the ministers at the church and was curious. Was the woman really going along for an adventure? If that was true, then she must regret her decision by now.

Bessie studied Maggie for a moment, perhaps wondering whether to confide in her. "I have several reasons. One is Evaline."

"You are very fond of her."

"I have known her since she was quite small. She was the daughter of my cook. When the woman was dying, she begged me to care for the child, who was only five. It was not a hardship. I loved her, and so did Mr. Whitney. We had no children of our own, so we spoiled her, he even more than I. She was never just a servant to us."

Bessie paused, scanning the company until she spotted Evaline and smiled. "We raised her almost as if she were a white girl, with the advantages of someone of wealth. She draws and paints and plays the violin beautifully. You have heard her of an evening at the campfire. Perhaps it was not wise of us to treat her so. She will always be a Negro. She will never be allowed to enter the front door of a Chicago mansion and be welcomed by members of society. If anything happens to me, the best she can hope for is to be a personal servant, someone who helps her mistress dress and handles social correspondence. That is a pity, because she is far too intelligent and too talented to be nothing more than a lady's maid."

"She might marry," Maggie said.

Bessie nodded. "She could not marry a white man of society, of course. There are a few Negro men who have risen to positions as doctors and solicitors, but not many. I suppose her best hope would be a coachman or a butler."

"Perhaps in California," Maggie suggested. Like Bessie, Maggie was watching Evaline as she walked along playing a game with Clara.

"That is what I am hoping. You see, she was treated abominably in Chicago. The son of one of my friends accosted her on the street and demanded she go to his lodgings with him. And more than once, when I sent her on an errand, she met hostility and perversion. People look down on a Negro girl who aspires to a higher station. There are those who would make her keep her place. You may recall that, early in our trip, two or three women in this company expected Evaline to do their washing. I had to step in. I hope things will be better in California, where I believe society is less rigid. At least I hope so."

"Evaline is a sweet girl," Maggie said. "She is so kind to Clara."

"She is that. I wonder that the indignities she has had to endure have not hardened her. She is too naïve. She trusts everyone. In protecting her and wanting her to have a happy life, I have failed her."

"Perhaps not," Maggie said. "You have shown her love. That is a great gift."

"Is it? Love imposes hardship."

Maggie considered Bessie's words and thought of her own situation. Her love for Jesse, brief as it was, had indeed brought anguish and pain, but out of that love had come Dick and Clara, and they were worth every blow of Jesse's fists. She would not tell Bessie about Jesse, of course. Like the others, Bessie believed Maggie's husband had been an honorable man. "You mentioned a first husband."

Bessie smiled, as if remembering. "He was young and very handsome. I believe I fell in love with him the first time I saw him, perhaps because he talked to me of books."

"Was he a businessman like Mr. Whitney?" She had met Bessie's husband once when she had gone to the Whitney mansion to fit a dress.

Bessie stared at Maggie a long time and did not reply.

"I am sorry. I do not mean to intrude."

"It is all right. I was just wondering if I should tell you my past. No one else here knows, not even Caroline. They all believe I was highborn, but I was not. My speech once was as crude as Penn's." She paused a moment. "Even Evaline does not know the whole of it."

"I do not need to know either," Maggie said. She already was burdened with too many confidences.

Bessie glanced at Evaline to make sure she was all right, then suggested she and Maggie sit for a few moments. Bessie made her way to a nearby tree and sat down in its shade, her back against the trunk. She stretched out her legs in front of her, then raised her chin and stretched to take the kinks out of her back. "Now you shall know my secret," she began. "I was born on a poor farm in Massachusetts and was destined to be a hired girl or a farm wife. We were all girls in the family, so I did much of the heavy work—plowing, seeding, harvesting, milking, and tending my sisters. My parents were hard and did not approve of frivolity. They did not believe in education for girls, either, and I did not learn to read and write until I was fourteen. That was when I went to Lowell as a bobbin girl."

"You worked in the mill?" Bessie was so refined that Maggie could scarcely believe such a thing.

"I was good at it. First rate." She grinned at Maggie. "I lived in a boardinghouse and loved my life. That was the first time I ever slept in a bed. The other girls complained about the food, but I was used to being hungry, and I could not stop eating. The mills had a school for the girls, and I was good at learning, too. I wanted to progress, so I determined to improve my speech, and studied the wives of the supervisors and owners to learn how to talk and dress properly.

"In time I advanced, but as I became more confident, I realized there was unfairness in the mills. The work of spinning, weaving, drawing-in, and dressing was dangerous and mindless. The girl I shared a bed with lost her finger in the machinery. We girls worked as hard as the men but earned only a fraction of what they were paid. Some protested, but I did not have the courage to do so, because I was afraid of losing my job. My family needed the money. The only other employment I could have gotten was as a domestic, and I might as well have gone back to the farm as do that miserable work.

"Then I met Abraham Lessing." Bessie smiled for a moment. "He was delivering supplies to the factory and noticed me because I was carrying a copy of Mr. Cooper's *The Prairie* that I had borrowed from the library. He asked if I liked it, and I said, 'You have read it?'

" 'Twice. I have read all of Mr. Cooper's books,' he told me. I wanted to ask him if he had read Mr. Longfellow's poems, too, but I dared not risk someone seeing me talking to a man. They were very strict and would have let me go.

"A week later, I heard someone whisper 'Miss,' and saw him sitting under a tree eating his dinner. I had thought of him for days. I sat down beside him, and we talked. After that we met in secret, until the mistress of my boardinghouse caught us and threatened to tell the mill manager or to summon my father. When I told Abraham we had been seen and could no longer meet, he put his arms around me and told me he loved me.

He knew of a minister who would say the words over us, and we were married that day."

Bessie wiped away a tear. "It did not last long. Barely a year later, he was thrown from his wagon and run over by horses. He was taken away and buried before anyone thought to tell me. I was seventeen and a widow, and I never knew where my husband lay."

Maggie reached over and took the woman's hand. A year! Bessie had had barely a year to love her husband. But then Maggie had loved Jesse for only a few months. "And then you met Mr. Whitney," Maggie said, when Bessie did not continue.

"Yes. I could not go back to the mill. Mr. Whitney was a bachelor, and I was employed as his assistant, to write letters and make travel arrangements, to have his clothes pressed and keep his social schedule. He was lonely, and we talked a great deal. He taught me refined ways, how to speak and dress as a woman of society, and he opened his great library to me. We fell in love and were wed. There were those who believed we had had an improper relationship and that I had tricked him into marriage, but that was untrue. When the women in Lowell would not accept me, Mr. Whitney insisted we move to Chicago, where society did not know us. I loved him in a different way from Abraham, but I loved him just as well."

• • •

Bessie did not seem inclined to say more, so Maggie rose, then held out her hand to help the other woman stand. The wagon train had passed them by, and they hurried to catch up. Suddenly Maggie pointed across the prairie and said, "Look! Indians." Up ahead of them, the wagons were forming a circle.

The two women ran for the wagons and reached them just as William yelled, "Ladies, get inside the wagon circle. Fetch your guns."

Maggie turned and looked for Clara, then saw that Dora had her by the hand in the center of the circle. She glanced over her shoulder at the Indians coming toward the wagons, thinking that they did not look like warriors. There were women and children with them, and the men were not painted. The lieutenant had said they were not dangerous when they brought their families along.

Someone must have reminded Joseph of that, but he said, "They are heathen. It could be a trick."

Maggie hurried to her wagon, looking about for anything left on the ground that might tempt the Indians. She took out a quilt and went back to where Clara was huddled with Dora. "Put the quilt over her. The Indians must not see her," she said, and she and Dora spread the cover over Clara. Some of the women hid themselves, too, but most huddled in the wagon circle, watching the Indians approach.

"They are not gentlemen," Maggie told Dora. "Observe how the women walk while the men ride horses."

"I heard the lieutenant tell us the Indian women are treated like draft animals. They do the drudgery whilst their lord and master plays games or sits and smokes," Dora replied. "So it is no surprise the men are mounted whilst their wives plod along. Still, look at how dignified the women are. They are quite majestic."

"It is clear the men have the best of it in all ways. See how they are dressed in beaded buckskin and fine shirts. The women wear only rags."

Dora gave her a sly look. "Indian men are not the only men who have the best of it in all ways."

William and Joseph went out to meet the Indians, a dozen of them, from an infant to a man in the prime of life, who did not deign to dismount. William approached him. "We have biscuits."

The man held out his hand. "Bis-ket."

Maggie went to her wagon to fetch biscuits left over from breakfast. She started toward the man, but instead she handed the pan to an Indian woman who was thin and had a look of hunger on her face. The woman took the biscuits, but rather than eat one of them, she gave the pan to the man on the horse. He shoved two or three

161

into his mouth, then fed one to the horse. He handed a biscuit to a boy beside him and ate the rest himself. Maggie was disgusted.

"Ko-fee," the man demanded.

Maggie brought the coffeepot, a tin cup, and a can of sugar with a spoon and poured coffee left from breakfast into the cup and handed it to the Indian.

He refused it. "Sugar," he said.

Maggie opened the can and added a teaspoon of sugar.

"More."

"No more," she said, holding out the cup.

The Indian grabbed it and drank it in one gulp, then made a face. "Cold."

Maggie took back the cup and pan and did not offer more. Instead, she touched the woman's arm and pointed to the wagon. She poured coffee into the cup, then added several spoonsful of sugar before handing the cup to the Indian woman, who gave her a bashful smile and drank.

"Present," the woman said.

Maggie went back to her wagon and looked about for something to give the Indian woman. She had not brought charms or other novelties. She spotted her sewing supplies and took out a safety pin. She had bought a dozen of the new invention when she and Mary had gone to a store for necessities. She had thought they would be useful to hold together torn clothing. Now she went to the Indian woman and fastened a pin onto the woman's frayed shirt. The Indian ran her finger over the pin and grinned. "Yes," she said. "More."

Maggie would not give away the rest of the pins, however, and shook her head.

By now Edwin, a driver headed to Salt Lake City, had joined the Indians and spoke to them in their strange language. William asked the warrior's name, and Edwin shook his head. "I cannot make it out. It sounds like Big Joe. That is not his real name, of course. Likely he was given it by passersby."

"That is good enough. Did he say what he wanted?"

"The usual—coffee, flour, sugar, bacon, trinkets," Edwin replied. "Guns, knives, and bullets."

"We can spare a little flour and sugar, but we will not give him weapons," William said.

"Oh, he knows that. It is just wishful thinking on his part. Maybe he believes he will encounter someone foolish enough to part with them. White people believe Indians are stupid because they cannot speak our language, but they are very clever. Sometimes I think them cleverer than us."

Big Joe said something in a guttural voice, and Edwin shook his head. The Indian spoke louder, and Edwin said no.

Big Joe looked angry and shook his head back and forth.

"What does he want?" William asked.

"Oh, he is only greedy. It is nothing."

"What?"

Edwin shrugged. "He is asking why there are so many women in our party."

The Indian muttered something, and Edwin spoke to him in the native's language. Then he told William. "I said we are taking the women to California to be wives of the miners."

Big Joe pointed to himself, then at a young man near him, uttering a demand.

Edwin hid a smile. "He wants one of the women for himself. And another for his son. He says he has always desired a white wife. His other wives are Indians."

Maggie gasped. "He has more than one wife?" Then she remembered Edwin was a Mormon and that polygamy was not a novelty to him.

"Ask him what he will pay for one of our women. We have two or three among us who are not compatible," William said.

Maggie looked at the minister, astonished, until he said that he was only joking.

"Perhaps you should not. Sometimes the Indians understand more of our language than they let on. He would take you seriously, and you would offend him if he thought you were playing with him," Edwin said.

The Indians had come inside the wagon circle, the women peering into the wagons and begging for food, the children, curious, picking up objects left on the ground. Now Big Joe rode around the circle staring at the women. After a time, he pointed to Mary and said something to Edwin, who shook his head.

"He wants her. He says she is strong enough to do a woman's work," Edwin said. "I told him she was not available."

The Indian grunted, making it clear he did not like being turned down.

"He says he has many horses and two other wives to help with the work," Edwin told Mary.

Mary stamped her foot and threw up her hands. "No!" she shouted. "No! No! No!"

Big Joe watched Mary for a moment, then spoke to Edwin, who translated. "He's offering three horses."

"Is that all!" Mary was offended.

"I believe you could get five," Edwin told her.

Mary let out a great laugh. "Not for all the horses on the prairie," she said.

"Then you have priced yourself out of the market."

After a lingering glance at Mary, Big Joe shrugged and looked over the other women, finally pointing to one who caught his fancy. She scrambled into her wagon and hid under a blanket.

"No women," Edwin said, then told William, "We need to placate him. He is insulted. Perhaps we can give him a slab of bacon."

"Perhaps we should give him a kick in the backside," said Joseph, who had been watching the negotiations.

"And start an Indian war?" Edwin responded. "Who knows how many Indians may be waiting over the hill. We would be foolish to rile him."

Big Joe spotted Evaline then and kicked his horse so that he was next to her. He asked something, and Edwin replied, then said to Joseph, "He wants to know if she is a white woman. He says she looks more like an Indian. If she is an Indian, then you can sell her to him, he says." Edwin paused. "I believe he has never seen a Negro before."

Evaline heard the conversation and shrank back. "No. You won't sell me, will you, Mrs. Whitney?"

"Of course not," Bessie replied. "Tell the man I would rather marry him myself than send Evaline with him."

Edwin shook his head. "No, ma'am. That is not a good idea. He might think you are serious."

"The whole subject is preposterous," Joseph said. "These are Christian women. They will have nothing to do with a heathen."

The Indian was insistent. He told Edwin that Evaline belonged with him, not with the company of white women.

"Get into the wagon and hide under the quilts, Evaline," Bessie told the girl. Bessie climbed

166

into the wagon behind Evaline and rummaged through the contents of her trunk. "Here, give him this." She handed Edwin a red silk scarf.

Edwin ran the scarf through his fingers, then held it up to the sun to let Big Joe see how the light made it shimmer. He raised it above his head, and the wind caught it and blew it around like a banner. Slowly, Edwin tied it around his neck. The Indian stared at the silk, then reached out and grabbed it and wrapped it around his head.

"You have saved his pride," Edwin told Bessie.

They watched as Big Joe pointed to the slab of bacon Joseph had set on the ground, ordering one of the women to pick it up. Then he turned and led his little band away, not so much as thanking them or even turning around to acknowledge the company.

"A white woman with an ignorant savage. The idea disgusts me," Joseph said. "How could he think any Christian woman would marry such a man?"

"You may think him ignorant, but there was a time not far distant when he was a prince. You would think differently if you saw him in his war paint, racing that horse across the prairie. You would be right to fear him then. They were a magnificent race," Edwin said.

"What changed him?" Maggie asked.

"We did. We white people." Edwin looked off in

the direction where the Indians had disappeared. "These Indians are beggars. You have not seen those who are fearless, the cream of a proud and intelligent people. Pray God you never will."

Nine

June 15, 1852
Fort Kearny

Maggie was fearful that Big Joe would return or that he would tell the other Indian men about the caravan of white women, and they would come and take them away. She kept Clara close to her the rest of the way to Fort Kearny.

The fort was a disappointment. She had expected a stockade, but there was only a collection of dilapidated buildings made of mud and sod. Hundreds of emigrants were camped on the rain-soaked ground a mile outside the fort, creating a sea of white-top wagons and milling and bawling animals, as crowded as St. Joseph.

William set up camp near the Platte River, where the women could wash themselves and their clothing. He said they would stay for a few days, since some of the wagons needed repairs and the oxen could use the rest. So could the women, Maggie thought. She and Mary used the time to repack their wagon while Winny searched for more items they could discard. Caroline and Bessie mended shoes and clothing and caught up on letters home.

• • •

At first, Pennsylvania House stayed close to the camp. On the trail, she had hidden in the wagon whenever another train passed them, afraid that Asa would be among the travelers. He had purchased mules, which were much faster than oxen, she told Maggie. Now, with so many emigrant groups arriving at the fort, Penn said, she was sure that Asa's company would be among them. He would be looking for her, waiting to snatch her up. Maggie understood. Like Penn, she, too, worried about the travelers who passed them on the trail. Her situation was even worse, she thought, because men who knew about the reward for her might be out there, and she would not know who they were. She told Mary about the reward, and Mary insisted that Clara, still dressed like a boy, keep company with her. No one would confuse her with the description the lieutenant had given of Maggie.

"Perhaps Asa has forgotten you by now," Maggie told Penn, although she knew that was not likely.

Penn shook her head. "I know he's out there. He'll find me one day."

"Well, you cannot live in a wagon all the way to California. You ought to visit the sutler's store. The fort is so crowded, and with all the soldiers about, he will not be able to hurt you there."

Penn thought it over and shook her head.

"You cannot live your life in fear," Caroline said. She had been helping Maggie repair a rip in a wagon cover, holding the edges together while Maggie sewed. "If God does not protect you, Joseph and William will. I will go, too."

Penn was still reluctant. "I don't need nothing there."

"We must get you a shawl," Caroline said. Women in the train had given some of their clothing to Penn, and she had picked up items abandoned on the trail, but there had been no shawls among the discards.

"I don't need one." Penn laughed. "It's hot enough to cook taters in a basket." She added, "Besides, I only got me a dollar."

"It won't always be this hot. You must have something warm to cover you for the mountains. William says the nights are very cold, and we may encounter snow before we reach California," Caroline told her.

"I can do without," Penn said.

"If it is the expense, there is money set aside. Besides, shawls are cheap here. I am told the sutler sends men out to rummage through the abandoned property in search of merchandise to sell."

"There's others that needs—"

"None so much as you. Besides, the others brought along warm clothing." When Penn still hesitated, Caroline said, "Maggie will come, too."

Maggie found Mary and asked her to watch Clara. Although Clara still dressed as a boy, Maggie did not think it wise to be seen inside the fort with her.

The store was a low building with a roof of poles, brush, and sod. Maggie was glad her skirt had been shortened and did not drag on the muddy floor as she and Penn searched the crowd, examining men's faces in search of Asa.

Penn stopped searching when she saw the array of goods. As if she were in a magical emporium, she looked in awe at the stock of bonnets and skirts, the scrub boards and washtubs and basins, the heavy china dishes and a set of teacups as thin and fragile as a moth's wing. Maggie wondered if, in years to come, their owner would regret leaving the cups on the trail or trading them to the sutler for necessities. She thought of the teapot packed in her trunk, the one she had taken from the Madrid farm for Mary. She would give it to her friend when the time was right.

A bolt of calico lay on the counter, and Maggie could not help but pinch the cloth between her fingers. It was cheap, but the red color was pretty.

Penn saw the fabric and touched it, too. "The flowers, they look real," she said.

"You like red?" Caroline asked.

"More than anything. It's the color of sunset."

Penn turned to look at a collection of jewelry in a glass case. She stared at a ring with a ruby stone, bringing her face up to the glass.

The sutler took it out and put it on his little finger, turning it back and forth to catch the light from one of the smoky lamps that lit the store. "It's real," he said.

"Real glass?" Penn asked.

The sutler snorted. "Real ruby."

"Oh, that's too bad." Penn looked disappointed. "I thought maybe it was real glass. I don't know a ruby."

"A ruby's better. Try it on." He handed her the ring.

Penn looked at Caroline for approval, and the older woman shrugged. Penn put the ring on her finger and held it to the lamp. "Someday I'm going to have me a real ruby ring."

"Only two dollars," the sutler said.

Penn gave her pretty laugh, the sound of bells tinkling. "You could ask a hundred dollars for all I care. I don't have no money to spend for a ring. Fact is, I don't have no money at all for nothing pretty."

"A dollar, then, on account of you like it."

Penn shook her head. "Like I said, I don't have so much as a nickel to spend on it."

"Then why did you ask me to take it out?" The sutler, annoyed, put the ring back into the case.

"I did not."

"We are looking for a shawl, a red shawl," Caroline said quickly.

"Ah, red. Everybody wants red. That will cost you." His eyes lit up.

"I do not want red," Penn said suddenly. "Blue. Do you have a blue shawl? I favor blue. Red puts me in mind of a bloody pig."

"Blue is more expensive than red. It is rare, and all the women like it."

"Well, I would not want a red one."

"Show her the blue ones, then," Maggie put in, frowning a little.

"Anything but red." Penn nudged Maggie with her elbow, and Maggie caught on, understanding then that Penn was a wily buyer. Maggie stepped aside.

The sutler pulled out a shawl that was a deep navy blue, almost black. "A beauty," he said.

"Not so's you'd notice," Penn told him. "It 'pears more black than blue."

He unfolded a second shawl. "There, the color of the sky."

"On a cold day," Penn told him.

"I cannot be all day showing you shawls. Them's the only blue ones I got. Now if you would favor red . . ."

"Oh, choose a red one," Maggie said, hiding a smile.

"I guess I can wait for Fort Laramie. I hear they got shawls cheap there."

"Laramie ain't so well stocked as here. Besides, it can get mighty cold at night 'tween here and there," the sutler said.

"I reckon I will just get cold, then." Penn nodded at Maggie and turned to go.

"Now just hold on. I would not want a little thing like you to get a chill. Might catch pneumonia. I could sell you a red one real cheap."

"I do not want red. I already said," Penn protested.

It was Caroline's turn to step in. "Now, dear, we do not have money to burn. Maybe—"

Penn stamped her foot so hard that Maggie jumped. "It ain't going to be cheap enough for me."

Caroline looked confused. She apparently did not understand Penn's bargaining tactics.

"Three dollars. You will never find a shawl in Laramie for twice that."

Penn only harrumphed. "That ain't cheap."

The sutler took down a pile of red shawls and sorted through them, pulling out one that was worn and faded. "I could let you have this one for two dollars."

Caroline nudged Penn with her knee, because the price was far less than what she had told Penn she would pay.

"I would not care to wear a shawl that was all tore up." Penn searched through the pile, setting aside each shawl until she came to a red paisley that was almost new. It was finely woven, and the colors were bright. She flung it around her shoulders. The shawl brought out the red highlights in her pale hair. "That one might do— for a dollar and a half."

"Robbery!" the sutler said.

"I do not like it that much anyway. Our trading's done." Penn started for the door.

"Now wait up. I could let you have it for a dollar and seventy-five. I will lose money, but I hate to see a body go cold."

Penn put her hand over her face to hide a smile. "What do you think, Mrs. Swain?"

Caroline looked as if she had expected to pay twice that much for a shawl, and one with only half the quality. "I do not want you to be cold either," she said, taking out her purse and putting the money on the counter before the sutler changed his mind. She snatched up the shawl and hurried Penn out of the door.

"Do you care for it at all?" Caroline asked when they were outside.

Penn had taken the shawl from Caroline and put it over her shoulders and was running her hands over it. "Might be the prettiest shawl I ever saw. And red! Red is my favorite color. I never in my life thought I would own a red shawl as fine as this. It is a dream."

"For a moment, I was not sure," Caroline said.

"You bested that man, and he has been in the business a long time."

"From now on, Penn should do the purchasing for us. She will more than pay her way with what she will save us," Maggie said.

Penn grinned at her two friends, then grasped Caroline's hands. "Thank you, Mrs. Swain. Nobody in my life ever bought nothing for me."

"That is what friends are for."

"I never had me a friend neither."

As Caroline put the coins into her purse, she suddenly took out a penny and handed it to Maggie. "I believe I saw sticks of candy back there. It would please me if you would purchase one for Clara."

While Penn and Caroline returned to the camp, Maggie went back inside the store. She waited while the sutler dealt with another customer, a large man in rough clothing. Maggie paid him little attention until she heard him say, "Give me that red ring there."

The sutler took it out of the case and set it on the counter. The man pocketed it and slammed down a dollar.

"Hey, that costs two dollars."

The man ignored him and left the store. The sutler, shaking his head, pocketed the coin. Maggie stepped up and pointed at a peppermint stick. The sutler took one out of a jar and handed it to her. Maggie held out the penny, but he shook his head and told her to keep it, saying, "Why should I make a profit today?"

Only a few women remained in the camp when the three returned. "Where have they gone?" Maggie asked Mary.

"Reverend Parnell took them to hear a harpsichord concert. A woman has agreed to play the instrument, which she has hauled all the way from Boston. It is said she plays poorly, and the instrument is out of tune, but it is a great diversion, and none have heard such music since leaving Chicago. Dora took Clara and Evaline with her, and a few of us stayed behind to watch the camp."

The three strained to hear the delicate sounds of the instrument, but it did not carry all the way back to the wagons. Still, they heard the squawk of the fiddles and the notes of a flute that accompanied it. Penn danced to the sound of the music, flinging her shawl over her shoulder, then waving it as she twirled. She grabbed Mary's hands and swung her around until Mary, clumsy at dancing, nearly fell to the ground. When the violins finished, Penn held the shawl in front of her and bowed to the women watching her. She smiled, and Maggie thought for the first time that without bruises and the haunted look Penn had worn most of the way from St. Joseph, she was pretty. She and the others clapped.

"More, more!" Winny called.

"You dance like a fairy," Maggie told Penn. "You should have a fine gown to go with the shawl."

"Red velvet with lace," Sadie said. "You have the tiniest feet I ever saw."

"And the dirtiest." Penn had stored her shoes in the wagon, and her feet were muddy from the damp earth.

Penn was a happy, joyous creature just then, and all it had taken to restore her was a shawl. *Well, a shawl and a wagon train of women who had made her one of them,* Maggie thought.

The music started up again, but Penn was finished with her dancing. She carefully folded the shawl into a triangle and wrapped it around herself so that the point was in the middle of her back and the black center was at her neck. She smiled again at the women, a little embarrassed now, but happy, as if she wanted to wrap them up in the shawl with her.

Maggie pinched the thick fabric, admiring the swirls of red and yellow, the touches of green and blue, rust and orange. "I believe it comes from Scotland. If you had a red velvet gown, you would indeed be the prime attraction at any ball in the city. Someday, when we are in California, I shall make you such a dress, and you will wear it with long white gloves."

"And a tiara, a diamond one like my mistress

had," Winny put in. "Only it would look so much better on you, Penn. Mrs. Fletcher looked like a crow with a crown."

Maggie laughed, and Winny smiled at her, knowing Maggie had seen her mistress.

"I hope you don't care about me dancing. I love it so," Penn said to Reverend Swain. He was the only man who had stayed behind with the women. "Dancing ain't a sin, is it?"

"Not when it brings joy to the Lord," he replied and took Caroline's hand. She smiled up at him, and he smiled back. Maggie had not seen him smile before and thought he looked less stern and doctrinaire.

"Thank you," Penn said. She made a clumsy curtsey and nearly slipped in the mud. Instead of being embarrassed, she laughed. Everything that afternoon seemed to make her laugh—and made Maggie laugh as well.

"We are truly banded together now," Caroline said. "We may bicker and disagree—and will continue to do so—but I believe we will go forward with a closeness other trains might envy."

As the others, all but Maggie, returned to their chores, Penn took off the shawl and carefully folded it. She would use it only in the coldest weather, she told Maggie. It would be a pity if such a fine garment was torn or dirtied. She looked up at the clouds and smiled when she saw a rainbow. She pointed it out to Maggie, who said it was as good an omen as she had ever seen.

Penn looked out over the wagons, their covers like clouds that had come down to earth. That was when she saw him, walking slowly toward her, a dark figure against the white wagon covers. His large hands hung loose; his powerful arms swung at his sides. He was a big man, with blond hair that curled around his neck, hair that was bleached by the sun. His face was bronzed. Even from a distance, his eyes shone bright blue with a touch of warning as he smiled.

"Asa," she whispered, too frightened to move. She held the shawl against her chest as if it were a shield.

Maggie gasped and swung around to stare at the man she had seen in the sutler's store.

Ten

Y ou look awful pretty in that red blanket. Awful pretty," Asa said, smiling again.

He sounded charming, but Maggie knew how cruel he was, and she was not deceived. She took a step toward Penn as if to protect her, but stopped when Asa glared at her.

"You ran away. You didn't even tell me you was going. You stole something from me. That wasn't nice, on account of I was so good to you. But it's all right. I found you. You can go on to California with me," Asa told Penn.

"I will not."

"Well, sure you will, woman. We been together two, three years. You belong to me. Besides, I come to get back what's mine. You took it from me." He reached for her arm, but Penn backed up until she was against the wagon.

"No. I didn't take nothing. You keep away from me, Asa."

"Aw, come on. You know you love me. I come on ahead of the others to find you. They wasn't ready to leave yet, so I come by myself 'cause I know you want me."

"Not no more. You beat me."

Asa smiled again. "I'm real sorry for it, but it weren't no more than a slap. Besides, it was your own fault. You made me do it. You was wrong making me mad, talking back the way you done. It ain't a woman's place to do that. But you'll learn your lesson once you give back what you stole, and I'll forgive you. I'll treat you real good now. You remember how it was when we met up. You sure was happy then."

"You changed. You said you was going to kill me."

"I meant nothing by it. You know that."

"Where's your brothers?" she asked.

"Oh, they's coming, both the other boys. Elias and me was waiting for Reed when I figured out you joined up with them spinsters." He looked at her darkly. "You remember how I kept Reed from hurting you."

"You done no such a thing." Penn shivered, and Maggie reached out a hand. "Reed's the worst of you Harvey boys." Penn turned to Maggie. "Reed put his thumbs on my eyes and said he'd gouge out my eyeballs if I didn't do what he said. He forced me. I told Asa, and he beat me instead of Reed."

"I'll do it again if I find him sniffing around you. You better not be sweet on him."

Maggie did not know what to do. Reverend Swain was gone, and the other women were back with the wagons. If she interfered, she would

183

likely be struck down by Asa, which wouldn't help Penn. She watched, wary.

"What you done with it, Penn?"

"I ain't stole nothing that weren't mine already."

Asa reached into his pocket, and Penn shrank back against the wagon, as if thinking Asa would hit her with something, perhaps his sap—a small leather bag filled with sand. He held out a fist to her and opened it. Inside was the ruby ring. "See, I brung you something. I knowed you liked it. This here is a wedding ring."

"You keep it. I ain't going to marry up with you, Asa."

"Take it."

Penn shook her head. "Go away. I got friends here that's going to protect me."

"All I seen when I was watching you was a bunch of women and a preacher that's already scared off. Now you take the ring. You said way back that you wanted to get married. You said you didn't want to be Pennsylvania House no more, just Mrs. Asa Harvey. Well, I guess now you will be. When that preacher comes back, he can say the words."

"I want you to go away. Please, Asa."

Suddenly Asa reached out and grasped Penn's hand and shoved the ring onto her finger. "I give two dollars for it. Now you take it. You do not want to rile me. You know that ain't a good thing."

Maggie would have laughed if she had not been so frightened for Penn. She had seen Asa put down only a dollar for it.

For a moment, Penn stared at the stone, which gleamed like a drop of blood in the sun. Asa put his arm around her. "You and me belong together. I'll treat you real good this time."

Maggie had heard those same words herself. Jesse had said them to her, and for a long time she had wanted to believe him, had indeed believed him. She knew that Penn was thinking maybe this time would be different. *No!* Maggie thought. *Nothing has changed. It is a trick. Do not believe him, Penn.*

As if Maggie had spoken out loud, Penn said, "No, Asa! You take that old ring. I don't want it. I don't want you." She removed the ring and flung it at him.

"Well, I want you, and I guess that is all that counts." The smile was gone now.

Asa leaned down to pick up the ring, and when he looked at Penn again, his face was twisted in anger. Penn attempted to move, but he held her against the wagon. Then he tried to pick her up, but Penn struggled, dropping the shawl in the mud. She stared at it, horrified, then used all of her strength to break away and rescue the garment. "You get away, Asa. I ain't yours no more."

"You are mine till I say you ain't, you God-damn woman. Now get over to the wagon before I whip you."

"No! I will not. You got to kill me before I go with you."

"I can do that."

Maggie knew she could not stop Asa by herself and yelled, "Mary!"

Mary, who had been sharpening a hatchet, came out from behind a wagon. She understood in an instant what was happening and called "Ladies!" The other women stopped what they were doing and followed Mary as she came to stand beside Maggie. They looked frightened and unsure of themselves. Maggie searched for Reverend Swain, but he was not there. He must have gone to the concert to escort the women back to the camp.

"Something wrong, Penn?" Mary asked.

Maggie answered instead. "That's Asa. He is trying to steal Penn away from us." She saw the hatchet in Mary's hand and wished she had her scissors with her. Sadie held a knife, and Bessie a hatpin. Winny grasped a piece of kindling, and even Caroline had picked up a rock.

"There ain't nothing wrong. Ain't your business," Asa said.

"It did not sound like a conversation," Mary told him.

"I said mind your business."

"This woman is my business—our business.

186

She is one of us. Now you go away and leave her alone," Mary said.

"I won't go back less'n I take her with me. Come on." Asa twisted Penn's arm behind her back, and Penn cried out in pain. "Ain't nobody going to stop me," Asa said.

"I will." Mary's hand had been at her side, and now she drew it out to show that she was holding a hatchet.

"Cross-eye bitch." Asa laughed, then made a sudden lurch toward Mary and, using his free hand, wrenched the hatchet from her. "God-damn woman," he said.

The women made a semicircle around Penn. Winny reached out and tried to wrest the hatchet away from Asa, but he shoved her down into the dirt.

"Any of the rest of you want to try stopping me?" He glared at the women. Then he asked Penn, "You want them to get hurt, do you? You come along with me now, or one of them's going to get fisted. Or worse." Asa struck the hatchet so hard against the wagon that it left a deep cut.

Penn whimpered. Maggie knew Penn would not repay their kindness with the hurt Asa would inflict on them. Perhaps Penn could run away later, but it was unlikely Asa would let her out of his sight. He would beat her, beat her that night, beat her so badly that Penn would never have the courage to leave him. At that moment, Maggie hated Asa as much as she did Jesse. She would kill Asa if she could, just as she had killed her husband.

"Now you wear this ring," Asa said, laying the hatchet on the wagon and forcing the ring back onto Penn's finger. "You tell them women we're married now. They take you away, they're breaking the law. It don't allow nobody to separate a man and his wife. Bible says I got the right to kill anybody that takes you away from me."

"No. It does not."

Asa looked up, startled and a little wary at the sound of a man's voice. Maggie turned around and spotted Reverend Swain. "I was doctoring an ox and did not hear the full discussion. Now I ask you to let go of Miss House."

Asa grinned at him. "You going to get involved in this, preacher man?"

"I already am. Miss House is one of my charges. She has asked you to leave her alone. I suggest you do so. You would not want to tangle with the authorities here."

Asa laughed at that. "The authorities? You talking about them soldiers? They're so drunk they can't pull out a gun without they shoot theirself in the foot."

"I am talking about the officers. They will not abide your taking a woman against her will."

"She is my wife."

"Miss House says differently."

"Well, she's been cooking my supper, living in my tent, sleeping in my blankets."

"Such activity does not make a woman a wife. Husband and wife are bound by the words of the Lord spoken over them."

"You speak them, then. That all right with you, Penn?"

Penn looked at Reverend Swain, then at the women around her. She could not answer, so Maggie spoke up for her. "No!"

"Didn't ask you." Asa tightened his hand on Penn's arm. "She don't mean that, does she, Penn? You tell him yes."

Mary stepped forward and slapped his arm. She was a strong woman, and Asa let go and raised his fist.

"Go ahead. Hit me," Mary said. "You like to hit women, do you not?"

Asa glared at Mary but lowered his arm. "I ain't talking to you no more." Then he added, to Joseph, "You neither." He picked up Penn, who kicked her legs and tried to get away.

"Let go of her," the minister demanded.

Asa paused long enough to say, "You going to stop me, preacher?"

"If I have to."

"How you going to do that? Maybe you'll cry for the soldiers." Asa gave an ugly laugh. "Or shout Bible words out at me."

"You will not take her!"

"Yeah, well, just you watch me." He tightened his hold on Penn, and she cried out.

"Do not hurt her." Caroline pushed forward until she was in front of Asa.

"Get out of my way." Asa held Penn with one arm, and with the other he shoved Caroline, who lost her balance and fell into the mud. Mary and Winny rushed to help her up.

"Sir! Your apology!" Joseph thundered.

"I am tired of you, Bible thumper." Asa slapped Penn, who was still struggling, then started dragging her toward his wagon.

Joseph lunged at him, hitting him on the side of the head.

"You!" Asa shouted. He let go of Penn and punched Joseph in the shoulder, knocking the wind out of the minister.

Joseph took a step backward. Then he charged. He hit Asa in the chest with his fists, striking blow after blow, while Asa, stunned at the ferocity, put up his hands in defense. Then Asa took a step backward and collected himself. "You go to hell! No preacher can get the best of me, God damn you!" He swung, but Joseph ducked.

"Do not take the Lord's name in vain." The minister swung again, but Asa caught his arm, then landed a punch of his own. As Joseph paused to catch his breath, Asa tried to knee him in the groin, but Joseph spun away, and Asa fell to the ground.

"Have you had enough?" Joseph asked, standing over Asa, his fists raised. Maggie looked at him, dumbfounded. She had never taken him for a man who could fight—or *would* fight.

Instead of answering, Asa grabbed Joseph and knocked him down, and the two rolled over and over in the mud. Asa rose to his feet and kicked at Joseph's head, but Joseph grabbed Asa's foot and pulled himself up. The two circled, each jabbing at the other. At last, Asa reached into his pocket and took out his sap.

"Look out," Maggie called.

Joseph glanced up, but it was too late, and Asa hit Joseph on the side of the head, stunning him. Asa moved in then, striking Joseph over and over again, until the minister fell to his knees. Asa kicked him in the groin, and Joseph toppled into the mud, stunned.

Not satisfied, Asa began hitting the minister in the head, until Penn grabbed his leg and begged him to stop. "Leave be. I'll go with you, Asa."

Asa backhanded her. "You'll go when I'm done with him."

"You will kill him!" Caroline cried, grabbing Asa's arm, but he flung her aside, too.

"He shouldn't have meddled with me," Asa said.

The other women moved forward. Winny

was the first to attack. She struck him with the kindling, while Bessie stabbed him with the hatpin, and Caroline flung her rock at him. The blows were like the bites of so many gnats, and Asa shoved them away. Sadie lunged at him with her knife. Asa roared when it sliced his arm. He grabbed the knife and started for Sadie, who lost her footing and fell to the ground beside the minister.

Maggie looked around frantically for a weapon and spotted the hatchet. She hefted it and started toward Asa, thinking to strike him with the flat side and knock him senseless. Asa saw her. He bellowed, reaching for the weapon.

At that moment, Maggie felt someone grab the hatchet from her. When she turned, Mary was holding it above her head. She held it only a second before she swung it at Asa, and the blade landed in his forehead. Blood gushed out, and Asa's eyes clouded. He reached for the weapon but stumbled and dropped to his knees. Then he toppled over, his hands opening and closing for a few seconds until they were still.

Mary froze, and Maggie had to remove the weapon from her hands and drop it into the mud. Mary started to crumple, but Maggie and Winny grabbed her and led her to a log beside the wagon.

Joseph shook his head back and forth, then slowly rose to his feet, stumbling a little as he righted himself. He pulled Sadie up, then stared down at Asa, bowing his head. His lips moved, but no words came out. Maggie could only wonder what he said in his silent prayer.

"I killed him," Mary said. "I meant only to knock him out with the side of the blade, but I killed him. The Bible says thou shalt not kill, but I did. It is a terrible sin, is it not, Reverend Swain? I am not much concerned with religion, but I believe there is a hell, and it is likely I shall go there." She began to shake.

Maggie did, too. Like her, Mary—Mary, the woman who always protected them—was in turmoil. Both of them had taken lives. Mary had done so to protect Reverend Swain and Sadie and Penn. *Surely the lives of three good people are worth the death of one crazed man,* Maggie thought. She wondered if Mary would believe that, or would carry guilt for her action just as Maggie did.

"You will not go to hell. You risked your life to save that of Miss House. And Mrs. Cooper," Joseph said. "It was only by ill luck that your hatchet instead of Mrs. Cooper's knife ended his life."

"Each one of us tried to kill him," Bessie said. "We are all complicit."

"You saved Joseph, too, Mary," Caroline added. "I believe the lives of three good people are worth that of a wicked man," she said, giving voice to Maggie's thought. "I should think the scales of heaven are weighted in your favor."

Maggie put her arms around Mary, who sagged against her. "Some men deserve death. He is one." She alone understood Mary's grief. The two of them shared that anguish.

Penn stood over Asa's body. "You ain't going to hurt nobody no more, Asa Harvey. You brung it on yourself. I don't hate you, but I'm glad you are gone for good."

"We must find an officer and tell him what has happened," Joseph said.

"No!" Maggie burst out. "What if they arrest Mary?"

"She would not be found guilty."

"They will charge me nonetheless. What I have done is sinful," Mary said.

"Is it not better to commit a lesser sin to prevent a greater one?" Maggie asked.

The minister smiled at her. "I believe you could be a preacher," he told her.

"Maggie is right," Caroline said. "Besides, an inquiry will take time. That would delay us, and it will give the Harvey men time to catch up with Penn. Who knows what they will do if they find her. We must think of the welfare of the other women. This accursed man should not have the power to keep us from completing our journey."

"Asa's brothers ain't far behind. If they catch up with us, it don't matter who killed Asa.

They'll kill me and maybe some of the others," Penn said, shivering.

"Then we cannot let them know Asa is dead," Maggie said. "We must bury him and leave."

"Bury him where? Is there sacred ground here?" Caroline asked.

Despite herself, Maggie smiled. "Why, right here. The oxen will trample the grave, and no one will ever know a man's body lies under the dirt." Before anyone could respond, she went to the wagon to fetch a spade and began to dig. The others took turns, and when the hole was deep enough, they laid Asa in it. Joseph said a few words over the body before the women covered it with dirt. They led several oxen over the grave until there was no sign of it.

They had barely finished when they saw the other women returning from the musicale. "Will we tell them?" Sadie asked.

"Not just yet, although I believe they may find out in time. We shall tell them to be ready to leave at first light. We cannot risk another day here," Joseph replied.

As the two cleaned the shovel, Winny whispered to Maggie, "Did you hear Asa accuse Penn of taking something from him? It must have been valuable or he would not have demanded it back. I wonder what it was."

"Maybe the dollar she stole from him. Whatever it is, he does not need it now."

Maggie took Mary's arm and led her back to the wagon. Mary shivered as if she were sick, and Maggie knew her friend was filled with grief. Would she have struck Asa, too, if Mary had not taken the hatchet from her? Maggie believed she would have. Still, she was glad she was not the one who had delivered the blow. When Mary turned to her, Maggie was surprised to see anger as well as sadness on her face.

"I misspoke," Mary said. "I said I was sorry I killed him, but I did not mean it. I am glad he is dead. I am glad Penn is safe. I would do it again. If someone comes for you, Maggie, I will kill him, too." She paused and said fiercely, "You and the others are more a family to me than any I left behind. I would give my life to protect you and Clara. And if it is a sin, then I shall gladly go to hell."

Maggie smiled at her friend and took her hand. "I do not believe you will go to hell for any reason." Later, she returned to her wagon and took out the china teapot with pink roses that had belonged to Mary's mother. She found Mary staring out at the prairie and handed it to her. Her cheeks damp with tears, Mary took the teapot and held it to her breast.

Eleven

June 18, 1852
The Great Platte River Road

A somber group of women left Fort Kearny the next morning. By then, those who had been at the musicale knew that something bad had happened in the camp, although they did not know what, because the women who had been present at Asa's death had kept the killing to themselves.

Although Asa was no longer a threat, Penn was more frightened than ever at the thought of his brothers catching up with her. Asa would have beaten her, but his brothers would kill her.

"Asa said he came on ahead of them. Surely they must be miles behind," Maggie told Penn.

Penn was not reassured. "I wish I knowed if they was by theirself or joined up with a company. They'll catch up, and when they find Asa ain't there, they'll come looking for me. What if dogs dig up the body? It ain't that deep. His brothers'll do me in for sure. And even though we turned his mule loose and throwed out his leavings like we done, they might find them." She looked up at her friend. "If it wasn't for you and Mary, I'd be dead already."

"Mary. It was Mary who saved you."

"You'd have struck him if Mary hadn't taken that hatchet from you."

Would she? Maggie wondered again. Would she have had the determination and the strength to kill Asa? A few months before, she would not have dared to strike a man with her hand, but things were different now. She and the other women were fiercely protective of each other. She had seen that when the dragoon attacked her. Instead of condemning her, the women had been solicitous, showing kindness by bringing her wildflowers and offering to watch Clara. Their kindness had helped her put the outrage behind her. Maggie would have sacrificed almost anything for them, and she knew that Mary felt as strongly as she did. The trip had given Mary a mission. Maggie realized that Mary considered the whole band her family. And they thought of Mary as their protector.

After Joseph's fight with Asa, Maggie viewed Reverend Swain in a different light. She had thought him dour with only touches of compassion, but now she knew that, like Mary, he would protect them—not just spiritually but physically. He was no longer the stern, distant preacher but their friend. That night, when the company was packing the wagons for the next day's journey, he said it was time to discard his pulpit.

"No! That ain't right," Penn said. "I'd throw out my new shawl before I'd let you do that."

"I would lighten our wagon to make room for it," Mary added.

"My rocking chair could go," Bessie told him.

The women agreed the pulpit should travel to California with them. When the minister heard them, he turned away and put his hand to his eyes.

Caroline's eyes were damp, too. "I always suspected there was greatness in him," she told Maggie. "But until this journey, I could not be sure."

"Have you told him?"

Caroline only smiled.

When the call came in the predawn to rise, Maggie was already awake. She roused Clara, and the two folded their quilts and emerged from the tent and began preparations for breakfast. Maggie had become as proficient as the men in dealing with the oxen and herding the cows. She sometimes rode a horse—astride now, after she and Caroline had ridden the horse left for them when Lavinia was dying—and once she even went hunting with Mary, although her aim was poor, and she shot nothing but sagebrush. The women who were not up to what was required of them had left the train at Fort Kearny. Three of them had joined the back-outs and were returning to St. Joseph.

While Bessie had said at the outset that she'd brought Evaline along to be her servant, Maggie noted that Bessie now did more for Evaline than the girl did for her. Evaline was a pretty thing, light skinned, her hair long and straight, and she had drawn stares from men in Fort Kearny. A few had made crude remarks. Bessie rarely let Evaline out of her sight now, watching over her just as Maggie watched over Clara.

From the start, Maggie had shared Clara's care with Mary and Bessie and Winny and other members of the company. After all, they were going west to find husbands and form families. That meant children. They loved children, and they adored Clara, who was a bright, happy girl with outgoing ways that were infectious. Despite her boy's rough clothing and her cropped pale hair, she was a pretty child. Whenever Caroline or Bessie made cookies or dried apple cake, they saved a portion for Clara. They told her stories, and Evaline drew pictures for Clara in her sketchbook. The two of them became companions, Evaline telling Clara that when they reached California, they would find a dog for her. Even Clara's fussiness and occasional tantrums appealed to the women. After all, the girl was only four, and it was acceptable for her to be cranky at times. Evaline or Sadie soothed her and insisted she lay her head in their laps when she was tired.

"You are very lucky to have her," Winny told Maggie one day, and Maggie knew it to be true. After the deaths of Lavinia and Asa, Maggie realized how fragile life was on the Overland Trail, and she became even more protective of Clara.

Maggie thought of little Dick and how he would have enjoyed the trip. Her son would have been old enough to help with the animals and take care of his sister. She missed him. So did Clara, who sometimes told her, "I want Dick." Thoughts of her son made Clara just that much more precious to Maggie. She had not been able to protect him, but she vowed she would keep her daughter from harm.

Mary had spotted a paper with information about Maggie and a description of her at the sutler's store at Fort Kearny. "I ripped it up. It must have come with an express driver, and that is why it was there ahead of us. I tore it into shreds and threw them into the river," she told Maggie.

"I knew of it already. Reverend Swain was given a copy, but he burned it," Maggie said.

"The description of you was good, but it could fit a thousand other women on the Overland Trail. I would not worry."

Maggie did worry, however. How many notices had been sent to the trading posts? What would happen to Clara if Maggie was apprehended?

"If I am found," she told Mary one day as they walked beside the wagon, Clara skipping ahead of them, "I want you to take Clara. I believe the others will back you if you claim she is yours."

"No one will arrest you," Mary said.

"Perhaps not, but I want you to promise."

"There are others better prepared to be a mother," Mary said.

"None better than you."

Mary smiled at that. "I will be her family," she said.

"Family means a great deal to you." Maggie stopped a moment to remove a sticker from her foot. She had decided to go barefoot to save her shoes, but the sand and rocks hurt her feet. She envied the women who had stopped wearing shoes weeks before and whose feet were now as tough as leather.

"It is why I came. I have always wanted one."

"What about your family in Illinois?"

"A family is more than being born in the same house. My mother was a good woman and loving, but my father was hard. He believed I was intended to work for his benefit, just as Micah and Louise did. I expect to have a family whose members love each other as you and Clara do."

"I thought Jesse was such a person. You cannot tell how a man will turn out."

"I will tell. Else I will not marry." Mary looked away. Her sunbonnet hid her face, so Maggie could not know what she was thinking. Then Mary turned back to Maggie and smiled. "We both agreed when we signed up for California that we were going to find husbands. But we had other reasons. You had a husband you did not want, and I was not sure I cared for one at all."

"Perhaps they will expect us to pay back the cost of the trip then," Maggie said.

"No, there was no time limit. We can tell them we are still looking."

"Twenty years from now?" Maggie asked.

"Fifty if necessary." Then Mary had a thought and turned to face Maggie. "What if you find someone suitable? Would you marry then, without telling him?"

"Telling him I had broken one of the commandments?"

Mary thought that over. "We have both done so. I think we should not concern ourselves much with the commandments."

Camping in sight of other wagon trains made many of the women feel safer than if they had been out on the prairie by themselves. The trains made both Maggie and Penn apprehensive, however, because they could not be sure Asa's brothers or Maggie's stalkers were not among them.

"At least Penn knows who to look for," Maggie told Mary. "I do not know who may be searching for me."

Mary scoffed. "Half the women in our train fit the description I read. I think you can forget about someone recognizing you."

That might be true, but Maggie was more comfortable when they were a distance away from other travelers. There seemed to be fewer of them now; whether that was because many had turned back or had taken different routes, she did not know. It seemed that before Fort Kearny, they were rarely out of sight of other emigrant trains. Now, they might go the better part of a day without encountering one.

Maggie knew that while she and Penn might feel safer with fewer other travelers about, the ministers did not. Two of their teamsters had deserted the train, joining faster trains at Fort Kearny, and William said he should have engaged more in St. Joseph. He did not care for the looks of the men along the trail who inquired about traveling with the women and so had hired no replacements. "I am concerned we will be attacked by Indians," he said.

"You need not worry so much," Maggie told him. "We were told it is unlikely we will encounter war parties. Besides, many of the women have learned how to shoot, just as we now are able to handle the oxen. I believe we could put up a good fight." The words were partly bravado, because Maggie herself was a poor shot.

Indians approached them once or twice to beg for flour and coffee or to barter. Winny traded a tin ring for moccasins, which many of the women now wore. Maggie gave up two of her precious safety pins to acquire moccasins for Clara and herself. The Indian women brought food to trade—jerky, antelope and deer meat, wild onions, berries, and a concoction called pemmican, a mixture of berries, meat, and fat pounded together that could be chewed along the trail to stave off hunger. The Indians sold braided lariats as well as buffalo robes, which the women considered useless for summer nights. Besides, the robes were heavy and might have to be thrown out later on. But Mary thought the buffalo skins would warm them if they encountered snow, and she traded her hair combs for one.

Maggie did not like the Indians staring at her, and she was wary lest they snatch Clara. The Indian women pointed at dresses and bonnets, necklaces and brooches. The Indian men studied the white women, too, always asking why there were so many of them and so few men.

"Mormons?" one asked, for even among the Indians it was known that the members of the

Church of Jesus Christ of Latter-day Saints practiced polygamy. Like the first savages the women had encountered on the St. Joe road, the Indian men tried to barter for white brides.

"Too many. I take," they said.

Mary seemed to be the woman who most intrigued the Indian men, probably because of her size and strength, but the men were interested in the others, too, and in Clara, who still dressed as a boy. One ran his hand through Clara's hair, which was so blond that it was almost white, then pulled it to see if it was real. Clara was terrified, and Maggie, outraged, slapped the man's hand away. He would have backhanded her if Edwin had not interfered.

William pondered the incident, then said, "He will lose face. An Indian woman would never dare strike her master, especially in front of others. We must placate him." He offered the Indian a handful of coffee beans and a crock of sour pickles. The Indian muttered something, and William handed over the blue bandana that he wore around his neck. The warrior was still angry, casting furious glances back at Maggie, but he rode off, his women following him.

"Will he cause trouble?" Maggie asked, still comforting Clara.

"He might," Edwin told her. "He has suffered an indignity. I wish we could have given him a horse. That would have satisfied him."

"If we gave him a horse, he would tell the others, and before long, we would be traveling on shanks' mare," Joseph put in. "I hope he does not come back."

"The fault is mine. I should not have struck him," Maggie said.

"The only amend would be to hand over your daughter. I suppose if I were a mother, I would have done exactly as you did if an Indian touched a child of mine," Edwin said. "A good mother would want to protect her child, and from what I have observed, you are indeed a good mother."

He smiled so openly at Maggie that she blushed. She realized that Edwin had been more attentive to her since they left Fort Kearny, and she wondered if the others had noticed. He had shown her how to make a fire of buffalo chips, the circles of dung that the women used for fuel, now that there were fewer trees on the prairie. He brought her wildflowers that he spotted in the tall grasses, and he asked her to repair a rip in his shirt. She had thought nothing of it, for she often mended the clothing of the others in the train and was pleased to do so. Edwin was a favorite among the women because of his youth and good looks and thoughtfulness. Some vied for his attention, but he seemed to treat them all the same—except for her. She was flattered, of course. It had been a long time since any man had complimented her. But it also made her uneasy.

No matter how carefully the women watched the Indians, they found items missing when they were gone. After Maggie complained that her thimble was no longer on a rock where she had left it, Edwin told her, "They have eyes in the backs of their heads. Never underestimate them. And never rile them. They have a long memory."

"Are they all so bad?" Maggie asked. She had given one of her safety pins to an Indian woman holding a small child. The mother was so loving that she reminded Maggie of a picture of the Madonna she had once seen.

"No," Edwin answered. "Many have been help-ful to white travelers who are sick or lost, but we reward them by cheating them. If I was an Indian, I would take what I could."

The ministers followed Edwin's advice to give the Indians coffee or sugar or biscuits. "I hope when they leave us, they will tell the other red men that we are their friends," Joseph said.

Edwin shook his head. "More likely, they will tell them of our strength—or lack of it."

Ever since St. Joseph, tales of Indian depreda-tions had spread among the emigrant trains. The emigrants did not speak from their own experi-ences but instead passed along stories told to them by others, embroidering them with each telling. Maggie heard tales of merciless killings, of men hacked to death, women raped and slaughtered, and children carried off. The travelers never told stories of white men who raped Indian women or shot Indian men for sport.

"Do they eat the children?" Dora asked Edwin after a woman told her about the kidnapping of a child.

"No, of course not," he replied. "They raise them as their own. In fact, Indians love children. They rarely hurt them but instead adopt them into their tribe. That may be why the Indian was so taken with Clara." His words did not reassure Maggie, who had heard of Indians who threw white babies into fires or bashed in the heads of those who cried too much.

They passed graves every day and stopped to read the names painted on rocks or wooden markers, wondering if the dead person might be someone they once knew. On occasion the cause of death was listed—cholera, for instance, which made Maggie think of Lavinia and hurry on for fear of catching the disease. There were inscriptions telling of the dead who had been killed in accidents. Mary pointed out one that read "Felled by a godless savage."

"How many Indians were killed by godless white men, do you suppose?" Edwin asked.

Maggie could not help stopping to read the markers, although not all were about death. A few days after leaving Fort Kearny, Maggie came across a buffalo skull with the words "Forever

Yours. E.M." painted on it. She pointed it out to Winny, who merely shrugged until she spotted a second skull several days later. "Love Always. E.M." was written on it. The next said "Meet me in Ft. Lar. E.M."

"They must be love letters," Maggie told the others.

"But what is their story?" Bessie asked.

"Perhaps we will find out in Fort Laramie," Caroline told her.

The women made a game then of looking for the skulls, but after a half dozen, there were no more.

"Perhaps she changed her mind," Winny said. The women were convinced the messages were written by a woman.

"Or she met somebody else," Sadie suggested.

"Maybe she was run over by a wagon," said Mary, who had thought the messages were silly.

"I think she ran out of buffalo skulls," Maggie told them.

Late one afternoon, not long after Maggie had slapped the Indian, Mary spotted a group of warriors on the horizon. The wagon train should have been corralled by then, but William had kept the women going in hopes of finding a camping place with water. "Look!" Mary shouted.

"I do not like it," the minister told her. He yelled, "Corral the wagons! Hurry! Indians!"

It was not the first time William had given such an order. The other instances had proven unnecessary, but still, the women were wary, and along with the teamsters they formed a circle with the wagons. Mary, Maggie, and others unyoked the oxen and herded them as well as the cows into the center of the enclosure, while the men took out their guns and positioned themselves beneath the wagons.

"They are not here to beg," Edwin told Maggie, as he handed her a rifle. Then he slid under a wagon with William.

The women were barely in place when the Indians swooped down on the train. Maggie knew that they were facing a war party. There were no women or children among the men. The warriors, who had stripped to breechcloths, their bodies and faces painted with hideous designs, yelled savagely as they neared the train and rode around the circle, looking for openings.

Maggie spotted an Indian wearing William's blue bandana. His face was painted in streaks of black and red, but she knew he was the man who had touched Clara. He had come for revenge with his band of warriors, and she was responsible. Had the man returned to snatch up Clara? She glanced back toward the center of the circle, where Clara was huddled under a blanket. Fear gripped her, and she knew she would kill the man before she would let him touch Clara—or he would kill her.

Edwin pointed out the Indian to William. "He is the one we have to get."

Some of the women were badly frightened and clustered around Clara, yelling in terror or crying and praying. "If only I had not come," one screamed. Perhaps none of them should have come, Maggie thought. She herself was almost paralyzed with fright.

"They say we must shoot ourselves rather than be taken by them," cried a woman near Maggie. *Could I kill my own daughter?* Maggie wondered. The idea sickened her almost as much as the idea that an Indian might steal the girl and raise her as his own. She glanced at the child she loved more than anything in the world and fought back hysteria.

Only a few gave way to their fear. After the soldiers on the St. Joe road had shown the women how to shoot, William had drilled them in firearms. They learned not only how to handle guns and circle the wagons but to build bulwarks, piling trunks and bags around the wagons to protect the shooters. Those who could handle guns found positions under the wagons, while others took out medical supplies to treat any who were wounded. Despite their fears, each hurried to carry out William's instructions.

It had all seemed simple when they practiced it. Now that the Indians were racing around the train, looking for ways into the circle, however,

212

Maggie was terrified. She would do what was expected of her, but as she crawled under a wagon next to Mary, a gun in her hands, she worried she could not hold the weapon steady enough to shoot. Winny, who was an even poorer shot than Maggie, dropped down on the other side of Mary. "I cannot shoot," Winny said, "but I can load your guns."

Maggie's hands shook as she aimed at a warrior who had ridden up next to her wagon, but instead of hitting him, she shot the horse of a second Indian.

"Good shot," Mary told her.

Maggie wished she had Mary's calmness, as Mary leveled her gun at a warrior and pulled the trigger, clipping his arm. He screamed and, holding his wounded arm against his side, made for Mary. He managed to shoot an arrow, but his aim was off, and the arrow struck the wagon cover. The man let go of his bow and came toward Mary, a hatchet in his hand. Maggie, her hands shaking, shot at him and missed. Penn dropped him.

The war party was small, made up of little more than twenty men. Still, they were not only ferocious but fearless. Maggie was stunned by their bravery. One Indian headed his horse toward the opening between two wagons and made it into the enclosure, using a war club to strike one of the women. He would have killed her if Edwin had not shot him.

Two of the Indians were dead then, but that did not stop the others. One came toward the wagons at a full gallop. Screaming, he raised a war club and knocked a teamster senseless. William shot at the Indian, wounding him, and the warrior fell from his horse.

At first, the Indians fought by themselves, each man attacking where he saw a weakness. But now, the warriors gathered a short distance from the wagons, then came toward the train as a group, yelling their war cries as if making a final assault.

"Get that God-damned bastard who is wearing my bandana," William called.

Ignoring the profanity that would have shocked him at another time, Joseph aimed for the big Indian. So did the others.

"Now!" William shouted, and there was a volley of shots. The Indian in the bandana dropped his bow and slumped over on his horse. He tried to straighten up, and Maggie watched him, mesmerized. The fear of Clara being murdered or kidnapped made her raise her gun and sight it on the man. She would not regret this killing. Joseph, too, raised his rifle and fired, just as another shot rang out. The warrior slid off his horse and was trampled. A second Indian came to the man's aid. He reached down and attempted to scoop up the body, but he, too, was hit and rode off, his shattered leg bleeding red against his white horse. The remaining Indians hurried after him.

There were no shouts of victory from the women, no cries of relief as the Indians disappeared. Several of those with guns stayed under the wagons, fearing the warriors would return, while the women in the center of the enclosure attended to the wounded. One built a fire and set a kettle of water on it to boil. Bessie took off her petticoat and tore it into strips to be used as bandages. William crawled out from under his wagon to assess the damage. A teamster was dead and two more injured, although their wounds would heal. One woman was mortally wounded, and a second was badly bruised where she had been hit with a war club, while Dora's broken arm hung loose. A warrior had struck her with a hatchet.

Two of the three cows had been killed. An ox lay dead. Another had been struck by an arrow and was kneeling and bellowing in pain from a broken leg. It would have to be shot. The train had already lost two oxen, and two others had been poisoned by toxic weeds after leaving Fort Kearny. William had filled a bottle with melted lard and poured it down their throats, then forced them to swallow fatty bacon, but he was not sure they would recover. If they did not, the train would have to abandon a wagon.

Edwin turned over the warrior who had been

shot dead when he breached the enclosure. "He looks like a white man," Maggie said.

"He is. I believe there are white men who have joined this band of renegades. Such whites are more savage than the red men. They are responsible for many depredations blamed on Indian tribes. It is rare for a small group of Indian warriors to attack a well-fortified train such as ours. Perhaps these outlaws did so because we have a preponderance of women. They did not expect them to be fighters."

"We will not worry about that now," William told Joseph as the two went to the severely wounded woman, who had an arrow in her breast. She lay on a quilt, Caroline and Bessie attending her. Maggie had rushed to Clara as soon as the fighting was done, but Evaline had kept the child from being frightened, and now the two were drawing pictures in the dirt with a broken arrow. Evaline offered to look after Clara.

"She will not make it," Edwin said, when Maggie joined those gathered around the wounded woman.

"Should we remove the arrow?" Joseph asked.

Edwin shook his head. "Sometimes the points are barbed. We do not know about this one because the arrow did not go all the way through her. If it had, we could cut off the arrowhead, then pull out the shaft. If the point is barbed, however, it would cause her more pain to remove it. She does not have long."

William said a prayer over the woman, then went to Dora. Joseph stayed behind.

"Am I dying?" the woman asked. Her name was Adela, and she was a widow. She had made a meager living in Chicago teaching singing and had a beautiful voice that stirred Maggie on the Sabbath when they sang hymns. She was older, older even than Mary, but she had been among the first to sign up for the trip, telling the ministers she thought God didn't intend for her to be alone the rest of her life. "You can tell me," she said.

Joseph took the woman's hand, as if not knowing how to reply. Maggie hoped he would not lie. It seemed dishonest to give her false hope. As she sponged the woman's brow with a strip of cloth, Maggie grieved for her. Adela had come west with such hopes for a new life. Would she have stayed behind if she had known what would happen to her?

"I believe our Lord will welcome you before the day is out," Joseph said. "You will be with Christ in heaven."

The woman gave a small gasp. Her breath was labored. "I had hoped to meet Him one day, but not so soon." She gave a little smile. "I shall tell Him of our adventure and ask Him to keep you safe. I believe He will be proud of us."

217

"I hope so," Joseph told her. "I am sorry it will end for you here."

"Do not be sorry. I am glad I came. How glorious to have had a little adventure at the end. I always feared freezing to death alone in my room in Chicago. Now I can see heaven above me." The words came slowly. "I shall be watching over you." She raised her hand and tried to take Joseph's. A moment later, she was dead.

Joseph grasped Caroline's hand then, and together they said a prayer. When he was finished, he asked, "What have I brought her to? She believed she would come west for a better life, and now it has been taken from her."

"She did not blame you. You gave her hope," Caroline said.

Joseph shook his head. "How many more will we lose before we reach California? How many will I kill?"

"Her death is not your fault."

"Perhaps not, but I feel responsible all the same." He turned away and wiped his eyes. "I killed a man, Caroline. I took the life of another human. The Bible says thou shalt not kill, and I did so."

"As you once told Mary, the killing was done only to protect the women. The Lord will forgive you."

"I am not so sure. It is different. My responsibility is greater. I am a minister of the gospel, charged with defending it. I know I cannot forgive myself. I broke the commandment." He covered his face with his hands to hide the tears.

"You did not kill that Indian. I did."

The minister looked up into the face of Mary, who towered over him. He shook his head. "I delivered the final blow."

"No, I did. I fired just a little before you. Your shot went wild. It was mine that took the Indian's life."

Joseph thought a moment. "How can you be so sure which bullet hit him?" he asked.

"I heard your shot a second after I fired. Perhaps yours was true, but if that is so, your bullet struck a dead man. Besides, Reverend, I am the better shootist."

"Then I did not kill him?"

Mary shook her head.

"*You* saved us, then," Caroline said. "We owe our lives to you, Mary."

The praise seemed to make Mary uncomfortable, and she said she would go to see about the other wounded.

"You have nursed?" Caroline asked.

"No, I treated the animals on the farm. Wounds and broken bones in a human cannot be so much different." She motioned for Maggie to join her.

When the two of them were out of earshot, Maggie asked, "Is it so, Mary? Did you truly kill the man?"

Mary smiled a little. "I am already responsible for one death. What matter that I should claim credit for a second? The Bible does not say you may kill once but not twice. Besides, the killing will not bring me the despair it would to Reverend Swain. We both know the guilt that comes from taking a life. I would save the minister from that."

"I am the one responsible for Adela's death," Maggie said, looking down and twisting her hands. "If I had not slapped that Indian, he would not have come after us." Two deaths now hung over her.

"Do not believe that!" Mary said fiercely. "You did what was necessary to protect Clara. She is worth breaking every commandment in the Bible."

Others had already seen to the wounds, which were serious but not life threatening. The two injured teamsters would have to ride in the wagons until they were healed. The woman who had been hit by the war club was weak and in pain, but William said no bones were broken, and she would recover.

Dora was the most severely injured. Her forearm was broken, and bones protruded through the flesh. She was conscious, her face racked with pain. William knelt beside her, examining the wound while women brought camphor, brandy, and ammonia from their wagons, not sure what would be needed.

"Perhaps the arm should come off," Edwin suggested. "I have never seen a break so bad, and she would not want gangrene to set in."

"No!" Dora screamed through her pain.

"I have set bones before," Mary said. "It will hurt, and maybe her arm will be crooked, but I believe we can save it." She held up the brandy bottle that someone had placed on the ground. "This will help, but laudanum would be better. Who has got laudanum?"

"I threw it out before Fort Kearny," one woman told her.

When none of the others answered, Mary said, "Then we shall proceed without it. The brandy will have to do." She held the bottle to Dora's lips and forced her to drink, waiting a few minutes for the liquor to take effect. She ordered Maggie and Sadie to hold Dora still while she and Reverend Parnell pushed the bones together.

The bone-setting was a painful procedure. Dora screamed. Perspiration ran down the faces of the two "surgeons," and they gritted their teeth as they set the arm. When Mary was satisfied the bones were in place, she laid a spoke from the back of Bessie's rocking chair against the broken forearm to keep it straight, then bound it with strips of cloth. "I think she will be all right," she said, as she sat back in the dirt. Dora had passed out, and Mary studied her for a moment. Dora's breathing was ragged, but she no longer moaned. Mary touched Dora's belly gently, then nodded. "I think she will be all right," she repeated, then said, "and she will not lose the baby."

It was then that Maggie realized that her own arm had been gashed during the fighting. The wound was long and jagged and soaked with blood, and it would have to be attended to. She might have asked Mary to care for it, but her friend was exhausted. And Reverend Parnell had disappeared. Maggie went to her wagon and took out needle and thread. Bracing herself against the wagon wheel, she stitched up the wound herself.

A teamster who was resting nearby watched the procedure and fainted.

Twelve

June 29, 1852
Fort Laramie

When they reached Fort Laramie, Joseph insisted that Dora see the post surgeon to make sure her arm was healing properly. He suggested that Maggie go along, too. Maggie knew her arm was fine, and she wanted to stay with the wagons, in case information about her had reached the fort. Still, she went, knowing that Dora needed her for support, since the ministers were aware now of her pregnancy. So Maggie walked the mile from where they had camped outside the fort to the surgeon's office, Joseph, William, Caroline, and Dora at her side. The man's services were in great demand because many emigrants had been injured or taken sick on the trail from Fort Kearny.

Dora's fever had subsided, but she was still weak and in pain and held on to Maggie as they slowly moved forward in the line. The sun beat down on them, and Caroline said she wished she had brought an umbrella to shade them. If she had, however, she probably would have discarded it on the trail. Sunbonnets would have to do. Dora was unsteady, and Maggie asked if she wanted to wait in the shade of a tree near the parade ground. The others would keep their place in line and come for her when they were near the door of the surgery.

Dora shook her head. It wouldn't be fair, she said, the others standing in the sun for her while she rested. Besides, being on her feet and moving around would strengthen her. She had spent too much time lying in the wagon. Maggie knew Dora would not admit her weakness for fear it would give the ministers another reason to leave her behind.

Dora had confided she was still frightened of losing her arm. Since the Indian attack, she had been inside the wagon, feverish, trying not to moan or cry out when the vehicle ran over a rock or dropped into a hole. She did not want to be a burden and refused to let the others tend her. Dora had expected to keep her pregnancy secret for a few more weeks, until after they left Fort Laramie, hoping that by then it would be too late for the ministers to make her return home. But now the whole company knew of her sin. The broadside she had read before signing up for the trip had said only women of good morals would be accepted, and here she was, unmarried and pregnant. "What is more immoral than that?" she asked Maggie.

"Abandoning a woman in need on the prairie," Maggie replied.

Maggie had been impressed with how well Dora had taken to the trail. As a schoolgirl from a privileged family, Dora had never known hard work or sacrifice. She had talked of being a teacher, but such girls romanticized the schoolroom, and it was more likely she had hoped only to marry the man who had seduced her and raise a family. What would have happened if Dora had not seen the broadsheet? She had signed up not because she wanted to go west for a husband but because she was desperate—like Maggie. And like Maggie, Dora would have had no idea of the challenges ahead. Still, she had met them. Dora never complained, never shirked her responsibilities, and even volunteered to do the chores of others who were tired or ill.

The women had formed a sisterhood, Maggie thought. Edwin had said they were less quarrelsome than the members of other wagon trains. He believed that was because they were women. Maggie wasn't so sure. She knew women did not get along with each other any better than men did. Perhaps they had formed a bond because they knew if they did not, they would never reach California. A man could quit a wagon train and join another, but women had no such opportunity. No train would want to acquire a single woman, one without a wagon or even a horse to call her own. Maggie was surprised at how such a diverse group had melded together: Caroline, the most religious woman Maggie had ever met, with Sadie, a prostitute; Winny, a maid, with the wealthy Bessie; Evaline with Clara. Even Lavinia, if she had lived, would have been one with them. Maggie wondered if the others saw how they had become sisters.

Maggie was aware that Dora did not want to see the surgeon. She was afraid he would say that the arm had not healed properly, that she should not continue the journey. As Dora, Maggie, and the others stood in line, Dora said there were emigrants more seriously ill and she should not waste the time of the surgeon. Indeed, a man in front of them lay on a stretcher made from two tree branches and a torn wagon sheet. He had a head wound and was unconscious. Behind them, an old woman sat on the ground coughing up blood. As the line moved, the woman scooted along with the help of an aged man. Maggie wondered why two such elderly persons would make the trip west.

For a moment, clouds blocked the sun, and those in line were relieved at a respite from the bright glare. But the clouds dissipated, and the sun seemed hotter than ever. Maggie loved the clear, early morning skies on the prairie, but long before noon, the rays were merciless, beating down on her head, her sunbonnet trapping the heat around her face, her eyes red from the glare. It was hard enough walking on the prairie, but standing still in the dirt of the parade ground was torture. Perspiration ran down the women's faces, mixing with the dust churned up by soldiers and horses. When she brushed her hand against her face, Maggie felt her cheek covered with grime. She reached out and put her arm around Dora, knowing that her friend felt the heat and dust even more than she did. "A few more minutes," she said. "Are you all right?"

Dora nodded and smiled, and Maggie wondered at her cheerfulness.

"I should be helping with the wagon. There is washing to be done," Dora said.

"It can be done without you," Caroline put in. "You should not exert yourself after being so badly wounded. And with the baby . . ."

Despite herself, Dora blushed. "I did not mean to deceive you. I did not know what else to do. I had nowhere to go."

"I understand," Caroline replied, then said no more, not giving a hint of Dora's fate.

"I sinned," Dora said, her eyes on the ground.

"Who among us has not?" Caroline replied.

By then, they had entered the surgery, a small, plain room lined with cots. A table stood along one wall—an operating table—and the surgeon sat at a desk. He looked tired, although he smiled when Dora pushed Maggie forward to have her arm examined. The surgeon barely glanced at it before saying, "You are fine. It appears from the stitches that the sewing up was done by a woman."

He did not wait for an answer but beckoned Dora forward. She sat down on a chair next to the desk, too nervous to speak. It was William who said, "Her arm was broken by an Indian hatchet. We reset the bones as best we could."

Dora held out her arm so the surgeon could examine it.

"We were attacked by Indians. Three of our number are dead, one of them a woman. Others were injured, but not as severely as this," the minister added.

"About average for a train of gold seekers," the surgeon said. "Some have had it worse, some better." He untied the bandages that held the spoke in place. "I believe you can dispense with the splint."

Maggie took the spoke. She would return it to Bessie to put back into her rocker.

"Will I lose my arm?" Dora asked.

"Not unless you don't want it anymore," the surgeon said, smiling. "It was set as well as I could have done. It will pain you some, and it will never be as good as new, but it will do. Had you a doctor who attended you?"

"A woman in our train."

"Are you the wagon train of spinsters, then? I have heard of you. There is much talk of you by those who have passed you on the trail. Many are betting you will not make it to California."

"Those who have observed us are betting we will," Caroline told him. "You should have seen us fight against the Indians. I believe we are as competent as any group of men—better cooks, too, and somewhat more polite."

"That would not be difficult." The surgeon nodded at Dora, who stood and stretched her back. "You are soon to become a mother," he said, glancing at Dora's protruding stomach.

Dora nodded, embarrassed.

The surgeon was not paying attention, however. It was not his job to take care of pregnant women, and he nodded at the next patient to come forward.

Outside, William left them to meet one of the men at the blacksmith's shop. Some of the oxen needed to be shod, and broken wheels and wagons required repair. The train was already behind schedule, so he wanted to hurry the work. Maggie was sorry to see him go. She knew that Dora had to discuss her condition with the ministers, and Reverend Swain, while he had softened, was still a man with high morals.

"I believe you will heal, and that is a relief. I am told the journey thus far has been easier than that ahead. We would not want to subject a sick woman to the hardships," Joseph said.

Dora considered his words. "You will let me go on, then?"

"Are you of a mind to return to Chicago?"

"Oh no. I just thought . . . I mean, the baby . . ." Her voice trailed off.

"It seems that one of every four women we encounter is expecting a child or has one at her breast," Caroline said. "I do not believe the trail will be that hard for you, if that is what you are thinking."

"Then I can stay with you?" Dora asked.

Joseph studied her a moment. "If I had known of your condition at the outset, I would have refused you. But you are one of us now. I have seen how you do what is expected of you, and more. We will not turn you out," he said.

Later, when Maggie was alone with Caroline, she asked about the decision. "My husband was angry when he learned of Dora's condition," Caroline said. Dora had lied to them. She had known the requirements for women making the trip west and had concealed her pregnancy. "We worried that if Dora remained, outsiders might believe we were taking a group of immoral women to California. We would then be compromised.

"Still, I pleaded for her, knowing she was desperate. I have never had a child, to my great regret and that of my husband. Nonetheless, I understand the heartbreak of a woman with a child she does not want. Like you, Sadie had guessed Dora's condition, and she told me, saying that I knew the alternative. If Dora had been left in Chicago, she likely would have been turned out. That could have meant her death as well as that of the baby. Sadie said that joining our company saved both their lives. I told Sadie she was becoming a Christian, but she replied that she had not gone that far." Caroline smiled. "Not all Christians are members of a church.

"I relayed all Sadie said to my brother and husband, and I told them that if we forced her to leave us, Dora would be in a worse situation than before."

"And you swayed them?"

Caroline shrugged. "My husband said we were only being practical by letting Dora continue. He knew that if we turned her away, we would be responsible if anything happened to her. He believed God would judge us."

"That was a powerful argument," Maggie said.

"I thought so myself. That is why I made it."

Fort Laramie was bigger and busier than Fort Kearny. The large parade ground was bordered by rows of barracks made from mud and straw, or adobe as it was called. Besides the surgery and the headquarters, there were a blacksmith shop, a sawmill, a public house, and a sutler's post.

Once she had escorted Dora back to the wagons, Maggie took Clara with her to the post to purchase fabric for sunbonnets. Many of the women from the train were there, although they merely wanted to look, not buy.

The selection of goods at the post was sparse, Maggie thought, turning her attention to the mountain men in their fringed buckskin suits decorated with beads. They smelled of camp-fires and animal skins. The trappers lounged about the room, smoking or chewing and talking of beaver they had trapped and buffalo they had slaughtered to any who would listen. They spoke of Indians they had slaughtered, too, and narrow escapes from savages and wild animals, and they lamented that their way of life was disappearing. "Too many pilgrims," one remarked, referring to the emigrants. They blamed the influx of travelers, but in truth, they had overtrapped the beaver. Besides, as Maggie knew from her days as a dressmaker, styles had changed, and beaver hats were no longer in demand. Now the men tried to sell themselves as guides on the Overland Trail.

Maggie studied the array of merchandise. The bolts of calico and rolls of ribbon, bonnets and hairpins, and packets of pins made her a little homesick.

"I wonder if I shall ever use my china plates again," Bessie said, coming to stand beside Maggie.

"You packed them in one of the flour barrels. They ain't going to break," Evaline told her.

"You must say 'are not' instead of 'ain't,' " Bessie corrected her.

"Yes, ma'am," Evaline said. Maggie knew that in the beginning, some of the women had thought Evaline uppity because of her fine talk.

Both women studied the merchandise on the shelves—the china, the bolts of fabric, the discards from the trail, and the liquor. Maggie remarked that she was glad they were abstainers since whiskey was five dollars a gallon. Bessie called the sutler over and asked him to take down the muslin and cut off three yards. She also purchased two yards of flannel.

"What do you need that for?" Maggie asked.

"A baby needs napkins, does it not? And shirts?"

"Miss Dora?" Evaline asked.

"Who else?"

"I did not think it was you having a baby."

Maggie frowned at Evaline's presumption in talking to her mistress that way, but Bessie only laughed and told the girl to mind her manners.

"You are nicer than you let on," Evaline said.

The sutler handed the purchased items to Evaline, who tucked them under her arm and waited with Bessie while Maggie chose the fabrics for the sunbonnets—green for Dora, red for Penn, and blue for the others. Then she purchased a length of yellow—yellow like the sun—since Clara had asked for a sunbonnet, although the little girl still dressed as a boy. The cap she had worn had been lost on the prairie.

None of them noticed a man staring at them until he approached.

"That's a right nice little gal you got there, ma'am," he said to Bessie. He pointed at Evaline.

Maggie was handing coins to the sutler and paid no attention to the man until she heard Bessie say, "Sir." Then Maggie turned and frowned. She did not like his looks. Or his smell.

The man removed his hat. "I could use such a woman, you know, make up my bed, wash my clothes, cook my supper. She cooks, does she?"

Bessie took a step backward. "She does not."

"Well, I ain't so particular about that."

Evaline stared at the man, fear in her eyes, and stepped close to her mistress. "What does he want?" she whispered. Bessie put her arm around Evaline. Maggie, alarmed, grasped Clara and moved closer to the two others. Clara took Evaline's hand.

The man smiled at Evaline, showing a mouth that held only half a dozen teeth. "Like I say, I'm looking for a gal to help me, warm my backside of a night." He turned back to Bessie. "I'd give a good price for her. I'm a buffalo hunter and make a fine living. How much do you want?"

Shocked, Maggie gasped, and Evaline crumpled against Bessie. Maggie knew little about slavery, had not thought much about the plight of those who were considered chattel. Now the idea that the beautiful young woman who had been so kind to Clara might be no more than an animal to be bought and sold sickened her.

Bessie looked the hunter in the eye. "She is not a slave, sir. She is not for sale."

"Well, I'll give you a little something anyway." He turned to Evaline. "How about it, girl? It don't bother me none that you're a darkie, and I'll treat you real good, buy you anything in this store."

"Get out of our way," Bessie ordered.

"Now don't be talking that way. I made you an honest proposition." He put his hand on Evaline's arm, and she screamed. "Don't be doing that, girl." He tightened his hand and moved it slowly up her arm, his other hand on the counter.

"Let go of her," Bessie ordered.

The post was crowded and noisy, and no one seemed to be paying attention.

"Let her go," Maggie repeated.

"Kill your own snakes," he snarled. "Whereat I come from, a white man's got the right to a colored girl like this. I expect she'll go with me. Ain't that right?" He grinned at Evaline, who turned her head aside at the foul breath. "Come on now."

Bessie tried to pull Evaline away, but the trapper held her fast. Bessie looked around for a weapon, but it was Maggie who spotted the

235

hammer lying on the counter next to the man's free hand. "Get away from her!" she ordered.

"Mind your business," he growled.

Maggie picked up the hammer and slammed it down on the man's fingers. He let go of Evaline and howled, screaming that his hand was broken.

As the hunter put his hand between his knees, whimpering and swearing, Bessie sent Maggie a look of triumph. "Well done," she said.

Maggie had heard of the rock mound ever since St. Joseph. Independence Rock was one of the most famous landmarks on the Overland Trail, and nearly all the travelers carved their names in it. However, she was unimpressed. The granite hump was only a hundred and thirty feet tall. Bessie, who had lived in New England, said it reminded her of a whale—a huge whale, of course, because the rock was nearly two thousand feet long and half as wide.

They arrived at midday on July 7, three days late, according to William's calculations. Wagon trains hoped to pass the rock by Independence Day. That way they were almost sure of making it to California before snow fell in the mountains, he explained. Still, William was pleased by their progress. They had made up much of the time they had spent at Fort Kearny and Fort Laramie. He would make sure the women did not tarry on the rest of the trip.

William said he would have preferred that they not waste the time visiting Independence Rock, but he knew that was impossible. For days, the women had talked of going there and carving their names in the granite dome, which they knew had become a kind of directory for those headed west. So William stopped the lead team near the rock, and the company made camp close to other trains that were gathered at the site.

"Take a chisel or a hammer and nails to inscribe your names," William instructed, after the company had unhitched the teams and herded them into the wagon enclosure. "Or axle grease or tar," he added, although the women ignored the last suggestions. Tar and grease would wear off over time. They wanted their names chiseled into the rock for eternity.

The men stayed to guard the wagons. They would go later. William led the women through the sage toward the gray dome.

"It looks like a giant lump of bread dough," Bessie observed.

"Unrisen, like my dough," Sadie said.

"More like spilled oatmeal," Mary told them. She took Clara from Maggie and set the little girl on her shoulders. Clara played with Mary's hair as if it were reins on a mule team. "Move out!" she called.

"Someday you will have a little girl like that," Maggie told her.

Maggie knew she was not the only one who appreciated Mary, who confided in her and sought her advice. She had seen how Mary was no longer the oddity she had been at home. On the trail she was the leader of the women. She laughed when the others spoke about the men they would find in California. In the evenings, she and Maggie gathered with them around the campfires while Evaline played her violin, another emigrant a mouth organ. Mary sang the hymns in a clear voice, although she did not dance as the others did. When the fires died down and the ministers read from the Bible or prayed, Mary seemed content, her heart full.

"The men will line up for you, Mary. You will have more suitors than any of the rest of us," Sadie told her.

"Who'll look at a puny thing like me when they can have someone as strong as you?" Winny asked. "Oh, you will have your pick, Mary. What will you look for?"

Mary blushed and shook her head, and Maggie realized later that she had not answered.

"I want someone who works hard," a woman said.

"Not a rich man?" Sadie asked.

The woman shook her head, and Dora added, "Me neither."

"I'll find a man that don't beat me," Penn said, blushing because she knew that although the women were aware she had run away from Asa because of his brutality, some thought it unseemly to admit such a thing.

Most of them murmured words of sympathy, however, and Mary said, "If your husband lays a hand on you, he will do it only once. I shall see to that."

"Come along. We must not dawdle," William called. He led the way to the rock, which up close was more impressive because of the names on it. Other emigrants were ahead of them, and Maggie heard the sounds of hammers as the travelers left their marks in the granite. One boy scrambled up the smooth surface of the rock, and with a nail he scratched his name high above the rest. Others used sharp rocks, chisels, even a hoe to record that they had been there.

Maggie walked along the rock, reading the names of emigrants, trappers, and explorers, a few chiseled into the stone more than twenty years before, lichen obscuring some of them. There were initials and names, dates and places. "Rich. York London Eng.," read one. Another was "E.E. MORRIS NEW YORK CITY." A third was simply "b.r. 1850." Someone had scratched a crude drawing of a wagon, and scrawled not far away was "Clara." "Look, Clara, there is your name," Maggie said, pointing to it. Clara did not know her letters, however, and the scrawl meant nothing to her. She was more interested in the drawing of an animal and said, "See, Mama, a dog, just like Dick's dog." Maggie remembered how Dick had made a friend of a stray that roamed the streets. The dog waited for him by the front door of the tenement each morning for the breakfast scraps Dick brought him. Then one day, he did not come. Dick found him lying in the street, run over by a hack. "Evaline says I can have a dog in California," Clara said.

"And you will," Maggie told her.

Several of the women in the party searched for familiar names and cried out when they found them. Maggie stopped at a name that read, "Susan Talman, 1849." "I wonder who she is," Maggie said to Winny. "Did she make it to California? Maybe she was killed by Indians or died of cholera. Perhaps she reached the gold camps and struck it rich. Or maybe she got disgusted and went back east. We could have passed her on the trail or seen her at Fort Laramie."

"Do you think someone will read our names and wonder about us?" Winny asked. "Maybe a hundred years from now they will read 'Winny Rupe' and ask who she was."

"More likely they will say, 'Winny Rupe. Oh, you know of her. She went to California and found a million dollars in gold. She married a rich man who became president of America,'" Maggie told her.

"What do I care about a million dollars. I just want to find my brother." Winny looked over the hundreds of names on the rock, then said in a small voice, "I did not know so many men went to California. How will I find Davy there?" They had walked partway around the rock by then, Winny searching for her brother's name. "I will read every mark if I have to. If Davy made it this far, for sure he would have left his name."

She lagged behind the others, reading each inscription, and when they were almost out of sight, they heard Winny yell. Maggie hurried back, and Winny pointed to a name scratched deep in the rock—"D. Rupe Chi."

"You found him!" Maggie cried. "All these names, and you found your brother's!"

Winny placed her hand over the name and grinned. "He made it this far. I know he got to California. He must have wrote me, but Mrs. Fletcher threw out the letters." She began to cry, and Maggie put an arm around her friend. "I feared I was the only one left, but now I know he is in California. Oh, Maggie, I will find him." Winny dried her eyes, then took out a nail and scratched "Winny. Sis."

"I intend to let them read my name," Mary said. Standing on tiptoe and finding a vacant spot, she chiseled her name in huge letters: "MARY MADRID. ILL. 1852."

She handed the chisel and hammer to Maggie, who inscribed her initials, M.K. She realized too late that she had enlisted in the company under the name Maggie Hale.

Sadie stared at the initials.

"I have changed my name," Maggie admitted. "I would be grateful if you would keep it to yourself." She chided herself for putting even her initials on the rock. What if someone who had heard about her saw them? The chances of that were slight, of course. Still, she had been foolish.

"Why did you change it?" Sadie asked.

"I fear . . . ," Maggie said, then caught herself. She stared open-mouthed at Sadie.

Sadie thought that over and nodded. "Most likely you fear your dead husband's family and are not wanting them to know you gone west. It was smart of you to pick another name." She laughed. "I expect I should've done the same." She took the chisel from Maggie and tapped it against the granite. When she was finished, Maggie's initials were M.K.H.

She handed the chisel back to Maggie. "What about Clara?" she asked. "You ought to make a record she's been here."

Maggie thought that over, then walked back to Mary's name, and under it she chiseled "C. Hale." She held up Clara so that the girl could touch the name. "There you are, Clara. You will be remembered here for a thousand years."

Maggie watched as Sadie carved her initials, then handed the implement to Penn, who scratched an *X* in the rock. When she saw the others watching, she reddened. "I can't write," she said.

"Then I shall write it for you," Mary said and chiseled "Penn House" on the rock. When she was finished, she frowned. "Are you afraid Asa's brothers will see it? If you want me to, I can scratch it out."

Penn laughed. "Even if they see it, it won't mean nothing to them. They can't read neither."

"You are still frightened of them?" Mary asked.

"Every single day. I know they are going to catch up with us."

Maggie feared that Penn was right. Just a few days before, they had exchanged pleasantries with a group of men who passed them on the trail. One mentioned that the soldiers at Fort Kearny had discovered the body of a traveler who had been buried where the wagons camped. When Joseph asked for particulars, the man replied that it had been the best bit of luck that the man's own family had arrived a day or two later and identified him. "Everybody is talking of it, because it was so bold, burying a man like that right where the wagons was."

"Was it robbery?" Joseph asked.

"Hard to tell. They found a sack of gold coins on him, but a brother of his says something was stole from him."

"What was it?" Joseph asked.

The man narrowed his eyes as if Joseph were too curious and shrugged. Then he asked, "Your women ain't been making white cake, have they? I'd give my right ox for a taste of white cake."

Joseph replied, "Not unless you can give them a dozen eggs. We have not seen an egg since the Missouri." He did not press the man further about the dead body.

"What about you, Reverend Parnell? Do you not want to inscribe your name on the rock?" Maggie asked, handing him the chisel.

He took the implement but did not use it. "*I* know I was here. I do not feel the need for others to know of it," he replied. He wandered off from the group then, the chisel still in his hand.

The day was pleasant, and Reverend Parnell had already announced they would be camping at the site, so Maggie felt there was no need to return to the wagons. Clara was running her hands over the names, stopping when she saw an animal chiseled in the stone. "Come on, Mama," she called.

Maggie felt carefree. "Come, let us walk all the way around the rock," she told Bessie.

Bessie looked to where Evaline was sitting on the ground, drawing in her sketchbook. "One day, someone will appreciate her record of the trip," Bessie said. "Before we left Chicago, we inquired of the editor of a newspaper whether he would like to publish her sketches. He said he would, then asked if I would write about the journey for him. When I suggested that Evaline do so, he said, 'Oh, does she read and write, then?' I am used to ignorant people believing that because she is a Negro, she is illiterate, but I would not have expected such an assumption from a learned man." Bessie shook her head. "I had hoped for a better life for Evaline in California, but . . ." She shook her head. "Perhaps California is no better than anyplace else."

Bessie invited Evaline to walk with them, but Evaline shook her head. "I shall be fine, Mrs. Whitney." Bessie looked around to make sure that Evaline was not alone and nodded. Then she linked her arm through Maggie's, and the two followed Clara around the rock. Up ahead, they saw that Reverend Parnell had stopped. He had told them he did not care to carve his name in the granite, but it was clear to the two that he was doing just that. They waited, afraid that they had intruded on something secret, and both began examining the wall, as if looking for names. There were fewer of them now, since this was on the far side of the trail. After a time, the minister finished what he was doing and walked on. The women waited until he was out of sight. Then they continued their walk until they reached the place where Reverend Parnell had stopped.

It took a moment for them to find what they were looking for. Maggie spotted it and pointed: "Anne & William Parnell, 1849." The names were weathered, and lichen spotted them. Maggie went closer, then saw a newly etched cross in the rock below the names. "Look," she told Bessie.

Bessie went to the wall and touched the cross. She drew in her breath, then said, "Reverend Parnell never told us he was married. I had thought him a bachelor. Surely he does not now have a wife in California."

"No. I believe the cross means that she is dead."

"Perhaps her death has something to do with this journey," Bessie said.

"He once said of us that we were all running away from something. I believe he is, too."

Bessie stared in the direction the minister had gone. "That poor man," she muttered. "No wonder he is so lonely."

Maggie studied her friend for a moment, then smiled to herself. Bessie could be a very determined woman. Perhaps she had decided on her third husband. Maggie started along the trail, then stopped and turned back when she realized her friend was not with her. Bessie still stood with her hand on Reverend Parnell's name.

Thirteen

July 25, 1852
The Mormon Trail

The rain started at midday on a Sunday. The wagon train still stopped on the Sabbath, not so much for religious reasons now as to let the animals rest and the company make repairs. William had found a good site near the Green River that had been occupied by others just a day or so earlier. That train had lightened its load and left behind hub hoops, wagon wheels, and harnesses. A window sash lay on the ground along with a clothes basket, a leather portmanteau, and a rag carpet. And there were ashes from what had been beans and bacon that the men of that train had set afire so that no one else could eat them. A pile of bricks lay nearby, which made the travelers laugh. How could anyone be so foolish as to transport bricks that far? Maggie held up a sad iron and asked, "What woman would want to come all this way just to iron clothes?"

That morning, Mary went with the men in search of six oxen that had wandered off overnight. Maggie watched her ride away into a glorious sunrise of pink and orange and lavender, the colors of a silk dress she had once made. The sunrise was followed by a brilliant blue sky, but it turned cloudy as the day wore on, and then the rain came. The land was still flat and brown, but it had grown prettier the farther they went from Fort Laramie, with hills and canyons, with bachelor's buttons and marigolds and asters—and berry bushes loaded with fruit. Maggie had been thrilled to find both black and yellow currants as well as wild strawberries and raspberries along the trail. Penn had discovered ice, too, ice that was perfectly clear and good, at a place called Ice Slough. None could understand how ice formed just a few inches below the surface of the grass. Clara put her bare toes on the ice and laughed. Penn dug up a quantity, and that night Maggie made a dessert with it, adding milk and sugar and strawberries. She gave her portion to Clara, who consumed it with delight and demanded, "More strawberry ice cream, please, Mama."

In camp, before the rain, Bessie and Sadie baked bread, using saleratus from a nearby spring in place of soda, and Dora made a crust for a pie. She would fill it with the wild fruit. Others aired bedding and washed clothes, scrubbing them on rocks and spreading them over bushes to dry, then sat in the shade of their wagons with their mending.

Maggie took out calico quilt pieces that she

had picked up from a pile of discards and began stitching them together. Sewing again gave her pleasure. She did not know if that was because she was turning discarded scraps into something useful or because selecting the colors and shapes to be made into a pattern made her feel like an artist creating a picture.

"What do you call the pattern?" Winny asked. She was mending Mary's petticoat, which had been torn when it was caught on a bush, and doing a poor job of it.

"I do not know. I am making it up."

"Is the quilt for Dora?"

"What a wonderful idea." Maggie glanced at Winny's big stitches. "Give it to me. I shall repair the petticoat. There is plenty of time to make a quilt for Dora's baby." She took the petticoat and ripped out Winny's crude stitches, wrapping the thread around her finger to save it. She was especially careful of her needle because she had brought only three with her.

The two sat quietly for a time, and Maggie remembered how she had loved sitting in the sun on the steps of the Chicago building in which she had lived. She had sewn while Dick played beside her with the little dog and Clara napped, her head in Maggie's lap. Those were her happiest days, when the children were small and Jesse had gone away. She missed Dick—she would always miss Dick—but she still had Clara, and that was some comfort. Maggie glanced down at the little girl beside her, who was arranging the quilt scraps by color.

It began to rain then, and the women gathered their sewing and went to their wagons and tents. Dora, whose pie was not yet done, stood over the campfire with a gutta-percha cloth over her head to keep the rain from splashing on the pastry. Maggie put Clara into a wagon, and those who had done washing collected the laundry from the bushes where it had been drying.

By the time Mary and the men returned with the missing oxen, they were soaked. Mary climbed into her wagon, stripped off her dress, and put on her dry one. The rain beat on the canvas wagon covers. The wind blew the drops inside, wetting quilts and blankets that were stored too close to the opening. Mary had discarded her feather bed at Fort Kearny but said she would keep the pillow even if she had to carry it on her head. Now she wrinkled her nose at the disagreeable smell of the feathers. "I had hoped to fish," she told Maggie. "I would have liked a dinner of fried fish, but I am afraid I would be washed down the river if I went near the bank."

Maggie would not have minded a light rain to settle the dust, but western rains were cold and heavy. And this one seemed as if it would last forever. The sky reminded her of the days in Chicago when coal smoke colored it a gray as dark as slate. The women strung their damp laundry inside the wagons and tents, which added to the wetness in the air. The rain depressed Maggie because it would not stop. She ate a cold supper that included Dora's watery pie, its crust the texture of soaked cardboard.

The rain saturated the ground, and William said he was afraid that if they left the campsite, the wagons would get stuck in the mud, which by morning would be as thick as pudding. The tents filled with water, and those who had slept in them crowded into the wagons to wait out the storm. Maggie hunched her shoulders and wrapped herself in a quilt when it was her turn to do chores or check on the animals, then hurried back to the shelter of the wagon. A few women tried to keep the campfires going but gave up, and for the second day they ate cold food.

Clara fussed about being cooped up in the wagon. She complained of the damp bedding and whined when Maggie gave her a slice of cornbread and cold beans for her dinner. "I want soup," she said. "I want ice cream."

"We have no fire to make soup, and the ice cream is gone," Maggie told her.

"I want strawberry ice cream," Clara continued.

"Oh, do be quiet," Maggie chided her. Maggie's nerves were frayed from the dampness, and she feared she was coming down with a cold. She had no patience for Clara. When she turned her back, Clara jumped out of the wagon and dropped into the mud.

Maggie climbed out after her, and the two tussled. Maggie hauled her up as Clara kicked, spraying mud over their clothes. "I want out," Clara screamed.

"Oh, Clara, how could you! Do not act like a baby. You are four years old," Maggie said. "Be still!"

A woman in the next wagon shook her head at Maggie, as if telling her to make her child behave.

"She is always so good. It is the rain," Maggie said, but the woman only frowned. Maggie held Clara tight and said she would tell her a story, but Clara put her fingers in her ears.

"I will take her," Mary said. "I am restless at being cooped up, too, and want to walk to the river to see how much it has risen. She is already wet, and I will keep a tight hold on her."

"I want to go," Clara insisted, pulling away from her mother.

"Do not cause trouble," Maggie warned.

"You cause trouble," Clara responded.

Maggie shrugged. "Oh, do take her," she said to Mary. She tied the yellow sunbonnet under Clara's chin, hoping it would keep the rain off her daughter's head. She watched from the wagon until Mary, Clara on her shoulders, disappeared,

252

a sense of guilt for her relief at having a bit of peace. When the two returned, Clara was soaked, and Maggie was brusque with Mary for letting the child get so wet.

She was relieved the next morning when the sun came out. The trees and bushes shimmered with drops of rain; the mountains smoked as the dampness steamed off them in the hot sun. Maggie was anxious to be under way and chafed that Reverend Parnell insisted they wait until late morning, after the sun had had a chance to bake the earth. "If the wagons get mired, we will have to double-team to pull them out. Better to get a late start after the ground is more solid," he said. Maggie rolled her eyes.

The women spread their bedding and damp laundry on bushes again, but they were packed and ready to leave, with the teams harnessed, long before the minister called "Move out!" They jockeyed for places in line then, forgetting their order of three days before. The oxen, rested, moved at a fast pace.

"Maybe the rain was not so bad," Winny told Maggie as they walked beside their wagon.

"Maybe, if I can ever get Clara's clothes clean again," Maggie replied, then glanced down. "And look at my hem. It is covered in mud." She still felt out of sorts.

The sky overhead was a brilliant blue, without a single cloud, and the grass, which had been brown from overgrazing by the trains ahead of them, had turned bright green and sparkled with wildflowers. "A day the Lord has made," Caroline exclaimed.

Maggie wondered how Caroline could always be so cheerful.

"The Lord makes each day," her husband put in.

"Yes, of course, but on some days, like me, He is not in such a good mood," Maggie told him.

She wondered if he would reprimand her, but to her surprise, Reverend Swain laughed.

They traveled all day beside the Green River. They had crossed rivers many times already, some of them fast and dangerous like the Platte could be in places. Others were mere streams, so shallow that, instead of riding across in the wagons, the women had removed their shoes, hiked up their skirts, and waded through them. The Green, normally more placid, was too deep and too cold for that. It was swollen from the rain and brown with dirt that had been washed off the riverbanks—and it looked treacherous. "The water is so muddy that it appears bottom side up," Mary observed.

"I believe you would need a spoon to drink it," Maggie said. She did not look forward to fording it.

By midafternoon the train had reached the crossing. William and Joseph stood on the bank of the river and stared at the water. "It is awfully fast. Should we wait to cross?" Joseph asked Edwin, who had traveled the Green before.

"Hard to say. I have never seen the water so high. The Green is usually more placid, but today it is as turbulent as the Platte. Without the rain of the last day, it would be much lower. There used to be a ferry here, but I see no sign of it."

"I believe we should do it," William said. "Due to our late start, we are well behind schedule. We could be here for days waiting for the river to go down. Besides, the oxen are rested and should have no trouble swimming across." He paused. "It could rain again, too. I hope that, unlike Jesus, the river does not rise."

He glanced at Joseph to see if his brother-in-law was offended, but Joseph ignored the remark and said, "I do not like it."

"You are too cautious. At this rate, we will not reach the Sierras before snowfall. The snow is far more dangerous than a river." When Joseph did not respond, William added, "I have traveled this route, too, Joe. If Edwin thinks we can cross, then I am of a mind to do so."

Joseph looked at the swirling river that foamed and whirled as it tried to escape the banks. "I pray you are right."

"Pray all you like," William said. "But you might also want to help us get the wagons across."

"I think we should wait," Caroline said, as two dead oxen swept past them in the raging water. "This is the worst river we have encountered, and I believe the women would be willing to camp a day or two until it subsides."

"I had not known you had selected such cowards to go to California," William told her in a waspish voice.

Caroline looked stung and said, "Thy will be done."

"William knows best," Joseph reprimanded her.

William turned to Edwin and asked, "How do you suggest we cross?"

Edwin walked to the willows lining the bank and studied the river for a long time. He returned and said, "I advise we wait until morning, when the water has gone down. Besides, it will take us a full day to cross. If we start this late in the day, only a few wagons will reach the other side, and it would not be safe to divide the women."

William sighed. "As you wish, but we must spend the rest of the day readying the wagons." He slapped at a mosquito that had landed on his head. When he drew back his hand, there was a spot of blood on it.

They were plagued with mosquitoes then, and Maggie wished for a hat with a veil like the one she had worn to the boat, then discarded on the St. Joe road. Her sunbonnet would have to do. What couldn't be helped must be endured, she told herself, then thought of Clara, whose skin would be covered by welts in no time. She placed the yellow sunbonnet on her daughter's head, hoping it would keep some of the mosquitoes away. Clara was still fussy and would be worse by the time they crossed the river.

The company talked about the best way to proceed. In any other train, Maggie thought, the men would have made the decision, but these women had shared in the work of driving the oxen and caring for the wagons. They knew as much about rivers as the men. Their advice was not sought, but neither was it rejected— especially not Mary's.

Although the river was swift, Mary believed they could swim the animals across. Reverend Parnell suggested sealing the wagon beds with tar and floating them to the other side, but Mary feared they might topple in the current. Finally, they agreed the safest way was to build a raft and take the wagons across one by one. They would tie a rope to a pine on their side of the river, then one of them would cross to the other side and attach it to a tree so that it could be used as a guide rope. There was time yet that day to make a raft by lashing together cottonwood logs.

By morning, the Green had gone down a little, but rain threatened again. "It is as good a day as we shall have," William announced.

"The water is still very high. Perhaps it will not rain. What would another day's rest hurt?" Joseph protested.

William threw up his hands in exasperation. "Wait, wait! Why not wait until December. Perhaps the river will freeze then, and we can drive the wagons across on the ice. You can wait if you like, but the women and I will be on our way."

Maggie stared at him in confusion. He was usually so calm, but he had been agitated these last days, always complaining of delay. Now Reverend Swain seemed to be the level-headed one. He, however, said nothing.

"We must keep to our schedule," William said to his brother-in-law's silent reproach. "I fear for snow in the mountains. You do not understand how it can be."

"No, of course not," Joseph said.

The two looked at each other for a time. Then William asked who would brave the water and carry the rope across to the other side. "Which is the strongest horse?" he asked.

"Miss Madrid's," Edwin told him.

"Then I shall take it."

"No, he will not let you ride him," Mary said. She had been standing with Maggie and the men, studying the river. "I will go."

"I will not allow you to risk yourself," William told her.

"You have no choice. Mine is the best horse,

258

and I am the only one who can ride him. Besides, I am as strong as you are."

"But you will be soaked," Caroline protested.

Mary laughed. "And Reverend Parnell will not be?"

The others tried to dissuade her. Only Maggie realized that Mary actually wanted to go, that she took pride in her strength and endurance, and she wanted the women to be proud of her, too. Mary was adamant, and at last William gave in. He tied the rope to a tree near the riverbank and gave the other end to Mary, who saddled her horse, checking a second and then a third time to make sure the saddle was tight, the stirrups in place. The minister instructed her to find a spot where the bank was not soft, a little ways downstream from where they stood.

" 'Tis a good thing she don't ride sidesaddle. She'd be washed right off in the river," Penn observed.

"At a time like this, propriety is of no consequence," Bessie told her.

"I am beginning to think it is of no importance at all on the Overland Trail," Maggie said. She watched Mary with admiration, thinking how the woman had been an inspiration to all of them. Mary had set an example. She was one of the reasons Maggie was different now—stronger, more self-assured. Maggie wondered what Jesse would have thought of her. If he were alive, would she still cower from him as she once had? And if she did not, what would he do? It was a moot point, since he was dead and could do nothing to her now, she told herself. Far more dangerous was the river.

They all watched as Mary checked the rope tied to her saddle horn, then urged the chestnut into the river. The horse fought her, but Mary prodded him, and he plunged into the water and was swept down the river with the current until he righted himself and began to swim. He resisted the force of the water as he made for the opposite bank. Still, the current was stronger, and it carried him along. Mary could not keep him on course. Suddenly the horse seemed to flounder and dip into the water, as if giving in to the river. Horse and rider were at the mercy of the swirling current, and Maggie feared Mary would be washed off into the water. A woman beside her gasped, and Maggie turned to see that all of them were watching Mary. It was as if they were all riding on that horse together. Mary pulled back on the horse's head and urged him on.

"Can she swim?" Bessie asked.

"What does it matter?" William answered. "If Miss Madrid is washed off the horse, her water-soaked clothes will pull her down to the bottom of the river."

The horse drifted and fought for traction as he and his rider were carried downstream. Then the chestnut caught himself and began to swim again. He reached the far side of the river, but the bank there was too high, and he could not get purchase. He was carried farther until finally he scrambled up onto dry ground. Mary dismounted and tried to wring out her drenched skirts. Then she raised her arm in triumph, and those watching, the men as well as the women, cheered.

Fourteen

The men had built a raft of large cottonwood logs and sealed it with tar. They believed it was safe, but it had to be tested before the women and wagons could be loaded. Now four men, including Edwin, who had crossed the Green several times, climbed aboard the raft. Edwin steered it into the river, using the rope as a guide. The raft caught in the current and twisted around, but the men righted it, and in a few minutes they reached the far bank. Mary helped them dock the craft. Three of the men stepped off. They would help unload the wagons after they were brought over. Edwin guided the raft back across the river. He would steer it back and forth.

Maggie had been ferried across rivers before, but she was apprehensive. So were the others. The raft might have been all right with four men on board, but the wagons were heavy, and each was filled with two thousand pounds of supplies. They could not be sure the cottonwood logs would not sink under the weight.

"Who goes first?" William called.

The women looked at each other; no one volunteered. Maggie clutched Clara and stared into the rushing water. Finally, Caroline stepped forward. "I will go," she said.

Joseph looked at her with concern and something like pride. "And I shall escort you," he told her.

"Hurry it along. We must all be over before the rain comes," William said, glancing at the sky, where clouds were gathering.

The men pushed the first wagon onto the logs and fastened the wheels in place with chains. Then Caroline and Joseph boarded and stood beside the wagon. "Do not look at the water," Edwin told Caroline. "It will hypnotize you and make you dizzy."

She nodded as she clutched Joseph's arm. Maggie could see fear on her friend's face. Along with the others, Caroline had encountered enormous challenges, but this was the first time she appeared to be truly frightened. She closed her eyes, as her husband gripped her waist to stop her shaking. Maggie knew they were both praying. Caroline leaned against her husband, her eyes closed, as the raft swirled in the water, caught in the current. She stood immobile as water lapped over the logs and splashed her dress, until at long last the raft bumped against the bank and Mary helped her out onto land.

Maggie, watching from across the river, had been caught up in the crossing, and when

Caroline and Joseph reached safety, she clapped with the others.

"At this rate, we will be finished by mid-afternoon. We should leave this place before the day is out," Maggie told Sadie. "I for one would like to be as far away from it as possible by nightfall."

After the first wagon was offloaded, Edwin piloted the raft back to where the rest of the company waited. "Who is next?" he called.

"We might as well get it over with," Bessie said. "Come, Evaline."

The girl, who had been drawing, closed her sketchbook and smiled at Bessie. "Shall you hold on to me or I on to you?" she asked.

"Either would ensure we would both fall off. Instead, we will hold on to the wagon." They waited until a wagon was secured on the raft. Then, along with other volunteers, they boarded the boat. The crossings went quickly after that, so quickly that William said they might even drive a few miles farther that day.

Most of the company was safely on the other side of the river when Maggie and Clara, accompanied by Penn and Dora, boarded. Maggie placed Clara in the wagon, then climbed in after her. Clara stood on a box of supplies so she could look out through the opening made by the puckered wagon cover, but Maggie lifted her down. "That is not safe. You might fall," Maggie said.

"I want to see out," Clara insisted.

"You can sit on my lap."

"I want out. I want Penn to hold me." Penn and Dora were standing on the raft outside the wagon.

"Penn cannot do that. She has to hold on to the wagon wheel or else she will fall into the water."

"She can hold me."

"No, Clara." Maggie held the wriggling child tight, annoyed that Clara was still obstinate. *What has gotten into you?* she wondered.

"No, Mama. Don't touch me. I am big. I can hold on myself." Clara pulled loose and went to the front of the wagon to see through the opening. The raft got under way then and swirled a little, and Clara caught hold of a box. "See, I can do it," she said. When the raft was steadied, she let go and twirled around. "Look, I do not have to hold on."

Before Maggie could catch her, Clara had climbed on top of the box again. Maggie rushed to grab her and held tightly to the little girl. "Behave, Clara! You will do as I say. The water is dangerous. Grab on to me."

Clara fussed, but she let Maggie grip her. The ride was smooth then, and Maggie told herself that she had worried needlessly about the crossing. The wagon box was deep. Maggie remembered how the men had chained it to the logs. She turned and stared through the opening and saw how far they had come. They were more than halfway now. She relaxed a little.

At that moment, a log submerged in the river struck the raft and sent it swirling. A box skidded across the wagon and caught Maggie's dress. She let go of Clara with one hand as she struggled to free herself, and at that, Clara jumped up onto the box, then climbed out onto the wagon seat.

"Look, there is Evaline. I see Evaline. She is drawing a picture of us. Evaline!" Clara called, but the noise of the river drowned out her voice, and Evaline did not hear her.

Maggie ripped her dress free and reached for her daughter, but Clara was standing on the edge of the wagon seat, trying to catch Evaline's attention. Evaline saw her then and waved, and Clara waved back with her free hand, then let go of the wagon cover to squash a mosquito that had landed on her cheek. The raft swirled, and as Maggie reached for her daughter, the craft was caught in the current and spun around, sending Clara tumbling off the seat. Maggie screamed, and Penn, holding on to the wagon, reached out for the girl, touching the tips of her fingers. She grabbed for Clara's hand, but Clara, instead of crawling toward Penn, tried to get to her feet. The raft lurched again, and Clara slid into the water.

"Clara!" Maggie called in terror.

Penn, holding on to the edge of the raft with

one hand, jumped into the water. "Where is she?" Penn yelled frantically. "I can't see her."

Maggie was out of the wagon then, searching for her daughter. "Clara! Clara!" she called, as if her voice would carry underwater. She glanced around the raft in the vain hope that Clara had clutched one of the logs and was safe. "Dear God, help me," she prayed, saying "help me" over and over again.

Once she thought she caught a glimpse of her daughter's yellow sunbonnet, but it was only a tree branch, and it sank into the churning, bubbling water. She stared at the spot where Clara had disappeared, thinking the little girl would pop up onto the surface. "Clara!" she screamed again as she went to the edge of the raft. She leaned forward, mesmerized by the water, ready to jump in, but Dora grabbed her. "You'll die," Dora yelled.

"I have to find her," Maggie said, trying to pull away.

"You cannot."

"Let go of me."

Dora held fast to Maggie's dress, risking her own safety, because another jolt would have sent them both into the river.

"She's gone, Maggie," Dora yelled.

"No. Let go. I will find her," Maggie said.

The men, who been on the other side of the wagon guiding the raft, failed to see Clara fall, but they heard the commotion, and Edwin rushed to Maggie and grasped her. "There is no hope, Mrs. Hale," he said. "No one, least of all a small child, could live in that current." He gripped her while Dora helped Penn back onto the raft. Penn was cold and shivering so hard that Dora held her tight.

At the far side of the river, Evaline had seen Clara fall into the water. She screamed and pointed. The others rushed to the bank while Mary jumped onto her horse bareback and forced him into the river. "Where is she?" she called, as she kicked the horse into the current. She looked at the raft for direction and then back at the women on the bank, but Clara had disappeared in the rushing water. She was gone.

Joseph, Caroline beside him, lifted Maggie off the raft. She was hysterical, at one moment calling Clara's name and at the other begging God to save her daughter. Caroline put her arms around Maggie and gripped her as if she were a small child. Maggie tried to pull away, but Caroline held her fast.

Sadie helped Penn, who was shaking, her teeth chattering, onto the ground, then wrapped her in a quilt and led her away to a wagon, where she could change into dry clothes, then sit by a campfire. The other women surrounded Maggie, their silence stronger than words of condolence.

Mary, who had ended her futile search for Clara and come back to the camp, joined them.

"She is with God," Caroline said.

"She is with little Dick," Mary added.

"But I want her with me," Maggie sobbed. "I must find her."

"God knows best," someone said.

"Then I hate Him."

"Do not blaspheme," a woman muttered.

"I think God would understand," Joseph told them gently.

"She was the best of us, the most innocent," Caroline said. "It is a crushing blow to lose her, but we must remember that God is with us in our grief. Your loss is greatest, but it is a tragedy for all."

"We had not counted her among the forty-four of you who joined the company in Chicago, but we must now, because she will always be one of us," Joseph said.

Maggie did not hear him. "Clara needs me. I must find her," she said.

They were all across now. There had been no more falls, no more accidents, and the women were safe—safe from the river crossing at least. They stood in small groups, silent, grieving, because Clara had indeed been one of them.

Maggie was not with them, however. She was following the two ministers along the riverbank as they searched for Clara's body. Caroline had tried to dissuade her, but Maggie shook her head. "She is my daughter. I must go. She will need me."

"Let her go," Mary told the others, then said to Maggie, "I will go with you." Maggie shook her head again, and Mary did not insist. Maggie trudged along behind the two men, absorbed in her own grief, paying little attention to what they said.

"I would follow this river a thousand miles if I thought we would find her," William told his brother-in-law. He stopped, then plunged into the willows lining the riverbank. The branches tore at his arms, which were already scratched and bleeding, his shirt ripped. "I thought I saw a splash of color, but it was only a bush," he said.

"We have come a long way already. I do not believe we will spot her. The water must have carried her for miles."

"Then I will continue to search for miles. You go on back, Joe. The women need you. You can offer them a solace that I cannot."

"They have need of you, too, Willie. You are far better at comforting the grieving than I."

"Not this time. I myself have too much grief. It is my fault. If I had not been impatient, we would have waited a day to let the water go down." He stretched out his hand at the river and said bitterly, "Look, the river has already subsided. And it did not rain."

"Blame God, but not yourself."

"Fine words for a minister, Joe. Yes, I blame God, but I blame myself, too, blame myself for so much. If I had not taken Anne west, she would be alive."

Joseph looked up, startled at the mention of William's wife's name. "Say no more of that. The blame is not yours."

Maggie glanced up as the two men stopped. She recalled vaguely the name Anne Parnell written on Independence Rock, but in her sorrow, the conversation meant nothing to her. She looked back at the river, searching. Clara might have been thrown up onto the bank. She would be cold.

Joseph looked back and said, "Walk beside us, Mrs. Hale."

"No, I shall follow." She held her grief close and did not want their words of comfort.

William studied her a moment but did not speak to her. Instead, he said to Joseph, as if Maggie were not there, "The blame is mine. This poor child's death is on my hands. We have no body to bury. So there will be no stone to mark her life. I used to think I was an instrument of the Lord. I even allowed myself to think that when I asked you to join me in putting together this company of women. I saw it as a way of making amends

271

for Anne's death. I thought she was directing me to do God's work. Now three of the company who trusted me are dead. How many more will die because of me?"

"And how many would have died if they had stayed at home—from tuberculosis or accidents or God knows what cause? They came willingly."

"Did Clara?"

Joseph thought about that for a moment. "I believe from what Mary has confided that you may have saved the child from a far worse death. You must let the Lord take this burden from you, Willie."

"He will not take it from Mrs. Hale."

"In time He will."

William didn't seem to be listening. He brushed away mosquitoes that were thick around his head. "Go on back, Joe. I shall continue the search alone." He turned to his brother-in-law. "Look at you, your clothes are torn, and you are covered with mud. What would your congregation think?"

"They would think—" Joseph stopped abruptly as Maggie screamed.

"There," she shouted. "There is Clara. We found her!" She pushed ahead of the ministers, then knelt in the water, holding her child's head in her hands. "Clara," she whispered. "It is Mama. Open your eyes. You are safe. I have you, Clara." She untied the ripped sunbonnet and threw it into the willows. She ran her fingers through Clara's wet hair, then touched the scratches on the child's face. "Wake up, Clara. There is a fire to warm you, and I will dress you in dry clothes. We will have soup for supper, and Penn will make strawberry ice cream." She picked up the child and held her close, water dripping from Clara's clothing.

"Let me take her," Joseph said.

"She is sleeping," Maggie told him.

Joseph reached for Clara, but Maggie would not give her up. "She is mine. I will carry her."

"She is too heavy. You must save your strength."

"She is mine."

William touched Joseph's arm, and Joseph was still. Together the two men, Maggie between them carrying Clara, trudged back up the river. Maggie was cold, her damp clothes weighed her down, and her arms ached. She stumbled along, tripping over dead branches, sliding in the mud, but she refused to relinquish her daughter. She would hold her forever. At last, they neared the camp, and William went on ahead to tell the women that Clara's body had been found.

Maggie saw them waiting for her and clutched Clara tighter, still refusing to let go of her. "She is sleeping. She is mine," Maggie said. "I want to hold her hand."

"She belongs to all of us, Maggie. She is gone. God is holding her hand now," Mary said, reaching for the child.

Maggie stared into the face of her daughter, touching the child's eyelids and her pale hair. Then, with a deep sigh, she relinquished the small body.

"I shall dress her in warm clothes. She will never be cold again," Mary said, then added, "Dick will keep her warm."

Maggie nodded.

"Wrap her in my blanket," Evaline said. Her face was drawn, and she had been crying.

"I picked flowers for her grave." Penn held a bouquet of wildflowers in her hand.

One by one, the women came forward, offering tokens or words of condolence. Maggie did not hear them.

The two ministers conducted a service for Clara, then buried her on a hillside far above the river. "Her final resting place should be dry and warm," Mary had said.

After the prayers were done and the hymns sung, the men began to dig the grave, but the women insisted on doing it themselves. Winny went first, taking a shovelful of dirt, then handing the shovel to Penn, who gave it to Bessie when she was finished, and so on until each of the women had taken a turn and the hole was deep enough. Just before Clara's body, wrapped in Evaline's blanket as a shroud, was lowered into the grave, Bessie reached down and cut a lock of the little girl's hair. Then Clara was buried, and the women shoveled dirt over the body and piled rocks on top of the dirt to keep coyotes and wolves from digging up the grave.

When it was over, the women walked solemnly back to camp. "How sad a thought to die so far from home," one commented, as she brushed tears from her eyes. "Her grave will be lost. Maggie will never find it again," said another.

Bessie stayed behind and unfastened a locket from her neck, one that she always wore because it contained a few strands of her first husband's hair. She removed the glass that secured the hair and held out her hand, letting the wind carry away the strands. Then she placed the lock of Clara's hair behind the glass. When the others were gone, Bessie came forward and gave the locket to Maggie.

Bessie left then, but Maggie stayed by the grave. She stretched her body beside it, her face against the damp earth. She could feel the cold in her bones. Mary found her there later on when she came back with a tin mug of tea and ordered Maggie to drink it. In her other hand, Mary carried a cross that she had made from two slats from the back of Bessie's rocker. Bessie had said they were oak and would last longer than pine or cottonwood. As Maggie held the cross, Mary pushed it into the ground at the head of the grave. Then, using a rock, she pounded it even deeper.

"The cross will last. Someday we will come back and find the grave and put up a proper stone," she said. To mark the grave even further, she lifted a huge rock shaped like an egg and set it in back of the cross.

Maggie ran her fingers over the crude letters that Mary had carved in the crosspiece, whispering each letter. "Clara Hale," Maggie said. "Her real name was Clara Kaiser."

"I know," Mary said. "But she is Clara Hale to all of us."

Maggie grasped Mary's hand and said, "I think she would like to live in eternity with the name of Clara Hale."

Fifteen

August 17, 1852
Great Salt Lake City

Clara would have liked the snow," Maggie murmured as she stared at the white mountaintops beyond South Pass. "I have never seen snow in summer."

"She would beg for snow ice cream," said Penn.

"That last Monday that we stayed in camp because of the rain, she wanted you to make ice cream," Maggie remembered. "That was before . . ." Her mind drifted off, and she could not finish.

"I'd climb up that mountain right this minute and get the snow for her," Penn said.

Maggie did not reply. She had barely spoken since Clara's death, but she had thought of little besides her loss. She once had told herself that her years with Jesse had been worth the pain because out of that agony had come Clara and Dick. Now both children were dead. The marriage had had no purpose besides heartbreak. Why had God given her a son and a daughter, then taken them away? What was the sense of it?

She tried to remind herself of the happy times, but she felt only grief. "Why?" she had asked the ministers.

Reverend Parnell had shaken his head and turned away, but Reverend Swain had replied, "I do not know the meaning of death, but there is meaning to life."

Some of the women maintained that it was best not to talk to Maggie about Clara, that Maggie would not want to be reminded of her loss. Those who shared Maggie's campfire believed otherwise, however. "You think she's going to forget Clara's death if you don't mention it?" Penn asked.

"Remembering Clara makes me happy," Evaline said. "I wish it would make Mrs. Hale happy, too." The night Clara was buried, Evaline stayed by the campfire for hours, drawing the girl's likeness. In the morning, she presented the portrait to Maggie, telling her, "It was Miss Mary's idea for me to draw it." Of course, Maggie thought. Clara was Mary's loss, too. And Evaline's. Caroline's and Sadie's and Dora's. The ministers'. At first Clara had been afraid of the two men. Jesse might have made her afraid of all men. But the preachers' kindness had eventually drawn her to them.

The picture Evaline had drawn was stored in Maggie's trunk, and several times each day, she took it out and stared at it as she fingered Bessie's locket, which she had not removed from her neck since Bessie had given it to her.

Those days following Clara's death had been hard for all of them, Maggie most of all, of course. The others tried to ease her grief by taking over her chores. When it was Maggie's turn, Penn harnessed the oxen and walked beside them on the trail, and Sadie and Bessie did Maggie's cooking. Dora, big with child now, took over the laundry. During the day, Maggie stumbled along behind the wagon, and at night, she sat staring into the campfire, until Mary told the others that Maggie was too caught up in sorrow, that doing her part would help heal her. So one night, Mary said, "It is your turn to cook, Maggie. You cannot sit idle."

Maggie, resting on the ground and staring out at the sage, looked up. At first she was surprised and then she was annoyed that others expected her to take over her duties when she was so wracked by sadness. She started to protest at the unfeelingness of Mary's demand, then saw the determination on her friend's face and rose and went to the wagon. She took out the beans and salt pork, the cornmeal and flour, and spent an hour preparing supper. Only after the meal was finished did she realize that as she had prepared it, she had put thoughts of Clara's death aside. The next day, without being asked, she went with Mary to harness the team.

Still, she treasured those moments of sadness that cloaked her and was reluctant to let them go. She had sorrowed over Dick's death, too, but she had still had Clara. Now she had no one.

She pondered all that, the might-have-beens, the what-ifs, wondering if she should have stayed in Chicago. She knew in her heart, however, that she had made the wise decision, the only one that would have taken Clara and her out of danger. Only it had not turned out as she had hoped. She should have been the one to die, not Clara. If only she could change places with her daughter. She could not, however. She was the one who lived.

Of course, she could join Clara. She could go back to Clara's grave and die. It was a coward's choice. Clara had not been a coward, and Maggie was not one either. Clara would want her to go on with the others, and to go on joyfully. That meant she must do her part. Nonetheless, the grief that weighed her down did not lift, and Maggie wondered if it ever would.

"We have crossed where the waters divide," William said one day.

"What's that?" Penn asked.

"At the west side of these mountains, the water in the rivers flows west, to the Pacific Ocean. On the east side, where we came from, it flows east."

"How does it know how to do that?"

"God tells it."

"Well, I hope He tells us how to get across them mountains."

The mountains rose ahead of them now, and Maggie was glad to leave the prairie, with its merciless sun. Although it was only August, the mornings were cold. In the early dew, the sage gave out a pungent odor.

Maggie was seasoned. She no longer felt the sand that worked its way into her moccasins. She walked miles on end without getting tired. Her eyes had stopped stinging from the campfire smoke. "We have been tried and not found wanting," Bessie told her. Maggie only nodded. Clara had not been found wanting, but that hadn't mattered. Maggie's thoughts were back at the Green River.

"The hardest part's behind us," Sadie continued.

"The hardest part hasn't even begun," William chided her. "There are mountains ahead and perhaps snow. We must hurry."

Sometimes they encountered travelers returning east who told them about the way ahead. "I would trade all the gold fields out there for just one acre of good Missouri land," one said.

"Turn back," another warned. "I seen hell, and its name is California."

Nearly everyone they encountered expressed wonderment that a group of women was going west to find husbands. Many had heard of the train of women from travelers who had passed them, and they stopped to stare. Some gave advice on which route to take.

William had hoped to take the train along an arid shortcut called the Sublette Cutoff because he believed it would save time, but the women protested. They wanted to follow the Mormon Trail to its end in Great Salt Lake City. Edwin encouraged them to take that route, promising that they would find a warm welcome among the Mormons—good food and a chance to replenish supplies.

"I would trade a week of my life for a fresh egg and a loaf of bread baked in a real oven," Bessie said.

The others began to talk about food then—puddings and cakes and pies. "Anything but vinegar pie," Penn said.

"Have they bathtubs?" Sadie asked.

"I would be happy just to be in a real house," Dora told Edwin.

"I believe the sympathy of our women will help you with your sorrow, Mrs. Hale," Edwin said to Maggie. He as much as the others had been solicitous of Maggie.

"We will need to find teamsters to replace the Mormon men who are leaving us," Joseph put in.

William looked at Edwin and the women, and shook his head. "I cannot fight all of you. We will take the Salt Lake route."

. . .

Maggie had not seen real civilization since she had left St. Joseph months earlier, and she was glad to reach Great Salt Lake City, which sat in a valley surrounded by mountain ranges. Penn stared at the buildings, most of them lumpy adobe squares set on streets that were white-hot from the midday glare. She pointed to a clapboard house and told Maggie, "I would like to live there."

Maggie nodded, not paying attention, and Sadie spoke. "Don't like it too much, Penn. Some polygamous Mormon is likely to snatch you up."

"Some what?" Penn looked confused.

"Polygamy. That is what Mormons do. It means they have more than one wife."

"They what?" Penn looked at Sadie in shock.

"Like in the Bible. The men have more than one wife," Maggie said, joining the conversation.

"I never was much for Bible reading on account of I can't read," Penn said. "How many do they have?"

Maggie turned to stare at a house where two women stood in the yard. "I do not know. Two or three. Maybe a hundred."

"A hundred! How could that husband remember all their names?"

"Maybe he gives them a number."

"Number Twenty-four, you come fix my supper," Penn said, and even Maggie smiled.

"Why, one man could marry all of us, and we wouldn't have to go on to California," Sadie remarked.

Penn thought a moment. "You think a woman could have two husbands here?"

Maggie shrugged. "Most likely it is against the law."

"When was the law ever a fair thing?" Mary asked.

"You mean the law lets a man have all the wives he wants, but a woman can't have all them husbands?" Penn asked.

Sadie smiled. "That is the way of it, since men are in charge."

"Well, maybe it's just as well. What would I do with two men ordering me around? What if they didn't want the same thing for supper?" Penn thought a moment. "I guess that's all right. I wouldn't want two men that could beat me. I already had me one."

"So did I," Maggie said softly.

"Then it's a good thing your husband's dead."

Penn asked Edwin what the polygamous wives were like. He laughed. "Why, just like women everywhere. I myself have two and intend to take more. Our women like nice houses and pretty dresses. They cook and wash and raise children. The women are happy with the arrangement. They help each other in times of trouble or loss. Those who are barren share the children of sister wives."

284

"Well, I wouldn't like it," Sadie told him.

"You might if your salvation depended on it," he replied.

Joseph, who had been listening, interrupted. "It is immoral. Polygamy is a sin."

"The prophets in the Bible practiced it," Edwin told him. "Abraham had two wives. Do you believe the Bible is wrong?"

"Nonetheless . . ." Joseph didn't finish.

"The first wife has to approve before her husband takes another wife," Edwin continued.

Caroline interrupted. "I would never say yes to a second wife."

"And I would never ask you," Joseph said.

"Still, it would be nice to have someone to help with the washing," Caroline added, glancing sideways at her husband.

"Caroline!" he said, and she bowed her head to hide a smile.

Maggie discovered she and the other women were of great interest to the Mormons. News that they were going to California to find husbands had made the rounds of the city, and several men called at the camp and asked to escort them to a dance the Mormons were holding that night. Most of the women said no, but a few agreed to attend, including Maggie. She had not wanted to go, but Mary insisted, and it was easier to give in to Mary than to argue with her.

When they arrived, they stared at the groups of women clustered around men. Several of those women were grandmothers, but many were barely into their teens.

"I expect those are their harems," Mary said.

"Look how pretty some of the women are. I thought they would be old and dried up. And their dresses!" Winny remarked, looking down at her own faded and patched calico. "What do you think of them, Maggie?"

Maggie had not paid attention to the women's clothing, but now she studied it. "Most appear homemade, but there must be professional dress-makers among them, for many of the garments are as fashionable as those in Chicago. Someone has studied *Peterson's Magazine* and *Godey's Lady's Book* and copied the latest styles."

"So many of the women are pregnant," Dora observed. "It seems that every third one is expecting a baby." She, too, had been reluctant to go to the dance, because her own pregnancy was advanced, and her arm, while healed, still ached from the break. She stared at the Mormons, who in turn stared at the little company of women.

"I wonder if they are appraising us as wives," Bessie said.

"We will be in your city only another day, so we will not be looking for husbands here," Maggie told a woman who greeted them.

"Sometimes it does not take that long. I myself

married a man after I knew him but two hours."

"I would not suppose one would decide so quickly about true love."

"True love!" the woman scoffed. "I had little choice. He wanted to take two brides at one time, and the other was already chosen. There were several who would have stepped in if I had refused."

"Marry in haste, repent in leisure," Dora whispered to Maggie.

The woman overheard. "Life may be difficult on this earth, but I shall have my reward in heaven. He is a high-ranking member of the church." She looked the women over. "It is a pity you are not among us. He is a good husband, and with so many other wives, he does not bother me too often."

Despite their drab clothing and skin roughed by the sun and wind, the women were quickly approached by the men, even Dora. No one cared about her state. Several men were attracted to Mary, who forgot to put her hand over her bad eye. That did not deter them from requesting her as a partner. By the time they left, the women believed the Mormons were decent, welcoming people, albeit with strange customs.

As they walked back to the wagons, Mary confessed, "I had a proposal of marriage."

"After one dance?" Winny asked. Then she inquired slyly, "Are you of a mind to accept?"

"He told me I would have my own bedroom, and he would buy me a plow and a mule."

"He is a romantic, then," Maggie told her. "Was he the handsome Dane you danced with?"

"It was the Dane's father, the man with one arm."

"Does he have teeth?"

"Of course. I counted three."

"Then we shall know where you have gone if you are not with us in the morning," Dora teased.

"Oh, I think I shall not marry him," Mary said, shaking her head. "It seems he saw me riding on the red horse, and it is the horse he admires. He said by way of proposal that he wanted me to sell the horse to him at a good price, but if I would not do so, then the only way he could see to acquire it was to marry me."

"He has a way with words," Maggie said.

The next day, Mary, Sadie, and many of the other travelers explored the city, but a few remained with the wagons. Dora, tired from the dancing the night before, stayed behind with Maggie, who was stitching a quilt. Stitching soothed her.

"Will you help me with the baby?" Dora asked.

Maggie looked up, startled. "Why?"

"I know so little about them, and I do not believe there are any other mothers among us. You are the only one."

"I should think you would not want me near it."

"You were not responsible for Clara's death."

Maggie shook her head. "Then why do I feel I am?"

Dora was silent a moment, then asked, "Did you want Clara? I heard you say your husband beat you. Did you want the baby?"

"Yes, after a time," Maggie said. "You did not want yours, did you?" She made a knot and bit off the thread. *Was there thread for sale in Great Salt Lake City?* she wondered. But of course there was. With a place so full of women, how could there not be? She would purchase some before she left.

Dora shook her head.

"But you do now."

"More than anything in the world. I love her so much." Dora put her hands over her stomach as if protecting the child.

"A girl, then?"

"I hope so."

"Some believe they are the best kind."

Edwin interrupted them. "I have been looking for a chance to talk to you away from the others." He smiled, and the two women nodded at him. "I have two houses. My first and second wives live in one of them. The other is rented, but I will ask the couple living there to move. There is a feather bed and pillows and a rocker and a rug. My father is a high-ranking member of the church, and I have had a blessing telling me that I will rise even higher. I am clean in my habits and have never hit either wife. I am the owner of a prosperous farm. My wives would not object to enlarging my kingdom. I believe I can offer a good life."

Maggie was bewildered and exchanged a glance with Dora, who looked confused, too.

"Well? Are you agreeable?"

"To what?" Maggie asked.

"To marriage."

"To you?"

He looked around and grinned. "I do not see anyone else."

"But which one of us is your object?" Dora asked.

Edwin grinned. "Why, both of you, of course. I would marry both of you in one ceremony. I have observed that you are compatible with each other and would be happy as sister wives. I have asked my wives, and they say they would welcome you."

Maggie and Dora looked at each other, and although they tried not to, both began to chuckle. "Oh, do forgive us. It is all so strange," Maggie said.

Edwin looked hurt. "I will be a good husband, and I chose you because you both are in need. You are going west in hopes of finding husbands, and I believe I am better than any of the men you will meet in California."

Maggie bit her lip to stop the smile, then said, "Edwin, we are sensible of the honor, but it would never do for me—or for Dora either, I believe." She glanced at Dora, who nodded. "It is quite out of the question."

"I would provide a home for your child," he told Dora, then said to Maggie, "And I would give you more children. I am a robust man."

"I can see that," Maggie agreed. Then, trying to spare Edwin's feelings, she added, "As you know, we have agreed to marry in California. It would cause us discomfort if we were to go against our promise."

Edwin argued for a moment, but nothing he said dissuaded the two women. Both tried to keep solemn faces. They waited until Edwin was out of earshot, then Dora burst out laughing, and Maggie joined her. Maggie laughed so hard that she doubled over, and when she stopped, there were tears in her eyes. "Imagine!" she said.

"Did he really think we would accept?"

"I believe so. I have never heard anything so preposterous in my life." Maggie wiped her eyes with her sleeve.

Dora studied her friend for a moment, then said, "I have not heard you laugh since . . ."

Maggie thought that over, then nodded. "I believe now I shall get better."

· · ·

Edwin must not have been too heartbroken that
Maggie and Dora turned down his proposal,
because he promised to escort both of them,
along with several other women, to a mercan-
tile that afternoon. Maggie went along to buy
thread.

Edwin pointed out the sights as they walked to
the business district—the stores and houses and
church buildings that the Mormons had erected
in only five years. The women spread out along
the street, dawdling a little, since it was a rare
day of leisure.

Penn stared at four women gathered in a yard
and wondered, "Is them those sister wives?"

"I believe so," Maggie said.

Penn started to reply, then stopped and gasped.
Maggie turned to see that her friend was watching
two men come down the street, one on horseback,
the other driving a wagon. Penn froze, a look of
anguish on her face. One of the men pointed at
her, and Penn started to run. He galloped after
her and grasped her arm.

"Looky who's here. Ain't it Penn House? We
been looking for you, Penn, been looking since
St. Joe." He jumped off his horse.

The other man caught up. "Ain't much of a
welcome you give us when we come all this way
just to find you. Elias there, he wanted to take
the cutoff, but I says you being a woman and all,

you'd want to go this way so's you could buy yourself some pretties."

"Where's Asa at, Reed?" Penn whispered.

"Funny thing, we was going to ask you the same thing, only we know."

"Know what?"

Reed turned to his brother. "Ain't that cute? She's asking about Asa, like she don't know he's killed."

"Asa's dead?" Penn looked down, as if she were sorry.

"Like you don't know."

"I'm real sorry, Reed," Penn said. "Me and Asa had us some good times."

Reed sneered. "Likely you killed him. We was at Kearny when they found his body. Soldiers said there was a bunch of women camped there. They said it was robbery, but Asa still had his gold on him, only he didn't have something else, something you taken off him in St. Joe."

"I don't know what you're saying."

"I guess you do, and you'll tell where it's at before long." He reached out and slapped her, and Penn fell to the ground, her mouth bloody. "Now you come along real quiet, and we won't do nothing to your friends."

Maggie hurried to defend Penn, as did Edwin and the other women.

"You have no business here, sir. You will release Miss House," Caroline said.

Elias stared at her while his brother came to stand next to Penn. "It ain't your business, lady. We're taking her with us," Reed said.

"No, you are not," Edwin told him.

"You going to stop us, Mormon?"

"I and the others." He nodded at half a dozen Mormon men who had come up behind the Harveys.

Elias turned and stared at the men. "Ain't your affair neither. She's our brother's wife, a grieving widow. We're taking her home."

"I wasn't never married to him, Elias. I ain't going with you," Penn told him.

"We'll ask you to leave the lady alone," one of the men said.

"God damn you, you go to hell!" Reed yelled.

"You will not take the Lord's name in vain, sir, not in His holy city."

Elias, furious, grabbed a pistol from his belt and aimed it at the man, ready to fire, but before he could pull the trigger, one of the Mormon men shot him. As Elias dropped to his knees, Reed reached for his own pistol and fired at one of the Mormons. In the melee, he, too, was wounded and fell to the dirt, writhing. The Mormon men put down their guns.

Edwin rushed to the wounded Mormon and put his head to the man's chest. "He's dead."

"So's this one, and the other's hurt bad," an elder said, examining the Harvey brothers.

Two Mormons gripped Reed's arms and dragged him to a wagon. Reed was conscious, and he glared at Penn, hatred in his eyes. "You killed them, Penn. You killed Asa and now Elias. You ain't never going to get away. I'll hunt you down. Don't you never sleep through a night without being afraid of me."

Edwin stood and took Penn's hands. "You do not need to worry, Miss House. He will hang—that is, if he does not die first."

Sixteen

August 21, 1852
The California Trail

The Mormons loaded the bodies of Elias and the dead elder onto the cart with Reed and hauled them off. "Reed'll get away and come for me. I'm not never going to get free of them Harvey boys," Penn said. "I can't never hide where he won't find me."

"We should be underway," Mary told the ministers, after the women returned to the wagons and explained what had happened. "Penn is badly frightened that Asa's brother will escape and come after her. And I believe she may be right."

"We leave tomorrow," Joseph said.

"Today," Mary told him. "Now."

"Some of you still have shopping to do, and there is to be a theater performance tonight to which we have all been invited," Joseph said. "We had hoped to purchase a cow, as our last one died near the Green River. Most important, we need to find men to replace those who have left us here."

"We are ready to leave now," Maggie said. "All

of us. We will help do the men's work. We are every bit as good as they are." The others nodded in agreement.

"It is foolish to leave so late in the day. We would go only a few miles. We do not need to rush," Joseph told them. "Reed Harvey will be locked up. He cannot follow us."

"We outnumber you," Mary said. "We leave now. The women have agreed we must protect Penn. You can catch up with us tomorrow."

Joseph sighed and asked his wife, "When have these women grown so bold?"

They made seven miles that day, twenty the next, and before the week was out, they were far from Great Salt Lake City. They were well over halfway on their journey now. Maggie believed the dust and the wind and the blistering sun of the Great Plains were done with. It would be cooler in the mountains. As conflicted as she was over Clara's death, she was proud that she had survived the hardships. At the beginning of the trip, she had wondered if she would be up to the mark. Now she found that she kept up easily with the others and was stronger than most. As the days passed, she felt more alive than she had at any time since Clara died. What was more, she did not worry so much now about being pursued.

She realized before long that she was wrong

about the trail ahead being easier. There were mountains all the way to California. In the distance, they were beautiful—majestic snow-capped monoliths, with forests of green pines, but Maggie knew that when she reached them, she would discover steep grades and rock out-croppings. She longed for the smooth swaths of prairie that made easy work for the oxen.

"I had thought there would be marked roads," Maggie told William.

He shook his head. "All we can do is follow the trails and when two cross, hope we choose the right one."

"But what about the guidebooks? Should we not consult them?" In Great Salt Lake City, she had seen half a dozen different guides to the gold fields.

"As useless as the maps to hidden gold mines. Some are written by men who have never crossed the Missouri." The California Trail, he explained, was well known to Fort Laramie, but soon after that, it split into one cutoff after another.

"Do *you* know where we are going?" Maggie asked.

"Of course," he said. "We continue west."

"How far?" she asked a teamster who had said he had made the journey before.

The man shook his head. "A right smart dis-tance."

. . .

Maggie sensed the uncertainty of some of the women. Despite the setbacks and even the deaths on the first part of the journey, they had kept up their spirits. They had formed a bond, but now that bond seemed to splinter. Some women began to question the wisdom of the trip. A few even wondered if they might have been better off sharing a husband in the Mormon city.

"Would it be so bad?" one of them asked Maggie. "I would have someone to help with the washing and cooking and caring for the children. It would be almost as if I had a servant."

"Unless *you* were *her* servant," Maggie replied.

"Edwin was quite handsome. Perhaps it would not be so bad to be one of three wives," the woman continued. By now the others knew that he had proposed to Maggie and Dora.

"He did not promise not to take more. You might end up one of ten or twenty."

As the emigrants considered the eight hundred miles ahead of them, some of them grumbled. Sadie looked at her hands, roughened and sunburned, and touched her face. "It must appear as weathered as leather," she said.

"Perhaps it is a good thing you do not have a mirror with you," said Maggie, who cared little about her appearance.

"Do you think men in California would really find us attractive? Perhaps they will remember the girls at home with smooth faces and reject us because we have grown old crossing the prairie and the mountains. What if no one wants me?"

"You are still the prettiest one among us," Maggie told her. "If you do not find a husband who suits you, then you can join me as a dressmaker. We are like sisters now."

"You do not intend to marry?"

"I . . ." Maggie did not finish. Although Jesse was dead, Maggie did not concern herself much with marrying.

There were disagreements and complaints among the emigrants now as they trudged along the trail. The harsh and tasteless meals affected their digestion, and the glare of the sun, stronger now at the higher altitude, burned their skin and gave them headaches. They encountered bodies of dead and dying oxen as well as discarded trunks and mining equipment, clothing and luxuries. Maggie picked up a comb someone had thrown away and shook her head. "Such a small thing. It could not lighten the load even an ounce."

One woman confided to Maggie that she no longer wanted to "see the elephant." But now it was too late. They had long since crossed the midway point, and it would take more time to go back to Chicago than to proceed to California. "Besides, where would I get the money to return home?"

Some began to argue among themselves. Penn complained after a wagon crowded in line in front of her, and Maggie was furious when a woman picked up a piece of kindling she had dropped and refused to give it back. Sadie lashed out at Dora for serving beans that were undercooked. "Did you not soak them?" she demanded.

Dora lowered her head and said, "I shall do better next time."

Sadie was not placated. "Edwin's wives don't know how lucky they are you didn't marry up with him."

"Sadie!" Caroline admonished her, then told Dora, "I once burned up an entire turkey when I was a bride. Undercooked beans are a small thing."

Sadie, appalled at her own words, hung her head.

Another woman turned on her tent mate when she discovered the woman not only was using her prize quilt but had put it too close to the fire and scorched it. "That quilt is the finest I ever made. I was saving it for my wedding night," she said, anger in her voice.

The culprit only laughed. "If you were not so ugly, your husband would pay more attention to you than to your quilt."

The woman was furious and slapped her tent mate, who slapped her back. In a moment, the two were on the ground, scratching and clawing at each other. Mary tried to separate them, but it was William who thundered, "Stop at once! Any more of this, and you both will be put out of the train!"

"You would not dare," one of the women said.

"I will not allow such behavior! If you would act like animals, then I shall cast you out to live like them."

Maggie looked at William in astonishment. Would he really banish the women?

"We will pray for them," Joseph said.

"Pray?" William thundered. "Discipline is more important than prayer." He shook his head and walked a little away from the camp.

The two women, chastised, did not look at each other, but the one who had scorched the quilt picked it up and folded it, handing it to its owner. "I am ashamed," she whispered.

"We must all do better or we will never make it to California," Mary told Maggie. Mary looked at the women around them. "We had forged a closeness, and now it is being sundered with pettiness. We must try harder to work together."

Sadie went to Dora then and said, "You are tired. I will clean the pots and plates for you."

As the women went back to their wagons, William asked Caroline, "What have I done to these women? What have I done to you?"

"You have given them a future. They complain,

but I believe not one in ten would want to go back to their lives in Chicago."

"Some have died, the little girl Clara among them."

"Might she not have died at home?"

Maggie, overhearing the remark, pondered it.

They had all heard of City of Rocks. It was near where the trail split, one part going to California, the other to Oregon. It was out of the way. Indeed, the stone city was difficult to access from their route, but the women begged to see it, and William, perhaps believing they needed some relief from their frightening experience in Great Salt Lake City, agreed to the delay. "We will consider it an excursion," he told Maggie.

She had expected a settlement of some size. Instead, she found herself in an encirclement of granite rocks in freakish shapes and of all textures and colors. Someone had used axle grease to write "Hotel" on one and "Our House" on another. Bessie declared it was the most wondrous site on the entire journey.

Evaline clapped her hands when she saw the rocks. "It is like a castle," she told Maggie, who knew how much Clara—and Dick, too—would have liked to play among the monoliths.

"To think we ever questioned whether Evaline should come on this trip," Caroline said. "She is one of the best of us." She told Bessie, "I believe her mother is smiling down on her—and on you. Not many women would undertake the responsibility of raising a Negro orphan."

"She brings me much joy. She is an intelligent girl, and she takes care of me."

"Indeed. She could not be more solicitous of you if she were your own flesh and blood." Maggie said, putting her hand to her mouth, embarrassed, hoping that Bessie was not angered by such an outrageous remark.

Bessie only laughed. "You do not offend. If she were white, I would indeed claim her as my own."

Evaline found Bessie sitting on a rock formation with Maggie. "Come, ma'am, you must see the rocks. Why, one of them is hollow. We must remember it in case of an Indian attack." She smiled at Maggie. "Clara would have played hide-and-seek in it." Many of the women were careful about mentioning the little girl, but Evaline had no such trepidation, and that pleased Maggie. She did not want Clara to be forgotten. Evaline held out her hands to the two women, who let themselves be led among the formations. She exclaimed over every monolith and column, every terrace and dome, each one more fanciful than the last. The excitement was contagious, and the two women were caught up in the girl's good spirits.

"We could live here," Evaline told Bessie, rushing from one rock to another. "We could plant your apple trees here and let them grow into an orchard." She stopped beside a boulder that was striated in purple and orange and gold. "Does it not look like a home from a storybook? I should have brought my sketchbook."

As the three walked back to camp, Evaline said it was her turn to prepare supper. "Beans! How would you like beans for your supper, ladies? And a surprise. I found a cluster of lamb's-quarters, enough for all of us."

When they reached the wagon, Evaline looked at the rock formations. "I should like to draw them at night. Do you think there will be a moon?"

Bessie turned stern. "Stay close to the wagons, Evaline. Who know what roams out there after dark?"

The sun had barely set when Maggie spread her tarp on the ground. The evening was pleasant, so the women had not erected tents. They wrapped themselves in quilts and blankets, and within minutes, the sounds of sleep were mixed with the lowing of the oxen and the stamping of the horses. There was no mooing of cows, however; the last one had died before they reached Great Salt Lake City, and there had not been time to replace it.

Despite the pleasant evening, Maggie could not sleep. She stared up at the stars, then watched as the moon rose, a half-moon the shape of a worn-out coin. The day had been a good one. She had loved the weird rock shapes and thought of City of Rocks as a fairyland, one that would indeed have enchanted Clara. The idea of Clara romping in the moonlight made Maggie smile. She was glad for the picture of her daughter that Evaline had drawn in her mind.

The night was peaceful, but still, sleep did not come. Maggie was not worried. After all, one of the teamsters was guarding them. They had been remiss in not finding more men, but the women themselves had proven capable of taking on many of the responsibilities of those who had left them in Great Salt Lake City. Maybe it was the fantasy of Clara that kept her awake, or her longing for both her children. Daytimes were crowded with activity, but the nights were lonely, and that was when thoughts of Dick and Clara swirled most in her mind.

After a time, she heard someone rise and walk quietly toward the rocks. Maggie sat up and spotted Evaline. The girl was in her nightdress, and she carried her sketchbook under her arm. She was going to draw the rocks in the moonlight after all.

Maggie turned over and closed her eyes, but again, she did not sleep. She began to think about Evaline out there alone. She might fall and break an arm or hit her head. There could be rattlesnakes or wolves prowling through the rocks. Maggie thought of waking Bessie, but she knew Bessie would be angry at the girl for disobeying her, and Maggie did not want to cause trouble for Evaline. Instead, she rose and quietly made her way to City of Rocks.

She crept among the monoliths, intending at first to call Evaline's name, but she did not want the girl to think she was spying on her. Then she saw her, perched on a rock. The moonlight on Evaline's white nightdress made her seem ethereal.

The girl was sharpening her pencil with a penknife. When she was satisfied with the lead, she put aside the knife and opened the sketchbook and began to draw, shifting a little so that her shadow did not fall on the paper. She drew quickly, glancing up at the sky from time to time as if wondering whether clouds would cover the moon and make it too dark to draw.

Evaline was such a pretty picture that Maggie lingered for a few moments to watch her. Then she turned back toward the wagons before Evaline could spot her and realize that she had been spied upon. That would spoil something pure and innocent. Maggie was almost sorry she had come, and she started back toward the camp. She was halfway there when she heard a cry, a cry so low that it did not carry to the sleeping women.

For a moment, she hesitated. The sound was probably nothing, but she couldn't be sure. Then Maggie heard a man's voice saying, "Little colored girl thinks she's too fine for me. Don't know her place."

Evaline murmured something that sounded like a plea, and then Maggie heard the man's voice again. "You make any noise, I'll kill you." There was the sound of cloth ripping—Evaline's nightdress, Maggie thought. She started for the camp to rouse the guard, then realized there was not time. She crept forward and saw Evaline lying on the ground. A man stood above her, and Maggie thought at first that he was one of the ministers. She saw him reach for Evaline's breast.

"Let's have a look at the little darkie," the man said. Evaline cried out, and the man slapped her.

The slap startled Maggie, and she took a step forward. She had hesitated when the soldier attacked her, but she would not do so now. "Stop it," she said. She could not control her voice, and instead of being commanding, it sounded weak and ineffectual. The man turned to her, and she recognized him as one of the teamsters, Green Holt. He was on guard duty that night.

"Get away," the man growled. "This is 'tween

me and her. Little whore asked for it. She been teasing me for a long time. She ain't never had a white man before. You go on back and keep your mouth shut or you'll get the same."

"How dare you threaten her! Stop it, or I will call the ministers," Maggie said.

"They can't hear you way over here." Evaline struggled, and he said, "You hold still, you black cat."

"Help me. Please," Evaline whimpered. She flailed around, and Maggie saw that several of the sketches had been torn out of the sketchbook and were crumpled on the ground. How could he spoil the precious drawings and the innocent girl who had made them! Maggie's anger gave her strength. "Stop it!" she yelled as loudly as she could. She grabbed a stick and hit Green Holt with it.

He wrestled the stick from her and flung it aside. Then he struck Maggie. She fell backward, and Green told her he'd take her after Evaline. He reached back again with his fist, but instead of striking her a second time, he screamed and pitched forward over Evaline. Maggie remembered the penknife Evaline had used to sharpen her pencil and thought at first that the girl had stabbed him. Then she looked up and saw a man standing over them with a whip.

The whip snaked through the air, and Green screamed again. He was lying on the ground, his hands over his head, when the lash hit him a third time. "Stop!" he begged. "I ain't done nothing."

"Scum!" the man with the whip said. "You will not have carnal knowledge of this girl! Stand up, you filth!"

The second man's back was to her, and Maggie could not see his face, but she recognized the voice of Reverend Parnell. She crawled over to the girl and covered her with the torn nightdress.

"Get up," William ordered, and Green slowly rose to his feet, his hands in front of him to ward off any more lashings.

"What you done that for?" Green asked. "She ain't nothing but a darkie whore. You can have at her when I'm done. You can even go first. Or I'll take the other one, even though she ain't fresh."

William hit Green across the face with the whip handle, striking him back and forth, breaking his nose. "You will not speak in such a manner about these women!"

Green put his hand over his nose, which was bleeding. "You ought to whip *her.* She asked me to meet her here. Begged me."

Evaline was so stunned she couldn't speak. Maggie thought of the dragoon who had attacked her, and she put her arms around the girl, both of them shivering.

She turned to see Joseph running toward them. Green's screams had awakened the camp. Several women held fagots, and Maggie could see their white faces. She tightened her arms around Evaline, knowing the girl wanted to creep away and hide. Maggie did, too. Her own nightdress was torn and stained, and she clutched it to her.

"I guess we got one or two more wants to try the whore," Green said. William stared at the man for a moment, then raised his whip handle and struck him again and again. Green screamed in pain, but William would not stop.

Joseph reached them and grabbed the whip. "For God's sake, Willie, it is enough."

"He accosted the girl," William explained. "I should kill him."

"You stopped him."

"We never should have come to this place. It is my fault. I should have insisted we stay on the trail." William shook his head back and forth. "I could not sleep, so I thought I would pray out here among the rocks. I brought the whip in case of snakes. I heard Mrs. Hale cry out. She got here first. Then I saw him—"

William reached for the whip, but Joseph refused to give it up. "You have punished him enough."

"No, Joe. Not by half."

"You are banished from our train," Joseph told Green.

The other men reached them, and one asked, "What did he do?"

"He attacked a member of our company."

The teamster looked around and spotted Evaline, sobbing in Maggie's arms. "It's only the colored girl. It ain't like he done it to a white woman."

William turned to him in fury. "I will not allow anyone to speak thus. Green Holt will leave our company. If you or any of the others say another word against this young woman, you will be asked to join him. I will whip any man who dares to touch her—or any of the other women."

The men muttered, stealing glances at Evaline. Maggie looked up to see several women halfway between the wagons and the rocks. Bessie was among them, and when she saw Evaline, she ran to the girl. She didn't say a word, only grabbed Evaline and held her.

Maggie put her arms around herself to stop her shaking, then felt a hand on her shoulder and looked up to see Mary, who picked her up and carried her back to the wagon. "You protected her. Now it is our turn to protect you," Mary said.

As they left the rocks, Maggie heard William order Green to collect his things and leave immediately.

In the morning, all the men except for William and Joseph were gone.

Seventeen

A ll of them?" Maggie asked when Reverend Swain told her. She was incredulous. "All of the men have deserted us?"

"It appears that way," Joseph said.

Mary, standing nearby, gasped, and the others stared open-mouthed.

"Joe and I searched the camp, but there is no trace of them," William continued. "Their belongings are gone, and they took several horses, along with as many of our supplies as they could carry. They probably would have taken Miss Madrid's horse, but he was tied close to where she slept. Besides, I believe they feared her wrath," William said.

"It is your wrath that frightens them," Joseph told him.

"Perhaps, but I could not stop myself. He called the girl a darkie whore." William's face was twisted.

"I understand. We are both charged with protecting the women."

William looked off into the distance for a moment, oblivious to the others. "I should not have been so rash. I offended the Lord. At times it seems as if I am not myself."

Joseph put his hand on his brother-in-law's shoulder. "Do not trouble yourself over it. The man committed a sin against the girl and against God. You did what was right. I hope, if called upon, I would have the courage to do that same thing."

Penn put her arm around Maggie and held her close. "You will be all right," she said, and Maggie understood all too well what Penn had gone through with Asa and his brothers. She was grateful for Penn, who had moved her quilt to Maggie's side and stayed with her through the night.

"We are in a precarious situation," William said. "We cannot proceed without the men."

The rest of the women were gathered around the ministers now. The entire camp was aware of what had happened to Evaline, and it sickened them. They were shocked that such a man as Green Holt had traveled with them for months, and Maggie believed that each must wonder what would have happened if she had been alone with the teamster.

Evaline blamed herself. When Maggie went to see her after sunrise, she had said over and over again, "I am sorry, Mrs. Hale. I did wrong, and you were hurt, too."

"You did no wrong," Maggie said, taking the girl's hand. "He is an evil man."

"If you had not come . . ." Evaline whispered.

She plucked at a thread on her fresh nightdress. Maggie had seen the remains of the torn gown in the campfire. Evaline's face was bruised and scratched, and it appeared she had rubbed it raw. "He spit on me. It felt like a burn on my face," she said.

Maggie nodded. Evaline clutched her arm. "Stay," she begged. So Maggie remained beside Evaline that morning until the girl went to sleep, then slipped outside.

Now she stood with the other women as William declared, "We cannot go on alone."

"We will have to go back to Great Salt Lake City and find other men who want to travel with us to California," Joseph said. "We will ask for Mormon men. I believe they are more trustworthy."

"How could you find them now when you did not before?" Mary asked. "Besides, backtracking would cost us weeks, and Reverend Parnell complains we are already late."

"Why don't we join another train?" Penn asked.

"Would they take us?" Sadie wondered. "Who wants thirty-seven extra women?"

"Surely there are men traveling in twos and threes who would join us," Caroline said.

William shook his head. "Have you studied those men? Several have asked to accompany us already because they are sick or out of supplies. I fear they would be little help, and even if they were healthy enough to do the work, we could not trust them not to rob us and be on their way, just like Green Holt and the others."

"Then we cannot go forward," Joseph said.

"I am afraid that is so. We must return to the Salt Lake and wait there. We will start out again in the spring."

Maggie glanced at Penn, whose face was twisted. She knew the girl was thinking of Asa's brother. Neither Penn nor Maggie was convinced that Reed Harvey would die or be hanged. What if he got away and found Penn in Great Salt Lake City? He would kill her. If the company went back, she might never leave the Mormon settlement alive. Returning could consign Penn to death.

Mary took Penn's hand. "I do not intend to wait a year to reach California."

The other women muttered their agreement.

William shrugged. "There is no other way."

"There *is* another way," Mary said, as the women quieted and stared at her. "We will go on alone."

"Without men?" William asked.

"Why not?"

"We cannot allow it," Joseph said.

"We know how to drive the oxen and how to make camp. We have learned how to repair the wagons and doctor the animals," Maggie said.

"What if Indians attack?" William asked.

"We are up to the mark with our guns. After all, we held off the Indians before," Maggie told him. "Mary can shoot as well as any man. So can Penn. I say we are as good as the men who deserted us. Maybe better."

"No," William said. "The worst part of the journey is ahead of us. It is too much to ask of you."

"If it was not too much to ask us to make this journey, why do you refuse to let us complete it?" Maggie asked. "If you do not care to go, then we shall continue without you."

"I believe we could do it," Caroline said, raising her chin. "Time will turn back before we will."

Joseph looked at her in shock. "You would go on without me?"

Caroline blushed. "Not willingly, Joseph, but I cannot desert these women. I believe God wants me to attend them."

Joseph stared at his wife. "Against my will?"

"Perhaps it is God's will."

Joseph turned and looked at the mountains to the west. Then his shoulders fell in defeat. "I believe we have been bested, Willie. The women will not go back, and we cannot stay here. We have no choice but to go on."

The women cheered at that, but William cautioned them. "It will not be easy. You will be challenged as you have not been yet. More of you could die."

"We might just as well die if we went back," Mary countered, glancing at Penn. Then she added, "We will put it to a vote. If more than five vote no, we will return to the Salt Lake."

The women looked at each other. Joseph and William, too, exchanged glances.

Maggie saw the look and added, "Only women vote." She raised her voice and said, "All wishing to go on, vote yes."

There was a chorus of yesses.

"Those who wish to return, vote no."

One or two opened their mouths as if to speak but did not, and in the end, the vote was unanimous.

"Let us move out," Winny called.

William held up his hand. "It is not so easy. With the men gone, we must leave at least one of the wagons behind, and that means lightening the loads again. You must go through your belongings once more."

Maggie suddenly realized what they were asking of themselves. Many of them were already exhausted. A few were sick. Still, Maggie would never vote to go back.

In the end, the company abandoned the two poorest wagons. The women searched their trunks and discarded items they had once thought indispensable. Mary took out her mother's teapot, touched her finger to the tiny pink flowers, and set it gently on a rock. Maggie stared at the teapot, and when Mary walked away, Maggie picked it up and hid it among her things. She would carry it in her apron if she had to and give it to Mary when they reached California.

Bessie refused to abandon her apple trees but added her rocking chair to the pile. Maggie placed the doll she had made for Clara among the discards, then turned away, tears in her eyes. She had nothing left that had belonged to either of her children. Winny, touched by the sacrifice, wrapped it in her spare dress, and in the doll's place, she left a framed drawing of her parents.

By late afternoon, the remaining wagons were packed, and William gave the order to move out, although they would not go more than a mile or two that day. The women were apprehensive, but they were excited, too, and proud of themselves. Not until they made camp late that afternoon did they realize how much work they had taken on. They were tired, and their muscles ached more than ever, and there was still supper to prepare, the animals to take care of, and wagon wheels to be greased and repaired. They were surprised at how much work the men had undertaken, work that now fell on them. Mary had already done men's chores, and she instructed the others. The women were silent, overwhelmed, as they realized what they had agreed to do. They had voted to continue, however, and they would not be deterred. In just a few hours, the excitement of going ahead without the men had worn off. Maggie understood now what it meant to be on their own.

Mary began greasing a wagon hub, but Maggie came up to her and gently shoved her aside. "I can handle this," she said. "You have done too much already."

Penn, watching, approached. "I shall help you," she said.

Winny heard the exchange and went to Dora, who was stirring a pot of beans. "My turn to cook."

"It is not," Dora said.

"Then let me do it because I want you to save your strength for the trail ahead."

The bond they had formed earlier was back. Maggie hoped the hardships ahead would not break it. She knew it would take all of them together to make it to California. Did she have a man's strength? So far she had proven herself, but California still was a long way off, and Reverend Parnell had said the journey ahead was harder than anything they had experienced. Well, she would try. She would tax herself to carry her share of the burden and more. There was no choice. Either they would work together or they would never make it to the gold diggings.

Evaline had ridden in the wagon all day, hiding herself under a quilt. That evening when the train stopped, she tried to get up. "I must be about supper," she said. "Surely it is my turn." She started to climb down from the wagon but stopped when she saw the women looking up at her. Their faces were open and friendly, sympathetic, but still she hesitated.

How different the reaction to Evaline's attempted rape was from what it might have been in Chicago, Maggie thought. There the girl would have been blamed, or she would pretend it had not happened. The trail was a different place, however. One of their number had been ill-treated. They all knew it, and they all shared Evaline's anger and resentment. "Come and help with the bacon," Maggie told her, taking the girl's hand.

But Evaline could not move. The others might want to take on her shame, but she kept it for herself. "No. I cannot face them," she murmured and slid back into the wagon, hiding under a quilt.

"She should be up. It does her harm to stay hidden," Sadie said.

"Working has helped me," Maggie put in.

"No. Leave her be," Bessie told them.

"You do her no favor. It will be harder tomorrow and worse the day after if she is left to brood," Sadie said.

"I cannot help it. She is a child."

"She is a woman, but I shall not interfere," Sadie told her, shaking her head.

Maggie and Sadie turned to the campfire. They all pitched in to prepare supper. Since Dora had already set a pot of beans on the coals, Penn mixed up cornbread. Their coffee grinder had been discarded, and Winny ground coffee beans by placing them on a rock and hitting them with a hammer. Maggie put slices of bacon into a frying pan.

Other groups were preparing their suppers, too, although a few of the women were so tired that they had already wrapped themselves in quilts and were asleep.

Maggie heard a commotion at another campfire. There was a clattering of tin dishes, and a woman yelled "Shoo!" Maggie turned to see what the noise was about and spotted a small black dog running away with something in its mouth.

"Catch him. He took my salt pork," a woman called, racing after the animal. Sadie reached for the dog and held him fast, but he had already consumed the food.

"Useless pup!" the woman said as she went back to her campfire.

"What is a dog doing out here?" Dora asked.

"Probably ran away or was left behind by someone who did not want to feed him anymore," Mary answered. "Look, there is a rope still attached to his neck."

"He has been following us. I saw him in the morning," Maggie told them.

"We shall have to get rid of him," said the woman whose salt pork the dog had stolen. "Perhaps we should shoot him. What if he is mad?"

"I do not think so," Maggie told her. "Look at him wagging his tail. He is friendly." She held out her hand, and the dog came close. "Poor thing. He is starving." She took a piece of bacon out of her pan and blew on it to cool it, then held it out to the dog. He snatched it out of her hand and ran off to eat it. He came back, and Maggie stroked his fur. "He is a tiny little thing. I believe he is a puppy. How could he survive out here, tagging along after wagon trains? I would think a coyote or a wolf would have gotten him."

"You had better put him out, or he will follow us all the way to California," someone said.

"How could we?" Maggie asked. "He will die if we do not take him in."

"Who wants him?"

"I know who will take him," Maggie said. She looked toward the wagon where Evaline was hiding, then coaxed the dog to her and began picking burrs and twigs from his coat. She untied the frayed piece of rope from his neck. "Tomorrow, when we reach a stream, I shall give you a bath, but for now, you will do." She rose and went to the wagon and climbed in with the dog. For a long time she sat and petted the dog while Evaline peered out from under her quilt. In fact, supper was eaten, the dishes put away, and the women sitting around the campfires singing before Evaline finally asked, "Who is that?"

"He is a mutt who has been following us. He has no name. I do not know what to do with him. One of the women suggested we shoot him."

"Shoot him?" Evaline rose up on her elbow.

"It is only a suggestion. Still, no one seems to want him. A bullet would be a more merciful death than letting him be attacked and eaten by a wolf or left to starve."

"You cannot kill him." The girl was horrified.

Maggie shrugged. "But who will care for him?"

"I will." Evaline put out her arms, and the dog jumped into them. She held the animal close, her tears falling on his fur. "I had a little dog at home. Whitey, we called him. We had to leave him behind. I shall name this one Blackie." She smiled. "Do you think Clara would have approved?"

Maggie watched for a time and then climbed out of the wagon. She went to Bessie, who was sitting beside the campfire. "Evaline will be all right," Maggie said. "The healing has begun." There was healing for her, too.

Eighteen

The train moved slowly. Maggie and the others packed and repacked the wagons. They took turns performing chores that the men had done. They lingered at their nooning, and for two days they started late and stopped early, making no more than a few miles. "At this rate, it will take us a year to reach California," William told them that night. "You must work together and work harder," he said. "The pass ahead is worse than any we have seen so far. The descent is the most difficult between the Missouri and California."

Maggie blew out her breath. She had heard of Granite Pass from an eastbound traveler and knew it would test them more than anything on the trip. "We shall make it," she said, although she was not sure.

"We have no choice," William told her. "But I wish we were better prepared. It will take everything we have to cross it."

The way up Granite Pass was no worse than what they had encountered before, and Maggie thought travelers had exaggerated its difficulty. She reached the top and once again admired the beauty of the far hills. In front of her, however, was a valley of rocks and formations so bizarre that Caroline remarked, "It appears the world has been broken apart." That broken world was a bizarre mass of limestone and sandstone and granite cones and tables and rock formations that made Maggie shiver because they brought to mind the strange shapes in City of Rocks. They shone red and green and yellow in the sunlight, like a devil's garden. They would have to descend miles over steep and twisting trails, through a series of mountains and valleys until the pass and its descent were behind them.

William said they would wait until morning to begin. "God knows where we could spend the night in that trail of horrors," he said.

Maggie wished that they had started earlier, because she lay awake much of the night worrying whether they were up to the task ahead of them.

The early morning was cold. Mary rose to place branches on the fire, and Maggie realized her friend had been awake and worried, too. "Do you think we can make it?" she whispered.

"We will try. It is that, my girl, or go back, and we have voted not to do so."

"I am glad we are going ahead. There is nothing behind for either of us. You will get us through, Mary. We will all pray."

"*We* shall get us through, you and I, and we will

leave the praying to others. Myself, I will place my faith in the wagons, not God."

"You are not a believer?"

"I am more inclined to believe the Lord comes to the aid of those who depend on themselves."

"Then He is surely on *your* side."

"*Our* side."

The two warmed themselves by the fire, and before long, the others awoke. Dora got up awkwardly, her distended belly huge in the dawning light. She rubbed her injured arm as if it pained her. Maggie hoped the baby did not choose that day to be born.

The rising sun sent long shadows across the east side of the pass, giving the rocks and defiles an even more devilish appearance. Maggie could see the remains of wagons and dead animals along the trail. From somewhere ahead of them, a dying ox bellowed. Maggie closed her eyes for a moment and said a prayer. She wished that Mary prayed, too, because God surely would pay attention to her. Maggie prayed that none of the women or their wagons or animals would be destroyed before they reached the bottom. She did not believe they could be so lucky, however. Like the other women, she hurried through breakfast, anxious to have the descent behind her.

William was nervous, too, and he yelled at the women to hitch the oxen. "No one is to ride inside the wagons. It is too dangerous," he ordered. "Joseph and I will be needed for the ropes, so you women will have to drive the wagons. If no one volunteers, we will cast lots."

"I will drive," Mary offered.

"And I," Maggie said.

Others volunteered, but the train still lacked one driver, so the women drew from blades of grass to see who would guide the oxen hitched to the final wagon. Dora had the shortest blade. She might have pleaded her condition, but she would not and started for the last wagon. Sadie exchanged a look with Bessie, then spoke up. "Let me go instead of her."

"No, the responsibility is mine," Dora said.

Sadie touched her arm. "Big with the baby like you are, you aren't strong enough. If you lost control of the wagon, you could run down the rest of us. Let me do it."

Dora thought that over. She had never used her pregnancy to avoid work, but it was clear that she was weak and exhausted. If she could not control the wagon, it could indeed careen down the mountainside. Finally, she nodded agreement.

The women loaded the wagons and were ready to leave when another train crowded in front of them. It was made up entirely of men. Both Maggie and Penn scanned the faces as they always did, but Reed was not among them.

The men looked at the women in disbelief. "Where's your men at?" one asked.

"We have none but our two guides. The rest have run off," Mary told him.

"You going to try this on your own?" He was incredulous. "Can't no women go down a pass like this without they have men."

"We intend to try," Maggie said. She raised her chin in defiance, although she was so afraid she almost shook.

The man called to the others. "This here's a wagon train of womens—womens! They think they can go by theirself."

The men stared, and two or three guffawed. "They expect us is going to help 'em?" one asked.

"Yeah, for a price. I say forty dollars a wagon ought to do it."

"For such a price, we might hire the United States Army," Mary told him.

Joseph came up to the men. "We thank you for your generosity," he said with sarcasm. "But we do not need your assistance."

"They're womens. You think they can drive them oxen down these mountains?"

"They have done so for a thousand miles. They are magnificent."

Maggie's heart swelled with pride. She might have expected such encouragement from Reverend Parnell, but Reverend Swain had been more critical. He was not a man to praise them without reason. He truly believed in them, she realized.

"Now move out," Joseph told the men, "or the women shall take precedence and show you what they can do."

As the men started off, one of them broke away. "You might chain a small tree behind your wagon," he told Mary. "The weight will hold it back." She thanked him, and he said, "Good luck to you, ma'am."

William let the men go a long way down the trail before he ordered the women to line up. "We do not want to crowd them," he said.

"And we want to study how they manage each curve and drop," Joseph added. "We will learn from their mistakes."

Just as Mary started down the trail, they heard the sound of a wagon far ahead as it careened over a cliff and crashed below. Men screamed. A mule made a hideous sound until there was a gunshot, and the animal was silenced. Winny crossed herself, and Caroline bowed her head in prayer. There had been a great deal of praying, Maggie thought. She hoped God was listening.

Mary glanced at Maggie, then at William, who did not comment on the tragedy but instead asked, "Are you ready, Miss Madrid?"

Mary could only nod as she urged the oxen forward. The other wagons joined in a line behind her. William and Joseph and the rest of the women walked along. The descent was treacherous. Frequently, the wagons had to stop while the women locked the rear wheels with chains to slow the wagons on the steepest parts of the descent. Maggie did her best to ignore the broken vehicles and dead animals scattered about, but she could not help but shudder at the thought that one or more of the emigrants who had shoved ahead of them had been killed in the accident. The wind came up, raising clouds of dust that settled in her hair and nose and made it difficult to see.

The last hill was the worst, too steep to allow the oxen to proceed on their own. The bottom was littered with the remains of more vehicles and dead oxen and mules.

"We must take each wagon down separately. We will have to use ropes, and we will need all the women to steady the wagon," William said. He and Joseph took two ropes and tied them to the rear of Mary's wagon. When he was satisfied the ropes would hold, William offered to drive the lead wagon down the final slope.

Mary shook her head. "You are stronger than I," she told William. "Your strength will be needed to hold the ropes steady."

"And you are stronger than I am," Maggie told Mary. "You, too, should help with the ropes. I will drive the oxen."

Mary started to object, but Maggie was right. It would take all of the women gripping the ropes to steady the wagon. If they could not hold it back, the wagon would crash down the final slope.

Maggie did not let the others see how frightened she was. She knew that if the women slipped, if they let go of the ropes, she could be crushed by the oxen or thrown over the side of the mountain. Still, if one of them was to die, perhaps it would be best if it was she. After all, Clara was gone, and Dick. California did not seem so important now. Still, Maggie did not want to die. She had not given up before, and she would not now. "Ready?" she called. The others nodded, and she cried, "Giddap!"

The women held tight to the ropes, slowly letting them out as the wagon made its way down the slope. The wagon hit a bump and swerved, knocking against her, and Maggie bit her tongue, tasting blood. Her nails dug into her hands. A woman cried out as she slid and let go of the rope. The others strained to hold the wagon steady. Maggie heard the wheels slide, but the women held fast, and at last the wagon was on flat ground. Maggie closed her eyes in a word of thanks. When she opened them, the women were gathered around her. Mary raised her fist, and the women cheered.

The men who had crowded in front of them

stared, their mouths open. They were digging a grave for one of their number who had been killed in the crash that Maggie had heard. The men had stopped to watch as the wagon made its torturous way down the slope, had stood there the entire time, waiting for the wagon to come loose, for Maggie to be killed. Now they looked at the women with awe. One of them stepped forward. "You need our help with your other wagons, do you? No charge."

William started to reply, but Maggie looked around at the women standing beside her wagon in awe, prouder of themselves than they had been for a thousand miles. She raised her hand to stop Reverend Parnell from speaking. Then, her head high, she replied, "Thank you for the offer, sir, but as you can see, we have no need of it."

They could have used the help, of course. Their other wagons had to descend the rest of the way into the valley, and the women ached from the strain of holding the ropes taut. But at that moment, not a one of them would have given her place to a man. Nor would they have wanted a man to replace a single woman.

Then Mary spoke up. "We should be happy to offer our help to you, should you need it."

By the end of the day, all the wagons were clustered beside a stream and the women sat around their campfires, happy and proud but too exhausted to talk. It was then that Dora announced that her baby was coming. The pains had started just as Maggie had begun the final descent. She had not only kept silent but had taken her place at the rope.

"Has anyone among us ever delivered a baby?" Caroline asked. The women looked at each other and shook their heads.

"I have helped mother cows. It cannot be that much different," Mary told her.

"I have given birth," Maggie said.

"I . . ." Sadie began, then stopped. "I have seen a baby born."

None of the others spoke up, so Maggie said, "Boil water. We will need clean rags, if there are any."

"In my trunk," Dora said. "Hurry. I think the baby will not wait longer." Her face was twisted, and Maggie wondered how she could have borne the pain so long without letting on.

Caroline went to the stream and dipped up a pail of water, then poured it into a kettle that she set on the fire. She dropped a length of twine into the water. Maggie found Dora's trunk and removed the rags and some tiny garments. *When had Dora found the time to stitch them?* Maggie wondered. The others made up a pallet on the ground and helped Dora lie down. In a moment, she began to moan and thrash about, trying not to cry out. Mary cleaned off a stick and told Dora to put it in her mouth and bite down when the pains got too bad. That way, she wouldn't bite her tongue. Bessie rubbed Dora's back. A few yards away, the rest of the women gathered around a campfire to prepare supper. And to wait. As tired as they were, none would sleep until the birth was over.

Maggie examined the girl. "The baby is crowning," she said. When the others didn't understand, she added, "I can see the crown of the head." She knelt beside Dora. "I know it hurts, but you must push. You will think your body will tear itself apart, but pushing expels the baby, and soon it will be over. And then you will feel such joy."

Dora didn't appear to hear. Sweat ran down her face, and she gripped the stick with her teeth. "I did not know it would hurt so much," she whimpered after a pain let up. Her face contorted again, and she bit down on the stick as she struggled to push out the baby.

"Good girl," Mary coached. She was kneeling beside Maggie. "You are doing fine. It will be over soon."

Dora began to pant. Then, as another pain hit her, she cried out, the stick falling out of her mouth. "It hurts. Make it stop," she begged.

"You walked a thousand miles and helped hold back a covered wagon. Birthing a baby, why, that's easy," Mary said.

"No it is not!" Dora pushed again, her whole body straining, and Mary said, "The head is coming out." She stepped aside, deferring to Maggie, who grasped the infant. Another push and the shoulders were out.

"Almost over. Once more, Dora. Once more," Maggie said.

The girl closed her eyes and gripped Mary until her fists were white. With one final push, the baby slid into Mary's hands. The infant twitched and began to mewl.

"We need to cut the cord," Maggie said.

Caroline hurried to her wagon and removed a pair of scissors from her sewing basket. She plucked the twine from the kettle of hot water, then cut a length. Maggie tied off the cord, then raised the baby in the air and said, "There, it is done." For the second time that day, the women cheered.

While Caroline and Mary cared for the baby, Maggie attended Dora. "We must dispose of the placenta," she said "Some say to bury it under a rosebush."

"A rosebush!" Caroline laughed. "Where do we find a rosebush in this God-forsaken land?" She began to laugh, and with the tension broken, the others laughed with her.

Mary wrapped the baby in the quilt that Maggie had made and placed it in Dora's arms, showing her how to hold the infant. Tears streamed down the new mother's face, although whether they were from joy or relief that the pain was gone, Maggie did not know. Dora held the baby close, then asked, "Is it a girl?"

In the excitement, Maggie had not told her. "A boy," she said.

"A boy?" Dora looked confused. Then she asked, "Is he all right?"

Maggie took only a second too long before answering. "He is breathing fine." She was not so sure, however. The baby's breath seemed shallow to her, and the infant was small, maybe too small. Still, she had not attended any births but those of her own children, so she did not know.

When the women were finished and Dora and her son were resting by the campfire, the whole company knelt, and William gave a prayer of thanks. They were all exhausted, and the prayer was short. As they returned to their blankets, Caroline began to sing the Old One Hundred, and Maggie wrapped herself in a quilt to the sounds of "Praise God from whom all blessings flow." As she drifted off to sleep, Maggie thought of the ebb and flow of life on the trail. The company had lost Clara, but it had been given a baby boy.

In the morning, one of the men from the wagon train ahead walked into the women's camp. "We heard a baby," he said.

"Born last night," Maggie told him.

"We thought so." He held out two wrinkled apples. "For the mother, to give her strength, although after seeing what you did yesterday, I am not sure she needs them."

Nineteen

The wagon train was even further behind schedule now. Every day mattered if they were to cross the Sierras before snowfall. Mary, who made the decisions with the two ministers, had insisted they give up Sunday rests to make up for lost time, and Joseph had not protested. Still, the morning after the harrowing descent and the birth of Dora's baby, she demanded a day's layover. They were all exhausted from the exertion, and none of them had slept through Dora's ordeal. Dora herself needed a respite. The day was hardly one of rest, however. Maggie cared for the baby. Bessie and Evaline washed clothes, Caroline baked, and Winny, Penn, and Sadie cleaned their wagon. Others repaired the wagons and mended the wagon sheets. The axle on one of the wagons was nearly broken through, and the wheel on another was shattered. So the women abandoned yet another wagon. They removed a wheel from the discarded vehicle and used it to replace the broken wheel on the other.

The remaining wagons were a sorry lot. The bright blue paint on the wagon boxes that had been so gay when they left St. Joseph had faded, and much of it was worn off. The wagon covers were gray from the dust and rain. The oxen were jaded, and after examining them William announced two could go no farther. Once more, he asked the women to discard anything that was not absolutely necessary.

"What about the trees?" William asked Bessie. She had brought the apple trees with her, had insisted at the beginning that they must go all the way to California. Under Evaline's care, they had thrived. She had watered them even when water was scarce and had washed the dust from the branches.

"I couldn't," Bessie replied. "They will be an apple orchard one day."

William looked away as if it were difficult for him to ask her to make the sacrifice. "We must lighten the load," he said.

Bessie turned to Evaline, who was holding the mutt, Blackie, in her arms. Maggie had asked once if the dog had forgotten how to walk, since Evaline carried him everywhere. She knew the dog helped the girl deal with her ordeal at City of Rocks. "We have already abandoned my rocker, my fine dishes, my fur coat, most of my clothes. I cannot sacrifice the trees," she said.

"I would not ask . . ." William let the words hang there.

Bessie turned her back and walked to one of the

340

slender starts, running her hand over the trunk. "What do you think, Maggie?"

"Perhaps you could take two with you."

Evaline looked up. "I would carry them, one in each hand."

"And who would carry Blackie?" Bessie asked.

The girl gave her a sly smile. "Perhaps I could teach him how to walk again."

Bessie nodded. "Someday you will be sorry, Reverend Parnell. You would come to call and tell me how nice it would be to sit among the apple blossoms, if only I had them."

"You could grow an orchard from two trees."

"If they live."

"I am sorry to ask it of you."

Bessie looked away, embarrassed. "The others have sacrificed so much more." Indeed, Mary had discarded the last of her farm implements, and Winny, to everyone's amusement, had tossed away her maid's uniform. Joseph had left his pulpit at City of Rocks. "I wanted to be treated like the others, so how can you not ask it of me," Bessie said.

Maggie spoke up. "You could plant the trees you leave behind right here, by the stream. Perhaps one day there will be an apple orchard in this place."

"Bessie's grove," William told her.

"Dora's grove," Bessie said.

After Bessie and Reverend Parnell left, Evaline

341

went to her wagon and removed her violin and set it with the other discarded items.

Dora spent the day resting. She had not known her body could hurt so much, she told Maggie. Each time she moved, she felt the ache. "But was not the pain worth it?" Maggie asked, handing Dora the tiny, whimpering infant.

Dora's milk had come in, and she tried to feed the baby, but he was a mewly little thing who did not seem to suck well. Dora held out her finger and let the baby grasp it as she marveled at his perfect fingers, the nails almost as tiny as pinheads. "Is he too small?" she asked Maggie. "Perhaps I miscalculated my months of pregnancy. Maybe he was early. He would be small if he was early, wouldn't he?"

"I think he is about right," Maggie reassured her, although she did not know. Her own children had been much larger.

"I never thought it would be a boy," Dora said. "I had not considered a boy's name. I do not know what to call him. He will not be named for his father, or for my father either. Maybe William or Joseph. Do you think they would mind?"

"I am sure they would be honored."

Dora looked pensive. "Those are awful big names for such a little thing. I shall wait. For now, he will be Baby." She held the infant in one hand and ran her hand through his pale hair, which grew in clumps and was as fine as silk thread.

Maggie understood what Dora was thinking, because Maggie herself had been overcome with emotion at the births of Dick and Clara. Dora loved Baby fiercely, and Maggie was aware that her friend had never known such love. Maggie would have sacrificed anything for her children. She knew too well that it did not matter how much you loved them, however. Love did not keep them safe.

Maggie fetched Dora a plate of food. "You ought to have fresh milk and butter and eggs, but beans and creek water are the best I can offer."

"I should be doing my part," Dora said.

"Nonsense. You have just given birth. You must take care of yourself so that you will be strong for your baby."

"It is not fair to the others."

"The others agree. You may believe this is your baby, Dora, but we think he belongs to us all." She turned aside and touched the locket around her neck. *Just as Clara had belonged to us all,* she thought.

One by one, the women came to admire Baby and to give Dora presents they had made for him—a dress fashioned from a worn skirt, a tiny cap knitted from twine, napkins made from aprons that would have been discarded. Dora was humbled by their kindness. The women begged to hold the infant and told Dora how fortunate she was. They talked of having their own babies in California. "I hope my confinement will be more pleasant," one said, laughing.

Maggie would have stayed with Dora in that place a week if she could, but she knew they must move on, and in the morning, she was ready.

"Move out! Move out!" came the call down the line of wagons, although there were only six wagons now. They had started with fifteen. The day was hot, and Maggie found it hard to believe they were hurrying to beat the snow.

She fell back into the familiar routine, riding in the wagon or walking beside it, stopping at midday to noon, then resting for an hour before taking to the trail again. For a time, the days were easier. The land was less mountainous, and the trail led past streams. Still, the novelty and excitement of the trip were long past, and Maggie was anxious to reach the end of the journey. After a while, the land grew drier, and the water turned alkaline, but she didn't complain. She plodded on, knowing it would get worse.

And it did.

The wind blew dust into every part of the wagons. Dora tried to keep it out of the infant's eyes and nose and mouth, but Baby cried from the irritation and kept the others awake at night. He did not sleep much and still did not take milk.

Maggie assured Dora he was fine, but she told Mary she was not so sure.

"Is it normal?" Caroline asked. "He does not seem to thrive."

"What is normal out here?" Maggie asked.

"If only we had a cow with fresh milk," Mary said.

"I do not believe he would take even that," Maggie told her.

"What about water? His skin is like parchment."

Maggie shook her head. "It is too harsh. It could . . ." She had meant to say the harsh water could kill him, but she stopped. She could not say that the second of the children in the train might die.

As Baby failed to gain weight and even seemed to lose it—there were no scales in any of the wagons—Maggie worried more than any of the others about him. She knew too well how quickly children could perish.

"Do you think he is all right?" the new mother asked Maggie over and over again. As the days passed Dora had resumed some of her tasks and worked now with the baby held against her chest in a sling made from an apron.

"Of course. With this start, he will be a tough little boy." But Maggie did not believe that. The baby was listless, and his cries were soft, as if he did not have the energy to scream. He seemed to be starving, yet the front of Dora's dress was wet with milk, and she complained of the fullness in her breasts.

The other women were too exhausted to do much more than smile at Baby. Maggie decided not to burden them with her concerns. She told Mary, who said she had noticed the child was doing poorly but had no idea how to help him. "I believe he may have been born too early," she said.

Maggie confided in Caroline, too. "Maybe you could pray for him," Maggie suggested.

"I do that already. I would rather supply him with milk and relief from the heat and dust," Caroline replied. Then she added, "I have seen such infants at the Kitchen in Chicago, and I do not hold out much hope for Dora's child."

The river disappeared, and the land grew desolate. For several days, the go-backs Maggie saw talked of the difficulties ahead. "Imagine the worst desert you can, and it is ten times as bad," one told her. "Nothing before compares to what lies ahead," said another. And a third said simply, "The devil designed the trail. You must travel through hell to reach California."

As they passed each eastbound traveler, Winny inquired about her brother. "Have you met a David Rupe, Davy he is called?" she asked. "Red hair, and eyes as green as the grass."

The men shook their heads. "I knew a Davy Brunning back in Kentucky," one told her.

"There was a Davy at the Goosetown diggings a time back," another said. "Don't recollect the last name."

"I bet he's struck it rich by now," Winny told Maggie. "They'd be calling him Mr. Rupe, not Davy. That's why they don't recall him."

Although she did not say so, Maggie was concerned that Davy had disappeared. Winny was making the trip to find her brother, not a husband. She would be devastated if he was not there.

It was odd, Maggie thought. They had all signed up to go to California to marry the miners, but many of the women didn't care about finding husbands. Winny wanted her brother. Mary had come for a new life for herself. Sadie hoped to get away from prostitution. Dora had signed up because she was pregnant. Caroline already had a husband. And she and Penn had run away from violent men.

To save the oxen, few rode in the wagons. Even Dora walked, with the baby slung across her chest. From time to time, he gave a feeble cry. It was so low that only Dora and Maggie, walking beside the new mother, heard it.

"I do not believe Baby will live much longer," Maggie told Caroline when they rested one noon.

"Such a cruel fate," Caroline replied. "If that is

347

the case, I worry that Dora herself won't survive. She has nothing else to live for." She thought a moment. "He must be baptized." She hurried away to find her husband, and that evening, Joseph performed the sacrament, drawing a cross on the baby's forehead with the river water.

Dora hardly seemed aware of the ceremony—Baby slept through it—and in the next days, she could barely keep up with the others. Dora slept only in snatches during the night, waking each time the baby mewled, trying to get him to take her breast, but he would not suck and turned away his head. He was feverish, and Dora tried to cool his body with water, but the water was harsh and turned his skin an angry red.

"Shall I carry Baby for you?" Maggie asked as she trudged beside Dora a few days later. The wind had come up, blowing so much dirt that Maggie had tied a scarf around her mouth and nose. She knew the dust in the air must make it hard for Baby to breathe.

Dora did not respond. She seemed to be moving in a trance.

"Here, let me hold Baby," Maggie repeated. She reached out her arms to take the infant.

Dora stared at her friend with unfocused eyes. Then she shook her head. "He needs no more care," Dora said.

"Of course he does." Maggie stopped as Dora's meaning sank in. "Are you saying . . . ?"

"He passed at our nooning."

Maggie closed her eyes against the tears. "Oh, my dear. Why did you not say so?"

"I could not. We are a day behind because of me. I would not ask for another half day to bury him. Besides . . ." She staggered, and Maggie put her arm around the young woman to steady her. "Besides, I could not let him go yet. How could I leave him behind in this terrible place? There will be no one to care for his grave."

Maggie understood, because she had felt the same anguish at leaving Clara's body near the Green River. She hoped wild animals had not disturbed it. The women had dug a deep grave, much deeper than the grave she and Caroline had dug for Lavinia. Still, she was horrified at the possibility the grave might have been desecrated, that wild animals might have fed on that dear body. She would make sure Dora's baby's final resting place was too deep to be disturbed. She did not want Dora to harbor such worries. "Only his body will be left. You will carry his soul in your heart," she said. "I shall fetch Caroline. She will tell the ministers."

"Not just yet. Wait until we stop for the night."

Maggie agreed. *Let Dora hold her baby for one more hour,* she thought. It was not a very long time. She herself would have held Clara and Dick forever. She walked beside her friend until William called a halt. Then she told him that Baby was dead.

As the news spread, the women grew silent, talking in whispers while they unhitched the oxen and turned them loose to find feed. They were quiet as they prepared supper and went about their chores. Just as they had felt a collective joy at the child's birth, they now shared the loss of him. Quietly, they approached Dora with their words of sympathy, but the bereaved mother barely acknowledged them. She did not speak or cry. In fact, she had not cried since she unwrapped the infant hours before and realized he was gone. She sat propped against a wagon wheel, her dead baby in her lap. Maggie brought her a plate of food, but Dora did not touch it. Winny clipped a few strands of the pale hair and said she would save them for Dora.

Bessie approached Dora and held out a silk scarf that had been a gift from her husband. It was as light as a butterfly, so she had not felt guilty about not discarding that bit of luxury. "Wrap Baby in this. He will wear something fine for eternity." She unfurled the scarf, pale yellow with gold and silver threads running through it. "I should be pleased if you would accept it," Bessie said.

Dora reached for the scarf, and as she did so, the wind caught it and flung it out like a banner. It shimmered in the sun. Dora stared at the silk, then spoke for the first time. "It is the color of his hair." She began to cry then. She put her hands over her face as she sobbed and gasped for breath.

Maggie picked up the infant from Dora's lap. "We will prepare him," she said. She and Sadie washed the dust and grime from the tiny body. What did it matter now that the water was harsh? They wrapped him in the length of silk and then the small quilt that Maggie had made. Because there was no wood for a coffin, they placed him in a burlap bag. Once again, the mourners dug a deep grave in the dry earth.

At twilight, they gathered at the gravesite for the burial. The words of the ceremony seemed too big for such a small soul in that hard land. So instead, Joseph read the Twenty-third Psalm, while William talked of God's love, which he hoped would surround Dora in her sorrow. Then, as they sang a hymn, each woman picked up a handful of dirt and threw it over the tiny body.

Later, as the women prepared for bed, Maggie volunteered for the first watch. She remembered what Mary had done after Clara died, and when the others were asleep, she peeled two boards from the side of her wagon and fashioned them into a cross. Then, using axle grease, she wrote "Dora's Baby" on the crosspiece and placed it at the head of the tiny grave. Like Clara, Dora's baby would at least have something to mark his final resting place.

Twenty

September 16, 1852
Forty-Mile Desert

Dora trudged beside the others in a trance, her arms folded against her swollen breasts. She seemed oblivious to the milk stains on the front of her dress, was unaware of the women who offered her words of sympathy. Every now and then, she muttered that she had sinned, that the baby's death was due to her transgression.

A pall hung over them all. William was edgy. It was apparent that the baby's death weighed on him as well. "How many more souls will I have caused to pass on before we reach the mountains?" he asked as he walked beside Caroline and Maggie.

When Caroline didn't answer, Maggie said, "We will not allow you to take the blame for the death of the infant, any more than we will blame his passing on Dora's sin. Do you think he would have lived had he been born in Chicago? Or Dora? She might have died in childbirth there. I believe you saved her by bringing her west. You also saved Evaline."

William did not appear to hear her. He strode

352

off, striking a stick against the earth until it broke.

"He is greatly burdened," Maggie told Caroline. Then she added, "It is your husband who has risen to the occasion. We are all grateful for it."

Caroline smiled a little and nodded. Joseph had indeed become their leader. As William sank into depression, Joseph had found strengths that had not been apparent at the outset. Over the last weeks, he, along with Mary, had made the decisions. Solemn and self-righteous at the beginning of the trip, he had become patient with the women's foibles, had laughed at faults that in the past would have annoyed him. His good humor buoyed them all. What was more, Maggie had observed, where he had once considered Caroline as no more than his helpmeet, he now seemed to treat her as a partner, asking her advice and, to Maggie's astonishment, taking it. "The women would not have made it this far without your support," he had told her. Maggie had seen the joy on Caroline's face at the words. *Would Joseph have given his wife such praise back in Chicago?* Maggie wondered. Caroline confided that Joseph had professed doubts and failings to her. "I believe he never did so before because he feared I would find him weak," she said. "It is just the opposite. I believe his humbleness gives him strength."

Maggie wondered if Reverend Parnell resented

his brother-in-law's leadership. After all, the trip had been his idea. But he seemed unaware of the change in their relationship.

Joseph came up to Caroline then and took her hand. He had become more affectionate as the weeks on the trail passed. He touched her as they walked, held her hand or patted her arm. Maggie knew that, despite the crowd of women and the lack of privacy, they had found time for marital relations.

"When we stop, I shall rub your feet. I know they pain you," Joseph said before he left to see a woman who waved him over.

As Caroline watched him walk away, Maggie whispered, "Have you told him yet you are with child?"

Caroline blushed. "How did you know?"

"I can tell." Caroline had lost weight during the march, and she had become less pudding-faced. Maggie had noticed the swelling in Caroline's belly the day Dora's son died and thought the Lord might be compensating them for the loss of Baby. As if one child could replace another! Caroline's joy would no more help Dora deal with her misery than Dora's baby had helped Maggie with hers. Still, she was glad for Caroline.

"The others, are they aware as well?"

"I have said nothing, and they are too tired to take notice."

Caroline smiled at Maggie. "We had given up

on children. I accepted that I had failed Joseph in that way. As a man, God perhaps does not know it would have been better to have waited until I reached California. Nonetheless, I accept His decision with gratitude." Then she added, "No, I have not told Joseph. I do not want to add to his worries."

When the women reached the start of the Forty-Mile Desert they made camp, and Joseph announced they would spend the next day preparing for the crossing. The oxen were jaded and needed a day's rest if they were to survive the grueling miles ahead. Two had wandered off the previous night and could not be found, and two more had been unable to rise in the morning. So another wagon was eliminated. Just five were left.

Before the little train started across the sand, William ordered the women to cut grass for the oxen and fill every vessel with water. They would build campfires to cook enough food for the journey ahead, although Winny remarked that the sand was so hot they could fry eggs on it. And the travelers themselves must rest. The next two days would be the hardest they had yet encountered. The oxen were weak, and Joseph said that if the animals were to make it across, no one could ride in the wagons.

Dora sank down beside a wagon and told

Maggie, "I must feed Baby. My breasts are so heavy with milk that they pain me."

Maggie looked at the woman sharply. Had she forgotten her baby was dead? "Rest. You will feel better if you can sleep," Maggie said. Dora did not argue. She lay down in the sand and closed her eyes. Maggie stared at her a moment, knowing Dora would not be able to walk forty miles under the relentless sun. Maggie would insist that Reverend Swain make an exception and let her friend ride in the wagon. She rose and went in search of the minister.

Just then, an eastbound group of men stopped not far from the women. Because it was late in the season, there were fewer travelers going east now. This group might make it no farther than the Salt Lake and have to winter there.

Winny, who was mixing cornbread, set the skillet in the coals and rose. She would inquire about Davy. Mary stood, too. The women had no guidebook and asked the groups they passed for directions. Mary said she was not sure why they did that, because each gave different advice. She could just as well determine on her own how to cross the desert. Still, she or one of the ministers always inquired. Mary looked around for Reverend Swain, but he was conferring with his wife, so instead she asked Maggie to come along.

"Hello, the wagons!" Maggie called as the three

women approached the group. Some twenty men were unhitching mules, leading them to water. She thought the train was made up entirely of men, but then she heard a baby's cry. There must be women among them. "How was the desert?"

A man looked up and shook his head. "We been to hell and back. I crossed going west and swore never to do it again, but here I am, God's fool for sure."

"We start across tomorrow. Have you advice for us?" Mary asked.

"Turn back is my advice."

"Have you heard of a Davy Rupe?" Winny broke in.

The man turned to her. "Seems like I have. Your husband is he?"

"My brother." Winny was excited. It was the first news of Davy since she had seen his name on Independence Rock. "Where is he?"

The man shook his head. "Maybe Dogtown. Maybe Goosetown. I cannot be sure. Cannot be sure that was his name neither."

When Winny looked away, discouraged, the man called to the others. "Anybody here heard of Davy Rupe?"

A second man joined them. "Some there is that changes their names."

"Not Davy," Winny said. "Have you come across him, sir?"

"Heard the name of Rupe, but can't recall the

Christian name. Was a year ago, maybe more, maybe less. Over by Hangtown seems like. That where you'uns be headed?"

"Goosetown," Mary told them.

"Close by."

"He was one of the Rough and Ready boys," Winny persisted.

"Ain't they all," the man said. "Ain't they all."

"We came to ask advice for the crossing," Mary told the men.

"I told 'em turn back is what I said," the first man remarked.

"My advice, too. It don't get better. Only gets worse." He looked over at the group of women and asked, "Where's your menfolk at?"

"We have two of them," Maggie replied.

"The rest of you's womens?"

Mary, Maggie, and Winny were used to the incredulous looks when men encountered their train.

"We heard of you. There's talk of you in the diggings from men that's passed you by. We thought it was a fairy story."

"Talk of us?" Maggie asked.

He nodded. "Men gone ahead of you spread it about there's a wagon train headed for Goosetown made up of women looking for husbands."

"The men are mighty excited about that," his friend added. "Seems like they're crowding into the diggings waitin' for you. Womens is scarce in the camps. How many you got?"

"Thirty-seven," Maggie told him.

"They're expecting a hundred, two hundred, maybe more. That ain't near enough to go around."

"But you have women with you, one anyway," Maggie said, glancing in the direction of the crying baby.

The two men looked at each other. "You thinking what I am?" one asked his friend.

The women tensed. They had become used to men who had mischief in mind when they saw the large group of women. "We are as able as any men," Mary told them.

"You have to be to get this far, ma'am. I would say more women make it than men. Now do not be sore at us. We mean no harm." He paused. "We got us a problem." He nodded in the direction of the screaming baby and said, "That there is the problem."

"A sick baby?" Maggie asked.

"Not sick. Hungry. She ain't had nothing to eat for more than a day, and I guess she will starve herself to death."

"We would give you milk, but the cows we started with are gone," Winny said.

"Her mother is ill?" Maggie asked.

"Dead, and so is her pa. The woman died out there on the desert. The man said it was his fault, that he never should have took her to California. They was going back home, but after she passed on, he went crazy and shot hisself. Now we got a baby and no women and not a thing to feed her. It grieves us sorely."

The second man added, "We got no milk, so we tried water, but she throwed it up. She licked whiskey off my finger and went to sleep, but then she waked up hollering worse than ever. We got no way to take care of her."

"You want us to take her?" Maggie asked.

"Sure it is she'll die if she stays with us."

Mary looked at Maggie and Winny. "Are we of a similar mind?"

"We are," Winny replied.

"Yes, we will take her," Maggie said.

The men grinned with relief and went to fetch the baby. They returned not only with the infant but with a sack of baby clothes and a gold ring that they said had belonged to the infant's mother. "We sure do appreciate this," one of them said. "I reckon she does, too."

Maggie reached for the baby and tried to quiet her screams. "Hush, you pretty thing," she said. She remembered holding Dick and then Clara when they were infants, how the tiny bodies felt warm against her breast. For a moment, she wondered if the child might be a gift to her. Perhaps providence was giving her another daughter. She knew better, however. "She is starving. We must hurry," she said, looking at the baby instead of at Mary and Winny.

"God bless you—and her," a man said.

Mary picked up the bundle of clothing, and the three started back to their wagons. As they did, they heard one of the men shout, "Let's move on out."

"I thought they were camping there," Winny said.

"Perhaps they are going on before we change our minds." Mary reached over and let the infant grasp her finger. "I wonder how old she is."

"We forgot to ask. I do not suppose they know anyway," Maggie said. "I should judge not more than a month."

They reached the camp with the squalling baby, and the women looked up, confused. "What in the world?" Caroline asked.

"A baby," Maggie explained. "A hungry baby with no mother. The parents are dead, and the little girl will be, too, if we do not take her."

"If Dora does not take her, you mean," Caroline said. "She is a gift from God."

"That is what we thought, that or a gift from those men, at any rate," Mary told her. "They did not know how to feed her. Where is Dora?"

The young mother was lying in the sand, sleeping. Maggie carried the baby to her and touched her arm. Dora awoke with a start, reaching for the baby. Then she stopped. "What . . . ?" She shook her head, confused.

"The men over there"—Maggie indicated a cloud of dust—"they left her with us. We believe God intends this child for you." She held out the infant to Dora, reluctant to give her up.

Instinctively, Dora took the infant and unbuttoned her dress. She put the baby's face to her breast, and the child began to feed. Dora stared at the little head and listened to the greedy sucking sounds. Then she looked up at Maggie. "Who is she? Where is her mother?"

"Her mother is dead. Her father, too. Without your milk, she will die as well."

"She's your miracle," Sadie said.

"No," Maggie replied. "Dora is her miracle."

Later, Joseph said they must find the baby's relatives and arrange to return the infant to them.

"How can we? We do not know who they are. We do not even know their names—or hers, either," Maggie told him. "The men did not tell us whose baby she is, and we forgot to ask." She glanced at Mary, who nodded.

Joseph thought that over. "Then it is clear she is Dora Mifflin's baby."

After he left, Mary said, "I am glad we did not think to ask."

Maggie smiled. She had not forgotten. And she saw no reason to mention the initials inside the wedding ring.

• • •

Led by Mary, the women started across the desert just at sunup, anxious to be on their way before the heat of the day. Still, the sun's rays hit them, and they were fierce. Before an hour had passed, Maggie was perspiring heavily. The desert was littered with broken and abandoned wagons and dead animals. The stench of the rotting dead was so bad that Bessie halted her wagon to search for a bottle of camphor oil that she and Evaline and the others could use to wet rags to cover their noses and keep out the smell. The air seemed impregnated with salt, which made Sadie beg for water. Joseph warned her that water was precious. They must be judicious, because they would need it later on.

Maggie walked barefoot, her moccasins long since worn through. The sand was so hot that it burned her feet, and she tied strips of burlap from an abandoned wagon around them.

"You should ride," Maggie told Dora. "It is all right with Reverend Swain. He told me so."

"I shall walk," Dora replied.

"Then let the baby ride." The infant, no longer hungry, was sleeping.

Dora shook her head. "I will carry her." She had used a shawl to tie the child to her chest.

Maggie studied her friend for a moment. The day before, she had been sure Dora would die before the crossing was done. Now the young woman was as strong as the rest of them, and her spirits were better than most. She hummed to the infant as they walked along and kept peering at the little face as if to make sure the baby was really there.

"Have you named her?"

"I thought of Caroline or Mary—or Maggie—but I cannot choose. What do you think of California?"

Maggie thought California was a terrible name. "I believe we are not in California but in a place called Washoe," she said.

"Washoe!" Dora exclaimed. "Why, that is the perfect name."

Maggie did not think it was any better than California and perhaps even worse, but she only smiled. "You do not need to decide now."

"I have done so. Her name is Washoe Mifflin."

"Washoe," Maggie told Mary later on. "Why did I not keep my mouth shut?"

"It is not so bad. You could have told her we were in the Forty-Mile Desert."

By noon, Maggie was drenched in sweat. The women could not stand to build fires but ate cornbread from the morning's breakfast and cold beans left over from the night before. Maggie tried to rest, but there was little shade beside the wagons, and she was anxious to be on her way. So she was glad that as soon as the oxen had rested and consumed some of the grass the women had cut and drunk a little of the precious water, Joseph called, "Move out!" One ox could not rise, and she and Mary unyoked him. They would lose more oxen before the crossing was done, Maggie thought, and would have to abandon another wagon.

Joseph and William drove two of the wagons, and the women took turns with the rest. Maggie was glad her stint was over. Now, head bowed, she walked beside Winny, both of them fanning their faces with their hands, although that failed to relieve the heat. Suddenly Winny yelled, "There is a lake! Look. Just a little ahead!"

Maggie looked up, excited. Perhaps the desert was not so deadly after all.

"It is a mirage," William called. "There is no lake, no water. It is an illusion, a reflection of the sky upon the sand."

"But I see it," Winny said, running toward where she had spied the water. When she reached the spot, she saw it was just a little farther on. She started off again, then stopped and began to cry. Slowly, she turned back to the company.

"Mirages are not unusual out here. We shall see more before we reach the river," William told her.

The sand was thicker now. The oxen strained to pull the wagons, and walking was harder. Bessie stumbled and fell, then forced herself to get up and continue. Maggie's sunbonnet trapped the heat around her face. She took small sips of water from a canteen but, mindful of Reverend Swain's warning, drank as little as possible. She glanced at Evaline, the dog at her side. The girl carried the two apple trees, and when the leaves wilted, she wet her handkerchief and rubbed the water on them.

"You must not. The water is too scarce," Maggie told her.

"I promised I would keep them safe," Evaline said.

"Not at the cost of your life," Maggie replied.

Evaline nodded and began to replace the cap on the canteen, but Blackie jumped up on her, and Evaline dropped the container. The dog tried to lap up the spilled water, but it sank into the sand. Evaline's eyes filled with tears, and she vowed to Maggie that she would drink no more water until they stopped to camp.

Late in the day, Joseph at last called a halt, and Maggie sank to the ground for a few moments' respite before making preparations to camp. There was to be no camp, however. "We will rest and eat supper," Joseph told them. "Then we will go on. We will march through the night and into tomorrow if we have to."

As dusk fell they started again, walking silently beside the weary oxen. From time to time a woman fell and could not rise and was put into one of the wagons to rest. Then after a while she took up the walk again, since none wanted to be thought of as a slacker. At one point, Maggie spotted a sign that read "20 miles to water."

"Only halfway," Sadie said. "Oh, I'd thought we were almost there." She uncapped her canteen to drink and discovered it was empty. She tossed it aside, startling Maggie, who stumbled, twisting her ankle as she fell.

"Oh!" Maggie cried out.

Sadie rushed to her. "It's my fault. Are you hurt bad?"

"Only a little." Maggie stood and grimaced as she put pressure on her ankle.

"Ride in a wagon," Sadie said.

"No, I shall tie a strip of cloth around my foot, and it will be fine." She reached under her skirt and unfastened what was left of her petticoat. Then she tore strips from it.

"That's a waste of a pretty garment," Sadie said. "I'd let you use *my* petticoat if I had one left."

"Likely I shall find another abandoned farther on." Maggie wrapped the strips around her ankle, then tested it. "All I need is a cane."

"A stick's going to have to do," Sadie told her. She looked around but saw nothing suitable. They were near an abandoned Conestoga wagon. It rose up in the moonlight like a ship. Telling Maggie to wait a moment, Sadie searched through the abandoned cargo and returned, raising her arm in triumph. In her hand was an ebony walking stick with a gold knob. She handed it to Maggie, then rushed to Dora to ask if she could carry the baby. Maggie started off, limping, letting the others pass her by, slowly dropping back. No one seemed to notice.

In fact, the women were all but oblivious of each other now. A few stopped to rest and were left as stragglers, until Joseph discovered them and urged them on. They stumbled through the starlit night, through heavy sand that seemed to get deeper the farther they went. Every few hours Joseph called a halt, and the women ate a little of the food they had prepared what seemed like days earlier and drank a small amount of water. More and more canteens were thrown to the side of the trail.

Maggie plodded along behind them, never quite catching up. She thought she might beg a ride in a wagon, but when she reached the stopping place, she discovered the others had gone on. Once she stumbled upon the two apple trees, their leaves withered, and knew Evaline had thrown them aside. Or more likely, Bessie had insisted they be discarded. Someone else would have to plant an apple orchard.

She recognized one of the company's oxen. It must have refused to rise and had been unyoked and left to die. She saw that another of their wagons had been abandoned so that the remaining oxen could be yoked to other teams to pull the four vehicles that were left. For a moment, she wondered if some of her things had been tossed out, but she did not have the energy to search. Moreover, she did not care.

She stopped for only a moment, then started on, slower now, guided only by the moon and the wagon trail that stretched west. Sometimes she passed other emigrants, but she was too jaded to greet them or ask if they needed help. Nor did anyone offer to help her.

She stopped only to rewind the bandage around her ankle, but after a while she could no longer do that. Each time she started walking, she grimaced from the pain and wondered if she could continue. The water had been gone a long time, and Maggie was parched. Her face, burned from the sun the day before, hurt her, and she thought her tongue was twice its normal size.

The sun rose, and in the daylight Maggie saw no one ahead of her. The desert stretched out as far as she could see. By now, the rest of the company would have completed the crossing. Surely someone would notice she had lagged behind and would come back for her. She concentrated on thoughts of Dick and Clara. The memory of her children kept her going. Each time she faltered, she remembered how she and Clara had started the journey together and knew she must complete it for her daughter's sake. Clara's death would mean nothing if Maggie failed to make the trip. As she struggled on, her thoughts of Clara changed. Now she touched the locket around her neck and wondered if, before a few more hours passed, she would join her daughter.

Twenty-One

September 19, 1852
The Sierras

Maggie did not know until Mary told her later that it was midafternoon before Winny inquired about her. The company had reached the river in the morning. They had drunk their fill of water, washed themselves and their clothing, then napped. Mary had examined the oxen to see which ones could continue. The company needed at least four teams for each wagon, which meant they must leave another wagon behind. So once more, the women pared their belongings, this time discarding even items they considered essential. They no longer cared about material things, only about reaching their destination.

Winny came across Maggie's things, which were untouched, and asked if anyone had seen her.

"She fell in the night, at the halfway marker," Sadie said. "I dropped my canteen, and she slipped. I found a cane for her, and she seemed to walk all right. I would have stayed with her, but I got caught up with Dora and her baby. I haven't seen her since." She wrung her hands. "It's my fault she got hurt, and I'll go back for her."

"No, I will go. I will take my horse," Mary said. She had not ridden the horse since before the desert crossing and had given him much of the water she carried. So the animal was rested enough to make the journey back across the sand. "If Maggie is injured, she will need to ride anyway." Mary had been busy with the oxen and had not slept. Still, she hurried to saddle the chestnut, then filled two canteens with water and set off.

It was the hot of the day, and she was weary, but not as weary as the travelers she encountered who were nearly finished crossing the desert. She passed a group of wagons and inquired if anyone had noticed a woman alone, walking with a cane. The people stared at her, then shook their heads, and Mary understood that in their stupor, they had noticed no one. A man asked for water, but Mary would not share the canteens. If one person wanted it, the others would demand it, too, and there would be nothing left for Maggie. "Water is ahead, not far at all. You will make it," she said.

Farther on, a man told her he had seen a dead woman. "I would have buried her, but I did not have the strength," he said.

Mary shuddered to think of Maggie lying in the road where anyone could tear at her clothes in search of valuables. She thought of the dead oxen and horses she had seen and wondered if

Maggie was already bloated. No matter what the condition of the body, Mary would bring Maggie back to be buried by the river. She would not leave her to rot in the sand. When Mary reached the body the man had spoken of, she realized it was that of an old woman. She kept on through the deep sand and then the alkali clay, baked as hard as a hardtack biscuit.

The sun was low, although it was still bright, and the heat continued. Mary wondered if she could see Maggie's body in the dark, for she had almost concluded that Maggie was already dead. Perhaps someone had taken the woman into a wagon, but that was unlikely. Would anyone pick up a straggler and let her ride while they themselves walked to save their oxen? There was little chivalry on the trail. In her search for Maggie, Mary had come across a man and woman fighting over a canteen of water, each demanding the other's share. The man, the stronger of the two, won and raised it to his lips. Mary urged the chestnut forward at the thought of her friend hobbling along by herself or lying in the sand dead. She would find Maggie if she had to go all the way back to the twenty-mile marker.

Maggie could no longer walk. She crawled now, the hot sand burning her hands and knees and scraping them raw. Her dress was torn, and she had lost her sunbonnet, so that her face was red and swollen. Her hair and face and body were covered in dust. She was barely aware that she still gripped the cane. Every now and then someone passed but did not stop. She looked up once to see two men staring down at her. "Hold on to us," one said, but in her delirium, Maggie did not understand they would aid her. She clutched the cane to defend herself, and the men shrugged and went on. Maggie's mind wandered. Two or three times, she thought she heard her children calling her.

She saw a tall figure loom up in front of her and tightened her hand on her cane when the figure stopped—a man on horseback. She had given up the hope that someone would help her and knew anyone who took notice of her was not to be trusted.

"Maggie?"

She heard her name and wondered how the man knew it. He dismounted and came to her. *Jesse,* Maggie thought. He had found her. He had come to take Clara. But he was dead wasn't he? And Clara, too. Maggie raised her cane.

"Maggie, it is Mary," a voice said.

Maggie looked up with eyes as red as the sunset that blazed across the sky. *Mary?* She was puzzled for a moment, because her brain was fogged.

"It is Mary. I have come for you."

"Clara. Do you have Clara?"

Mary swallowed hard, then said, "Clara is at the river."

"Oh," Maggie said. "Do you have water?"

Mary took the canteen from the horse and held it to Maggie's mouth. She let her have only a few sips, because the water had to last until they reached the camp.

"More," Maggie pleaded, and when Mary said no, Maggie began to cry.

Mary put her arms around her friend and brushed the sand off her face. "You are safe, Maggie. The others are waiting for you. I've come back to fetch you." She picked up Maggie and set her on the horse, then mounted the chestnut herself. From time to time, she gave Maggie sips of water, but Mary herself never took a swallow. She sang a little, and Maggie relaxed, finally falling asleep. Mary held her tight.

When she awoke, Maggie was confused. At first, she did not know where she was or why she was on a horse. She turned her head to look at Mary, and then, slowly, she remembered. "You came for me," she said.

Mary nodded.

"I would not have made it. I heard angels singing and Clara calling me. She wanted me with her."

"We wanted you, too," Mary said. "Your family here wants you."

Maggie, her mind clearer now, thought about

375

that. In the hundreds of miles since St. Joseph, she had seen other companies fight and break up, had known of partners who robbed each other on the trail. Some travelers left behind their sick to die alone. The women had done none of those things. There had been bickering and slights, even hostility. But over the hundreds of miles, they had come together until now they were as one. If Mary had not returned for her, Sadie would have, or Bessie, or any of the others. Just as she would have gone in search of them.

As if knowing what Maggie was thinking, Mary said, "Being part of our group of women has been the greatest adventure of my life." It seemed that Mary was talking to herself as much as to Maggie. "If I do not find a husband, if something happens and I do not make it to the gold camps, I will be satisfied, because I know I have been part of a remarkable journey with you and the others. We are sisters. We are a band of sisters."

Mary and Maggie returned near midnight. The women should have been asleep, but most only dozed, uneasy about their friends. Mary, they knew, had not slept for more than thirty-six hours. How could she stay awake to repeat part of that awful journey?

Then suddenly the two women were in their midst. William lifted Maggie from the saddle and set her on the ground. Penn fetched an ointment she had made when they reached water and spread it on Maggie's inflamed face. Joseph knelt beside Maggie and examined her ankle. She grimaced as he turned it from side to side, then gently pressed the bone. When he was finished, he announced the bones were not broken, but the ankle had been sprained and was badly swollen. He bound it tightly with strips of cloth and told Maggie that she must ride in the wagon until the ankle would support her weight.

"No," Maggie said, mindful that any weight would make it harder for the oxen to pull the wagon. "I am not an invalid."

"You *are* an invalid," William told her. "If you do not take care of yourself, you will be an even greater burden." He looked abashed at what he had said and added, "It is not your fault. We must thank God your foot was not worse injured."

"We should let her rest another day," Joseph said, but William held up his hand.

"No, we move on tomorrow. I will not allow more delay."

"What does one day matter?" Caroline asked.

William looked at his sister a long time, then muttered, "It matters. Oh, yes, it matters."

They had reached the river, but to Maggie's consternation, the sand did not end. In fact, it seemed to be deeper, and the oxen strained to pull the three remaining wagons. The heat was stifling, and although she knew the way through the Sierras was even more challenging than the Forty-Mile Desert, Maggie could not wait to be in the mountains, where it would be cooler.

They passed an eastbound wagon and stopped to ask about the trail in front of them. The men looked over the women and shook their heads. "You think you have seen the elephant, but you seen only his tail. The body lies on ahead," said one.

"Perhaps we should turn back, then," Mary said in jest.

"We have already crossed the Rocky Mountains," Winny told the men.

"Pah! They are mere hills compared with the Sierras. You will wish for the desert again before you are done."

The Sierras were indeed impressive, giant towers of granite piercing the sky, more awe-inspiring—and more frightening—than anything the women had seen before. The wagon train followed a trail beside the river, then turned into a pretty canyon, where cottonwoods gave way to pine trees. At first the trail was easy, and Maggie thought the difficulty of crossing the mountains had been exaggerated. Before long, however, the road became a twisting trail blocked by logs and boulders, some as large as a wagon. Steep rock walls rose hundreds of feet on either side, casting the deep chasm in shade. Everywhere lay the carcasses of both wagons and animals that had fallen victim to the trail.

The women's three wagons barely made it halfway up the steep trail before night came on and they were forced to stop. They secured the wagons, then chained the oxen to keep them from running away. There was no place to pitch tents, so the women slept on the ground, under the stars.

Maggie declared that the wagons moved so slowly that she was more comfortable hobbling along with her cane than riding under the canvas wagon cover. The truth was, however, that she felt safer on foot than in a wagon, which might at any moment veer off the side of a cliff. And safer surrounded by women, if Asa's brother had escaped and was behind them. Edwin had said Reed Harvey would hang, but Penn was sure he was following her.

The next day, the canyon opened onto a valley, but Maggie found little relief. The train still had a hundred miles to go, and the way led through distant mountains. There would be no more fifteen-mile days. The journey would take a week, perhaps two, and every mile of it would be treacherous.

Other parties were camped in the valley, and they viewed the women with curiosity. A few men offered to guide them—for a price—but were turned down. "We made it this far. Why would we need a man to tell us what to do?" Mary asked.

As Mary and Maggie were yoking the oxen one morning, a bearded man in ragged clothes approached them and said he would offer his services in exchange for food. Joseph recognized him. He was one of those who had abandoned the women at City of Rocks. It was Maggie, however, who spoke. "We do not care to mix with thieves and deserters," she said. "Go on your way."

"There is forgiveness," Joseph told her.

"Not for horse thieves. At the first opportunity, he will abscond with Mary's horse and who knows what else. We would need to set two guards at night, one for the camp, the other to watch him."

"I was wrong. I should not have listened to the others. It has not gone well with me," the man said.

Mary scoffed. "You mean because you are afoot?"

"All the animals are dead. They did not make it across the desert. Green Holt died when a wagon ran over him, and the rest of us, we quarreled." He paused. "You could use the help over the mountains."

"We do not need your help," Mary said. She turned and went to her horse and mounted it, as if she were afraid he would steal the chestnut.

"You have your answer," Joseph said.

"But I am starving."

"And you want the help of those from whom you stole food? What happened to the provisions you took from us?"

"You mentioned forgiveness."

Joseph nodded. "Yes, we do forgive, but we are not fools. None of us would trust you, and our safety is my concern."

He turned to Caroline, who said, "I agree he cannot join us, but we will share our supplies." She went to a wagon and returned with cornmeal and flour and a small piece of bacon that was covered in mold. "We scrape off the mold before we eat it," she said, handing the food to the man.

Maggie told Caroline, "You are a better Christian than I."

"No," Caroline said. "Perhaps I am just someone who is more fortunate."

Maggie thought they had seen the worst of the mountains, but the pass they encountered now was more treacherous than any other. It took all their oxen hitched to one wagon to pull it to the top of the pass. As they started up, they heard the terrifying sound of a wagon ahead of them that had fallen over the side of a cliff, splintering on the rocks below. Maggie blanched, and Mary grasped her arm. "There is nothing but to continue," she said.

The wagon made it to the top. The women

unyoked the oxen and returned with them for the second wagon. And the third. When they were finished, a man who had watched them told his companion, "Now we truly have seen the elephant—a trainload of women getting not one but three wagons up the Devil's Ladder. The wonder of it!" He went up to Mary and Maggie, took off his hat, and bowed.

Twenty-Two

The women made their way across one blue range of mountains after another, along narrow trails, past boulders and giant pine trees, climbing up steep trails beside deep chasms, as they slowly moved westward. They wondered how those ahead of them had made it that far before tossing out saw blades and axes, gold pans and washers. They found a spinning wheel and, to Joseph's amusement, a pulpit.

The trail was crowded with gold seekers hurrying to reach the mining camps before the snow. From time to time there were curses directed at travelers and recalcitrant oxen. Most of the emigrants were men, but a few women were among them. The women's train passed a man crying over the crushed body of a child, a woman screaming that the death was his fault. They saw hollow-eyed women hunched over as they trudged up the steep inclines, women who had left behind everything that mattered to them to follow their husbands' dreams.

Maggie stopped to comfort a woman who sat beside the trail sobbing. When Maggie offered aid, the woman replied, "There is none can help me. All is lost for a devil's dream of gold."

Not all of the gold seekers were depressed, of course. The closer they came to the diggings, the more the men became animated. Some of them whistled or sang "Oh! Susanna" as they walked along. They talked of the gold they would find and how they would spend it. At night, around the campfires, the men spoke of riches. Their women did, too, but most of them talked of the gold they hoped would take them back home to buy fine houses and farms that would impress their families and neighbors. "My feet are reluctant going west, but oh how I shall skip when we are eastbound," one woman told Maggie.

Those demoralized women were so different from her friends, Maggie thought. Her band grew more excited the closer they were to the gold country. They asked each other how many weeks, how many days. They talked of the husbands who waited for them, of the fortunes they might find. Were their hopes too high? Perhaps in a year or two, some of them would be among the disgruntled go-backs.

With so many travelers crowding the trail, Maggie and the others became sociable. At night they could see a dozen campfires dotted across the mountains. They visited nearby emigrants, inquiring where others had come from and recalling the names of friends they might have in common. The women in the camps looked at

Mary and Maggie and Winny in awe, asking if it was true they had come west on their own, had actually volunteered to make the trip in search of husbands.

"Perhaps you will decide when you reach the diggings that you do not need a man," one suggested. "How I do envy you."

"We have proven that we do not need them. The question now is, do we want them?" Mary said.

Winny inquired of eastbounders whether they had heard of Davy Rupe, but none seemed to know of him.

"If you will agree to marry me, I will turn around and go with you to look for him," one man told her.

"I have no need of a go-back," she replied.

Now that they were close to the gold camps, Maggie discovered that they were an even greater curiosity. Travelers ahead of them had spread the word that a wagon train of women looking for husbands was soon to arrive, and the women learned that a welcome was planned for them at Goosetown.

"What will they think of us, dirty and brown as beans, dressed in rags?" Dora asked.

"Perhaps they will not want us," one woman worried.

Joseph reassured her. "There will be a hundred, maybe a thousand suitors for each of you. They will be grateful for the strongest, bravest women in Christendom."

The snow started in the middle of the night, surprising them all. The September days had been warm, and there had been no feel of moisture in the air. The snow, heavy and wet, woke Maggie, and she shivered as she rushed through breakfast, then helped yoke the oxen. William, frantic, hurried them along, shouting for them to be on their way before the blizzard worsened.

"We must wait a day until the storm is over," Joseph told him, as he studied the thick flakes that descended on them. "The trail is obscured. I believe we face a greater danger from stumbling over a cliff than we do from outwaiting the snow."

"You do not know," William told him harshly.

"Listen to Joseph, brother," Caroline said. "We are only days from our destination, and the men there know we are coming. You or Joseph could ride on ahead and ask them to rescue us if the snow does not stop."

"You do not know!" William told her.

Maggie and Sadie glanced up at his loud words. "Know what?" Maggie asked.

"I will not see you perish. I should never have allowed us to visit City of Rocks. I bear the fault for the wasted time."

"I am against it," Joseph said. "I will not

allow you to let them face even more danger."

"You are a fool, Joe. Do you want the women to die?" William's voice rose so that he could be heard above the wind.

"Some will surely die if we go on today. We cannot see five feet ahead of us."

Reverend Parnell turned away. His back heaved, and Maggie realized he was sobbing.

"What is it?" Caroline asked. She put her hand on his arm. "Willie, what is it?"

He shook off her arm, but she persisted. "What is wrong?"

"Anne," he said at last, using the back of his hand to wipe his eyes.

"Anne?" Maggie remembered the name carved with William's on Independence Rock.

"His wife," Caroline murmured.

"I have told you only that Anne died on the trail. In truth, my wife died because of the snow. She was murdered."

Caroline gasped. "I knew Anne had perished in California, but you have never given me the details. How could it be that she was murdered?" she asked.

"She was. I found her frozen body in the snow."

"How awful for you, for her." Caroline put her arms around her brother. "You have never spoken of it, and I did not want to intrude by asking. Was she truly *murdered?*"

"I consider it so."

"What happened?" Joseph asked.

William bowed his head for a moment, then looked out into the storm. "We stopped two days to rest. A blizzard came on, like this one. It was not far from here. If we had been just one day ahead, we would have missed it. I and another man volunteered to go to the diggings for help. I thought Anne would be safe in camp. When we returned, she was lying in the snow, curled up, frozen. If we had not wasted those days, we would have been safe on the other side before the blizzard started."

"But murder?" Joseph asked. "Was it not a tragic accident?"

"The others, they refused to let her shelter with them. I had protected her against mistreatment the entire trip, but I was not there, and the others turned their hatred on her. She had been violated. She sought shelter among some rocks and must have died in her sleep."

"How beastly. They were degenerates," Maggie said.

"Why would they do such a thing?" Caroline asked.

"I believe you know the answer," William said. "Oh, they told me she had chosen to be by herself, but I knew them, knew the way they had dishonored her. I should have known they were waiting until I was away. If only I had insisted she go with me, but I deserted her." He stared off into the soft whiteness that blanketed the harsh landscape, hiding the detritus of thousands of gold seekers and their wagons.

Despite William's insistence that they leave, Joseph prevailed, and the women camped that day, huddled in the wagons and tents, taking turns at keeping the campfires going. The night turned bitter, but in the weak dawn they saw that the snow was slowing, and by midafternoon it had stopped. Joseph said they would move out the following morning.

The melting snow exposed the scarred earth and turned the trail to mud. The oxen strained to pull the wagons through the foul mire of dirt and animal waste that littered the trail. Mary walked beside the lead team, urging the animals on. They were stubborn, however, and the train moved slowly. Once she slipped in the wet earth and rose covered in mud. She laughed as Maggie helped her up and said, "Oh, what a bride I must appear to be."

"None of us looks appealing," Maggie replied, helping Mary brush off her skirt. "We would be taken for little more than washerwomen." She paused. "Have you grown anxious for a husband, then?"

"Not anxious, but curious. After all, this was the reason we signed up."

"It was the reason the ministers signed us up."

"But not the reason we came." Mary paused. "Are you still worried about being recognized?"

Maggie thought that over. "I am not the frightened woman I was when you first knew me. Now I think of the future, not the past. But yes, I fear a little, although not near as much as I did before."

"It will not be long," Mary said. "Once we counted this trip in months. And then weeks. Now it is only days, and soon it will be hours. It does not seem possible. I wonder what lies ahead for us."

Maggie stared off into the distance. "I shall miss you when this is over. The others, too. I hope we will not be separated."

"We will not ever be separated, except perhaps by distance. What we have come through together will always keep us close. I do not believe a husband could be as dear to me as you and the others," Mary said. "You are more than a family to me."

Maggie grasped her friend's muddy hand. "I would not have made it without you, Mary. None of us would."

Touched, the large woman turned away. "You give me too much credit. We are all each other's strength. Our band of sisters has accomplished what no other women have, and we have done it together, each one contributing. I do not wish a single one would have turned back." She seemed embarrassed at her sentiment and struck the lead ox with a stick, urging him on.

Knowing that they would be at Goosetown in a few days, the women were more excited than they had been since the first hours of the trip. In the evenings, they washed and mended their clothes and studied themselves in the sliver of mirror that one of them had kept. Their faces were tan and leathery, and Bessie and Evaline rubbed bacon fat into their skin to smooth and soften it, then laughed, telling each other they smelled like pigs. Maggie and Dora washed each other's hair in the melted snow. Dora braided her hair, while Maggie fastened hers into a twist on top of her head.

"I did not know we were so vain," Maggie said, as she repaired a collar on Sadie's dress. "We have come thousands of miles through desert and mountain, driving oxen, fighting Indians and weather, and now are we reduced to frail woman-hood?"

"We will never be that," Bessie replied. "We will never go back to what we were."

"No," Maggie said. "For that alone I am grateful." Then she asked, "What kind of a husband will you look for?"

Bessie shrugged. "One who will be kind to Evaline," she replied, "and one who is not perfect."

"I'd rather have a kind man than a rich one," Penn told them.

Maggie turned to study the girl, thinking how much Penn, too, had changed. She had joined them as a frightened young woman. Now she was strong and sure of herself. Mary did not believe Penn would ever again let a man hurt her.

"Then you do not care about riches?" Maggie asked.

Penn straightened her skirt. "Maybe I'll get rich on my own."

Dora laughed. "How? Will you learn to pan for gold?"

"Who knows?"

"If you do not find your brother, will you look for a husband?" Caroline asked Winny.

"I will find him," Winny insisted. "Or he will find me."

One by one, they stopped their sewing and primping and wrapped up in quilts and blankets, and despite their excitement, they fell asleep, not waking until the sky in the east was pale.

Maggie did not have to be hurried to eat breakfast and yoke the oxen, because with the end of their journey so close, she could not wait to reach the diggings. With the wagons packed, she moved off over the mountain trail with the others, Mary in the lead again, as she had been since they started into the mountains, her chestnut horse tied to the back of the wagon. Maggie led the second wagon, while Dora walked beside her, holding the baby. Maggie wished the animals would hurry, but they plodded along, just as they had for months, too dumb to know their journey was almost over. There were still mountains to cross, but after what they had come through, those mountains did not seem so formidable.

They reached a wagon that was bogged down in the mud and stopped. A man cursed his oxen as he whipped them, but they could not pull the wagon out of the mire. "Give me the borrow of your oxen," he demanded of Mary.

"I am not inclined to do so," Mary muttered, then looked at the harried woman beside him and the brood of thin and bewildered children and relented. She added her oxen to his, and they pulled his wagon onto dry ground.

The man did not thank her but said, "You ought to trade me a pair of my oxen for yours. Mine are used up."

"You abused them. You are lucky they have got you this far," Mary told him.

"So you would leave me here with the wife and brats?"

Mary looked him over and replied, "Your wife and brats are welcome to join us. You, sir, can sit with your wagon and poor oxen until kingdom come." The retort pleased Maggie, who knew Mary would not have dared utter such an impertinence only a few months before.

The man cursed her, but his wife looked up, and Maggie saw the trace of a smile on her lips.

"I believe she was tempted," Maggie told Dora, as they started on their way.

The day had turned cold, and the mud along the trail was slippery. Harsh, stinging snow began to fall, making the ground slick with ice.

They were on a downward slope now, a treacherous place where the trail was narrow. The mountain was on one side, and a steep chasm dropped off hundreds of feet on the other. "We must go lower to get out of the storm, no more than a mile," William told them. "It is too dangerous to camp this high up."

Mary and Maggie hurried the oxen, but the animals would not go faster. The trail was too slick, and the wind had come up, swirling snow and making it difficult to see. Other travelers, anxious to reach the diggings, passed them. Some were on horseback, but others walked. A man cursed Maggie's oxen for blocking the trail. Another forced her close to the cliff edge as he pushed by her on the inside. She glared at him, then turned to discover another man, on horseback, who had come up behind her. He had been following them for an hour or more, she realized, but now he was moving fast, and it seemed that he might shove her aside.

Instead, the man dismounted and put his hand

on her shoulder, and Maggie was wrenched around. "There you are!" the man screamed. "I knew you were one of them. It took me a time to recognize you, but I do! Come with me, or I will kill you!"

Maggie looked at the bearded face contorted with hatred, and for a moment she thought the man was someone after her for the reward. Then slowly she recognized him. "Jesse!" she cried, shrinking back, nearly falling against the wagon. She had believed he was dead. All these weeks and months she had thought she had killed her husband, had been comforted by the belief he would never hurt her again, but she was wrong. "You are dead. I thought you were dead," Maggie whispered, trying to wrench herself away.

"If you had your way, I would be. You tried hard enough to kill me."

"You would have killed me. And Clara."

"It was my right."

"We were told there was a reward."

He laughed, and the sound chilled her. "I put it about that there was."

"You have the money?"

He only smiled. "Who'd be the wiser?" He dug his fingers into her shoulder. "Where is Clara?"

"Dead. Clara is dead."

Jesse's face turned white in anger. "You killed my daughter."

"She drowned. I could not save her." Maggie

paused. "What does it matter to you? You never cared about her."

"She belonged to me. So do you."

Maggie stared at him. The shock of seeing her husband alive had worn off. She looked at him now in fear.

Still, she said, "I will not. You will not hurt me ever again."

"You come with me, or someone will be hurt," Jesse told her. "Maybe one of these women. You will be responsible."

She thought how Penn had stood up to Asa. Maggie would not falter either. She looked around then, frantic to spot one of the ministers, but they were far behind, pushing a wagon that was mired in the muck.

Only Dora was beside her, her arms protecting the baby, not sure what to do. Then Mary, who was walking just ahead beside the chestnut horse tied to the wagon, turned and stared at Jesse. She realized something was wrong. "Maggie?" she called.

"Jesse. This is Jesse. He is alive," Maggie managed to say.

Enraged, Jesse slapped Maggie's face. Then he struck her with his fist.

Mary stopped the oxen. "Leave be," she ordered, her whip in her hand. "Let go of her or I'll whip you."

"It is not your business. I do what I like."

"No," Maggie cried. "Not anymore."

"You tried to kill me. You have to pay for it," Jesse said. "I nearly died."

"How often did you try to kill her?" Mary asked.

Jesse didn't answer. "She murdered our daughter."

"Clara fell from a boat. Maggie tried to save her. Maggie would have died, too, if she had not been held back."

"What does that matter? She will come with me."

"Leave be, Jesse." Maggie backed away from him until she reached Mary's wagon. Jesse followed her.

Penn came up to them then. "Who's that?"

"Maggie's husband," Mary told her. "He is not dead. He wants her to go with him."

"He ain't going to take her any more than you let Asa take me." Penn reached into her pocket for the pistol, but Jesse leaned over and brushed it out of her hand.

"You're nothing but worthless women. You back off before you get hurt."

We are not worthless women. We have survived two thousand miles of hardship that would have defeated many men, Maggie thought. *I am not the woman who once cowered before you.* She straightened her back and faced her husband. "I am not afraid of you, Jesse. Not now. Not anymore. I have friends to protect me." Both Penn and Dora moved close to Maggie and put their arms around her.

Jesse looked about and saw that the rest of the women had come up and were surrounding them. They did not know what was happening, but they sensed the danger Maggie was in. Sadie had picked up a rock, while Winny held a tree branch in her hands. Even Caroline held a stout stick. The two preachers joined them, and Joseph said, "You can see for yourself that you are outnumbered. If you hurt Mrs. Hale or anyone else, we will report you to the authorities in California. They deal harshly with men who harm women."

"Mrs. Hale. Is that what she calls herself? She is Mrs. Kaiser. My wife." Jesse, angry, glanced around at the group. He let go of Maggie and took a gun from his belt.

"You can threaten us all you want, but Mrs. Hale is not going with you," Joseph said.

"I say she is." Outraged, Jesse lunged at the minister, who fell back against the wagon. Mary grabbed Jesse and wrestled his gun from his hand. He fought for the weapon, pushing Mary down into the mud. She tried to right herself, but the mud was slippery, and she slid. She grasped Jesse to steady herself, but he stumbled and landed on top of her.

Before anyone could grab them, the two fell

against the wagon, knocking the chestnut horse off balance. He reared, and the wagon shifted. The oxen tried to steady themselves, but they were tired and balky, and their hooves slipped in the mud. A wagon wheel slid off the edge of the cliff. The oxen struggled for purchase, but the weight of the wagon was too much. It fell over the cliff, dragging the oxen and the horse with it. Mary and Jesse, caught beneath the wagon, tried to brace themselves, but there was nothing to grasp, and they slid into the abyss.

Maggie stared in terror as Mary disappeared in the white.

Stunned, the women were silent, listening for Mary's cry, but the only sounds were the oxen bellowing and the wagon crashing and splintering as it bounced on the rocks and landed hundreds of feet down. When all was still, Maggie rushed to the edge, but in the swirling snow she could see nothing, only a vast field of white obscuring the horror far below.

Twenty-Three

Maggie was silent as she stared into the white. For a moment, she could not move. Then she spoke, her voice choked and raw. "I will fetch a rope. Mary will be hurt bad. We will find her."

"And the man," Caroline added.

"He can go to hell," Maggie said. "I am only sorry he did not die months ago, before we left Chicago."

Maggie started for the wagon, but William took her arm. "Miss Madrid is gone. No one could have survived such a fall."

"You do not know that," Maggie told him.

"I do know it, and so do you. You have seen the remains of men who have fallen into canyons that are only half so deep as this one."

"Maybe she survived. She could have been caught on a tree branch," Maggie said. "We cannot leave her. Remember the stories we heard about men with cholera who were left behind by their friends for dead, but they recovered?"

William shook his head. "Miss Madrid did not have cholera. No one could live after a fall of hundreds of feet. It is likely she hit a rock or was crushed by the oxen or the wagon long before she reached the bottom. I am so sorry . . ." His voice trailed off as he himself was overcome with sorrow.

"Then we will bring up her body," Maggie told him. She yanked away her arm and clenched her fists. Tears ran down her face and froze on her cheeks. Nothing on the entire trip had prepared her for the loss of Mary. Or for the fact that she was responsible. Two of their number had died because of her—Clara and now Mary—the two she cared about most. She had considered that she or Penn or some of the others, even the ministers, might die, but Mary was invincible. Maggie would not have survived the trip without her. None of them would. Maggie would not even have had the courage to sign up for the journey in the first place. How could she desert Mary now? "I won't leave her here for the bears and panthers to rip her apart. We will take her with us to the diggings and bury her there."

William shook his head. His eyes were wet. "How will you find her body, Mrs. Hale? We cannot see more than a dozen feet into the depth. And if you do find it, how will you bring it up?"

"We'll find it. I'll go with you," Penn spoke up. "Me and Maggie'll fetch her. If she's dead, we'll bury her in my red shawl."

"I'll go, too," Sadie offered. "We'll bring her up with a rope."

"All the ropes we have tied together would not reach half the way down that canyon. You would endanger not just yourselves but the rest of us. It is hard enough to follow the trail in the snow. Do you really believe you can safely descend hundreds of feet when you cannot see where you are going? How could you find her?" Joseph asked. "You would perish yourselves."

"Then we shall camp until the snow clears," Maggie said.

"Until summer?" William asked. "This is the first of winter's storms. The snow may not melt in these canyons until June or July."

"We cannot leave her to freeze," Maggie cried.

Penn put her arms around Maggie and held her as the two sobbed. The others wept, too.

"Only her body will be frozen. Her spirit is alive in us. She is in heaven, where she is looking out for us, as she has these many months," Caroline spoke up. "I believe we must ask ourselves what Mary would have wanted. Would she have wished her friends to risk their lives to find her body? She herself has no use for it now. She has deserted it to be with God." She glanced at Maggie and added, "And Clara. Clara is not alone now."

"She almost made it to California. All these months and thousands of miles. She would have reached the diggings in just hours," Dora sobbed. "She was so close." She let her tears spill onto baby Washoe's head.

"She did make it," Caroline told her. "She made it because *you* will arrive safely. You will take Mary there in your hearts. I believe Mary's mission was to bring the rest of you through this journey. Her strength is in all of you. We will go on because Mary showed us the way. Perhaps, like Moses, she was given a glimpse of the Promised Land, and that was enough."

Maggie stood in the snow, oblivious to the cold, contemplating Caroline's words. It was not enough, of course. Mary deserved better. She had wanted to complete the journey, but still, she had had a sense that she would not. Maggie remembered Mary saying that if she did not reach the gold camps, she was still glad she had come.

Mary was dead, and Joseph and William were right. It would be folly to try to recover her body. Mary would not have wanted her and the others to risk their lives just to bring back her remains. Anyone who descended into the canyon would likely not return. She went to her wagon and found the bundle containing the few things she had not discarded. She reached inside and removed the china teapot that she had planned to give to Mary at their journey's end. Running her hand over the tiny roses, she thought of how much the teapot had meant to Mary. Then, slowly, she raised it above her head and threw it into the canyon where Mary had disappeared, listening as it hit a rock and shattered into a thousand fragments.

"We must go on before the snow worsens," said Joseph. "I will take the first wagon."

Maggie stared at him. Since leaving the desert, Mary had always led the first wagon. There were only two wagons now. William said he would drive the second.

"No," Maggie spoke up. "I will take the lead wagon." Mary was dead. Now Maggie would see them through.

"Evaline and I will drive the second," Bessie said.

William started to protest, but Joseph stopped him. "It is up to the women. This is their train—Mary's train."

Maggie moved toward the wagon. As she did so, William turned to Joseph. "Another woman dead, and it is my fault," he said. "Of all of them, why did it have to be Mary?"

"Perhaps, as Caroline suggested, her mission was done. She more than anyone brought our band of women through. Because of you, Mary found her purpose."

William considered the words. "Do you believe that?"

"I do, and you must, too."

William slowly nodded, and in a minute he set off toward the wagons. Joseph would have followed him, but Caroline touched his arm.

"*You* have found your purpose on this great journey, too, Joseph. You have risen to the challenge. I suspected there was a greatness in you, that you were intended for something better than overseeing a church in Chicago, and in the hundreds of miles we have come, I have seen evidence of it," Caroline said.

"It is William who has led us."

"Yes, in the beginning, but you have taken over where William faltered. I am proud of you."

"And I you," Joseph told her.

Caroline closed her eyes for a moment at the rare compliment. Then she smiled at her husband and said, "I believe the little one who will join us in just a few months will be proud of both of us."

"Are you saying . . . ?" Joseph stared at his wife. "After all these years . . ."

"I would not tell you before for fear you would worry about me. But now that the trip is near done, I believe it is time you know."

Joseph smiled. "You are even more beautiful this moment than the day I married you." Then, despite the snow and the cold and the sorrow of Mary's death, he picked up Caroline and swirled her around as snowflakes covered them.

That evening, the two ministers held a memorial service for Mary. There would be another in a proper church, when they reached the diggings— that is, if there was a proper church.

For the moment Mary's friends wanted their grief assuaged by prayers and hymns. After camp was set up and supper finished, they gathered between the two remaining wagons. As befit the site, the service was informal. The ministers led the prayers, and the women sang. "She was the ablest and purest of us," William said in a eulogy, then asked if anyone else wanted to speak. Almost all of the women did.

Maggie went first and told of meeting Mary in front of the Chicago church, the two of them encouraging each other to attend the meeting. "She was like a sister to me." Maggie started to say more, but she broke into tears.

"Mary saved me, and you all know that is the God's truth," Penn said.

"She gave me my daughter," Dora told them.

One by one, the women recalled how Mary had helped them or strengthened them when they were too wretched to continue. They cried as they spoke and held each other's hands. When they were finished the camp was silent, except for the wind. Caroline said, "We are filled with sadness, but we must remember Mary with joy.

We will complete our journey in her name." She did not say more. That was enough.

Maggie was ambivalent as she started down the trail the following morning. She mourned Mary, but as each step brought her closer to her destination, she began to think of what lay ahead. She would reach the diggings in a day or two, and then she would have to decide her future. The snow continued on and off, and it muffled the sound, but after a time Maggie thought she heard the noise of an eastbound wagon train—a large one, she concluded, because as it came near, it was very loud. Why would anyone start east in the snow?

As she led the two wagons into a clearing, she heard a man shout, "There they are! There's the women!" A cheer rose up, and a hundred men rushed toward the wagons.

"We come to bring you home!" a man shouted.

Maggie looked at them, astonished and then embarrassed at her own slovenly state. She turned to the others. A few were patting their hair into place and straightening their dresses, but most just stared. For an instant she looked for Mary, then realized Mary was gone. *She should have had this moment,* Maggie thought.

The men surrounded the wagons, but a broad man with a bushy red beard, who appeared to be their leader, held up his hand to stop them. "We are anxious to make your acquaintance, but we are gentlemen. Now hold on, gents, and do not rush the ladies!" He paused. "Be there a Winny Rupe amongst you?"

"Davy!" Winny cried. She pushed through the women and embraced her brother. She turned to her friends. "I knew it. I told you Davy was here!"

"I knowed when I heard a band of women from Chicago was headed for Goosetown that you was one of them. I been writing you every month to come."

"I never saw the letters. They must have been tore up," Winny said. Then she asked, loudly enough for everyone to hear, "Have you made a fortune, Davy?"

"Enough so I can meet my promise. You will not be a hired girl no more, Win."

"He serves as the judge of Goosetown," a man shouted.

"Good enough for me," Winny said.

William and Joseph came forward and introduced themselves. "I hope you men are worthy of these women. They have overcome hardships you can only imagine. I have never seen such courage. They are women unlike any others," William said.

"Woe to the man who does not treat them right," Joseph added.

"We will take care of him," Davy laughed.

"No need. The women will," Joseph told him.

"How are we going to choose a wife?" a man shouted.

"You will not. The choice is up to the women," Joseph replied. "When they are ready, they will ask you."

"These are decent men. They've come to carry the ladies in. Their walking days are over," Davy said. "We brought wagons for them."

"I could pack one or two on my back," a man shouted.

The men cheered, but the women only looked at each other. Then Maggie spoke up. "We are grateful to you, but we have made this journey without your help. We will finish it on our own."

"A particular lot they are," one of the men muttered.

Caroline heard him. "Most particular. I hope you are men enough for them."

The trip to Goosetown took the rest of the day and then one more. When the caravan at last reached the camp, the men stepped aside and cheered as thirty-six women, their backs straight, their arms around each other, walked by themselves into the diggings.

Twenty-Four

September 30, 1852
Goosetown

"Come with me. I got something to make us rich," Penn told Maggie after the excitement had settled down. The men had unloaded the wagons and turned out the oxen and were preparing a party, while the women had retired to primp a little. Men had moved out of a dozen of the nicest cabins and turned them over to the women. They had board floors and beds made of logs that were covered with pine boughs and buffalo robes and stood back among the pine trees, away from the frenzied mining activity. The women could use them as long as they liked, and the first couple that married would receive one as a wedding present.

Goosetown was nothing like the bucolic rural towns of Illinois that the women had left behind. Most of the homes were crude—tents or cabins of raw logs chinked with mud. There was no evidence of refinement—no curtains or flower boxes at the windows, no signs of paint. The stream that ran through the diggings had been dug up in the search for gold, and the banks were lined with piles of rocks and sand. Mining equipment littered the land. The sun was out, and the crooked streets were muddy with snowmelt. A general store charging usurious prices occupied an enormous tent, and half a dozen saloons were set up in dirt-floored cabins. There was a hodgepodge of other enterprises—a barbershop, a smithy, a Chinese herb shop, and a washhouse among them.

Still, if the landscape was raw and the air filled with shouts and curses, there was a contagious sense of excitement and hope. Maggie felt revived after the long trip. This valley, surrounded by mountains, was a new land, a place to start over.

She and Penn hurried to where the two reverends stood watching several men recover gold from a sluice box. Both ministers were sipping from tin cups. "You were right, Willie. I came near selling my soul for this coffee," Reverend Swain told his brother-in-law.

Penn turned up the hem of her dress and pulled out a basting stitch. She removed a folded piece of paper, wrinkled and torn in spots, from its hiding place and unfolded it, smoothing it with her hand. "Here," she said to Joseph. "You take it."

Maggie stared at the paper, curious.

"I bought it of a man in St. Joe. I told Asa it was give to me, but I paid five dollars for it. He wanted more, but it was all I had. He said I was

411

a nice girl, and as he was dying and couldn't go back to California, he wanted me to have it. Asa didn't pay no hundred dollars for it. He lied. I was the one bought it. Asa stole it from me, but I took it back when I run off in St. Joe. That's what them Harvey boys was after. It's genuine."

"Genuine what?" Joseph asked.

"A map. A map to a gold mine. I was going to keep it for myself, but after what we gone through, I figured we all ought to share. It's a fortune." Penn beamed at the minister.

William, who had been concentrating on the gold extraction instead of listening to Penn, glanced at the map and smiled. "A fortune?"

"She paid five dollars for it," Maggie told him.

William turned to Penn. "You what?"

"The man sold it to me wanted more, but it was all I had. It was the money I saved up for three years. I sewed that map in my skirt and walked most of two thousand miles with it. It's genuine."

"Genuine like this?" William took a similar map from his vest pocket and unfolded it. "There were hundreds peddled in '49. I paid two bits for it and kept it to remind myself I'd been suckered. I guess folks still get taken in."

Penn stared at him, her mouth open. "You mean it ain't real?"

"No more than a thousand others that have been sold along the way."

"The map was what Asa and his brothers were after," Maggie said.

"That man promised me it was genuine," Penn told him. "He promised me."

William studied the map, then handed it back. "The X there that shows where the mine is—that is the middle of the ocean."

"Then it ain't real?"

William shook his head. "I am sorry."

Penn crumpled the map and dropped it in the mud. "I should have give that worthless thing back to Asa. Them Harvey boys is dead because of it." Penn stomped off.

To Maggie's surprise, few of the women were anxious to marry right away. They took their time choosing husbands. They had become too independent to rush into matrimony, and while they had come west as brides, some were not sure they even wanted to marry.

Dora was the first to find a husband. She sat one day with Maggie on a log in the sun, her infant in her lap. As the two women rested, a man came up and asked, "Would you let me hold the baby? It has been a long time since I have touched a little one. I have washed my hands." He held them out for Dora's inspection.

Dora tightened the blanket around Washoe, then gave her to the man. He cradled the infant in his arms as if he knew what he was doing. He looked down at Dora and said, "I had a wife and son once, but they perished."

"That is Washoe—Wash for short," Dora said. Then she added, "She is not rightly mine. She was given to me. My own died."

"You are blessed to have her." The baby cried a little, and the man shushed her and rocked her in his arms. Then, reluctantly, he handed her back to Dora. "I hope you find a father for her. He would be a lucky man to acquire a wife and daughter on the same day." When Dora didn't reply, he said, "You are a widow, then."

Dora looked him full in the face. "I never was married."

Maggie touched Dora's hand. She was proud of her friend for speaking the truth.

The man took in the meaning of what Dora had said. "Out here, what matters is the worth of a person, man or woman. This is the place to start a new life." He and Dora talked for a long time. At last he said, "We are told the women are to choose their husbands."

"What do you think?" Dora asked Maggie.

Maggie nodded.

"I have a ring," Dora said, holding up her hand. Baby Wash's mother's ring rested on her finger.

Maggie rose, giving her seat to the man. Later in the day, she stood beside Dora as her friend recited her wedding vows.

• • •

Penn borrowed a gold pan from a burly miner, who showed her how to swirl the water in it and look for specks of gold. "I bought a map to a gold mine in St. Joe," she admitted to him.

He grinned at her. "Me the same. Give a ten-dollar gold piece for it."

"Mine was five. That makes you the bigger fool," she said.

He laughed. "I guess I am."

"Asa would have struck me dead for saying that," Penn told Maggie, when she confided she had found her man. "I told him I wouldn't live with him unless the words was spoke over us. He said he was of a similar mind."

"I believe he could stand up to Reed Harvey," Maggie told her.

"I ain't worrying about them Harvey boys no more." In fact, Penn did not have to. Sometime after that, an emigrant told her that he had attended the hanging of Reed Harvey in Great Salt Lake City.

When she looked over the camp with all its single men, Sadie told Maggie, "I could make a fortune if I returned to my old ways." Then she added, "I do not care about a fortune. I came here for a husband, and I intend to find one." She was studying herself in a mirror and frowned. "I have gotten old."

Maggie shook her head. "You were pretty when we left Chicago, the prettiest among us. The trail has given your face character. Now you are beautiful."

"Beautiful enough for Davy Rupe?"

Maggie grinned. "If you can tear him away from Winny."

"I would not want to."

Winny acted as both maid of honor and best man when Sadie married Davy.

Winny herself never married. She lived with Davy and Sadie for the rest of her life, a beloved aunt to their children. "I came west to find my brother," she told Maggie once. "I found him and a sister, too. Why do I need a husband?"

Bessie did not appear to be interested in any of the Goosetown men. A number of them approached the cabin to inquire about Evaline, but she told them the girl was too young to marry. "You have found no one among the miners to your liking?" Maggie asked one day as they walked along a creek where men were working sluice boxes in their search for gold. Several stopped what they were doing to stare at the women.

"Oh, I have," Bessie said.

Maggie smiled a little. "Of course. Does he know?"

"Not yet."

They came to the temporary chapel where the

weddings had taken place. It had been many days since the women arrived, and by then the ministers had performed two dozen weddings. William saw the women and came over to them.

"Bessie has made a choice," Maggie said.

"A fortunate man. Who is he?" William asked.

Bessie turned to Maggie and said, "You are too forward."

"One of us has to be." It was not her place to intrude, but she feared Bessie had turned timid. Maggie said to Reverend Parnell, "I believe Bessie would marry a man of God."

"A preacher?" William frowned. Then his eyes widened. "I know of only one among us who is unmarried. But he is not much of a man of God now." He looked at Bessie. "You have seen my weaknesses over these past months. I am unworthy of you."

"I have seen a man, a good man in almost all ways. I would not want perfection. It would be too difficult to live with such a person. I would like someone with flaws, just as I am flawed."

"I find it difficult to believe that about you. You are a kind and generous woman."

"I have lived a life of deception."

William frowned. "And you are overburdened with it."

"I am. And worse, I have burdened another. I intend to make amends by telling her the truth." William studied Bessie as she faltered and glanced back toward the cabin where she and Evaline were staying. Evaline sat with Blackie, drawing in her sketchbook. Maggie smiled at the scene, remembering that Evaline had promised to find a dog for Clara when they reached California.

Bessie took a deep breath. "I will tell you first. Evaline is not my charge. She is my daughter. My first husband was a Negro. So you see, I am a deceiver. You may think I am unworthy of you." She took a deep breath and went on. "My second husband knew of Evaline's parentage and loved her as if she were his own. But I never told Evaline. I intend to do so now. Before the day ends I hope she will call me mother. I will tell everyone. I know it will shock them—and you."

William smiled at her. "No shock to me. I suspected as much."

"You did?" Bessie's eyes widened. "Any man I marry would have to accept her as his daughter, too."

"I find that no hardship, but a blessing. You see, my wife, Anne, was a Negro."

Maggie had been approached by several men who wanted to marry her, but they did not interest her. As she walked one day along the creek, watching the men work the diggings, she was thinking she might set up a dressmaking shop. The women she had come west with certainly needed clothes, and the men had plenty of gold dust in their pokes. She stopped to observe a man who was bent over a gold pan. A boy of about five worked beside him. She stared at the two until the boy looked up and grinned. "Papa," he said to his father, then pointed at Maggie.

The man stood up. "You are one of those women," he said.

Maggie nodded. "I have not seen you before."

"No, I did not think any of the women would want to take on two children." He glanced behind him, and Maggie noticed a second boy barely beyond babyhood. The child reached out his arms, and Maggie yearned to pick him up, but it was the man who lifted him into the air. "Their mother is dead."

"Not want to take on two children?" Maggie repeated the man's words. "I can think of nothing so joyous." She reached into a bag she carried and took out Clara's doll. Winny had given it to her when they reached the diggings, and she had kept it with her. She handed it to the older boy.

"I am Robert Kane," the man said.

"I am Maggie Hale." She should have told her real name, but she was no longer Maggie Kaiser. Maggie Kaiser was dead—just like Jesse Kaiser.

"Will you sit?" he asked.

"I would rather play with the children," she replied, and Robert handed her the younger boy. "He is Ezra. The older one is Jeff," he said.

419

After a time, she took Evaline's drawing of Clara from the bag and showed it to Robert. "I had a daughter once," she said. "And a son." Then she added, "I tried to kill their father, but I did not. He is dead, however."

"I am sorry for you."

"He was a cruel man. I do not grieve for him."

"You have that right."

Maggie was cautious. She wanted to be sure before she opened her heart to another man. She made Robert wait a week before she proposed to him.

Epilogue

1902
Goosetown

Maggie's marriage was a good one. She and her husband had three children of their own. The first, a girl with pale hair like Clara's, they named Mary. The boys were William and Joseph. After the gold ran out, they stayed on in Goosetown and farmed.

When they had been married forty years, Maggie and Robert retraced part of the trail that Maggie had traveled with the women. The journey was easier now. There were railroads and good wagon roads. The couple covered part of the distance on horseback. Maggie had not forgotten the trail. She remembered the twists and turns, the climbs and crossings. Most of all, she remembered the Green River, the place where the raft had crossed it, the place where Clara had perished.

She was solemn when they reached that spot, dismounting and trudging up the hill, more winded than she had been forty years earlier. "There," she told Robert, pointing to a group of trees. "I remember there were saplings. Look how they have grown. Somewhere close is a rock that is shaped like an egg. Mary placed it there. Clara's grave is beside it."

She started toward the grove, but just then, she spotted a man working in a field. The land was no longer wilderness but had become a farm. The man came over to them.

"I was through here in 1852 with a group of women," Maggie told him.

"They tell of you still."

"You have heard of us, then?" Maggie smiled. "Thirty-six of us made it to California."

"And one did not," the man said.

"Several did not."

"One you buried here."

Maggie touched the locket with the strands of Clara's hair that she still wore. "How did you know? She was my daughter. She drowned. She was four."

"A girl, then. We thought she was a grown woman."

"You know of her?"

The man nodded. "We found the grave. It must have been a deep grave, because wild animals never dug it up. You will see that there are still rocks on top of it. There was a cross, too."

Maggie's eyes filled with tears as she remembered Mary pounding the cross into the ground. "It was made from the spokes of a rocking chair."

"Part of it was broken off, and we could make

out only one name. Come." He led them into the trees, then pointed to a small plot of ground surrounded by an iron fence. Inside, beside the remains of the cross and the egg-shaped rock, was a headstone. "We considered it to be sacred ground, so we never planted here."

Maggie went inside the fence and knelt beside the headstone. Chiseled into it was "Clara. 1852?"

"Her name was Clara Hale. She drowned," Maggie said, her voice filled with emotion. "I was afraid she would be forgotten."

The man shook his head. "She is written up in a history book about the county. We have all wondered about her. We placed the gravestone. The wife, Ella, tends the grave. She puts flowers on it. She says she knows that somewhere someone may still be grieving for her."

He introduced himself as Ephraim Tanner before he left them alone. Maggie and Robert stayed by the grave for a long time, Maggie sitting beside the mound of dirt and rocks, holding her husband's hand, feeling the grief of that awful time. After she composed herself, she and Robert went to the farmhouse. Ella Tanner invited them to sit on the porch. She brought a pitcher of water and glasses, because it was a hot day. "We think of her as a part of this place," she said. "She was here before us. That's why we call it Clara Farm." She cleared her throat and glanced away so that she would not embarrass Maggie, who was crying. "Would you like to take the cross with you?"

Maggie thought that over and shook her head. "No, Clara is part of this land now. The cross should remain with her."

To mark the fiftieth anniversary of the women's arrival in Goosetown, the town commissioned a statue of Mary. It was made by the noted artist and sculptor Evaline Whitney Parnell. Her Overland Trail sketchbook, first published in 1855, had become a classic. The statue was dedicated at a ceremony attended by all twenty-one of the wagon-train women who were still living. William was an invalid, but Bessie had come with Evaline. Joseph was there, along with Caroline and four of their five children. Maggie and Penn, both widows, were accompanied by Maggie's daughter, Mary. Sadie and Winny brought Davy. Sadie still wore a gold nugget around her neck that Davy had given her in place of a wedding ring. She preferred it to the diamond ring he had bought for her after selling his mining interests and taking her and Winny to live in a mansion in San Francisco. Dora was accompanied by Wash. Now fifty, Wash wore a worn gold ring. Dora saw Maggie looking at it and said, "You must remember. It was her mother's. There are initials inside."

"Did Wash ever find out who she is?" Maggie asked Dora.

"She never tried. She says I am her mother."

The dedication included fireworks, a picnic, and speeches. The women, many old and bent and one in a wheelchair, recalled the excitement of the trip, the beauty of the land, the companionship. Few talked of the hardships. They remembered Clara and Lavinia and Adela, the woman who had died during the Indian attack. Most of all, they remembered Mary. Maggie spoke for all of them when she recalled Mary's strength and her love and said they would not have finished the trip without her help. "She was the ablest and purest of us," Maggie said, recalling the words of Reverend Parnell a half century earlier, spoken the day Mary died.

It was a wonderful gathering, Maggie thought, as she chatted with her friends from so long ago. "We have grown old," Maggie told Caroline. Joseph shook his head. "Caroline will never grow old." Maggie knew he had never seen Caroline as she really looked but had always considered her beautiful.

"Come, Mother," Evaline told Bessie at the sound of a train approaching. "The train has arrived. Father will be anxious for us to return."

Penn tightened a worn red shawl around her shoulders while the others gathered their belongings and made ready to leave. But just then a portly couple as old as the women hurried up.

"We are late," the woman said. "It could not be helped. We made our disappointment known to the conductor, but he did nothing." Distressed, she looked around. "Why did you not delay the ceremony and wait for us? You knew we were coming. When I heard of it, I sent a telegram. We expected to be part of the occasion." She held out several pages of paper. "I have prepared a speech." With the back of her hand she wiped perspiration from her face.

Maggie, confused, glanced at Penn, who shook her head. Dora frowned, and Joseph and Caroline exchanged a glance. The others, curious, stared. Maggie couldn't imagine who the couple was. There had been so many telegrams back and forth among the women, and even newspaper reporters, that she was not surprised she had missed one or two. The event had been reported in all the California papers and picked up across the country. Maggie had been interviewed a dozen times. Perhaps the woman had been a member of the wagon train. Maggie had thought that they had all been accounted for. She went over the names of those listed in the program as dead. Had she made a mistake? Was this woman one of them? Perhaps she was among those who had started out but turned back.

"I read of it in the Chicago newspapers, and my

wife sent word we would be here. It is strange that you went ahead without us, for who could be more important than us?" the man said.

"Than you?" Maggie asked. She was tired and leaned on her cane, the one Sadie had given her so long before.

"Mary would not have joined the train had we not urged her to go. Why, you might say that none of you would be here if it were not for us."

"Who are you?" Maggie asked.

"Why, we are Louise and Micah Madrid," the man said. "I sold half of our farm and gave the money to Mary for the trip. We encouraged her to go."

"And I presented her with my prized china teapot. I should like to know what happened to it."

"It was broken" was all that Maggie could think to say. She stared at the couple. She remembered how they had called Mary a fool, how they had mistreated her, how Mary had had to threaten Micah with a lawsuit to get a fraction of her inheritance. Most of all, Maggie recalled how happy Mary had been once she was away from them, how she had bonded with the women as she had never done with her brother and his wife.

Louise held her chin high and announced in a loud voice, "Mary was our sister." She looked around for acknowledgment.

Maggie glanced at Penn, then at Dora, Sadie, Bessie, and Caroline. At Wash and Evaline. The women exchanged glances, then clustered around Maggie. She rested her hand on the cane's knob, silver now since the gold had worn off long ago. "I remember," she said. She did not tell them what she remembered, did not remark on how they had belittled and exploited Mary. She would not dishonor Mary's memory with pettiness. But one thing she would not accept. "You say she is your sister," Maggie said. Her back stiffened, and she raised her head. "No. Oh, no." She felt Penn's arm tighten around her. "She was not *yours*. She belonged to us. Mary Madrid was *our* sister."

Acknowledgments

I've been intrigued with the westward movement ever since I was six, when my parents, my brother and sister, and I went west from Virginia to Colorado in a 1939 Plymouth. For years, I've wanted to write a novel about a strong group of women on the Overland Trail during the gold rush days. The problem was finding my story, and when I finally did, it was a mishmash. Thanks to my agent, Danielle Egan-Miller, for making me switch from a cast of thousands to a focused approach. Thanks to the wonderful people at St. Martin's Press—Elisabeth Dyssegaard, who suggested I further condense and clarify the tale; Jennifer Enderlin, who always has my back; and Alan Bradshaw and India Cooper, for final editing. I'm grateful to writer friends Arnie Grossman, Wick Downing, and Harry MacLean for their encouragement. I'm indebted to Will Bagley, one of the West's premier historians, for his input. Will helped me keep Overland Trail history straight by suggesting a number of changes and corrections. He also pointed out that too many men in the story are bad guys. So?

I can't say it often enough that my family is

my strength—Bob, Dana, Kendal, Lloyd, and Forrest. My sister, Mary Dallas Cole, props me up with her love and support. I am blessed to have her and my brother, Michael Dallas, to whom this book is dedicated. Mike was an exceptional high school English teacher in Clear Creek County, Colorado, who made a difference in the lives of so many students. Although unpublished, he is the better writer in the family.

I've written about western history for fifty years. Still, *Westering Women* required considerable research. These are some of the best Overland Trail sources I used:

The Great Platte River Road: The Covered Wagon Mainline via Fort Kearny to Fort Laramie. By Merrill J. Mattes. Lincoln, NE: Nebraska State Historical Society, 1969.

With Golden Visions Bright Before Them: Trails to the Mining West, 1849–1852. By Will Bagley. Norman, OK: University of Oklahoma Press, 2012.

The Plains Across: The Overland Emigrants and the Trans-Mississippi West, 1840–60. By John D. Unruh, Jr. Urbana, IL: University of Illinois Press, 1979.

Hard Road West: History and Geology along the Gold Rush Trail. By Keith Heyer Meldahl. Chicago, IL: University of Chicago Press, 2007.

The California Trail: An Epic with Many

Heroes. By George R. Stewart. Lincoln, NE: University of Nebraska Press, 1983.

Covered Wagon Women: Diaries and Letters from the Western Trails, 1840–1890. Vols. 1–11. Glendale, CA: Arthur H. Clark, 1983–1993.

Overland Days to Montana in 1865: The Diary of Sarah Raymond and Journal of Dr. Waid Howard. Edited by Raymond W. and Mary Lund Settle. Glendale, CA: Arthur H. Clark, 1971.

The Shirley Letters: Being Letters in 1851–1852 from the California Mines. By Dame Shirley (Louise A. K. S. Clappe). Santa Barbara, CA: Peregrine Press, 1970.

Covered Wagon Days: A Journey across the Plains in the Sixties, and Pioneer Days in the Northwest; from the Private Journals of Albert Jerome Dickson. Edited by Arthur Jerome Dickson. Lincoln, NE: University of Nebraska Press, 1989.

Journal of a Trip to California: Across the Continent from Weston, Mo., to Weber Creek, Cal., in the Summer of 1850. By Charles W. Smith. Publisher not listed.

A Frontier Lady: Recollections of the Gold Rush and Early California. By Sarah Royce. New Haven, CT: Yale University Press, 1932.

Books are produced in the United States using U.S.-based materials

Books are printed using a revolutionary new process called THINKtech™ that lowers energy usage by 70% and increases overall quality

Books are durable and flexible because of Smyth-sewing

Paper is sourced using environmentally responsible foresting methods and the paper is acid-free

Center Point Large Print
600 Brooks Road / PO Box 1
Thorndike, ME 04986-0001 USA

(207) 568-3717

US & Canada:
1 800 929-9108
www.centerpointlargeprint.com